WORTH HIS SALT

WORTH HIS SALT

ROWAN WILDER

BRONWYN
BOOKS

For Rebecca,
giver, fighter, and weaver of worlds.
Your stories matter, both in their strength and their vulnerability.
I can't wait to see you bring them into the world.

Worth His Salt can be read as a stand-alone romance, but it was written as part of the Fakari Islands series—a collection of romances that, together, chart a bigger story for the islands. You don't need to read other installments in the series to enjoy this book.

For those who do want to read the bigger story, a quick note on chronology. While this is the second Fakaris book to be published, it's the first in the in-universe timeline. To read the stories chronologically, start with this book. *In Her Own Rite*, the next book in the series, is already available for reading and purchase at all major booksellers.

THE WINDSWEPT
FAKARI ISLANDS
HALLU
HALLUK
HOUSE
NORTH
HARBOR
SAROE
THE
RING
THE
CLIFFS
TEMPLE
MOON
LAKE
FIKARIG
COMMON
HOUSE
WESTEL
SOUTH
HARBOR
OESTER
HALSSEL

FAJJE
THE RUINS
MARIT
KEIST
TOWARDS THE
DISTANT SOUTHERN ISLES

The Fika

and extended family and friends

A *fika* is a Fakari pack unit, usually made up of three to five families, who share pack life together. The names of official members of the *fika* are bolded in the family tree below. Other members of the extended family and community are also shown.

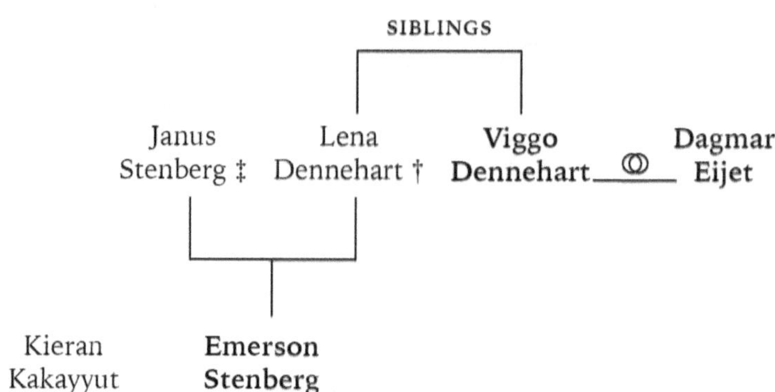

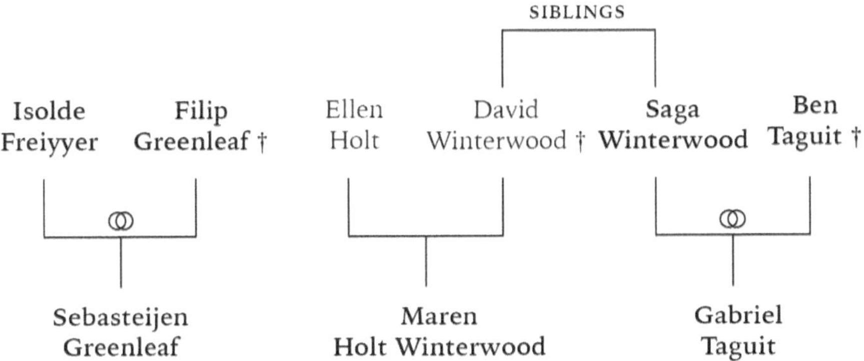

KEY

† Person is deceased
‡ Person is estranged
⦾ Mates

SENSITIVITY WARNING

Worth His Salt is a steamy enemies-to-lovers shifter romance. Readers should know that it contains elements that may be personally difficult for some. In particular, the male lead lives with chronic pain and disability after an injury that occurred three years before the book takes place. The incident in which he was injured is also described on page through memory in one chapter. There is also explicit sex shown on page—always consensual, and always enjoyed by all!

For a full list of trigger warnings, which will include spoilers, please see **rowanwilder.com/whs-cw**. If you would like to ask about a specific trigger without risking spoilers, feel free to DM me on Instagram at **@rowanwilderromance**.

1

MAREN

The last time I was on a boat, I threw up thirteen times.

That was during college orientation, when I made the mistake of choosing whale watching over the food tour for my day trip. My roommate insisted—and at the time, I wasn't in the habit of saying no to people who insisted on things.

In the immortal words of Julia Roberts: *big* mistake. *Huge.* The wind was rough and the waves were choppy, and not only did my tour group not see a *single* whale, but we all ended up hurling repeatedly over the side of the boat. It was probably Boston Harbor's most colorful day since 1773.

I learned two valuable lessons that day. First: always pick the food tour, and second: never let someone pressure you onto a boat. Those lessons have served me well in the years since, and I can't help but wonder now—as the ferry rocks back and forth so strongly I worry about a repeat incident—whether I could have arranged for an island-hopper instead.

The answer is no, of course. The Fakari Islands are hard enough to get to as-is.

First I had to book a last-minute flight from New York to

Halifax, then take a six hour bus to the northern tip of Nova Scotia. The bus ran so late that I nearly missed the ferry, and since it only runs three times a week, I did *not* have the luxury. After some extensive pleading and flattery, I was let on last, sweaty and exhausted just in time for a twelve hour boat ride.

All this just to visit Halssel, the only one of the islands that's actually open to visitors. Which is to say: my plan B.

The original plan—scoring a meeting with Saroan Salts' owner on Saroe, the biggest of the Fakari Islands—fell through after a dozen unanswered emails and phone calls. Which felt okay when I had the luxury of time; after all, you can wear anybody down if you try hard enough. But now...

I swallow as the memory from two nights ago comes back to me. Let's just say there's a reason I needed to get as far away from my real life as possible.

The ferry lurches as it meets a particularly rough wave, and my hands clasp the side of the boat so hard my knuckles pale. Behind me, I hear a few older women gasp as a splash of seawater sprays onto the deck. I feel the anxiety start to coil in my gut, and instinctively reach into my pocket for my hand cream, unscrewing the cap and squeezing some out into my palm. As I rub it over the fronts and backs of my hands, the familiar scent of lavender and witch hazel hits my nostrils.

Breathe in, two, three, four, I think, closing my eyes. *Out, two, three, four...*

My stomach is finally starting to settle when I hear another commotion from the deck. I open my eyes to see a group of tourists crowding at the front of the boat and follow their gaze. Up ahead, the first of the islands is coming into view in the distance.

Oh my God.

The shape is instantly recognizable: the mountain in the back and cliffs on either side, with a colorful harbor nestled in front. The buildings around the harbor are far away enough that they look like robin's eggs, painted in deep reds and bright blues and yellows. You can just start to make out the wooden stilts that keep some of the shops on the dock above the water.

I raise my chin, trying to catch a glimpse of the other islands. In the haze over the water you can only see Halssel clearly, but I make out the shadows of a few of the other islands—Westel, Oester, and Saroe—in the far distance, hovering like ghosts in the mist. Just then, the ferry lurches again, and an older woman appears beside me, grasping for the boat's edge.

"Sea sick?" I ask.

She nods grimly. "I'm not much of a boat person."

"Me, either." I laugh uneasily as we hit another wave. "How long are you on Halssel for?"

"Just a few days. My wife has wanted to visit the Fakaris for years, and I finally scheduled it for our anniversary. You?"

I glance down at the lilac carry-on suitcase I've brought with me, with my giant purse resting on top.

"A week. Maybe eight or nine days, max."

"A *week*?" Her eyebrows shoot up. "There's not much to do on Halssel, is there? What do you have planned?"

"I'm traveling for work," I say. Sort of. Basically. I'm manifesting.

"I see."

I lean in. "Actually, between you and me, I'm hoping to be let onto Saroe."

She makes a face like Robert DeNiro—eyebrows raised, mouth downturned, nodding slowly like I'm an idiot.

"Well," she says diplomatically. "Good luck. I don't think anyone's been to the other islands since the nineties."

"Yep! I'm hoping they'll make an exception."

I start as we hear a loud grinding sound coming from the floor below us, and look up to see the ferry driver pulling on the brake as we near the harbor. As the boat slows towards the dock, my eye catches a sign off of the main entrance to the harbor: *Welkommitet Fakarieilat*. Welcome to the Fakari Islands.

My heartbeat quickens to a patter, and I can feel it pulsing in my throat. This is real. It's actually happening.

The ferry finally comes to a complete stop, and the gate in front lowers onto the dock so we can disembark. As the older couples around me begin to get off, I hoist my heavy brown purse over one shoulder.

"Happy anniversary!" I call to the woman, who's grabbed the hand of another lady wearing a matching knit cap. She waves politely and mutters something to her wife. Probably along the lines of *that girl is gonna need a miracle.*

She's not wrong. But luckily I'm used to making my own miracles.

I turn to the docks and try to take note of all of it. The iron waves crashing against the rocks of the shore; the early May sun catching the spray; the smell of salt in the air. Finally, pulling the little suitcase behind me, I step onto the dock and start to worm my way through the other tourists. Although we're the only ferry of the morning, the market is already humming with energy. Shopkeepers are preparing their stalls for the new visitors, and I can see a woman setting up tables outside of a small cafe. To the left is a gravel road leading up to the cliffs, with little red cabins nestled alongside.

I follow the main street forward, looking for the storefront I've all but memorized. Around me, handfuls of tourists are admiring traditional Fakari goods—hand-knit sweaters with intricate patterns, thick wool blankets, and hand-thrown pottery sold out of wooden stalls parked in front of traditional brick-and-mortar stores. I see a man selling dried fish, and a woman my mom's age organizing jars and sachets of herbs under a sign for Moon Lake Apothecary. And there, at the end of the market street, I finally see what I've come here to find: Saroan Salts.

The stall is smaller and a little less elaborate than the ones around it. Splayed across its tables are jars upon jars of different kinds of sea salt in varying colors: tan, white, deep teal green. An older couple in matching yellow raincoats is admiring the goods, the woman examining jars one by one as her husband takes a moment to sample some salt with bread and olive oil.

Behind the booth are two young men, both tall and broad-shouldered. They share the same olive-toned skin and broad, blunt features that I recognize as uniquely Fakari: features that the addition of my mom's genes have rounded out in my own face. The one in front seems slightly older, sporting dark stubble and thick black hair. The other one has curly, wind-tousled hair and an open, friendly face. He disappears into the brick-and-mortar store behind the stall as I get closer.

I shove my nerves down as far as they can go, and walk towards the stall with my shoulders back, doing my best to project confidence.

"*Morlaa'kut*," I say to the tall one. The words feel awkward and foreign in my mouth, but I give what I hope is a winning smile.

He looks up at me, his dark eyes critical.

"Good morning," he says dryly—in English. "Welcome to the Halssel."

"Thanks so much! It's my first time here. Do you work for Saroan Salts?"

He looks pointedly at the glass jars he's leaning over to put on display, and I follow his gaze. Each jar sports the same teal-and-cream label, with the Saroan Salts logo displayed in the middle above the product name: *Traditional sea salt. Smoked salt. Samphire salt.*

"Oh, of course you do, sorry! I've been up most of the night on the ferry."

I laugh, but he doesn't crack a smile. Instead he stands up straight, crossing his arms in front of him.

"How can I help you?"

"I'm looking for Mr. Greenleaf, the company's owner. We've been emailing for months."

"Have you?"

His tone is challenging, and I instinctively feel my smile tighten.

"Yes. I'm here about a meeting for Puur, the wellness brand."

"Did he agree to see you?"

"Well—"

"Hey, Seb?" the other man asks, stepping out from the store-front. "We're low on rosemary salt. Do you remember if Finn packed any this morning?"

"Gimme a second."

"Wait. You're—*you're* Seb Greenleaf?"

My eyes slide over him again, taking in his broad frame and the faded jacket he's wearing over a flannel shirt. He can't be much older than 30. I'd been expecting someone closer to my mom's age.

I feel my cheeks grow warm. I hate being unprepared. What I hate more? Being caught in a lie. Or, well, *half*-lie.

"Mr. Greenleaf, I've been trying to reach you for months," I sputter, tumbling into my sales pitch. "My name is Maren Holt, and I work for Elspeth Waters at Puur. Well, sort of, but I'm here on behalf of Puur. They're—*we're*—really interested in selling traditional Fakari salt through the online store and pop-up loca-tions. Puur is a thriving wellness brand—"

"Not interested," he says, turning away to lift a box of salts from the shelves behind him. He hands it to the other man and gives a nod towards the storefront, where the worker disappears with the box.

"I… but Mr. Greenleaf."

"It's Seb."

"…*Seb*, this would bring Fakari salt to a whole new demo-graphic. The magazine is ready to dedicate an entire cover story to this, and set up a generous arrangement."

"I saw your emails. We're not interested."

"I…" I stop, flustered. "Has someone else already reached out to you? Someone from Goop? Or Naturi?" If that's true, my one shot is over. Elspeth was clear: she needs the exclusive on the next big thing. If another brand has gotten here first, she'll have to scrap the story—and my job opportunity with it.

"No, I'm just not interested."

"Well, why not?"

"We don't do business with mainlanders."

The irritation in his voice catches me off-guard, and I feel the edge of anger rising in my gut. Before I can suppress it, I snap, "What do you call this then?" and gesture at the market around us.

Seb looks up. I can see his face a little better now. Strong jaw, the edges of his facial hair just a little messy. Broad, strong features and big, dark eyes, where I can see the pupils are ringed with amber.

For a moment, I feel something in me still. He feels familiar, almost like I've met him before. The world around me goes soft as I try to figure out what it is. And then in a flash it's over, and the sounds of the market come back to hit me in full force.

"This is a *market*… for *tourists*," he says slowly, like I'm stupid. He starts arranging the glass jars before him again. "We focus on small trading and hospitality. Not selling out to magazines that peddle vagina candles and jade eggs to bored, rich housewives. Now, if you want to buy some salt, let me know. Otherwise, get out of my way."

My indignation hits me so hard that it takes everything in my body not to snap, *Okay, well fuck you!* I bring my fingers to the bridge of my nose, and the smell of my hand cream gives me just enough calm to make myself intelligible.

"Please," I say. "Think about this for a moment. This deal could be life-changing for everyone at Saroan Salts. Elspeth is ready to make a generous offer for exclusive trading rights. It's

a massive influx of money that could do a lot for your company."

He turns to grab a crate from the table behind him, and I start to talk faster.

"I've read everything on your website—well, all two paragraphs of it. I know you're trying to make sea salt the traditional Fakari way. I'm sure you need more money to scale. That's *exactly* why this deal could be so good for you. The money could fund a change that would impact your business for years."

"Look, I'm *not interested,*" he says, setting a crate of soaps down with force. As he crosses the stall to pick up another box, I notice he steps with a limp. I bring my eyes back up to his face.

"So tell me why not," I say.

"I don't need to explain myself to you."

"Well, I'm not leaving until I get a satisfactory answer, so it might be in your best interest to try."

He rolls his eyes. "Typical," he mutters under his breath.

"What's that supposed to mean?"

"Your behavior. It's typical. A great example of why we don't make agreements with mainlanders."

"And what if I'm not a mainlander?"

He gives me a sardonic look, his eyes meeting mine and then very deliberately dropping down. I suddenly become hyper-aware of my appearance—cute outfit obscured by my colorful oversized coat, cheeks flushed with the fresh morning air, curls probably having crossed the line from 'adorably windswept' to 'tumbleweed' on the ferry ride over. His gaze feels deliberately mocking as it rakes over my body, and for a moment I'm reminded of the way I felt in middle school gym, when the popular guys jeered at me as I ran by and my thighs jiggled. That was back when I still saw my generous curves and soft, rounded body as a weakness. I've fought long and hard to love myself—my big legs, wide hips, and soft stomach—and I'll be damned if some dumb salt trader tries to make me feel less-than.

Defiant, I cross my arms and raise my chin, daring him to mock me as he finally meets my eyes.

"And what if I'm a horse?" he asks.

"Ex*cuse* me?"

"Nothing. Just that you couldn't reek more of the mainland if you'd tried."

"Excuse *you*! You don't even know me."

"You're right, I don't. But I know the islands, and you're not from here." He turns from me as though our conversation was over. *The hell it is.*

"My last name's Winterwood," I say, so loudly that I see the heads of the elderly couple snap up from the corner of her eye.

Seb turns around to face me.

"What?"

"Maren Holt *Winterwood*. My dad was from Saroe, the big island."

I've surprised him now, I can tell. His eyes take me in again, but this time I see no trace of mockery—just genuine confusion. I watch him register my features, taking stock of my full lips, strong brow, and the wide cheekbones hidden beneath my round cheeks. Finally, he brings his gaze to my eyes with intensity, as though searching for something.

"You're David's kid," he says finally.

"Yeah, I am." It's weird hearing my dad's name on his lips. "Wait, did you know him?"

"Gabe?" Seb calls over his shoulder, ignoring the question.

The other stall worker ducks his head out from the door to the store behind them. "Yeah? What's up?"

Seb turns around and jerks his thumb to me.

"Your cousin's here."

2

MAREN

The other one looks at me, his brow furrowed.

"What?"

"That's David's girl," Seb says, and he shoves past Gabe to walk into the shop.

"Oh my God. Maren," Gabe says, walking out from around the stall. He comes up to me and gives me a bear hug, slamming me into his chest so hard that I lose some of the air from my lungs. "I can't believe you're really here."

"I... uh... " I mumble against the wall of his chest. He takes a step back, eyeing me.

"Man," he says, nodding slowly. "My mom always swore you'd come back one day. This is wild."

"Sorry, I... This is really embarrassing, please don't take it the wrong way—"

I realize there's no gracious way to end the sentence. As I stop talking, recognition dawns on his face.

"You don't know who I am."

I shake my head. "No. Sorry."

"Right. I'm Gabe." He extends a hand. "Gabriel Taguit. My mom is your aunt Saga. Your dad never mentioned a sister?"

"Um, maybe. I don't know, he died when I was little. And my mom never really talks about..." I gesture around vaguely. *Him. The islands. Any of this.* "Well, to be honest, she never really talks about anything except like, my career and my health. She doesn't know I'm here. If she did, she'd probably kill me."

I laugh in a way that's supposed to offset how awkward this is, but it doesn't help. Gabe stares at me for a long moment, and that's when it finally really hits me that I'm looking at family—the only living relative I know of, other than my mom. It's like seeing myself through a filter: a weird, warped-reality version of me. His curls are looser than mine, but the same color my hair would be if I didn't highlight it to honey-brown. His skin is almost exactly the same tan, if maybe a shade darker than my own. But it's his eyes that get me. Big and deep, rich brown—just like mine—but ringed with amber.

He has my dad's eyes, I realize. The thought almost makes me choke up.

Gabe seems to be having a moment, too, but he snaps out of it first.

"So why are you here, after all this time? I saw you talking to Seb?"

Right. The deal. "Yes! So, I work at Puur, the wellness magazine. Or, well, I will, if I can get this to work. They want to introduce Fakari salt to the American demographic, and they're willing to give it a cover story in the magazine to help promote it. I write the story, I get the job, and Saroan Salts gets a deal that's gonna change lives. Do you think you can help me get Seb on board?"

He looks over his shoulder in the direction of the storefront. "Nah, sorry. Seb makes his own decisions. But even if I could convince him, I don't know if that makes sense. We like to keep to our own here—I don't think most people would be interested in a magazine cover story."

"Do you think you could at least get me onto Saroe?"

He gives me a long look, then nods. "I think you should meet my mom."

WE WALK BACK towards the dock, and Gabe slows down as we near the stall for Moon Lake Apothecary. The woman standing there—Saga, Gabe called her—is the one I saw earlier. She has the same golden skin tone as her son, with dark hair streaked with silver and slicked into a braid that falls over her shoulder. As we approach, she looks up and warms visibly at the sight of us.

"*Heij, piu,*" she says to Gabe, and then notices me. "And who is this?"

"Mom, this is Maren."

Her eyes go wide and she whispers something under her breath. Within seconds she's coming out from behind the stall, wiping her hands on her apron and pulling me into a hug.

"Oh, sweetheart. I always knew you'd come home." She pulls away and I see her cheeks are wet.

"I knew the *agaayit* would bring you back. Look at you," she says, resting a hand on my face. "Eyes like your father."

She looks into them intently, as though searching for something, and I let out an uncomfortable laugh.

"It's so nice to meet you," I say. "This is wild. I never knew I had an aunt. I— I don't know, I can't believe this."

"Your mother never told you?"

I shake my head. I'm expecting disappointment, but she just nods.

"Then there must be a lot you don't know."

"Probably?"

Thunder rumbles in the distance, and we both look up to see a wall of clouds knitting together up ahead.

"Come," Saga says, putting her hand on my shoulder. "Let's get you inside. I want to know everything about you, and you can ask me anything you like. Gabriel, will you mind the stall?"

He nods and walks around it to take a seat, and Saga gestures for the main road.

I follow her down to the docks and then right, up the hill to a little cafe. The wind is starting to blow harder, and I can feel the first traces of drizzle hit my cheeks. Saga pulls open the heavy wood door and gestures for me to get inside.

I step in. It's a small space, just a handful of tables clustered under the windows, with a counter and a bakery display case on the far wall. There's some kind of flute music playing in the background—I assume traditional Fakari music, but I'm not sure if that's really what the locals listen to or just a show for us tourists. Saga follows me in, and across the room a waitress with thick red-brown hair looks up.

"*Heij* Saga," she says, walking over. "Good to see you. And who's this? A customer of yours?"

"This is my niece, Maren."

The waitresses' eyebrows raise and disappear behind her bangs. She gives me a long look.

"David's girl," she says, and I wonder how many people here actually knew my dad. "*Wilkommit*, Maren."

"*Takka.*"

"*Katalltet Fakari?*" She seems surprised, and I shake my head.

"Oh, no, I wish. I just looked up some phrases on the flight to Nova Scotia."

"Well, your accent's pretty good! You must have picked up some things from your dad."

"Maybe." I smile awkwardly. If my mom is to be believed, I'm *too* much like him: undisciplined, impractical. But he died when I was so young that I'll never know for myself.

The waitress gives me a long look, as though searching for something in my face the same way Saga just did. I find myself clearing my throat, wanting it to end.

"Maren's just come over on the first ferry out," Saga says, putting a gentle hand on my shoulder. "I'd like to treat her to some breakfast. Can we choose a table?"

"Oh, *iija*—yes, of course! Pick anything. I'll get you two some menus."

I walk forward with Saga and choose one of the tables on the far end of the cafe, with a view of the tourists' cabins and the cliffs. It's drizzling and overcast, but there are already traces of sun peeking out intermittently from between the clouds.

"The weather changes fast here," I say, taking a seat

Saga sits across from me and slips her worn brown coat off of her shoulders.

"Does it?" She pulls her braid over her shoulder. "I suppose. We get sun and rain most days. And winters are pretty cold for mainland standards. Or, so I assume, based on the coats I see tourists wear. I've never been."

"You've never been to the States? Or Canada?"

She shakes her head. "No need."

"Well, I can see why. It's gorgeous. I've been obsessing over photos for years, but it's way more beautiful in person."

"If you think this is nice, you should see the other islands," she says.

This is my chance.

"I'd love to," I say quickly. "That's why I'm here, actually. I'm trying to write a story about the Fakaris."

"A story?"

"Yes, specifically about Fakari salt. I have memories of my dad telling me about the salts, and I want to understand how they work—the healing properties and the, like, cultural history. I feel like this could be a *huge* hit in the States. When I saw online how Saroan Salts is trying to bring back the traditional way of salt harvesting, I thought it was the perfect opportunity for a collaboration. If I write the story and *Puur* starts selling the salt, just imagine how much the business would grow."

"And this… story… is the only reason you're here?" she asks.

I hesitate.

"It's the most important reason."

The waitress comes over, dropping two laminated menus on the table. I pick one up. It's cutesy, with a swirling font and drawings of each of the baked goods. I see a curled cinnamon bun and a loaf of dreamy-looking walnut dessert bread.

Saga eyes me for a long moment, as though weighing her options. Finally, she says, "Listen, Maren. The islands are very careful with outsiders. Your dad was Fakari—you're not an outsider to me. But other people may see that differently. And if you're coming here as a journalist, or for a trade agreement, I don't think that's going to go over well."

I swallow. "I *need* to be here. I don't have another option." I pull the tube of hand cream from my pocket and squeeze some into my palm again, rubbing it over my hands. As the calming scent hits my nostrils, I see Saga wrinkle her nose.

"What's that?" she asks.

"Oh, it's hand cream. I have really bad eczema. Here, it's natural," I say, extending the tube to her. She shakes her head, leaning away slightly, and I find myself a little offended.

"Let me see your hands," she orders. I drop the tube on the table and extend my palms to her. She looks over them, eyeing the rash like a fortune teller.

"I can make you something for that," she says, looking up. "A few weeks on the islands and this will clear right up."

"Oh, I doubt it. I've tried everything, and this stuff is the only thing that works. But thanks anyway."

She looks at me for a long moment, and not for the first time this morning, I feel strangely uneasy.

"Maren, I don't know about this story," she says finally. "But you're family, and I think you have a right to be on the islands. I'll talk to the others and see what we can do."

"You can't just bring me yourself?"

She shakes her head. "It doesn't work that way. The council has to make a decision."

"Right. The council." This is the only thing my mom ever told me about the Fakaris. *It's like a cult, Maren. All these secret councils and codes. And God forbid you ever try to break with tradition, or they kick you out, just like your father!*

For a second I wonder if this is a mistake, and I'm gonna get *Midsommar*-ed and memorialized on some awful true crime podcast. But Saga says,

"I'll talk to them tonight and try to get an agreement. If they let me bring you, you can stay with me for a while. But listen—it *cannot* be just about this story, alright? If that's the only reason you're here, it won't happen. You don't need to tell me what else this is about, but I need you to tell me honestly if there's another reason."

I think of what happened two nights ago in the parking lot. Why I had to get out.

"There's another reason," I say finally.

"Alright. *That*, I can work with. Now let's get you some breakfast."

3

SEB

"She's pack. That's the end of the story," Saga says.

We're in Saroe's common house for a pack council meeting. Different elders sit on the floor in one big circle, with non-voting community members behind them to listen in. Saga's perched cross-legged on a bed of pillows across from me, with her son Gabe behind her.

"You've gotta be kidding me," I snap. "She's here to make a deal. She doesn't give a shit about us or the islands—she just wants money. We're seriously gonna risk pack security for *that*?"

"We don't turn away pack members," says Heimig, one of the elders. "Are you suggesting we break five hundred years of tradition?"

"I'm saying *fiyeka pakka*," I say, bristling. "She's not pack. That rule was made for people who leave the islands and come back, not people who have never even been here." I turn to Gabe for backup. "You saw the girl, man. There's no wolf in her."

"*Fiya pakka, amariuk ot nekkat*," Saga said, her voice tight. *She's pack, wolf or not.* "Maren is David's daughter, and my niece. We don't know how the wolf appears in people who aren't fully Fakari. But if she has Fakari blood, she *is* one of us."

I bristle. "You saw her eyes. She reeks of wolfsbane and mainland chemicals. If she had a wolf, she couldn't stand that stuff."

"Come on, Seb," she says. "If she'd been raised here, you would have grown up in the same *fikarig*."

I think of the *fika* I grew up in—a few families choosing to live together and share pack life under one roof. Saga and Gabe; Emerson and her aunt and uncle; my parents and me. I try to picture the mainland girl growing up alongside us: exploring the woods in the summers, celebrating holidays, and taking trips to the north island when we got old enough. I can't.

"Yeah, but she *wasn't* raised here," I say. "That's the point. She doesn't know our ways, and she doesn't have a wolf. She may have Fakari blood, but culturally she's all mainland. There's a reason we stay separate."

"You were on the mainland yourself, for a while," Heimig says.

"*Exactly*, so I know how they are," I say, my voice getting louder. "They're competitive. They lie. Their whole way of life is built around hierarchy and power. Mainlanders are one and the same. Pack life is totally foreign to them."

"You say that like you can speak for everyone," Gabe says. "We met good mainlanders, too. The doctors who took care of you—"

"No," I snap. "There may be good people, but their way of life is broken. Isn't that the whole reason we stay isolated? To keep their culture off our shores?"

"The man's got a point," says Kieran, sitting behind Heimig. He can't vote in decisions yet, but council rules allow anyone to contribute to the discussion. "Our separateness keeps us safe. Look at what happens to the packs stuck on the mainland—the whole structure breaks down. The closer a pack gets to mainland culture, the worse the fall."

"Oh, come on," says Gabe. "You guys think we'll turn into the Manhattan pack from letting one girl in?" The Manhattan pack are the worst offender—half of their wolves work on Wall Street, and all cower under an hierarchical power structure with an alpha at the top, calling the shots.

"I'm saying it doesn't take long before it starts to happen," I say. "Think of the ones that share our way of life—Badlands, Arctic Gates, Crater Lake. They've had to fight not to lose the cultural independence *we* already have. Why would we give that up for some half-blooded mainland girl?"

"That mainland girl is my niece, *igaa*," Saga snaps. *Pup.* "Show some respect. If not for her, then for me."

"I— ugh." I can feel my wolf inside me, prowling, wanting to be let out. I force myself to take a breath. "It's not personal. It's just… Our ancestors fought to protect our safety and cultural sovereignty. Are we really going to give it up for a foreigner?"

"She's *Fakari*. She came here to learn where she comes from."

"She came here to sell us out to a *wellness magazine*," I say, my voice dripping with distaste. "If she's begging to be let onto the islands, it's only to buy more time to write that story or strike a deal. And what happens when she goes running back to the mainland? What if she tells people what she saw here?"

"Come now, Seb," Saga says, her voice softer. "Your father would have done anything for David to come home. Why are you so against bringing his daughter here, when it's clearly what fate wants?"

"You speak where fate whispers," I snap.

"I *listen* where fate speaks." She holds my gaze. "Your father was the one who opened our borders, once."

"And he's the one who closed them after David died. He learned from his mistake. I thought we did, too."

Saga shakes her head, and I can feel I'm losing this.

"Come on," I say, growing desperate. "Of all times, is *this* the moment to bring a foreigner here? We *know* something's wrong with the islands, and that the ancestors are upset. We see things are getting worse. If we do this now, we risk worsening their anger."

"You're making connections where there are none," Saga says. "Maren is half Fakari. If anything, it's clear to me that the ancestors are calling her home."

"Enough," Heimig said, raising his hands. "We've heard what both parties have to say. It's time for a vote. We either let David's daughter onto the islands or we don't. Those in favor?"

A ring of hands goes up, Saga's among them. I look around and see that most of the younger council members have their hands raised, too. That's no surprise—the younger generation has always been more open to cultural integration. What throws me off-guard is how many of our parents' generation are voting in favor.

They're blinded by the love they had for David, I think. A love that cost my father his life. My inner wolf snarls in anger.

"Against?" Heimig asks.

I raise his hand, looking around the room. There's a few hands from our parents' generation, and the oldest members of the council—our grandparents' age—have their arms raised. It seems like an even split. I set my jaw, feeling my wolf snap with rage inside me.

"Tied," Heimig says, finishing his count and glancing at the council secretary. "What's the precedent for something like this?"

Saga doesn't give him the time to answer. "The family exception. In the past, we've let in extended family in the case of a tie. Think of Ingela's sister, back in the nineties. When in doubt, we err on the side of pack."

"This is insanity," I say. "What are you talking about? If it's a tie, we do nothing. We regroup."

She shakes her head. "Not in the case of family."

"You're stealing the vote!"

"No, she's right," says the council secretary, looking up from his notes. "The last time we voted on an extended family member, it was an even tie, and we ruled in favor."

"Then it's decided," says Heimig. "We let David's daughter onto the islands. Saga, she's your ward. Caring for her is your responsibility until she can find her own way."

"No, stop," I say, rising to my feet. I wince as my weight hits my left leg, and straighten. "It's not that simple. How are you going to tell her about us, huh? What happens when she sees a pup freaking out at the grocery store and thinks we're overrun with wildlife?"

"I'll keep her at our *fikarig* for a few days and try to break the truth to her slowly."

"And then what? She goes running back to the mainland to write her article? I don't think salt is going to be the headline of *that* story."

"She won't go back," Saga says, shaking her head. "She may think she's here for the story, but there's something else driving her return. Once she finds it, I don't think she's going home."

"That's a pretty big gamble. You're betting the security and the independence of the islands on a *hunch*?"

"The council's decided, pup," Heimig says. "Pack code is clear."

I shake my head and storm out of the common house.

The night is cool and clear, and I can hear footsteps following me as I rush past the gardens and gym in the direction of the lake. I sniff the air—Gabe, with Kieran and Emerson behind—and pick up my pace. My leg aches with the movement, and at the sound of their footsteps growing faster, I shake my head, letting my body snap and unfurl into my wolf form as I break into an all-out sprint. I don't have time for their shit today. I need to be alone.

I race to the lake, and I sense Kieran and Gabe shift, too, but they don't rush to keep up. Kieran yips at Gabe and I hear them slow, giving me some space. *Good.* I run through the brush and bramble, jumping over roots and ducking under fallen branches. My heart is racing in my chest, and I feel the anger pulsing through me. The edge of the forest is nearing, but I know I need more time to come back to my senses. I take a left and keep running, faster and faster, until my heart is all wolf and the edges of the man disappear into the farthest corners of my consciousness.

I finally emerge at the lake twenty minutes later, panting and on the edge of exhaustion. Sure enough, there are Gabe and Keiran in their wolf forms, waiting at the water's edge. Gabe's wolf is smaller than mine, his fur a light gray-brown. Kieran's wolf is big and white, towering over the rest of us. With them is Emerson, in her human form as always, long blonde hair spilling over her shoulder. She's holding a ball of clothes to her chest, and looks over at me as I near them.

"About time," she says.

I snap towards her in a mock bite, and even though I get nowhere near her, Kieran snarls at me, a warning. I shake my head and shift back into my human form, coming to sit beside them.

"Sorry, Em," I say. "Rough day."

"It's okay," she says quietly. Kieran growls again.

"It *is* okay," she says, giving him a look. "Calm down, please."

She tosses me my sweater and sweats, which flew off when I shifted. I pull them on, fastening the magnetic clasps along the side until I'm covered. Most Fakari clothing is designed to accommodate a shift, whether through clasps that allow it to fly off without tearing, or the loose, flowy fabric worn by the older generation. Gabe shifts into his human form beside me and pulls on his own clothes. When Kieran stays in his wolf form, Em leans back against him, resting against the fur of his chest.

"I just can't believe this," I say. "This is so shortsighted."

"Come on, dude," Gabe says, fastening his sweater. "She's my cousin. It can't be that bad."

"She's all mainland," I say. "Saga can't see it because she's still fucked up from losing David, and she just wants this to work. But anyone with a nose can smell that that girl doesn't belong here. Watch: in six weeks she'll be back on the mainland, telling everyone who will listen that we're shifters. And then how long will it be before the American government is at our shores?"

"Take a breath," Gabe says. "You lost. It is what it is—let's make the most of it."

I bristle.

"My mom always said she'd come back, and here she is," he adds. "The article is just a surface-level reason. There's something deeper drawing her home."

"The ancestors," Em says softly.

I say nothing, and we spend the rest of the evening watching the moon rise over the lake in silence.

4

MAREN

I open my eyes to see the early morning light streaming in through the curtains.

Wait—those aren't my curtains. It takes a second to remember where I am. But then I hear the soft whistle of the wind and the roar of the ocean faintly in the distance.

Oh, right. The Fakaris.

Oh my God. I'm actually here.

I roll over in bed and reach for my phone, which fell to the floor in the middle of the night. Turning on the screen, I see that airplane mode is still on, meaning my mom hasn't had the chance to reach me. For a second, my thumb hesitates over the screen. Then, finally, I tap open the shortcuts menu and turn on my service.

It takes my phone a second to connect to cellular data. And then, when it does—*BAM.*

A barrage of text messages and notifications appears. I see four or five from Mom right away.

Mom: I couldn't reach you last night. I'm
worried, please call me.

Mom: Maren, where are you? I'm serious.
Call me.

Mom: I saw the news clip from the
parking lot. I know it was you. I TOLD you
this would happen if you didn't listen. Call
me right now

Mom: Maren, we can fix this. I can fix this
if you just PICK UP THE PHONE

Mom: MAREN!

Heat floods my cheeks as I skim through her messages and then set our chat on mute. I go over to my email. At the top are a few confirmations from my last-minute flights and ferry bookings, but between them is an email from Elspeth's assistant, asking for an update with her on cc. I tap on it and type out a quick reply.

> *Hi Fallon and Elspeth,*
> *Thanks for checking in! Things are going great so far. I'm*
> *at the islands and making connections, gathering good*
> *info for the article. It's going to be a gorgeous cover.*
> *Connection is bad here, so if you don't hear from me for*
> *a few days, just assume everything is going great!*
> *Sincerely,*
> *Maren Holt*

Feeling the drum of nervousness in my chest, I swipe down the options menu and turn my data off again, then climb out of bed. I was too tired for my evening routine last night, so I just stripped off my clothes and dumped them on the chair at the foot of the bed. Now I turn to the purple suitcase and get to unpacking my skincare and makeup pouches. I pull out the white zip-up pouch and blue bag, and head into the tiny bathroom.

Some people are raised with religion, but my mom raised me to believe in something more reliable: skincare. I start on my routine her dermatologist gave me, screwing open droppers and ceramic jars of cream as I go. Exfoliant. Toner. Essence, serum, moisturizer, and sunscreen—in my mom's immortal words, even the best skincare routine is worthless without sunscreen. And I mean immortal almost literally, because she hasn't raised an eyebrow since I was in middle school.

Next, I turn my attention to my body, stripping off the over-sized gym shirt I slept in and slathering myself with moisturizer. I take note as I run my hands over myself. Thick bronzed arms; full breasts and stomach, and an ass and thighs like a Pixar mom (without the itty-bitty waist). This is just about the only area of my life where I don't kowtow to my mother. To her, my body is just another thing about me that's too much—a symbol of my lack of discipline, and as a result, her failings as a mother. But I know my body isn't a thing to be perfected, but a tool for experiencing the world. It's the one thing in my life that's *mine*. It's the one place in the world where I'm home.

A ripple of anger surges through me as I remember Seb yesterday, using those mocking eyes to try to make me feel insecure. He'd be lucky to ever even get near a woman with half my talents and a fourth of my ass.

I finish moisturizing my legs and get dressed, opting for a white sweatshirt dress and Air Jordans. My hair is big and messy today—it gets bigger every day after wash day—so I clip it up and out of the way. Finally, going over to my makeup bag, I pull out a smokey perfume and spritz it in my neck and over my sweatshirt. And with that, I'm ready for the day.

A day full of nothing, I remember. A day full of waiting to see if I'm even allowed to step foot on my dad's home island.

I lift my chin defiantly. That's okay. I'll find something to do.

I walk back into the main room of the cabin and look out of the window. It's slightly overcast, but the cliffs look gorgeous this morning. Saga won't be back with news until eight or nine at the earliest, she said. I might as well enjoy a walk.

THE WIND IS COOL, and I feel it brush against my bare legs as I make my way along to the cliffs. It's not a far walk to the edge; the cabins are half-way up, and these cliffs don't go too high. But even with the houses so close and the harbor not too far down, it's so quiet up here that it almost feels like a different world.

I'm not used to quiet—not back in Boston, and not in my brain. Back home I *always* need to have something on in the background: a podcast, a playlist, a YouTube video, an audiobook. If my phone dies while I'm on a run, I end early and go home, or else it feels like my mind will explode. But it's weird—the higher I climb on the cliff, the quieter the world gets, and my brain starts to get quieter, too.

I reach the top and look out to the gray sea below, taking a deep breath. The air is so clean and clear here that it almost feels too big for me, like my lungs expand to new places when I take it in. It feels *good*. Instinctively I close my eyes and lift my chin, enjoying the wash of cool breeze on my face.

When I open them again, I'm surprised to see that I can make out a part of the next island in the distance. Now that yesterday's fog is gone, the banks of—it must be Westel, I think, trying to remember the geography of the islands—are visible. If I'm right, then that's the smallest of the islands other than this one. I can see almost the whole shape of it, though only the shore is clearly visible, the rest growing hazy along the line of the horizon.

I fix my gaze on the shore, trying to remember what I know of the island. Then, suddenly, I see something at the edge of one of the banks move with lightning speed, and my eyes follow. A group of animals running through the trees to the shore. With a gasp, I realize.

Wolves.

Adrenaline cracks through my body in an instant, and I freeze. They're so far away; I know that logically. But my body recognizes a predator—*remembers* instinctively what these animals can do—and I turn rigid, afraid to even move a muscle.

They're too far away. They can't hurt you, I think to myself as memories flash through my mind. Fur and teeth and blood. The sound of crying. A gunshot.

Anxiety ripples through me, and I feel that awful thing in my gut: the part of me that ruins everything, desperate to take over. Instinctively, my hand reaches to my pocket for my hand cream. I rub some into my palms and bring them together, drawing them close to my chest as the familiar scent of lavender and witch hazel helps my mind grow soft. Safe.

I'm fine. They can't hurt me.

Even as my mind stills, I stay there, watching them. The wolves walk along the shoreline, two of them yipping at each other playfully. They look younger, and after a minute, I think I can tell which one's the leader of the group. It moves his head towards the trees, and the pack follows its lead away from the water.

I watch as they disappear and let out a long, low breath.

Wolves. This place has secret councils, and possibly a cult, and definitely *wolves.*

Maybe coming here was a mistake, after all. But before I can even entertain the thought, I hear my mom's voice in my head, from just before she arranged my Puur pitch.

This is the last time I'm going to save you from yourself, Maren. It's time to grow up and show that you can be trusted with your own life.

No—I need to be here. Turning around, I head back to the cabins and the harbor below.

To my surprise, it's Gabe, not Saga, who finds me later that morning. I'm sitting at a table outside the same cafe as yesterday when he walks up.

"Hey. Good news! The council okayed you."

"Yeah?" I jump up, clapping my hands in front of me. "Oh my God, *amazing*. Okay, that's perfect. I can be packed in five minutes."

He laughs. "Yeah, I figured you'd want to leave right away."

"Oh, sorry. Do you have to work?"

He shakes his head. "I was going to—I usually work the salt stall on Wednesdays, but Finn's taking over for me. Mom put me on Maren duty."

"What's Maren duty?" I cross my arms in front of my chest instinctively.

"You know. Showing you around and stuff. Helping you get settled."

"Oh." My hands fall to my sides again. "Okay, great. Then I'll grab my stuff."

"What's this?" He nods to the table where I was sitting. I look down, where a pile of books and a large paper bag shows the spoils of my morning.

"Oh, this is just stuff I bought for research." I close the cover of the book I was reading and turn it to him. "I got a book on Fakari history and culture, a guidebook on basic Fakari phrases. See? *Ije kommet ei Fayaanestit Staatuk*. That means I'm from the US."

Gabe smiles. "I know what it means."

"Also! I got this super cute sweater." I reach down into the bag and pull out the thick wool. It's a rich red, with a wheat-like pattern along the bottom hem and edge of the sleeves in a tradi-tional Fakari style. I hold it proudly up to my chest.

"The guy told me that this pattern symbolizes the abundance of island life."

Gabe snorts. "Who told you that? Tobias? He'll say anything to make a sale."

I lower the sweater. "Wait, really? So what does it mean?"

"I don't think it means anything. I think it's a sweater."

"Hm." I look down at the item in my hands. Maybe I should return it.

"But I'm sure it'll look great," Gabe adds.

"Yeah?"

"Of course." He smiles and claps a hand on my shoulder. "You're one of us—it's practically your birthright. Now come on, we'll get your stuff and take the boat to Saroe. And once we're there, I'll get you a better language book, too. This one only has the basic phrases. Wait 'till I teach you to curse."

GABE HELPS me pack up my stuff, and after I check out of my cabin, he takes me to a little boat off the side of the harbor. It's a white motorboat with a faded logo on the side, and I can see some old blue tarps folded on the seats. He steps down into it easily, grabbing my suitcase and pulling it in after him. As he brushes off the seats, I lean against one of the large wooden stakes of the dock, trying to figure out how to get in.

He looks up. "Oh, here, let me help."

Gabe reaches to offer me a hand, but it's not quite as much support as I'm hoping for. I step gracelessly into the boat and almost immediately fall onto my ass.

"Thanks," I mumble.

"I guess you don't have many boats in... where did you grow up again?"

"I'm from all over—my mom moved us around a lot when I was little. But most recently Boston."

"No boats in Boston, then?" He starts untying the rope from the harbor's edge.

I think of my freshman orientation trip again. "Actually,

Boston's on the water. But for me it might as well have been landlocked."

Gabe gets the boat going and then takes me around the east side of the island, pointing out Westel and Oester as we pass between them. It's hard to hear him over the sound of the motor, so we don't talk much as we go. Instead, I take in the part of Halssel I hadn't seen yet, admiring the mountain and the rich green forest along the back of the island. Eventually, Saroe comes into view: first the rocks of the shore, then the low green hills, marked with tumbling waves of gray-green grass. As we get closer, I can make a row of houses along the coast, all stone builds and tiled roofs.

We near the harbor, less busy and colorful than the one on Halssel. I see a half-empty parking lot to the left, and a couple shops in front, with vendors and fishermen eating lunch on the benches facing the sea. As Gabe starts to dock the boat, I realize they're staring at us.

"How many people know I'm coming?" I ask.

"Oh, everyone."

"Everyone?"

I eye a group of fishermen. They're muttering something to each other, and one of them gestures towards me with the hand he's using to eat an apple. I meet their eyes with a raised brow, expecting them to look away, but they just keep staring. One of them lifts an arm in greeting.

"Yeah. Word travels fast on the islands," Gabe says. "And we haven't had new people here since... well, since your mom's time, I guess."

Right. My mom. It's almost impossible to imagine her here, but of course she was too, once, or she and my dad would never have met. That was back in the nineties, during the short window of time the Fakaris opened up their shores. They closed down again when I was a kid, for reasons she never explained to me. Maybe if my dad had been alive, he could have told me why.

Gabe helps me out of the boat, then lifts my bags onto the dock before hopping up himself. He dusts off his hands and leads me towards the harbor. As we pass, I notice the people around us eyeing me curiously.

"It's about a twenty minute walk to the *fikarig*," Gabe says. "We don't drive much around here, but you didn't bring too much stuff, so I figured we could walk."

"Okay. It'll be cool to see the island, anyway. What's a *fikarig*?"

The word feels clunky on my tongue, even after spending this morning sounding out phrases from my guidebook.

"Oh, it's a house you share with your *fika*, your—ehm, well." Gabe gestures awkwardly, like he's trying to find the right word. "I guess it's kind of like a chosen family. A *fika* is usually four or five families who share life together. You live in the same house, and you share holidays and vacations."

"Like a commune..." I say carefully.

"Sort of. I guess."

Cult confirmed.

We walk over a cobblestone street, passing a shop with crates of apples and fresh vegetables outside.

"*Fi-ka-rig*," I say again, sounding out the syllables.

"It literally translates to communal house," Gabe adds as we pass a bookshop. "It's where the name Fakari comes from, actually. Because the islands are our shared home."

"Oh, no way! The guidebook didn't mention that. That's beautiful."

He shrugs. "Yeah, I guess it is."

"So who else lives in your *fikarig*?"

"Well, me and my mom. Emerson—she's our age, too—and her aunt Dagmar and uncle Viggo. And then there's Isolde, and you met her son Seb already."

"Wait." I stop in my tracks. "Seb *Greenleaf* lives with you?"

He nods. "Yeah. We're basically brothers. I mean, we're not actually related, but we grew up together."

I swallow, bringing my hand to my head. "You're telling me I'm going to *live* with Mean Surly Salt Dude from yesterday."

He laughs. "If you wanna look at it that way."

I shake my head. Communal cult life is *not* going to work for me.

"God. Tell me Emerson is normal, at least."

"She's great. She's quiet, but she's really kind once you get to know her. And our friend Kieran—he's not officially in our *fika*, but he might as well be—basically lives with us, too. I think you guys would get along."

We start walking again and I nod, thinking. "So it's like, mostly normal people, and then Seb."

Gabe smiles. "Yeah, but even Seb—I don't know, he can be a little hard-headed, but he'll grow on you. His heart's in the right place, his head is just—"

"Up his own ass?" I offer.

He snorts. "I guess."

We take a left. Up ahead, I see the cobblestones give way to a path that winds through trees and towards rolling green hills.

"But hang on, that's three families in your *fikarig*, right?" I say as we turn down the road, towards the trees. "You and your mom, Em and her family, Seb's mom and him. But you said four or five."

I sense Gabe hesitate. "Uh, yeah. It was four, originally. With your mom and dad."

My head snaps up. "*What?* My parents lived in your commune?"

"Your parents were part of our *fika*, yeah. Or, they were supposed to be. You'll be staying in what would have been their bedroom."

Oh my God. I don't know why I never thought about where my dad lived when he was here. I guess my mom has shared so little about him and the Fakaris that my questions never got that far.

I look up at the hills and trees ahead of us, stone fences marking the plots of land of different families—or *fikas*, I guess—in the far distance.

"I had no idea," I say quietly. "It must have been so hard on your mom when they left."

"It was hard on all of them."

From his voice, I can hear that there's something more there, but he doesn't elaborate. We walk in silence for a few minutes as I pore it over, trying to imagine how it would have been.

"Still," I say finally. "That's not a lot of people for three families, right?"

"Seb's dad died a few years ago," Gabe says by way of explanation. "And mine passed away when I was a kid."

"Oh God, I'm so sorry. I know how hard that is."

"Yeah," he says, nodding. "Thanks."

My thoughts turn to my own dad, and the few memories I still have of him. He died when I was six, so the images in my mind are fragmented and soft around the edges. But I remember how I felt around him; the way he laughed. And at the thought of him, I suddenly remember the wolves I saw this morning.

"Can I ask something?" I ask.

"Yeah, of course."

"Is there a lot of wildlife on this island?"

"Oh, uh, we have sheep, mostly for wool. Some foxes and rabbits. Why?"

"I saw some wolves in the distance this morning, when I was on the cliffs."

"Oh *Halssel*?" he asks, looking over. "That shouldn't have happened. We have codes—"

"Codes?"

"I, uh... yeah." He swallows. "Like... wildlife control, I guess?"

He sounds unsure of his own words, and it makes me nervous.

"There shouldn't be any wolves on the tourist island," he adds.

I shake my head. "No, I saw them in the distance, on the coast of another island. Westel, I think. But that's not—I mean, there's no wolves *here*, right? On Saroe."

He hesitates for a split-second, and I feel a chill spread up my spine.

"There's nothing that would hurt you here," he says carefully. Somehow, I don't feel any better.

"I hate wolves," I mutter. "Awful, horrible animals."

"Oh yeah? Why's that?" His voice is delicate, probing.

"You don't know?" I ask, looking up. "That's how my dad died. A wolf attack when we were camping. Your mom never said...?"

Gabe says nothing, and I feel something tense in the air between us. I'm about to ask about it when he gestures up ahead.

"There. That's the *fikarig*," he says, clearing his throat.

I follow his gaze. Off in the distance and a little to the right, I see a large white home with a thatched roof and a sage green door and shutters. There's ivy up one side, and to the left of it is a second structure—an add-on to the house, I think, made of brick. It stretches behind the home and has some kind of turret on the side. The house is nestled between the trees, before the forest turns to fields.

I swallow, taking it in. My parents' old house.

My new home.

5

SEB

When I get to the *fikarig* for dinner, I smell it immediately.

Witch hazel, chemicals, and some cloying perfume that reeks of artificial smoke.

The mainland girl is *in my house*.

Maren, I remind myself. The mainland girl is named *Maren*. The same Maren I've heard Saga cry about every year on David's birthday and the anniversary of his death.

I shake off my shoes on the mat, shutting the front door behind me. I should be happy for Saga—glad that she finally gets back some family after everything she's lost. But I know how this ends. In just a few weeks Maren will leave us, and Saga will be worse off than when she started. And I know *exactly* how badly that kind of loss fucks up a *fika*.

I hang my jacket on a hook in the hallway. It's still pretty cool outside for May, but the house is warm with the heat of whatever Gabe's making for dinner. The air is rich with the scent of herbs and fish, and I can hear the sound of chatter from the kitchen. Gabe and the mainland girl, talking about something.

Maren. Her fucking name is Maren, I remind myself again. And she'll be staying with us for a few weeks, even if I think that's the worst idea in the world. I hate it, but I should do my best to be nice.

I follow the sound of their voices, walking towards the kitchen.

"Okay, now do idiot," Gabe commands from his place before the stove.

"*Nagaayit,*" Maren tries, and Gabe laughs.

"Almost, that's plural. It's *nagaayu.*"

I lean against the doorway. "And *nagaaya* for a woman."

Maren turns around. She looks different today. Her hair is up this time, and she's wearing some kind of weird little dress that looks like a hoodie, exposing the soft skin of her thighs. Either that, or she forgot to put on pants. But no, that's not what's changed.

She looks happy, I realize. Until her eyes land on me.

"Well," she says. "If it isn't my favorite professional acquaintance."

"If it isn't the *nagaaya* who yelled at me at the market."

It's supposed to be a joke, but I see her upper lip curl in distaste. Over her shoulder, Gabe mouths *What the fuck, dude?*

Damn. So much for being nice. "Sorry, I—"

"Well, maybe if your customer service weren't so abrasive, I wouldn't have to yell."

She crosses her arms over her chest, and immediately I feel my inner wolf recognize a challenge. The words come out of my mouth before my brain can register them.

"I'm not usually abrasive to customers. Just people who lie so they can speak to a manager."

"*Excuse* me?" she asks. Behind her, Gabe turns back to the stove, apparently ready to keep himself out of this.

"You had an appointment with Mr. Greenleaf, didn't you?" I ask. "Weird. I didn't see it in my calendar."

"Sorry for assuming the head of a company wouldn't be some dude who dresses like the manager of a Hot Topic," she says, stepping towards me.

What the hell is Hot Topic?

"I should have known to expect it, actually," she adds, "considering that your business is barely off the ground. Maybe I should have reached out to one of the bigger salt companies, run by people who know how to recognize a good deal when they see one."

"Thanks for the business advice," I say, crossing my arms. "I've always wanted professional feedback from some girl who doesn't even work at Puur."

At this, I see Gabe's head snap around. Maren sputters, her eyes growing wide.

"I didn't say I worked at Puur, I said I was here on *behalf* of Puur, which is true," she says. "I *will* work at Puur once I write this article and secure a deal. I have Elspeth's word. And how do you know that?"

"I looked you up. There are zero articles there written by you. I did find an article on a different website, about choosing a vibrator based on your zodiac sign. *Charming.*"

"Oh, so you *can* read," she says with an empty laugh. "I'm so relieved. I did wonder, after all those emails you blatantly ignored."

"I love to read. I read your whole LinkedIn profile, actually."

From my periphery, I see Gabe's eyebrows raise to his hairline, and he turns slowly back to the stove. I should rein myself in, but my wolf's in charge now.

"Very illuminating. What was it, a semester of fashion school, then half a computer science degree, then you *did* actually graduate, but in marketing. Part of a linguistics master's—I saw beekeeping in there somewhere, *that* was a surprise—"

"Sorry I contain multitudes, bro." She raises an eyebrow.

"Not all of us can stay in our hometowns and live with our moms when we're thirty."

I feel my jaw tense.

"Oh, yeah, it must all seem very foreign to you. The idea of community. Actually forming relationships and staying in one place."

"What's that supposed to mean?"

"You're a tourist."

She rolls her eyes. "Cute xenophobia. Did you find it in the back of your great grand-dad's closet, along with that ancient sense of style?"

"No, really," I say. "Not just here on the Fakaris. In life. A hundred jobs, a bunch of half-degrees. You're afraid to sit still. So why *would* I be a tiny part in your latest non-career? Really, why bother to get to know you at all? You'll be gone in two weeks anyway."

She blinks, and I can see something in her eyes, wide and soft and vulnerable. For a second, I want to take it back; say sorry, start over. But then, in a flash, that look is gone. She steps towards me, getting so close there's just inches between us, and the world grows still.

"It must be so hard," she says. "It must be so *exhausting* to hold on so tightly to every little thing in your life."

Her voice is quiet but controlled. Unnerving. My wolf starts pacing, anxious to be let out. *Not now*, I think.

"Tell me, is it embarrassing?" she asks, her voice almost a whisper. "Standing next to someone who isn't afraid to try something new, or admit when something doesn't work out? Or does it just make you scared, because you know you'll never be brave enough to take the same kind of risk when it matters?"

I swallow.

"I could never be scared of a woman who forgot to wear pants to dinner," I say, and turn to walk out of the kitchen.

6

MAREN

Aunt Saga comes back from work just after Seb leaves for upstairs. As soon as she sees Gabe and me at the stove, she claps a hand to her chest.

"Oh, how many times I've dreamed of seeing you two together in this house."

Gabe looks over. "*Heij, Ama.*"

Hey, Mom, I translate mentally. I can still feel the adrenaline coursing through me from my brief interaction with Seb. *Asshole.*

Saga smiles at Gabe and then looks over at me, her eyes misty. "Your father would be so happy to see that you're home, *piu.*"

"What's *piu?*"

"It's a term of endearment. Like sweetheart, or love. Don't worry. I'll teach you so much Fakari you'll be a professional translator in days."

"I've taught her some words already," Gabe says, turning off the stove. "Come on Maren, show her what you can do."

"*Uikbaane,*" I say.

Gabe barks out a laugh as Saga looks at him in horror and swats his arm.

"Gabriel! She can't even form a sentence, and you already have her cursing."

"I can say a few sentences already, actually!" I try to bring to mind the phrase I recited to Gabe this morning. *"Ije kommet ei Fayaanestit Staatuk."*

Saga shakes her head. *"Nekka. Tik kommtet ei Fakarieilat."* She pronounces the words slowly for my sake.

I blink as my brain pieces the words together. *No. You come from the Fakari Islands.*

A weird feeling forms in my chest. She really believes it. I wonder if I ever could.

"We finished dinner," Gabe says from over my shoulder. "Maybe you guys can set the table while we wait on Em and Kier."

I press a smile. "Uh, yeah, sure! Just show me where everything is."

Saga gives me a quick tour through the kitchen, handing me a stack of plates and silverware as we go. It's a large space, but it feels homey, with cool tiles on the ground and the Scandinavian-style cabinets painted a rich shade of dark green. She grabs the glasses and leads me into a dining room to the left, which Gabe hadn't thought to show me when first he let me into the house.

The room is large, with cream-colored walls and a view of the garden on one side. In spite of its size—there's a massive dining table in the middle, able to seat twelve people at least—it's made to feel smaller by dark wooden beams stretching across the low ceiling.

Saga rolls out woven place mats before each seat as I put the plates down. We'll just be eating with the six of us today, she tells me; Emerson's aunt and uncle are working late, along with Seb's mother.

Just as we finish setting the table, I hear the front door open and two voices: one low and rich, followed by a woman's gentle laughter.

"Ah, you're home!" calls Saga from behind me. "We're in the dining room. Come say hello to our new houseguest!"

A minute later, the two of them appear from the hallway. I see the girl first. She's beautiful—slender and willowy, with long blonde hair that falls down her back and around her delicate face. Behind her is the man I assume is Kieran, the family friend. He's built like a brick house: tall and broad, with reddish-brown hair and a thick beard. The rest of his tanned, angular face is covered with a spray of freckles.

"Oh, you must be Maren," the young woman says, walking towards me. "It's so nice to meet you. I'm Emerson. Or Em, if you want."

"It's nice to meet you, too!"

I pull her into a hug, and instantly feel her narrow shoulders stiffen in surprise. It's only as I pull away that I realize maybe hugging people in introduction is one of those cringy Americanisms you hear European people complain about.

Emerson's posture softens slightly as I step back, and I'm about to apologize when I see her smile, gray-blue eyes crinkling at the corners. She really is beautiful; she reminds me of a watercolor painting, soft and delicate in comparison to Seb, Saga, and Gabe's rich, deep coloring. The guy behind her steps forward, extending a hand.

"I'm Kieran," he says, and I take his hand and shake it. It's massive; *all* of him is massive. I glance between the two of them. Standing next to each other, they look like an Abercrombie ad.

"I like your outfit," Em says, looking down at my dress and shoes. "The dress is so cool. I only ever see clothes like that on TV."

"Aw, thanks. Believe it or not, I got some feedback on it today."

Her brow furrows. But just as I'm about to rat Seb out, Gabe appears behind me, carrying a sheet pan of the fish he taught me to make earlier.

"Alright, everything's ready. I thought we'd have traditional Fakari food for Maren's first dinner on the islands. *Kalgaali*—that's white fish, Maren—with mixed vegetables and some *bakka* bread on the side. Can someone get Seb?"

Kieran nods and turns out of the dining room to head for the stairs.

"So how about your outfit?" I ask, gesturing to Emerson's blue scrubs as she steps to the table to take a seat. "Are you a doctor?"

"I'm training to be a healer under your Aunt Saga."

"You're a healer?" I ask Saga, taking a seat myself. "I thought you owned the apothecary."

"I do both," she says. She sits as Gabe comes in carrying a tray of flatbreads—*bakka*, he called them. "I became a healer when I was Emerson's age, and I opened the shop about fifteen years ago."

"And healer as in…" I realize I don't know how to ask the question, but Saga catches my drift.

"We practice essential medicine the way you know on the mainland—setting bones, handling cuts and burns, that sort of thing. But we primarily practice traditional Fakari medicine. There are a few licensed doctors on the islands who practice Western medicine, but for anything beyond routine care, like a surgery, we transfer people to the mainland."

"Really?" I say. "You send people to the States? On the ferry…?"

"The agreement is with Canada," Emerson says. "For emergencies, it's not too long of a helicopter ride to Toronto."

Across the table, I hear Gabe clear his throat like a warning. I turn to see Kieran and Seb enter the dining room, and Kieran takes a seat next to Em. Seb, with a brooding look on his face, walks around the table to sit behind the only empty plate. Directly across from me.

I glance between the others, trying to figure out what just happened. Kieran starts loading food onto Emerson's plate, and as he glances at me, I figure it's a lost cause.

"So what do *you* do for work, Kieran?" I ask, changing the subject.

"Uh, I'm a carpenter. I make furniture." He passes the dish of vegetables across the table to Gabe.

"He's being modest," Emerson says. "He has his own workshop, and he makes *beautiful* pieces. Actually, one of his dining sets was just featured in a mainland magazine. What was it called, again?"

"*Architectural Digest,*" he mutters.

"Oh my God, for real?" I say. "That's wild. That's so cool, Kieran! Congratulations!"

He smiles uncomfortably, but I can see Emerson warm at the praise.

"So *some* magazine coverage on the islands is appreciated," I say lightly, glancing pointedly at Seb. He bristles and I look away, reaching for some bread.

"And Gabriel here used to work for the apothecary, before he began helping Seb with Saroan Salts," Saga says across the table.

I turn to Gabe. "Yeah? What do you do?"

"Careful," Seb grumbles. "Anything you say can and will be printed in *Bored Housewives Weekly.*"

"Only because *Surly Asshole Quarterly* wasn't hiring," I say sweetly. "The readership is too low, since the subject matter is so agonizingly boring."

To my right, Kieran snorts.

"Sebasteijen," Saga admonishes. "Be nice to our houseguest."

"What? She just called me an asshole!"

"She's not wrong," says Kieran, and I decide I like him.

"Plus, you called her a *nagaaya* earlier," says Gabe.

"*Sebasteijen!*" Saga says again.

"I was *trying* to be funny," he says, serving himself and then setting the dish firmly onto the table. "But fine, okay. Forget it."

As I put the last vegetables and a cut of the fish on my plate, Kieran clears his throat and raises a glass.

"Let's eat. *Kutetkuk*," he says. The others repeat after him.

"*Kut-et-kuk*," I manage to get out, a half-step too late.

"Anyway," Gabe says, looking to me. "I do whatever has to get done for the business. Right now, that's a lot of physical work. We harvest the salt the old-fashioned way, so it's a lot more labor-intensive than at the bigger plants."

"Oh, that's interesting," I say, taking a sip from my drink, some kind of sparkling elderberry mix. "What does that mean? Labor-intensive how?"

Across the table, I see Seb stiffen.

"I promise I won't write anything about what you tell me, Seb," I say with a look. "I really am just curious."

Gabe says nothing and glances at Seb as if waiting for permission. Finally, Seb looks up at me. Under the heavy shade of his brow, the amber in his eyes glimmers.

Damn it. He's kind of hot, I realize. I hate myself for noticing.

"Making salt is easy," Seb says finally. "All you need is seawater and heat. Making high-quality salt, *consistently*, is harder. But most of the salt companies around here do that just fine, the same way salt is harvested all around the world."

"But you're trying to do something different, right? You're making it the traditional way." I stalked his company's bare-bones website enough to know that. It's why I reached out to him in the first place.

Seb stays quiet, and I wait for him to say more. He opens his mouth and then hesitates, and I let out an exasperated sigh.

"Come on, dude, what do you think I'm gonna do? Start a rival salt business?"

He cracks a smile. "Maybe, after the Puur job falls through."

Saga gives him a look.

"Seb," she murmurs, but he stays silent. Finally, she turns to me.

"Seb isn't just interested in making traditional Fakari salt," she says. "He's trying to uncover and revive the *way* our ancestors made, and used, salt long ago. That method has been mostly lost to time. Did your father ever tell you about the *Fakari Eijna*?"

I shake my head.

"It's our ancient book," Saga continues. "It contains our people's earliest myths, but also codes for living and an early history of our people. And in the earliest stories, salt already makes an appearance. It can be used to heal people, or to prepare them for important milestones. It has certain... ceremonial purposes."

At this, I see Seb stiffen out of the corner of my eye. I keep my gaze locked on Saga, willing him not to ruin this.

"Over time, certain traditional means of making things gets lost," she continues. "Do you know about the black churches of Norway, for example?"

"No. Only from pictures."

She nods. "The churches are made of wood, but they need to be re-sealed regularly with a special tar to protect them from the elements. The Norwegians still do this today, but they no longer have the original recipe for the tar—it's been lost to time. What they have now is a weaker, less effective tar, which needs to be applied more often to do the same job."

"How did the recipe get lost?" I ask.

She shrugs. "That just happens. Imagine it's three hundred years ago. You are a shoe cobbler; your father was a shoe cobbler, and his father was a shoe cobbler. You intend to teach your children how to make shoes. But you don't have to write down how, right? Because to you, everyone knows how to make shoes. Why would you preserve that knowledge for a future generation when you can just teach your child, and she will teach her children..."

Saga's voice trails off as I take another bite.

"So making salt was a family business?" I ask.

She nods. "Traditionally, yes, it was a trade passed down from each generation to the next. Then, a few hundred years ago, there was a… pause."

"You shouldn't be telling her this," Seb mutters, his voice low.

"No, please," I say, leaning forward. "I'm really interested. Why did they stop?"

"It's a long story, and we don't have all the details," Saga says. "But in short, they knew they would need to stop in advance, so they harvested a lot of extra salt, as a stockpile for future generations. Enough for one hundred years, until we could resume the production again. But the pause took longer than they'd planned. And when we were ready to begin again…"

"No one knew how to do it anymore," I say.

"Well. They knew how to make sea salt," Saga says. "Just not quite the same way. The way we do it now creates virtually the same—"

"It's *not* the same," Seb says, turning to her. "You know that's true; the *Eijna* describes effects we just don't see today. If you didn't believe that, you wouldn't have mentioned the book."

"What kind of effects?" I ask.

Saga turns to me. "We use the salt for healing, as you remember from your father. But also for ceremonies, such as the coming-of-age rite to become a council elder. The *Eijna* describes how salt was used in the preparation leading up to, and the healing after, that rite. What we read there isn't… *exactly* how it goes today."

Seb mutters something to her in Fakari. It holds the cadence of a warning.

"We still use some of the ancient salt for the rite," Emerson says quietly, next to me. "We have the original stockpile the ancestors left us, but we've been rationing it for generations."

"Rationing like how?"

"Where you used to receive 20 grams of the ancient salt, now it's one gram, and we fill in the rest with modern stuff."

"So you're trying to figure out how they made the ancient salt?" I ask, turning back to Seb. "Are you close?"

He says nothing.

"We're getting closer," Gabe says. "Most of the places here use modern heating methods to get the water to evaporate, and you get left with the seasalt. We're trying to use geothermal heat, the way the ancients did."

"That... *sounds* really modern," I say.

"It isn't," Seb cuts in. "The Fakari people have used geothermal energy for as long as we have records. We know people have been using hot springs for healing since before the first settlers came."

"But... they also used it to make salt?" I ask. "How?"

There's an awkward pause.

"We don't... we don't quite know," Gabe says finally. "We can't get enough heat yet to get there, so we're using radiators for now. I mean, they're powered by geothermal energy, but—"

Seb makes a comment in Fakari, and Gabe shuts up. I take a bite of fish, thinking it over.

"You should say that on the website," I say. "Even if you're not there yet, that's an amazing story. It's super interesting. People would totally want to support you."

"We don't need foreigners knowing island business," Seb says dismissively.

"So why sell to us *dirty tourists* at all, then, if we're so worthless to you?"

"'Cause he needs money," Kieran mumbles.

Seb bristles, but across the table, Gabe nods.

"No, it's true. The way the other plants use heat is cheaper. The geothermal radiator is expensive, so we produce a lot less. We need more money, either to get more power or move to a location with better access to a geothermal heat source."

"So why do you care so much about this?" I ask, looking across the table at Seb. I can feel the wheels turning in my head, trying to understand the human angle—both for the magazine article, and for me. "What's the motivator for you?"

He stares me down, and as I catch a glint in his eyes, an irrational thought hits me. I realize somewhere deep down that I hate Seb Greenleaf, just a little. The look in his eyes—as though I have to earn not just his trust, but his *respect*—makes something in me want to commit arson. As he glares at me, I vow that the next time I see a hate comment online, or a man telling people to "return to tradition" on Twitter, I'm going to picture his perfectly punchable face.

I sit up straighter, refusing to break his gaze. Gabe clears his throat uncomfortably.

"Like Em said," Seb says finally. "They used to give you the ancient salt for your rites. Now it's a fraction of that, with mostly filler and none of the same properties. I think that matters."

"Why?"

His voice is icy. "It. Just. Does."

I stare, wondering. It's clearly personal, and figuring out why will be the key to a good magazine article for me—and any decent marketing copy for him, if he had an ounce of sense. But if I'm honest with myself, I don't think I want to get to know him well enough to find out.

"Fine. So tell me about the rite, then," I say, looking over at Saga. "What's the coming-of-age ritual you mentioned?"

"*Agaayu,*" Seb mutters, putting his glass down hard on the table. Next to me, Em jumps.

"It's a test of personal strength," Saga says carefully. "We only do it in the winter, under certain conditions."

"Like what?"

"The *kiyyulit* need to be visible. You call them the Northern Lights."

"Oh my God, I totally forgot you can see the Northern Lights here!" I say. "That's amazing. But it's too late in the year now, though, right?"

"Yeah, they only come out from October to March," Emerson says, glancing at me.

"Not that that would have made a difference this year," Kieran mumbles.

"Huh?" I look over at him, but Gabe supplies the answer.

"We didn't see the lights this winter," he says. "No one was able to do the rite this year."

"Oh." My brow furrows. "Is that… typical? That it's so rare to see them?"

"No," says Saga, and an awkward silence falls at the table.

I glance between them. This conversation is *weird*, and not for cult reasons (although, yes, I did check for wiretaps and art of great leaders in the bathroom). I feel like I'm only getting twenty percent of the story, and I want to know *everything*—about Fakari medicine; about the salt and why the ancients stopped making it; about the *Eijna* and the rite. But just as I'm about to ask my next question, Emerson cuts in.

"Enough about the islands—you must have heard way too much today already. We want to hear about *you*. Where did you grow up? What do *you* do for work?"

I take another bite of my food. I'll have time to figure this stuff out, I think, so I *do* tell her—about Boston, my degree, and (spitefully, in Seb's direction) my brief stint as a beekeeper, among other things. Slowly, the weird mood at the table eases, and the conversation warms up, though that's probably because Seb leaves the house just after dinner.

I spend the next few hours with Gabe and Emerson, cleaning up the dishes and drinking cheap wine on the *fikarig*'s back porch. Kieran has a date and leaves early, but I stay outside with Em and Gabe until the sky turns a dusky blue.

"I think I'm going to bed," Em says finally, getting up. "Did Gabe already show you to your new room?"

"Yeah, thanks." I'd expected more personal affects, but the room is mostly bare. Just some handmade wooden furniture and linen sheets, and a couple Fakari ceramics on the windowsill and dresser. No art, no photos. If Gabe hadn't told me, I'd never have known it was once intended for my parents.

"And I should get some more work done tonight," Gabe says, getting up. "Seb wanted me to make some changes to the website. Unless you want me to stay, Maren?"

"Nah, that's cool. It's been a long day. I guess I should probably turn in early, too."

"Alright. I'll walk with you," Em offers, as Gabe gathers our wine glasses.

I follow her into the house, up the stairs to the second floor landing. She takes a left and says goodnight, and I turn to the right, past the door to Saga's space and down the corridor to the part of the house that was designed to belong to my parents. The door to my room is still open from earlier, and the one next to it—probably a linen closet or a bathroom or something—is closed.

I walk into my room, shutting the door behind me and climbing onto the queen-sized bed. Next to it, my phone is lying on top of a little wooden bedside table. I pick it up, and briefly consider turning on cell service again to check for messages. But then I remember my mom's texts from this morning—*I know it was you. I told you this would happen if you didn't listen*—and decide against it.

I can't deal with that now. Not yet.

Instead, I walk to the dresser and pick up the books I bought this morning. Taking a seat on the bed, I start reading about Fakari history and culture. I'm hoping for information about salt traditions, or maybe the rite, but there's nothing; just stuff about knitting and wool, and the way different salts are used for different kinds of healing. After a while, my eyelids start to grow heavy, and I feel myself getting drowsy. I lie down, trying to muster the energy to go wash my face. And then, reflected on my black phone screen, I see it.

Light.

Not just any light. Dancing, vibrant light, like I've seen in the movies.

My head snaps up to the large window next to my bed, and sure enough, there it is. The Northern Lights, right outside my window: so bright and colorful that they reflected down off of my dark phone screen.

It's not what I expected them to look like at all. In the movies they're green and blue with hints of purple. These are vibrant pinks and reds, streaked with violet, dancing so fast it almost looks like the sky is on fire.

I scramble to the window, heaving to push it open and craning my head outside.

They're gorgeous, taking up almost the whole sky—so big and beautiful that I don't think I've ever felt smaller, somehow. I sit on the edge of the sill, leaning out as far as I can. And then, out of the corner of my eye, I see him.

Outside, walking towards the house with his head craned up at the sky, is Seb.

He's barefoot with a bundle of clothes under his arm, wearing some kind of loose pants and no shirt. His hair is wet, and on his face is some kind of inscrutable look of wonder, and maybe something else.

I stare at him for a minute, trying to figure it out.

Fear, I realize. He's looking at the sky with fear.

A breeze brushes past me, whispering over my skin and trailing down. As the wind shifts direction, Seb looks away, briefly broken from his trance. He takes a deep breath, then turns his head and looks directly at me.

I freeze as our eyes meet. I want to close the window and climb back into bed; to hide from him and the way he makes me feel. But I belong in this house, I remind myself. Saga believes it.

Ije kommet ei Fakarieilat—I am from the Fakari Islands, in my own way.

Seb looks at me for a long minute, then heads towards the front door of the house. I hear it open and close, then the tread of his uneven footsteps on the creaky wooden stairs. Eventually he makes his way across the second floor landing, and for a second I think he's going to come to my room and tell me again that I should get the hell out of here—that I don't belong. But his footsteps pass by, and then I hear another door open and close, and the sound of him pulling back a chair.

It's not a bathroom or a linen closet next door. It's Seb's room.

I look up at the lights again and take a deep breath.

God. We're not just going to be living under one roof. We're sharing a wall.

7

SEB

I can *feel* her.

I turn around in bed, casting my gaze to the wall between us. It's two in the morning, and I can't sleep. Not because of Maren snoring, although I'm pretty sure that's the sound I hear—the heavy rise and fall of her breath through the wall. But because I can *sense* her in this house, her presence strong and foreign and invasive.

I crane my neck to look at the window above my bed, where the *kiyyulit* are still dancing in the sky. You'd think that after a winter of darkness, I'd be thrilled that the ancestors are showing their favor to us again. How many nights did we worry about their absence? How often did I go to the temple, burning *loter* to pray for their return? Saga will probably take this as evidence that they're happy we let Maren onto the islands, but that can't be the full story. After a year of darkness, I can't convince myself that the ancestors painting the sky red as flames is a good thing.

I heave a sigh and roll onto my back, staring up at the ceiling. Any other night, I'd be happy to be up this late. The more tired I am when I drift off, the less likely I am to face the dream. But that's the thing: I'm *not* tired. I can feel my wolf pacing inside my chest. We're on strict orders from Saga not to shift anywhere near the *fikarig* until Maren knows the full truth, but I was able to get some of my wolf's energy out near the lake after my swim. Still, he's antsy now that we're back at the *fikarig*, and I don't know why.

He must recognize a threat in Maren the same way I do.

I need to calm myself, so I close my eyes and recite a few verses from the *Eijna*. The syllables come out quick and soft as a whisper, and I let them wash over me, lulling me to peace and a sense of safety. After a minute, I find one verse that helps my mind go quiet. I recite it over and over, until I hear the words grow lazy and my mind goes soft. The words fall farther away, until I'm slipping into a dream.

I'm in the ring at the top of the cliffs on the night of my elder rite. My steps are even; my shoulders are light. It's only three years ago, but the kid in that ring is a version of me that doesn't exist anymore. The version of me that died there, along with the future I thought I had ahead of me.

Some part of my brain—the part of me that's still awake— realizes what's happening: that I'm slipping back into nightmare.

Wake up, wake up. Turn back. Don't do it.

But it's too late. In the mist before me, an enemy starts to take shape. I see its head and body emerge from the mist; yellowed, golden eyes staring at me. I hate those eyes—hate this beast, and what it did to me. How I only have myself to blame.

The version of me standing in the ring fumbles to find my knife, even as the last sliver of my conscious mind fights it.

Don't do this. Turn back. Save yourself.

But I'm stupid, and I draw my blade. The wolf lunges, and the edges of my mind fade to black, until I'm fully living out the memory of the night that destroyed my life.

I wake up the following morning in a sweat, and glance at the clock hanging above my door.

7:30. I've slept for less than five hours.

I bring a hand to my head, remembering. It doesn't come for me every night, but at least a few nights a week—and this time, it felt more real and visceral than it has in a long time. The blood, the searing pain; the feeling of the beast digging into me, bringing me to the edge of death. The moment I prayed to die, and the miracle that somehow saved me.

I let out a low breath, trying to collect myself. *It's over. It's behind me now.* So why did it feel so real last night?

I can still hear the rhythm of Maren's low breathing through the wall. Clearly her presence has thrown me off—my wolf must recognize the threat she poses, and the stress worked itself out in my nightmares. And then I realize: if I can hear her breath like this, she's still asleep. That means that, so long as the others are up, there's a chance to talk to them alone before she interrupts.

I heave a sigh and swing my legs over the edge of the bed, rising to my feet with some effort. My left leg aches, but I set my jaw and bite back any part of me that wants to complain. She could wake up any minute.

As I make my way down the stairs and towards the kitchen, I can hear the soft patter of voices. I round the corner and see Em, Gabe, and Saga seated at the kitchen table.

"*Morlaa'kut,*" Em says to me. *Good morning.*

"*Morlaa',*" I mumble. I see Gabe's made scrambled eggs for everyone, but I just grab a white and blue painted mug and come to sit beside him at the kitchen table.

"You were out late enough to see the *kiyyulit,* weren't you?" Saga says to me, her voice quickened with excitement. "What a gift. The ancestors are pleased we've brought Maren home."

"I wouldn't be so sure," I say, reaching for the ceramic pot Em's used to make coffee. I pour some into my mug, the scent of roasted beans and cinnamon hitting my nostrils. "A year of darkness, then bright red lights covering the whole sky? Seems like a bad omen."

"Red and pink just means a stronger solar flare," Gabe says. "We've seen it before, here and there."

"Not like this," I say, setting the pot down. "Not so much red, or this big and vibrant. And not after a dark winter."

"We've never had a dark winter before," Em says.

"Exactly."

Em's mouth twists, and she shakes her head. "It's too early to know what it means, but we know the ancestors are doing something. That's a good thing, right? They're speaking to us again, after a year of silence."

"Absolutely," Saga says.

I say nothing, and take a sip of my coffee.

"So what's the plan, then?" Gabe asks, turning to his mom. "Are you telling Maren today?"

Saga shakes her head. "Not yet. I want just another day or two to ease her into the idea."

"Great idea," I say. "Another day where the whole island can't shift? Let's see how that goes."

"Just not around *her*," Saga says. "I've warned the neighbors to be careful during the day, just until the next council meeting. I'm sure we'll have told her by then."

"The next council meeting?! That's a week from now. You think you can keep up this charade for a *week*?"

"She needs time to settle into life here," Saga says, looking at me. "It'll make it easier when I do tell her if she already feels at home. And in the meantime, we'll make sure she's here at night, and that Gabriel or Emerson are always with her during the day so she doesn't get too far on her own."

I scoff. "Yeah, she really seems like the type to like being babysat."

Saga gives me a look. "You would do well to be kinder to

David's daughter, Seb. See it as a way of honoring the ancestors, if you have to. He was your father's best friend."

"Yeah, and look where that got him," I mutter over my coffee.

"*Seb*," Saga says. I see the pity in her eyes, and I hate it.

"What, am I wrong?" I snap. "If David hadn't left, my dad would still be alive. And now I'm supposed to show deference to his daughter? *Please*."

"Not deference," she says gently. "Just kindness."

I take a gulp of my coffee and push my chair back.

"Whatever. You all enjoy safeguarding the mainlander today, I'm going to the salt plant to get some work done. I'll see you for dinner."

"We were going to take her swimming at Moon Lake," says Gabe as I get up. "You want to join? Could be fun."

"*Nekka*," I snap. *No*. "It won't be."

8

MAREN

"Hey, guys."

I walk into the kitchen to see Emerson and Kieran sitting at the breakfast table. Em's wearing an oversized teal sweater over a long floral dress, her hair down and loosely wavy. Kieran is hunched over a plate of scrambled eggs, still visibly half-asleep.

"You're over early," I say.

"Oh, uh... Kieran stays over most nights." Her cheeks redden with the words.

I glance between the two of them, remembering the date he had last night. Not my business. But I'm *definitely* curious.

"He's heading to work soon," she continues. "Gabe and I were thinking about taking you swimming today. Do you have a bathing suit?"

"Not with me." I glance around the kitchen. "Man, that coffee smells *so* good. Do you guys have extra mugs?"

"Cabinet above the sink," Em says, gesturing. I follow her gaze and open a green cabinet door to find a row of white ceramic mugs, each decorated with intricate blue patterns. Grabbing one, I turn to sit at the table with them.

"Yeah, I figured you might not have brought anything. I thought I could take you into town and we can find you something before heading to the lake."

"You think they'll have something cute in my size?" I don't know how things work in the Fakaris, but shopping for plus sized clothes in Paris with my mom a few years ago was an absolute nightmare.

"I'm sure. If we head out soon, we can get back from the lake around two. Which will be perfect, because I need to study and Gabe has some work to do."

"Okay! Sounds perfect."

EM LEADS me back towards the cobblestone streets of the town center. There's a soft breeze in the air, and the light feels golden —May here feels closer to spring than it usually does in Boston.

"Do you mind if we stop at the bookstore first?" she asks. "One of the new textbooks for my healer's training came in."

"Yeah, sure," I say, minding my feet as we walk. The island is hilly, and while the people around me don't seem to have any trouble with walking over cobblestones at an angle, I'm less confident. Em takes notice and slows her own steps to match my pace.

"It's just down the street," she says, pointing. "It's one of only two bookstores on this island. The other one is closer to the western shore, and I almost never get out there anymore."

"Do you guys order books from the States?"

She nods. "Some, yeah. But books about Fakari topics are printed here on the islands. So this book isn't coming in from abroad, but from the printers."

I nod as she gestures to the right, at a blue wooden door sunk a few steps below street height. We take the three steps down, ducking our heads as we step inside the bookshop. There's a few tables of books near the front, each covered in different themed displays—one on gardening, another on poetry, and at the far end what looks like a travel collection. Behind the tables are rows of shelves, and I can see steps leading down to a bigger collection downstairs.

"*Wilkommet*," says a man from behind the counter to our right. He's older, maybe in his 60s, with short white stubble across his chin and thinning, gray-blonde hair.

"*Heij* Heimig," says Em, walking up to the counter. "You called about the new book?"

"*Iija*, and I see you've brought a new friend with you." He nods in my direction and smiles, his gray eyes glinting. "It's very nice to meet you, Maren. I'm Heimig. I own the shop and serve on the island council."

Ah—that's how he knows me. He was one of the ones who voted on my right to be here.

Heimig extends a hand, leaning over the counter, and I take it.

"Nice to meet you, too."

"You know, I grew up just down the road from your father," he says, staring at me. "Quite a family resemblance."

I nod awkwardly. "I wouldn't know. We didn't keep many photos of him in the house."

"Oh?" he says, still holding my hand and looking intently into my eyes. "That's a shame."

His gaze is eerie, and my mind immediately goes back to the way Saga and the waitress stared at me on my first day. I feel the urge to pull my hand away.

"Heimig? The book?" Em asks.

"Oh, yes, of course." He lets go, and I let out a low breath.

"You'll be happy, actually, Emerson. The printers also sent over the first few of your set of texts for next year, so you can pick them all up today. I'll go down to the storeroom. Just a moment."

He nods at us and walks down the steps to one of the other rooms in the bookshop.

I walk over to the table on travel books, eyeing them. There's books on Iceland and Ireland, and a travel guide to Nova Scotia. But I also see some books on the other Fakaris. *Hiking Routes of Keist,* reads one, featuring a woman with walking sticks walking over a low mountain path, bright orange wildflowers on either side. There's also *Saroe Teiyye Seijstrider,* which I gather from flipping through the first few pages means something like 'Saroe through the seasons.'

It's the book on Fakari ruins, though, that catches my eye. The cover features a photo of large, mossy stone arches peeking out through the mist. It looks like a dilapidated former church or monastery.

I pick the book up just as Heimig returns to the front room of the bookstore. Flipping through the pages, I admire glossy photos of moss-covered stones on Saroe, something that looks like part of a former castle, and then those church-like ruins from the cover again. I look down at the caption below. It's written in Fakari, but my eyes skim the caption, looking for words I can make out. *...norderligst Fakarieilat, Fajje, beijatema 'eilat uq tod'...*

The north-something Fakari island, Fajje, something something.

"Hey. Ready to go?" Emerson says behind me.

I turn to her and point to the caption. "What does this say?"

Emerson looks over my shoulder, her long blond hair falling out from behind her ear as she leans forward. She squints and translates the paragraph for me.

"Ruins of the churches left behind by 15th century missionaries on the northernmost Fakari island, Fajje," she translates, *"nicknamed 'the island of death' for its history of atypical burial practices. Ruins are free to explore, dogs permitted. Closely nearby are the Fakaris' only European-style graveyard...* and then some details about how to arrange a visit."

"Huh," I say, turning the page.

"Would you like to buy the book?" Heimig asks from behind the counter.

I hesitate for a second, then shake my head, putting it down.

"No, that's fine. I was just looking. But, actually…" I hesitate. "You must have copies of the *Eijna*, right? The Fakari myths and legends book?"

His eyebrows raise appreciatively. "Ah, so you're interested in Fakari culture already! Just like your father. Saga must have been speaking with you. Yes, of course, we have many copies—"

Next to me, I see Em's posture shift just slightly, and Heimig's eyes fall to her face. I turn to glance at her but she's already looking back at me, smiling.

"…Although, of course, the only copies we have are in Fakari," Heimig adds. "And you'll be needing an English copy, I assume."

"Um… Yeah, I guess?"

"I can order one for you. We could have one by the end of the week."

Emerson shifts beside me again, too quickly for me to see clearly.

"…Or, next week, perhaps," Heimig adds.

I glance between the two of them. Something weird is going on.

"I'll take a Fakari copy now, actually," I say, my voice a little sharper than I mean it to be. "And a Fakari-English dictionary. Which I assume you'll have to have in stock, since they're the official languages of the islands. Right?"

I smile firmly. No one is getting in the way of what I want to know.

"Yes, of course," Heimig says, giving me a polite smile. "Just give me a minute and I'll get that ready for you."

I nod as he disappears downstairs, then glance awkwardly at Em. I expect her to be annoyed, but the look in her eyes is something closer to humor. I wonder if she cares what I'm reading, or if she's acting on someone else's orders.

We say nothing as we wait for Heimig to return. He enters the room a moment later, slightly winded, and rings up the two books under his arm for me.

"That'll be K64.97 *króna*," he says.

I reach for my wallet and tap my card against the machine. I have zero frame of reference for what that costs in dollars, but that's a problem for tomorrow-Maren. A moment later, a green check mark appears on the payment portal.

"I'll give your *fikarig* a call when your English *Eijna* comes in," he says as he slips the two books into a paper bag and hands it to me. "Enjoy the rest of your day on the island, ladies."

"*Takka*," Em replies, and she leads me out of the door.

"Some light reading for you, then?" she asks me as we reach the street.

I shrug. "There's not much else to do at the house until I can start working on my article. And this can probably help, you know? I could use it for context, or something."

"Yeah, maybe," she says, and her voice has a strange edge to it. For a second, I think she's going to say something about the article, but then she adds,

"I have to do some studying tonight. Maybe we can read together. I can help you with your Fakari if you get stuck."

I blink. "Oh! Yeah, sure. To be honest…"

She looks up at me. "Hm?"

I let out a breath. "I kinda thought you didn't want me reading this."

She shrugs. "I don't think I could stop you even if I did. And I don't."

I nod. "Well. Okay. What are you studying for?"

"I have my end-of-year healer's exams coming up," she says, leading me up the hill we came from and towards another shopping street. "Then I'll have finished my fourth year of training, and I can start doing rounds."

She beams, bringing her hands together as though she almost wants to clap with excitement. "I can't *wait*."

"How long is the whole degree?"

"About five years, depending on how you stack your courses. The first three years are mostly school, and then you start combining it with apprenticeships and stuff. I'm apprenticing with Saga."

"That's long. How did you make yourself finish?"

Her brow furrows for a split second.

"I don't know. It didn't feel long. I just knew it was what I wanted to do, and that made it easy."

I nod, considering. I've never felt that way, about anything.

"How did you know you wanted to be a healer?"

She leads me to the right, down a new cobblestone street going up. I can see a few clothing shops up ahead.

"I shadowed a couple different people at the end of high school, just to make sure. I looked into other jobs, too, and I even interned at the museum for a while. But I just kept coming back to this. Working with people, helping them… I don't know. It just felt right. I knew it was what I was meant to do. There was never anything else for me."

She gestures to a shop to the right, where I can see various bathing suits and towels in the window. "This is us."

I nod and follow her inside, turning her words over in my brain. Wondering what it feels like to just know, somehow, where you belong.

9

MAREN

We get back from the lake mid-afternoon, and Em, Gabe, and I leave our bathing suits out to dry on the back porch. Em did manage to find a few options for me, and I settled on a black one-piece with sheer cut-outs on the sides. Once I realized you can actually find plus-size options here, I was dying to look at other clothes in the neighboring stores. But Em flat-out refused, insisting that it was *so* important we meet Gabe at the lake as soon as possible—even though he ended up being late. Just another split-second interaction to add to my long list of cult vibes.

I let Em shower first—today's gonna have to be wash day for my hair after swimming in the lake, and that routine takes at *least* an hour. While Gabe gets an early start on dinner, I curl up in the living room with my new books and a notebook for translating. I start with the table of contents, going word for word.

"*Aalde…*" I mutter, flipping through the dictionary. Meaning *ancient, old.* I write it in my notebook.

"*…Aspreija…*" *Origins.*

I translate the titles of the four major divisions of the book.

Ancient origins; Fakari gods; something like 'legends of mortals'; and lastly, the moral codes. Is it insane to try to translate this book myself, when I barely speak a word of Fakari? Almost definitely. But every time I lose interest, I remind myself of the half-dozen moments this week that someone cut themselves off to spare me from getting a straight answer.

If you don't tell me, I'll figure it out myself.

I'm in the middle of searching for the Fakari word for salt when Saga walks into the living room, two older women behind her.

"*Heij* Maren," she says, shaking off her shoes on the mat. "You went to bed too early last night to meet Dagmar and Isolde. They live in the *fikarig* with us. Here, say hello."

The other two women pass her and walk into the living room, one with a short, soft frame and pale blonde hair cut to her shoulders. The other is tall and lean, with sharp, angular features and dark brown hair that falls in waves around her face. This one must be Seb's mother, I think—and when she gives me a curt nod as the shorter one pulls me into a gentle hug, I see immediately where Seb got his charming disposition.

"It's so nice to meet you, Maren," says the shorter one, pulling away from me. "I'm Em's aunt Dagmar. You'll be meeting my husband Viggo tonight. And this is Isolde."

She gestures at the woman beside her, who extends a hand.

"Nice to meet you," I say to her, taking it. "Thank you for welcoming me into your home."

"Of course," she says curtly. "Saga was adamant."

I smile politely, but something in the air grows firm and unpleasant. Just like the other day on the cliffs, I get that uncomfortable feeling in my gut—something tense and frustrated, wanting to get out. Instinctively, I drop Isolde's hand and check my pockets for my hand cream, but they're empty. I haven't seen it since I brought my stuff to the house last night.

"What are you working on?" Dagmar asks, looking down at my notebook and tilting her head.

"Oh, um, the *Eijna*," I say, only half paying attention as I double-check my pockets. "I wanted to learn a little more about Fakari culture and history. The man at the bookshop didn't have any English copies, but I thought it might be a nice way to improve my Fakari, too."

Dagmar and Isolde exchange a look, and it's at that moment that Saga comes up behind them.

"She's reading the *Eijna*," Isolde informs her tersely.

I look up. Something unspoken is happening, just like between Em and Heimig at the bookstore. The feeling in my chest grows more irritated, and at the rise in frustration, I think of what happened in the parking lot the other day. Where the hell is my hand cream?

"Why don't we give you two some space," Dagmar says to Saga, and with a nod, she and Isolde disappear from the room.

"What's going on?" I ask, my voice tighter than I want it to be.

"Nothing, *piu*. We just haven't had the chance to talk properly, just the two of us, since you've arrived. Why don't you sit?"

She gestures for the couch next to us, and reluctantly I take a seat, glancing at Dagmar and Isolde's backs as they walk from the room.

"So you're reading the *Eijna*. That's wonderful. What motivated you to pick it up?"

I sigh. "I don't know. There's so much about this place that I want to know. I thought this might help."

"There are better ways to learn about your culture than from a book of legends. Or, more interesting ways, at least. Especially if you don't..." Her brow furrows as she looks at the books again. "You're reading it in Fakari?"

"Heimig didn't have an English version. Or, pretended not to, after some kind of wordless exchange with Emerson. Kind of similar to the look you shared with the others, just now, actually."

Again, the words come out harsher than I want them to, and I find my cheeks warm just slightly. Man—I need a nap or something. But Saga's eyes warm with humor, and I let out a breath I didn't realize I was holding.

"You feel people are keeping things from you," she says.

"I guess."

She nods. "I understand. That may be my doing, in part. I want you to get to know these islands, Maren. It's your birthright. I just don't want to overwhelm... What are you doing?"

I'm patting my pockets again, looking around the space around me.

"Sorry, I'm just looking for my hand cream. Have you seen it anywhere? I usually don't leave the house without it, but I guess with the move yesterday, I must have left it somewhere."

She eyes me, her gaze wary. "I haven't seen it. How long have you been using this hand cream?"

I shake my head, looking around and then finally giving up. "I don't know, a couple years? Why?"

"Just curious."

I think of the look she gave it in the cafe the other day, and my words come out clipped, defensive.

"My mom found it for me. I had some issues in high school, and the medication for them gave me a rash. We had to keep tweaking the meds and creams until we finally found a combination that did it for me. This was the only thing that kept it under control."

I swallow. Emphasis on *kept*. The supplements and creams Mom's been giving me have gotten less effective in the last few years. Just another way I'm disappointing her.

"What kind of issues?"

I purse my lips.

"I have a big personality," I say finally. "I had a hard time reining it in for a long time."

She nods slowly. "What did that look like?"

"I don't know," I say, bringing my hands to my head. "I don't really want to talk about it right now, okay? I just want to find my hand cream. The smell helps me feel better when I get stressed out."

"Okay," she says, placing a hand on my arm. "I'll help you look, alright? After dinner we'll search together. And let's have a chat somewhere tonight or tomorrow about the *Eijna* and anything else you'd like to know."

"Yeah, okay. Thanks, Saga."

DINNER IS FAIRLY UNREMARKABLE. I meet Em's uncle Viggo, a tall man with thinning blonde hair and a booming voice. The presence of all the elders at the table, plus Kieran and me, seems to keep the energy at dinner in check. Seb comes home from work just before we sit down and is visibly sulking, but doesn't snap at me today.

"Did you have fun at the lake?" Dagmar asks me. "Emerson mentioned you all went together."

"Yeah, it was nice," I say. "The water is so clear, and the weather was gorgeous."

"You were at Moon Lake? Was Seb with you?" asks Isolde.

"No, why?" I glance over at him, but Isolde answers the question herself.

"Oh, it's just close to the Saroan Salts plant, and to the pools where he goes swimming. I thought maybe he'd joined."

I look up at him. If bad moods were visible, there'd be a dark cloud emanating from his body at a three-foot radius.

"I prefer to swim at night," he says, by way of explanation.

Of course he does. I bet he prefers to swim any time I'm not around.

"Is that where I saw you coming from last night?" I ask. "When you were coming up the hill."

He nods wordlessly, and I set my jaw. Would it kill him to at least *pretend* to have a normal conversation?

"Where do you swim?" I ask.

He sighs, like my presence is the biggest imposition in the world. "There's a few hot springs near the lake."

"Oh. Like geothermal pools?"

He nods, and an awkward silence falls at the table again. That anxious, scratching feeling in my body starts up.

"Well. I hope you'll have a nice time swimming tonight," I say tersely. "I was going to go on a walk, so maybe I'll see you around."

"You wanted to go on a walk?" Saga asks, glancing around the table. "Maybe Gabriel can accompany you."

"I have some work to do for the web shop," he says. "I was going to do it this afternoon, but we spent more time at the lake than I expected. I can't get too far behind."

"It's fine, I can go by myself," I say.

"Emerson?" Saga asks.

"I'm sorry, not tonight. I really need to study. Kier?"

"I have a date," he says.

"Really, I'm fine going on my own."

"I'm sure we can find someone to go with you," Saga says.

I let out a low breath. They don't want me to leave the house by myself—that much is obvious. This, even as Saga promised she'd tell me anything I'd want to know later today or tomorrow.

I take another bite of my dinner—a tomato-based dish with something I've never had before called halloumi. I *need* to get out of the house and run off some of this extra energy I'm feeling. After dinner, I'll search for my hand cream, and then I'm getting out of here—whether Saga knows about it or not.

10

SEB

Today was supposed to be a day of harvesting salt crystals —work I usually find meditative, especially when doing it alone. But when I came in this morning, something had gone wrong with the radiator and it shut off by itself. That means that the water never got hot enough to produce the salinity we needed, which means there was no salt to harvest. Now, we're three days behind on production—more, if the humidity keeps up.

I stew over dinner, berating myself. I should have gone to check. Saroan Salts is profitable, but barely, and the margins are so low right now that it feels impossible to scale. Upgrading to a better location will always stay a dream if I can't get my shit together as a business owner. At least my sales are low enough that this won't have a major impact on stock, I think.

Just another failure.

Gabe seems to notice I'm out of it, and he tries to pull me from my thoughts once or twice over dinner, but I won't be moved. I run the numbers again in my head, figuring out how much extra stock we have and how far this will put me back. At some point, Maren asks a question, but by the time I realize she was talking to me, the conversation's already moved on.

I stay lost in my head over the meal, then help Gabe and Viggo clean up the table after. I'm about to head out of the front door for my nightly swim when I see Maren walk into the hall, the hood of her sweatshirt pulled up around her face. She's clearly trying to be quiet, and I stop in my tracks.

"Maren, is that you?" Saga calls from the living room, and she freezes.

"Yeah," she says, turning to the right to look to the living room. "I couldn't find the hand cream, so I was just gonna go for that walk."

"Oh, perfect. Seb was just leaving for a swim."

Not perfect. I don't want Maren swimming with me for a hundred reasons, none of which I care to explain to either of them.

"It's late," I manage. "You must still be tired from traveling. You should stay here."

"There's not much for me to do here," she says. "I forgot to bring a converter, so my laptop and phone are dead and I can't charge them until the shops open tomorrow. And I just really need to get out of the house."

She raises an eyebrow, daring me to fight her on this. She wants a babysitter about as much as I want to babysit.

I grit my teeth. I don't want to explore with Maren. Not the house, not the island, not anything. But a quick glance over my shoulder at Saga tells me she's not budging. And if I were Maren, I'd probably be doing the same thing she is right now.

"I wouldn't mind exploring by myself," Maren adds. "I'm happy to just go out on my own—"

"No, of course not. You're our guest," Saga says. "Seb will be more than happy to take you."

I look at Saga again. I haven't been *more than happy* to do anything in years, and she knows it. But she smiles at me, and I know I can't win.

"Fine. I'm going swimming. Do you have your bathing suit?" I ask.

"I have everything I need," Maren says coldly.

I give her a look up and down. She doesn't have a bag with her, but I'm not her mom. And I *am* going swimming, whether she gets in the water or not.

"Fine," I grind out. "Then let's go."

I lead her to the door of the *fikarig* and we walk down the steps, turning left towards the wooded path. It's a warm evening, and the air has just a trace of humidity. I can hear the crickets chirping as we start towards the lake, Maren looking resolutely at her feet as we go.

Ask her a question. That's what people do: they talk in awkward silences—they get to know each other. But I don't *want* to know her. I don't want to ask a question, only to be met with an answer she doesn't even realize is practiced—perfectly tailored to get some kind of desired reaction from me. The mainland art of constant performance.

"So, do you... Are you..."

My mouth tries to form something stupid and superficial I can ask her so my brain shuts up. But I start before I can finish the thought, and the words hang in the air, lifeless.

"You don't seem like the kind of person who has a hard time finding the words for things," she says. "What? Do I make you nervous?"

I scoff. "No."

"What then, hm?"

"Nothing."

"Come on, talk to me."

I sigh. "Well, right *now*, you're irritating me."

"Yeah, that sounds more in-character."

"Oh, because you're so relaxed?"

"*You* try being chaperoned all day and tell me how you like it."

She gives me a look, and I see a dare in her eyes. It's not like she's dying to go to the hot springs with me. She'll be even less thrilled when she sees the size of them.

"Yeah, you're right," I offer. "It'd piss me off, too."

We walk the rest of the way in silence, and I lead her through the woods in the direction of the lake. The smell of chemicals on her skin has faded slightly now, giving way to something else. It's warm and rich, like honey. This must be her natural scent, beneath all the garbage she's been caking on herself for years. I hate that it smells kind of good.

As we reach the path that heads down to the lake, Maren starts to turn left, following it down.

"No, the springs are further ahead."

"Oh, okay." She walks back up to follow me, and I lead her another fifty paces or so down the way, towards the secluded area off the side of the lake where she and the others went swimming at noon. As I bow my head down under the arch made by tree branches, she follows, placing her hands on her head to keep that coiled mane of hair from getting caught on a tree branch.

"Woah. This is gorgeous," she says as they come into view.

My response comes out more like a grunt than I intend it to, and drop my bag near the water's edge.

"How many of them are there?"

"The pools?" I ask, pulling my shirt over my head. "Three on this side of the lake. This is the biggest one—the other two are farther back." I want to tell her that she's welcome to swim there alone, instead, but Saga would have my hide.

Maren squats down by the water's edge, eyeing one of the blue solar-powered lanterns that have been set up around the perimeter of the water. The water in the hot springs is bubbling and tinted a blue-gray from the buildup of salt. She eyes it with curiosity.

"And coming here is free?" she asks.

"Of course. It's a natural resource."

I'm expecting her to make a snippy remark, but she just nods wordlessly, looking back down at the water.

I slip off my shoes and take a breath. I'll have to take off my sweatpants before getting in, revealing some of the scarring on my leg peeking out from under my swim trunks. She's to the left of me, and especially crouched down, she'll see it immediately.

It's not that I'm ashamed, necessarily. But I don't think I could handle her eyes on me, taking in the mangled flesh and the scar. Wondering, the way people do; spinning stories in her head where I'm the victim. It's bad enough that everyone on the islands knows what happened to me—that I almost died, the closest anyone's come to failing their rite in decades. But somehow, having her not know and fill in the gaps feels worse.

Maren glances at my hands on the waistband of my sweats and seems to register my awkwardness. She averts her eyes to her feet, where she begins untying her own shoes with great focus. Grateful for her momentary kindness, I turn my back and step out of my pants, then lower myself into the water before she has a chance to see my leg in the lamplight.

The water is warm, enveloping my body and sore muscles immediately. Within seconds, I feel close to weightless, and I breathe a low sigh of relief.

Across from me at the water's edge, Maren rises to her feet, kicking off her shoes. She strips off her clothes, revealing a black bra and a small black triangle for underwear. My eyes rake over her before I can stop myself. She's gorgeous: generous curves, the softness of her stomach giving way to wide, rounded hips and strong, shapely legs that taper down to her feet. I bring my eyes up to her face and I see the defiant raise of her chin, her eyes meeting mine in challenge.

That's what my wolf likes most, I think before I can help it. She's daring—not afraid of my gaze, of my words, of my inner challenger.

She wants to fight. And my wolf wants to play.

"Like the view?" she asks.

"You're directly across from me. Where else am I supposed to look?"

She crouches down to the surface of the hot spring.

"I wasn't planning on swimming tonight," she says, by way of explanation for her attire. "I left my new bathing suit to dry on the porch. I hope you don't mind."

"What you wear is none of my business."

"Could have fooled me with that snippy remark in the kitchen yesterday."

I stifle a noise. She's fast—for everything I say, she has a clever retort, delivered faster than my brain can even register she's speaking. I turn my attention inward, where I feel my wolf feeling playful towards her in a way I'm definitely not.

Down, boy.

"You should follow me on Instagram," she says lightly, lowering herself into the water. "There's a slew of other thirsty men who follow me there. You'll be in good company."

"I'm not *thirsty*," I snap. I don't know what it means, but I can guess. There must be a legion of men on the internet who long for the shape of Maren's body the way sojourners crave an oasis in the desert. But just like that oasis, she's a mirage: a figment of whatever you want her to be, before she disappears and you're left alone with nothing but scorching sand.

"You say that, but you were staring directly at my ass."

"No, I'm not." I was staring at the strong curves of her thigh, like an idiot. What the fuck is wrong with me?

"Whatever, dude," she says, and lets go of the edge of the spring, so that the water comes up to her shoulders.

"Oh, God. This feels amazing." She runs her hands through the water, her eyes wide with wonder. "It's so... I don't know. Fizzy, or something. Light. They should charge for this."

She says it like it's a joke, but I roll my eyes before I can stop myself. Typical. Mainlanders are more concerned with money than the public good—and you can tell from the state of their world. I dip myself below the surface of the water before I can let out a bitter retort.

As the water envelops my body, I can feel the pressure of the salinity push gently against me, willing me back towards the air. When I come back up, I run a hand over my hair to pull it from my eyes, and look up to see Maren gazing happily at the sky, taking in the stars.

I watch the reflection of the blue lamplight on her face. Her hair is thick and wild, piled on top of her head with a large clip. I wonder for a moment what she would have been like if she were raised here. One of the curls at the nape of her neck has gotten free, and I can see that the water from the spring has caused it to re-coil itself. For a second, I wonder what she'd look like swimming with her hair down—if the water would make all of it coil up, or weigh it down so it washes around her body.

What the hell? Why do I care?

"You swim here every day?" she asks, looking up at the trees above us.

"Every day."

"Why?"

Because it's the only thing that helps. But I don't want to talk about my leg, so instead I say,

"If it's good enough for the ancestors, it's good enough for me."

She scoffs. "You sure care a lot about the ancestors."

"I'd take that as a compliment if you didn't sound so judgmental."

She lowers her gaze from the stars to look at me and smiles sweetly.

"Your instincts are correct."

"I care about honoring the past," I say, my voice defensive. "About preserving what's at risk of being lost. Is that so bad?"

She snorts. "It wouldn't be, if that was what was going on."

I feel my inner wolf snarl. "What the hell is that supposed to mean?"

"Sorry. None of my business."

"No. Say it."

She shakes her head and lets out a sigh. "Just, like. You say it's about preservation. But what you're actually doing is trying to resurrect something that's been gone for hundreds of years already. So, like, which ancestors are you honoring? Because for the past few hundred years, your ancestors weren't making your kind of salt, either."

I run my tongue over the edge of my teeth, feeling a snarl forming somewhere in my chest. I cough to cover it.

"Sorry," she says after a second, and her voice is softer now. "Like I said, none of my business. It's just really hard for me to put my knives back once they're out in the open."

"You brought your knives to the hot spring?"

"I bring my knives whenever you're around." She smiles apologetically.

"I guess that's probably at least partially my fault," I manage.

"Probably." She winks this time, and I feel something in me respond. My inner wolf, idiot that he is, likes this—even the fight. I clear my throat, trying to cover the sound of a satisfied rumble in my chest.

"So what makes the water feel like this?" she asks.

"Like what?"

"So... light."

"It's the salinity of the water."

She nods, waiting.

"What?"

"I want to hear more about it."

I shake my head. "Well, *I* want to enjoy a quiet night at the hot springs."

"Yeah, but I'm here, so that's not happening. Now tell me about the water."

I can feel my eyes roll back into my head, and try to bring them back to her face. I shouldn't tell her anything—whatever I say has a 50% chance of being reprinted in a mainland magazine next month. But this is David's kid, and as much as I hate him, I can practically feel the spirit of my father hovering over my shoulder, prompting me to *play nice*. He'd probably jab me in the ribs if he knew how I'd been acting to her all week. And if he didn't, Gabe would.

"The salt has healing properties," I say finally. "But the salinity also makes you feel like you're floating. It eases the weight of your body."

"And the heat? Is that natural, too?"

I nod. "Heated by the island's geothermal energy."

"Like your salt plant."

"Yeah." *In theory.*

"Okay." She sits up, nodding at me. "See, this is another thing we could say if you wanted to sell these salts. Salt baths? Soaks? They would *kill*. Why aren't you leaning into stuff like that?"

"This isn't about money for me, Maren," I say, my voice clipped. "I don't want to sell out our ancestral knowledge to a bunch of mainlanders who will move on to the next trend in a week."

"Sorry, but that's bullshit. You need money to get more power for the plant. Gabe said so."

I cross my arms, and the motion sends a wave of water towards her. It reaches her and gently washes over her skin, and I do my best not to notice the beads of it running over the smoothness of her chest and shoulders. *Agaayu*, what the fuck is wrong with me?

"Listen, you don't have to give away any information you don't want to," she says, leaning forward. "But even just saying that Fakari people have used salt baths for centuries to heal sore muscles and injuries, and selling a set of simple bath salts, would be *so* smart. And I can help get it in front of the right people to sell."

I want to brush her off, but a part of me hesitates. I think of the stupid second radiator we can't afford.

"What else?"

"What do you mean?"

"What else would you do, if you were running the company? To make it successful?"

She thinks for a moment, looking up at the dark night sky.

"I guess I'd start with the storytelling. Your website should be giving artisanal quality, traditionally made, honoring the past." With every suggestion, she moves her hands and shoulders, like she's dancing to show her own excitement. "Right now it's giving free Wordpress template."

I set my jaw. It *was* free.

"Then what?"

She looks away again, thinking. "I'd beef up the descriptions of the cooking salts you're selling. I'd explain what makes each one special, and why someone would want to choose, like, a smoked salt over juniper salt. You could look into making some finishing salts—you know, the ones that chefs sprinkle on top of a fancy dish, right at the end? Expand into other cooking prod-ucts that let you build up the brand, like salted honey. And *then* I'd expand into other markets. Bath salts, body scrubs. If those are a big success, you could even grow into other bath-related products that don't use salt, like how those Icelandic spas sell moisturizers and stuff."

I stare at her.

"What?" she asks.

"You can just *do* that? Come up with stuff like this on the spot?"

She grins. "Must be that half of a marketing degree you mentioned."

I stare at her for a long moment, debating myself. This is such a bad idea.

"Maybe... maybe we can help each other."

Her eyes light up, and she leans forward.

I sigh. "I need K65,000 Fakari *króna* to upgrade to a bigger plant, with access to the better geothermal heat source, for a year. That's something like $50,000. If you..."

I hesitate. I don't really want her involved. But Gabe's only able to help me part-time, and I've barely been breaking even this year. Upgrading the space feels a million miles away.

"If you help me get the first K25,000 *króna*, I'll do your interview. You can get your cover story and your mainland job."

Her face lights up.

"But, listen to me," I add. "You're *not* writing about the most vital parts of island history and culture. It's salts *only*. And I get final say on whatever you print."

She beams, doing that shoulder dance thing she did a minute ago. "Baby, I can get you the whole 65. *Especially* once the interview's out. But yes, deal."

She extends a hand to me, her fingers skimming over the water. I reach for it and shake, ignoring the way it feels to briefly be in her spotlight—to have her shimmer with delight from something I said. To have her call me baby, even as a joke. She's a mirage, I remind myself; none of this is real. And in just a few weeks, she'll be back in her country, pursuing her next deal or career.

"Why do you want that interview so badly, anyway?" I ask, letting go of her hand. "You really want to work at a place that sells jade vagina beads to the 1%?"

"Those jobs pay well, you know."

My lip curls in a sneer before I can stop myself. "So it's about money."

She shakes her head, and her voice comes out a little softer than before. "No, that was a joke. You want to know the honest truth?"

"Yes."

"This whole job thing is kind of a favor. My mom knows the magazine's founder, Elspeth, through a friend of a friend of a friend. I don't have a lot of writing credits, but the magazine agreed to this specific article idea because there's a lot of interest in the Fakaris, since they're so mysterious and secluded or whatever. I said that, since I'm half, maybe you'd all let me in..."

She shrugs apologetically. "It was a stretch, but they agreed to give me a job if I could get them the article. My mom doesn't know what the article is actually about—I think she'd kill me. But she really, really wants me to land this job. She had to pull a bunch of strings to get me the interview after I fucked up the last gig."

"The beekeeping?"

She smiles and shakes her head, her curls bouncing with the motion. "Nah. Last year I was interning at the State Senate and I… may have stabbed a senator. On camera."

"*What?*"

"With a pen!" she says, bringing her hands up to convey her innocence. "And he seriously deserved it. Trust me."

"What did he do?"

She sighs. "He'd been making these gross comments for weeks. And then when we were all posing for a photo on the front steps and I guess he thought I couldn't react, he put his hand on my ass and, like, fondled me. So I stabbed him." She raises her eyebrows and smiles. "I'm not gonna let a photo op get in the way of some swift justice."

I can't suppress a grin. Yes, she's over-the-top—but there's something about Maren that makes it hard to look away. I don't think she would let a freight train get in the way of whatever it is she wants to do.

"Anyway," she continues. "It wasn't like I wanted to work in politics or anything. But my mom's cousin was a senior aide there, and she had already pulled some strings to get me *that* job, after I'd messed up the last one."

"Let me guess. You stabbed a bee who tried to sting you?"

"Will you get over the beekeeping thing? My God." She rolls her eyes. "For your information, this one involved zero bodily harm. I figured out my boss was buying his wife jewelry on his company card and passing it off as business gifts, so I told HR on him. He got fired, but as a result his whole team ended up getting axed, including me. My mom says my self-preservation instinct isn't very strong."

"Sounds like it's more than strong enough," I say, thinking of the pen.

She shrugs. "She says I have a hard time keeping my instincts in check."

That gives me pause. There's no wolf in her eyes. But for a moment, I wonder...

"Anyway. She says this is my last shot to make something work. And maybe she's right."

"So your mom wants this, not you."

She shrugs. "I mean, my mom wants what's best for me."

"What do *you* want?"

She stares at me, something happening behind her eyes.

"I... I don't know. I think..." She swallows, her brow furrowing, and I'm pretty sure I'm getting her thoughts in real-time. "I mean, I guess I just want what everyone wants. To feel like I'm a part of something, you know? To feel like I belong somewhere."

The thought is interrupted by the sound of a howl in the distance. Maren's head snaps up, and she starts to scramble for the edge of the spring.

"We should get out of here," she says, pulling herself up over the edge of the water.

"It's okay. It sounded far away," I say. But she's visibly

shaken, and with trembling hands she pulls her sweater over herself, then tries to step into her jeans as soon as possible.

"No, we need to get out *now*. I saw a whole pack of wolves on one of the other islands the other day. There could be more of them. We need to get back."

"Maren—"

Her head snaps to me. "If you don't want to come with me, fine. But I know what they're capable of, and I'm leaving *now*."

I register the fear in her eyes. The howl is harmless—probably just a gang of local teenagers having fun on a Friday night. But she's scared, and I can't let her be out here by herself, or Saga will kill me.

"Alright, alright." I pull myself over the water's edge and turn my back to her, stripping off my swim trunks and stepping into my clothes. By the time I have my pants on, she's fully dressed, the wetness from her bra soaking into her shirt, outlining the shape of her full cups. *Agaayu.*

"It's a fifteen minute walk back," I say.

She nods and starts walking briskly towards the path. I try to keep up, but she's whipping through the woods, almost running, and my left thigh burns.

"Hey, hey, slow down," I say, reaching for her arm. She looks over her shoulder at me just as we hear another howl in the wind, and I see the panic in her eyes as the sound hits her.

"We have to hurry," she whispers.

"It's fine. Seriously, we're gonna be home in just a few minutes."

But she's looking over my shoulder now, and I turn to follow her gaze. Some thirty, forty paces from here there's a teenage girl sitting at the lake's edge with her back to us. Around her are three teens in wolf form—two hiding in the trees, the third stalking slowly towards her with his head low, trying to sneak up on her.

"Oh my God," she whispers.

Fuck. I knew Saga's plan was hopeless.

"Maren—"

"I... Oh my God," she says again, then looks around wildly. "What do we do?"

"I don't—" I stammer. "Listen..."

"You have to distract it," she hisses. "If you go over there and make some loud noises, I can help her—"

The wolf hears Maren's whispering and snaps his gaze to look at us. I can see now that it's Joris Groenberg, a kid of about 15 or 16. That must make the girl at the water's edge his girlfriend, Elsie.

I shake my head slightly at him, trying desperately to communicate something I can't with words. Joris isn't old enough to sit in on council meetings, but he must have heard about Maren, right? If he can just leave...

Joris nods his head at the other two wolves, a signal. But Elsie's still looking out at the water, oblivious, and Joris walks closer to her, trying to catch her attention.

"Maren—" I say.

But as I look to my right, Maren does the last thing I'm expecting. Her eyes grow big and I see her breathing tear through her body, the fear overtaking her. Suddenly her frame snaps forward, and I watch as her body breaks, sprinting towards Joris in a haze of white teeth and black fur.

I should run after her, but I can't move.

I've seen that wolf before—on that horrible night, and in my dreams for the three years since.

Black fur. Strong build. Golden eyes.

The wolf from my rite.

11

MAREN

My body acts before my brain can understand what's happening. All I see is the girl, who turns around and stares at me, wide-eyed. I scream for her to get out of the way, but it's drowned out by the sound of a wolf, snarling and yapping, seemingly so close to me that he must be just over my shoulder.

The girl scrambles to her feet and runs out of the way, and somehow I realize I'm on the ground, on my hands and knees. How did that happen? My body is racked with adrenaline and fury and the desperate need to protect. The wolf who was sneaking up on her scrambles as I get close, but I see now that there's two others. One of them runs up to me, baring his teeth, seemingly ready to attack. I try to shove him away in a fit of terror, but it's all happening so fast that I don't even see my own hands, and all I make out is fur and claws and blood. I'm panicking, gasping for air, and then I hear Seb yelling, running towards us.

I can't do this I can't do this I can't do this. The other two wolves are on me, pressing me into the ground, pushing my arms and legs down. I hear the girl scream.

I'm going to die, I think. I'm going to die on this stupid fucking island, and I'll probably be immortalized on that awful true crime podcast, after all. But then I hear the pounding of footsteps and the deep shout of a man's voice. And the last thing I see is Seb over me, pulling the others off of me, before everything goes dark.

WHEN I WAKE UP, I'm in my room in the *fikarig*, and my head is pounding. I smell honey and peppermint, and open my eyes to see Saga sitting on the edge of the bed, her brow furrowed in concern.

"*Heij*," she says softly as she sees my eyes open. "You're awake."

I sit up, running my arms over myself, checking for cuts or bruises. My body is sore and the fear is still rattling through my bones, making me shiver, but I seem otherwise unscathed.

"What happened?" I ask, looking at her. "Where's Seb? Is he alright?"

"Seb's fine, *piu*. He brought you home."

"I... Oh my God," I say, looking around the room, trying to get my bearings. "I asked Gabe about this. He said there was nothing here that would hurt me. How could this... How the hell—"

"Maren," she says, placing a gentle hand on my leg under the blanket. "This is my fault."

"What?"

"I'd hoped I could get you settled in here a little bit before we tell you. I wanted you to get a feeling for Fakari life before you found out. And I wanted the chance to spend a little more time with you, too, to see if my suspicions were correct."

"What are you talking about? What's going on?"

She nods her head just slightly, eyeing me.

"Maren, Seb told me what happened in the woods when you saw those wolves. You ran to them. You wanted to defend the girl, right?"

I nod.

"Did you realize what happened when you ran to them?"

I swallow, my breathing growing shallow. "They attacked me."

"But do you realize what happened to *you?*"

I shake my head. "I don't... I don't know. Sometimes my anger just takes over me. I was running at them before I could think about it."

Saga nods again, and I can see the words she's trying and failing to form. She looks at the ceiling and lets out a low sigh. I feel the anxiety and frustration rattling through my body.

"Tell me what's going on," I say.

"You were flipping through the *Eijna* this afternoon, *iija?*" she asks. "Did you read anything interesting?"

I shake my head. "I just translated the table of contents."

"One of our most treasured legends is of Tayyakuk, a mythical hero we consider the first Fakari islander. When he came to the Fakaris, he wrestled with the moon goddess for the right to call the islands home. When he won, she gifted him with the powers of the wolf as a reward. And this, we believe, is why the Fakari people each still have the gift of the wolf today."

"What... what is the gift of the wolf?" I ask, even as some part of my body already knows.

"Maren," she says, her voice careful. "The wolves you saw at the lake shore this evening were not wolves—not true wolves, anyway. They were Fakari teenagers who had shifted to their wolf skins. And when you attacked them, you, yourself, shifted."

"I... *No.* What are you talking about?"

This is either some kind of terrible prank, or the cult uses hallucinogenic drugs I haven't been introduced to yet. I need to get out of here. I reach for the blankets and try to pull them off of me, but I realize I'm naked underneath.

"Oh my *God*, where the hell are my clothes?" I ask, pulling the blanket to my chest.

"*Piu*, please listen to me," Saga says, her words coming faster. "Your father was Fakari and he had this, too—every one of us does. Me, Gabriel, Seb. We didn't know if you'd have a wolf within you, because you're only half Fakari by blood. But what happened tonight shows that my suspicions were correct—you *do* have a wolf. This cannot be the only time this has happened."

I blink, biting my lip and feeling a stinging in my eyes. The parking lot. The last time my mother pulled me out of school. And the time before that. All the times we moved from city to city.

"Tell me, *piu*," she says gently.

"No. You're crazy. This is crazy."

She stares at me patiently, waiting.

"Stop looking at me like that," I say, and I can hear my voice waver, on the edge of tears. She just places a gentle hand on my foot, over the blanket.

"I don't—I don't *know*, okay?" I say finally. "I've always been different. My mom always said I have temperament issues. It's hard to rein in my feelings when they get strong enough. And sometimes, when I think there's a threat, I… I just sort of attack before I can think about it. But it's not *this*. I'm not some kind of *creature*. I'm not a monster."

"You're not a monster, *piu*. You're Fakari. The *agaayit* have blessed you with a wolf. It's a part of your nature—you cannot fight it."

I swallow, feeling tears sting my eyes.

"I don't *have* a wolf. I *am* a person."

"Okay," she says gently. "Be that as it may, *we* each have a wolf. I do, Gabriel does, your father did."

"*No*," I say, and I can feel my throat grow thick with tears.

"My father was *killed* by a wolf. And none of this… none of this is possible. You're playing some kind of joke."

Saga nods and stands to her feet. I see her pool her energy, and then her body snaps forwards, changing shape and form. Her clothes—a loose teal wrap knit sweater and flowy gray pants that billow out before tightening at the ankles—now stretch around her body, and I watch as her face and body shift into those of an animal. In a moment, the wolf—*Saga*—is standing at my bedside, looking up at me with wide, gentle eyes.

Saga's eyes. Deep, dark brown, ringed with amber.

"*No*," I say. This can't be happening. I bring my hands to my face and hear the shuffling as she shifts back, then feel the pressure on the bed as she takes a seat near my feet again.

"It's okay if you're not ready to talk about it," she says. "But your wolf is a part of you, and the longer you suppress her, the harder it will be to rein her in when she gets out. I suspect you've already been noticing that."

I swallow, thinking of the way the last six months have gone —how that clawing feeling in my core has gotten harder and harder to ignore in times of stress. My mom thought my medications needed changing, but maybe...

"But how could I have this…" I pause. "This *thing* my whole life and not know it?"

"I think…" Saga says carefully. "It's possible your mother knows about your nature. She knew about David."

I look at the ceiling, trying to imagine my mother—powerful, pristine, impeccable—living on an island with fucking *werewolves*.

"That's… that's not possible."

"It's why they left," she says gently. "She didn't want you growing up with this."

"I… I thought my dad was kicked out," I say weakly.

She shakes her head. "No. He left for your mom. For you."

I take a deep breath, feeling it rattle through my chest. It's like I can't get enough air.

"I think she may have been helping you suppress your wolf, without you knowing," Saga continues. "The hand cream you've been using contains witch hazel, which is a herb that suppresses our nature. There are others that do this, too: wolfsbane, St John's wort. When ingested, spirulina in combination with turmeric."

I blink as twenty years of my mother's pills and wellness supplements come to mind. *Oh God. Oh God.*

"But why would she *do* that?"

"If David didn't die at the hands of a wolf... if instead he..."

Saga lets her sentence trail off, and the memory comes back to me in all of its horror. My dad and I were camping, and there were hunters nearby. I was always told that he defended me from a wolf attack, and that's how he died. But all I remember is the sound of a gunshot and the weight of the wolf's body as it hid me.

As it *shielded* me from the hunter.

They never found Dad's body. Just the wolf. After a few months, they called off the search—but my mom never seemed to think there was hope after they carted the wolf's body away.

Oh God. Oh God.

"Are you saying he was *hunted*?"

"Not on purpose—not by people who knew he was a shifter. But that's what we understood, from the little information we gleaned from the news and your mother before she broke contact."

She sighs, looking down at the blanket.

"It's a very difficult thing to be separated from your *fika*, or the rest of your pack. It's a primal, instinctual feeling—it leaves you restless. I spoke to him in the months before his death. It was wearing on him to be away from us. If your mother saw that struggle... If it was ultimately his... *nature* that got him hurt, I can only imagine that, with a mother's love..."

"No, stop." I put my hands to my ears. "It can't be true. She can't have known. How could she not tell me?"

"She would have known about the witch hazel, *piu*. There are shifters on the mainland, too—including in Manhattan, where you moved first. Once you know about this world, there are ways to learn more. To get what you need to suppress this."

I blink, the tears stinging my eyes.

"My whole life she's tried to make me something I'm not. And now it turns out that was never going to be possible, because I have a whole fucking *werewolf* inside of me, that she *knew* was there and never even told me about."

Saga nods. "It's a lot to take in."

"You're telling me." My head aches, and I lean back against the bed, eyeing her. "Is that sweater wool?"

"Yes, why?"

"Are you seriously telling me that you're a wolf in sheep's clothing?"

Saga smiles. "If it'll make you laugh, then yes."

I bring my knees to my chest, the blanket gathering around my body.

"Can I be alone for a while?" I ask.

She stands. "Of course, *piu*. I brought your *Eijna* up here, in case you want to do some reading. Help you process. I've left an English copy, too."

I nod, resting my head against my knees, and hear her walk from the room into the hallway. Before she shuts the door, I hear her pause. She says something in Fakari, and I hear Seb clear his throat from the hall.

"You want to see her?" she asks him, this time in English.

"I…" His voice trails off, and I'm surprised to hear that it comes out raw. He must have been shaken by this evening, too. A moment later, he answers.

"*Nekka*. I don't."

Saga shuts the door, and I pull the blanket higher up over myself and turn over in bed. My mind is a blur as I start reliving almost every moment in my life. That time in middle school when I shoved Clara Weir for calling me a hippo—did I shift, or just get angry? When my mom tried to get me to take those powdered shakes in college, was that really diet food, or just another way to drug me without my consent? I start to feel that antsy, horrible feeling building again in my body, and that in itself makes me start to panic. Is that *her*? The wolf Saga says is inside me?

I swallow and think of my mom: her perfect makeup, flawlessly coiffed hair, the tailored pantsuits and elegant cashmere sweaters. I was never good enough; always too big, too loud, too reckless, my humanity just too irrepressible for her. But, it wasn't really my humanity, was it? It was *this*—this animal.

Wolf, I tell myself, trying to push down the bitter feeling of the word. It's a wolf. And that's the part of me she didn't want— the part that came from Dad. Maybe that's why she never wanted to talk about him, never told me about my family. Never wanted me to go to, or even *think* about, the Fakaris.

To protect me, comes a voice from inside myself. Yes, this was a part of Dad, but it was also the thing that killed him. Maybe she just wanted to keep me safe.

I stare at my phone, thinking. I don't have to deal with this. My mom was able to keep it mostly under control for decades. Yeah, it's been getting harder—but now that I know, we could fix it together.

I finally let myself think about the parking lot a few nights ago: the man who tried to mug me, and the rage that burst from me out of nowhere. That horrible, clawing feeling just tore out of me, and I attacked with a power I didn't know I could muster. It was as he ran away, bleeding, that something in my brain came back online. I needed to run, as far from that experience as possible.

Run here, to the Fakaris.

Oh, the irony.

I look at my phone again, considering. My mom can fix it. She'll pay someone to squash the video of the incident, and if I want to, I can go back to my old life. I can write the article, or a different one; I can get the job at Puur, or the next place. I can be the perfect, high-achieving daughter she always wanted.

But then I hear her voice in my mind. *It's time to grow up and show that you can be trusted with your own life.*

She lied. She gaslit me for years about who I am, and drugged me to keep from finding out.

"Fuck this," I mutter to myself. I stand up and walk across the room to my purple suitcase, zipping it open to reveal its contents. Locating the pouch of creams and medicines, I tear it open, searching for everything she ever gave me. Green powder to add to my breakfast—"full of antioxidants," she claimed. I check the back, reading the list of ingredients. Sure enough, spirulina. I remember the turmeric capsules she gave me this summer, and pull out the bottle to drop it next to me. Next are face creams, vitamins, sunscreen—of course she wouldn't poison my sunscreen, I tell myself. But then I remember that she got this directly from her dermatologist, and add it to the pile just in case.

Once I get to the bottom of the bag, I look at the pile of products next to me. Skin tightening creams, vitamins, powders: a dozen things to make me into whatever it is that she wants. Something I can never, ever be.

I don't need her approval. I don't need the article, and I don't need the job at Puur. I'm going to succeed on my own terms, and I'll do it as the total opposite of everything she ever wanted me to be.

I swallow, thinking of the deal I made with Seb. I'll make his product line more successful than anything my mom has ever thought me capable of. And I'm going to do it *my* way, without any of her money or connections to help.

Not for him, or for her. For *me*.

12

SEB

"You want to see her?" Saga asks.

"I..."

I hesitate. I've been standing outside Maren's bedroom door for hours, pacing, waiting for her to wake up.

But I don't *want* to see her. I don't want to do anything with her. I want to understand how to make any sense of this.

Saga raises an eyebrow, waiting for my response.

"*Nekka.*" I shake my head. "I don't."

I turn and head down the stairs, running my hands over my head as though trying to wake myself from a dream. Gabe is sitting on the living room couch, and looks up as I reach the bottom of the stairs. Seeing my face, his brow furrows.

"Hey. You good?"

I put my hands up as though waving him away, and rush out the front door.

The purple-blue sky from earlier this evening is black now, and as the humid air hits my skin I find myself bringing my hands to my head again.

I don't understand this. I don't understand how—

I pull off my clothes, shoving them onto the wooden bench on the porch, then let my body shift. It folds forward, my limbs bending and changing, and then I'm on all fours and I'm running, running, running.

How could the *agaayit* do this to me?

A growl escapes me and I find myself snapping, gnashing my teeth. I need less of this—less thinking, less feeling. I give the reins to my wolf and let myself run, watching the light of the moon recede as I enter the dark cover of the forest.

I REACH the temple at the edge of the woods and shift back. There's a clothing box outside, and I reach in to pull out some sweatpants and a ratty black sweater someone's left behind. It's not much for entering a holy place, but the *agaayit* have seen me in worse shape than this.

My left thigh aches as I walk up the steps and turn to the alcove where *loter* are stored for visitors. I grab a handful and count them—five in all—then write my name and the number in the logbook so someone can be in touch in a few weeks with my tab. My eyes scan the list of prior visitors this month. Wim, Tamu, Ingela—no one close to my own age. That's no surprise; I don't know many young people who bother with the old gods. But without my dad here, it's the closest I can feel to him and the way he raised me, and I need that more than ever tonight. Strips of paper in hand, I pull open the heavy wooden door of the temple and step inside.

The room is awash in candlelight, wooden beams and arches glowing softly above the sacred space. I stop to dip my feet in the water of the selenite basin, wiping them off with one of the towels provided, then walk towards the niche for Keijgur, god of justice. With every step, I feel the pain searing in my thigh. A reminder, as though I could ever forget. I come to stand before his idol and dip the tip of the first *lot* in the pool of oil before him, then bring it to the candle in front of the statue.

I mutter the prayer in Fakari, the syllables coming out of my mouth as muscle memory before my mind can process their meaning. *Mighty Keijgur, god of justice, hear the cries of your servant as he brings himself before you…*

The oiled tip of the *lot* touches the flame, and I watch as the fire grows bright for just a moment, consuming it in blue and orange. I finish the opening prayer and bring my eyes up to the carved stone of the statue's face.

"How could you let this happen?" I ask as the fire engulfs the edge of the paper. My voice is hoarse, and I hear it echo off the wooden beams around me.

"How could it be *her*? Haven't you all taken enough?"

The words taste bitter in my throat. It's the *agaayit* who give and take, and we're supposed to be grateful for all of it. But how can I be grateful for *this*?

I watch as curls of fragrant smoke waft upwards.

"I was raised in the Fakari way. I've followed your edicts all my life." My words come out bitter, spiteful. "I memorize the *Eijna*. I restore the ways of the ancestors. And you repay me with *this*?"

I swallow, momentarily fearful that speaking to the gods in anger will result in worse things in my life. But anger is fuel for the work of achieving justice. And Keijgur, of all the gods, will know that.

"After my rite, I *consecrated* myself to you," I spit, dropping the last of the *lot* before the flame burns my fingers. "Three months of study, fasting, and prayer. And *this* is the life that awaits your servant? Haven't I suffered enough? Why?!"

I look down at the remaining *loter* in my hands and think of Dad. He was the one who first brought me here as a kid. My first memory of saying prayers with him was at this very statue, asking for David Winterwood's return. And later, after he'd realized that was a lost cause, to Tinnúr, the god of peace and security—asking for David and his family to have a good life.

David and his wife and *daughter*.

Maren. The thought of it makes my stomach roil with something close to grief.

"I don't accept it," I say. "I know the *agaayit* can do anything. Change this. Change my fate. Make it different somehow."

But as I look up at the wooden statue, unmoved, I know I have no choice. The gods make these decisions, and we need to live with them—no matter what they cost us.

I look around at the other alcoves in the temple and think of the hundreds of prayers of my father's that went unanswered. My own unanswered prayers for him, near the end. And I bring my gaze back to my hands, at the *loter* I have left. I don't understand how prayers work—sometimes I wonder if they even do. But even in my rage, I know I can't leave this temple having only brought up my own anger.

I walk to the alcove for Tinnúr and dip the edge of one strip of paper into the oil. As I bring it to the flame, I whisper the opening prayer in Fakari.

Gracious Tinnúr, champion of peace…

The fire glows hot as it touches the oiled paper, and the smell meant to awaken this god is different from the one Keijgur's flame, his oil infused in some different way. I take a breath as the smoke curls upwards.

"Thank you for the life of my father Filip," I say woodenly. "See to it that his spirit be brought into full unity with the ancestors. And please bring peace to my mother Isolde, consoling her in the loss of her mate…"

I drop the last edge of the paper before it reaches my fingers, and dip the next *lot*.

"Bring healing to Saga and her son Gabe for the loss of their husband and father, Ben. Bring his spirit into unity with the ancestors."

I watch the flame lick its way down the strip of paper, and let go. Then the next, and this one makes my throat burn.

"In honor of my father Filip, I ask for peace for the spirit of his friend David. Bring his spirit into unity with the ancestors."

I can't help myself.

"…In spite of his abandonment of our people, and the pain his choices caused."

As the fire consumes the end of the paper strip, I look down at the last *lot* in my hands. *David and his wife and daughter…*

My father would want me to burn *loter* for Maren. And I have, for years in this *agaayit*-foresaken temple, before knowing who or what she was to me—how she'd one day doom me to my father's fate. I can't bring myself to do it now.

I swallow and bring the last *lot* to Tinnúr's oil.

"And bring *me* peace," I say as the edge of the flame touches the last *lot*. "From the anger for what I've lost, and the knowledge of the loss that lies ahead."

Licks of fire eat up the paper, and this time I let them reach all the way to my fingertips, letting even the last edges of the paper go up in smoke. I stand there for what must be five, ten minutes, stewing. Cursing the Winterwoods and everything they've taken from me.

13

SEB

The following morning, I wake to loud noises from the kitchen.

I sit up in bed, listening for what's going on. The sound of clanging pans. A heavy thud, then ceramic shattering. Saga yelling something.

I run downstairs and into the kitchen to see Kieran and Saga in human form, yelling at Maren's wolf. At the sight of her, I feel a jolt of adrenaline surge through me.

"*Piu*, I need you to shift back," Saga's saying.

"What the hell is going on?" I ask.

Kieran shrugs. "I made a joke. It didn't land."

Maren snarls and her tail whips back and forth, knocking over a wooden chair. I almost want to ask where Em is, but I already know. She can never handle violent outbursts, no matter who they come from.

"Come, Maren," Saga says, her voice practiced in its gentleness. "Take a deep breath. Try to quiet your mind. Let the human take over."

Maren snaps out a bark, snarling at her.

"She can't," I say. "She's too angry, and she doesn't know how to control her shift yet."

Maren whips her head at me and snaps at me, too, as if angry that I'm talking around, not to her. Over her shoulder, Saga brings her hands to her face.

"Oh, I've been so foolish. We've gone about this all wrong."

"You think?" I look down at Maren's wolf. I can smell her anger in the air, but there's something else, too. Fear, I realize. She's looking back and forth between us, and I can see her front paws raising nervously, like she wants to pace.

I hesitate, feeling the resentment curdling in my gut. But as her tail whips back and forth another time, almost knocking over Saga's cabinet of ceramics, I sink into a squat.

"*Heij*," I say, meeting her at eye level. Her wolf's eyes are unnervingly familiar—eyes that have haunted my dreams almost every night for three years now. But now that I know Maren at least a little, I recognize that there's something distinctively *her* about them.

It wasn't her, I think. Not *this* Maren—the one raised on the mainland who doesn't know shit about the Fakaris. Yes, it was her spirit, somehow. But this Maren can't even control her shift, let alone meet me at the top of cliffs. I try to separate them in my mind.

"Look at me," I say to her. "I know it feels like the wolf's in charge, and you can't find yourself in there. But you can. Take a breath. Try to find the edge of your reason."

Her eyes dart back and forth between me and Saga, uncertain.

"Do as he says, *piu*."

Maren brings her eyes back to me and shakes her head slightly, like she's trying to wave a bad thought away. We all watch her for a second as she searches herself, but I can scent her frustration in the air before I see it in her eyes. Her gaze comes back to me and she snarls.

"Yes, you can," I snap. "Stop being an idiot and get out of your own way. You're letting your emotions get the best of you."

I hear Kieran snort from the other end of the kitchen, and I give him a look. It must be pretty rich hearing me give this speech to someone else, after what he's seen me go through.

Maren looks down again, and I hear a whining from the back of her throat. A moment later her body is folding forward, her legs and arms spilling onto the cool stone tiles of the floor. I look away, even as my body recognizes her nakedness.

"I'm going back to bed," I grumble to Saga, and turn to leave the room as Maren scrambles on the floor for what's left of her torn clothes.

"*Nekka, weijtet,*" Saga orders, asking me to wait. I keep walking, and she follows me out of the kitchen.

"You have to train her," she whispers to me in Fakari.

"I don't have to do anything."

"You owe it to your *fika* to do this. She doesn't know how to shift."

"All of us shift," I say, walking to the stairs. "You can teach her, Kier can teach her. Hell, anyone but Em could show her how to do this." Emerson has a wolf, if Kieran is to be believed, but I've never seen her out of her human form.

"You have the closest experience to this, and you know it," Saga says.

I roll my eyes. "Please."

"You do. After your rite, your anger had you shifting without meaning to almost daily. You had to learn to restrain your inner wolf. Help her learn to do the same."

"*No,*" I say forcefully, reaching the foot of the stairs.

"Your father would want this, Sebasteijen," she says quietly.

I turn around in a flash. "My father is dead. And thanks to David, I might add. So I have no idea what he'd want, because I can't ask him. And the last person I owe any help to is David's kid."

"Do it for me, then," she says, her eyes pleading. "Or Gabe. Do it for the ancestors, who brought her back here with a purpose."

"*No,*" I spit, and I head up the stairs.

14

MAREN

"Listen, I'm sorry," Kieran says.

"Don't look at me," I say, clutching the tatters of my pajamas to my naked body. "Get out."

He looks pained, and brings a hand to the back of his neck. "No, seriously, I should have—"

"Get *out*," I spit, feeling heat rise in my face. Without meeting my gaze, he nods and leaves the room, and I'm left sitting alone on the kitchen floor, butt-ass naked.

Saga comes in a minute later, holding a large folded blanket.

"Here, *piu*," she says gently. "You can wrap this around yourself until you get to your room. And we'll buy you some new clothes. There are special ways to accommodate shifting in clothing. We'll find something."

"I don't *want* to find something," I snap, surprised at how angry the words sound as they come out of my mouth. "I don't want this."

"I know, *dennani*," she says gently. "It gets easier."

"What's *dennani*?"

"My daughter."

I look up at her face, her dark eyes gazing at me with tenderness. She looks a little like Dad, I think—the parts of Dad I'm able to remember. I wonder if she looks at me and sees him, too. The thought makes my anger soften, just a little.

"Do you think if my dad hadn't died, I would have known how to control this?"

She nods. "I'm sure he would have taught you."

I hang my head, trying to imagine the person I'd be if my mom hadn't kept this from me. Would I have had to fight so hard, all these years, to love myself? Would I have spent all this time feeling so listless, so unsure of where I belonged? Of whether I belonged anywhere at all?

I stare at the cold stone floor, wondering, and feel Saga's hand come up to stroke my hair.

"Tayyakuk was a hero to our people," she says softly. "His wolf gave him the strength to defend and build up the islands. Your wolf feels like a liability now. But maybe, in time, you will be able to see her as part of what makes you strong."

"Right now she's mostly the thing that makes me naked before breakfast."

I can hear a soft exhale of breath as she smiles. "She's only just started coming to the surface—it makes sense that she's harder to reign in. With time, you'll learn to work with her."

"How?" I ask, looking up at her.

"With practice and patience. Children are usually coached by their parents as the years go on. But some people's wolves are especially strong, and they need some extra training to learn to work with them."

I think of the conversation I heard her have with Seb in the hallway. I couldn't translate the Fakari fast enough to know what they were talking about, but I could tell from Saga's tone that she was asking him something.

"Is Seb one of those people?"

She nods.

"But he doesn't want to help?"

She hesitates. "He may... need some convincing."

I grimace, pulling my blanket tighter around myself. "What's his issue with me?"

"Nothing you did wrong, *piu*."

I snort. "Yeah, I know that much."

THREE HOURS LATER, I walk into a large room on the third floor and find Seb. He's hunched over a table at the far end of the room with a stack of books in front of him. The whole room is wallpapered with books—it must be the house library. Seeing Seb at a desk, I start to back out and close the door quietly, but he turns over his shoulder and sees me.

"Oh. It's you."

"Yeah," I say, and stop. I feel the heat rising in my face, thinking of this morning's outburst. "I was looking for Gabe. Sorry, I'll see myself out."

"He's not home," he says, turning back to the open book in front of him. "He's selling salt on Halssel today."

"Okay. Well, tell him to find me later. It's about the website."

He turns in his seat to look at me. "What about the website?"

"None of your business."

"It's literally my business. Saroan Salts is my business. I own it."

"Got it, thanks." I cross my arms. In the hand that's not on the doorknob I'm holding a notebook, and as soon as it comes into view, Seb's eyes zero in on it.

"Tell me."

"No. The website is Gabe's job. So if you see him, just tell him to find me, 'kay?"

"Come here," Seb says, waving his hand as if to summon me.

"I'm not *coming to you* on command. I'm not a dog."

He rolls his eyes and stands up to walk over to me. In just a couple of strides he's in front of me, reaching for the notebook. Instinctively I pull my arm away.

"Come on, show me."

"No." I move my arm behind my back.

"Why not?" he asks, reaching around my body.

He's just inches from me now, and I put my free hand between us, pushing him back.

"Because I didn't invite you to my personal space. And because I said no, and the second you show me you don't listen when someone says that to you, I'm just gonna dig my heels in harder."

His brow furrows for a flicker of a second, and then his gaze drops to my mouth and then back up to my eyes. I suddenly become aware of the fact that I'm touching his chest, and I drop my hand like I've been burned.

"You're right," he says, stepping back. "Sorry."

He turns around and starts walking back to the table.

"Gabe should be back around seven," he adds over his shoulder, and his voice sounds like gravel.

I swallow. I don't get what just happened. Something strange is tugging in my core, spurring me to try again.

"I... I can show you if you want," I say. "It's for our deal."

He reaches the desk and turns, leaning against it, his arms crossing over his chest.

"The deal's still on?"

"Yeah. Why would anything be different?"

"Well. 'Cause you're..." He gestures towards me.

"'Cause I'm Fakari?" I say coldly, daring him to deny it.

"'Cause you're *pakka*."

Pack. The word comes out easy, like it costs him nothing. But somehow the admission—so easy, so casual—hits me, some primal thing in my gut. I know he's just referring to this shifting thing. But still, the idea of being part of a pack, a community...

"If anything, this... wolf stuff..." I hesitate, the words still feeling too ridiculous to say out loud. "*This*, whatever it is, just gives me more reason to try. I need something to go right. I want to do something without my mom's hands all up in it. I don't care about the Puur job right now, I just... I need a win. On my own terms."

"Even if it's for me?"

"In *spite* of the fact it's for you."

He nods. "Are you still going to write the article?"

"I don't know. I'm just taking things one step at a time. And step one is this." I lift the notebook.

I see his jaw flex, and he nods, gesturing to the table next to him. I walk over and rest the notebook on top of it.

"Okay. I read all the pages on the website—I mean, all two of them, you're almost less talkative online than in person—and I have new copy for you. I think we should emphasize the known healing properties of the salt, the ancestral connection—"

He huffs a breath, and I put a hand up to stop him before he interrupts me.

"—*without* giving away anything you don't want to. We don't need to talk about the *Eijna* or the rituals. I took a look at the way Icelandic sea salt is marketed, and there's this salt company in the Netherlands doing really cool stuff. They *also* talk about reviving traditional ways to make sea salt, and they don't have a whole magical wolf situation going on, I assume. If they can do it, so can we."

He hesitates, then nods.

"And I think we can lean into the mysterious feeling the Fakaris have for a lot of Americans," I add. "Since no one's allowed past Halssel, we can kind of play up the exclusive feeling —like, this is the *only* way to get access to this wisdom and these healing properties, short of being from the islands yourself."

I keep my eyes on the notebook, not wanting to see his expression until the whole pitch is out.

"We should have a page that makes salt suggestions based on

what you need. And a customer service email for if you want help choosing. I can run it, if you want—to be honest, I don't trust you with email. And I have a few contacts with big social followings I can send PR packages—"

"Can I see this?" he asks, gesturing to the notebook, and I nod.

He picks it up and scans over the paragraphs I've written out. I finally look at him, and I see his mouth twitch with what seems like displeasure. He turns the page, reading the rest of it, then swallows.

"It's fine," he says finally.

"It's better than fine. It's good, and you know it."

He clears his throat.

"What you're doing right now isn't working," I add. "That's why we made this deal in the first place. You need to let me make the changes I want to, or it won't work."

"Fine."

"Good. And we need to run Instagram ads—the best website in the world isn't gonna work if people don't know it exists. I think $300 for the first month is a good starting point."

"*What*?! Are you insane?"

"That's nothing. It takes money to make money," I say, crossing my arms over my chest.

"Yeah, thanks, Mr. Monopoly. I know that, because I took out a loan when we started the business. Which we paid back in a year by *not* making stupid financial decisions."

"Not investing enough into your marketing *was* a stupid financial decision, and it's why you need me. I'll go fifty-fifty with you on the budget for the first week, if it'll get you to agree."

His brow furrows again, his dark eyes meeting mine. "What? Why would you do that?"

"Like I said. I need a win. And I *know* I can make this work."

He holds my gaze, and I can feel the frustration crackling in the air between us, but I refuse to look away. Finally, after what must be two minutes, he says,

"Fine. I'll pay the full $300. I don't need your financial help."

I roll my eyes, even as I feel a strange little bubbling of happiness in my chest. All my emotions feel closer to the surface since last night, and the satisfaction of winning an argument feels better now, too. I wonder what other feelings these creams and supplements have been dimming.

Seb sets my notebook back on the table, and as he does my eyes wander over what he was reading.

"Is that the *Eijna*?" I ask. The text is Fakari, and there's an illustration on the right-hand side that looks like something folkloric.

"No, it's a history book."

"About?"

He says nothing, and I cross my arms.

"My dude," I say. "You really need to stop acting like you're being charged by the word for everything you say to me."

"I'm not your *dude*, dude."

"So then what are you, to me?"

It's a set-up: I'm expecting him to snap back with something quippy, but when I look up there's a weird expression on his face. I stare at him for a second, confused, but he seems to shake himself out of it and moves past the question.

"The book is about our salt traditions," he says, clearing his throat. "What we know of the old rituals, the ones mentioned here and there in the *Eijna*."

I nod and lean over, examining it. "And how much do we know?"

He shakes his head. "Next to nothing. This book came out this year, so I was hoping for some new insights or discoveries, but it's just a summary of what we knew already. We're sure there were different multi-step rituals—before the elder rite, before battle. Some of that has been preserved—or a part of it, at least. But for how the salts were made, or how they were originally used in the elder rite, we have next to nothing."

"They didn't bother writing it down?"

"If they did, it's not in places where we know to find it."

I look up, meeting his gaze. "You should look at what was recorded by outsiders."

He scoffs. "What outsiders? We've been closed-off to Europe and the mainland for centuries."

"No, seriously. I saw photos of ruins from an old church on one of the other islands. There must have been more than just that. If the people who were doing these traditions didn't think to write them down, outsiders who witnessed them definitely would have."

Seb rolls his eyes, and they flash gold before coming back to me.

"As if any Fakari person would have gotten close enough with a colonist to let them see our way of life. We forced them out as soon as we had the chance."

"That can't be true. If it were, no one would have had time to build that church, and the Fakari language wouldn't have Dutch and Danish influences. And you wouldn't have fully Fakari people here who look like Emerson, as well as people who look like you or Gabe."

His mouth flattens into a firm line. "The only churches we have here are on Fajje, and barely any Fakari people have lived there *since* the time of the colonists, *because* of their influence. We've always stayed separate."

"I'm just saying—"

"Listen, I'm not saying that outsiders have nothing to offer —"

My head rears back. "Woah, where did *that* come from?"

"—I'm just saying that Fakari culture has *never* made space for outsiders, and that's why we've been able to preserve so much of our culture in the first place."

"You're wrong," I say, shaking my head. "Trust me. I wrote a paper on this in undergrad."

At this, he lets out a cold laugh. "And which career was that for, again?"

"I swear to God, if you bring up beekeeping again—"

"I was actually going to ask."

"It wasn't beekeeping, you self-righteous dickhead," I snap. "It was a class on the history of American religion. I wrote my paper on women's diaries from the 1800s, and how they tell a more comprehensive history than other records—specifically *because* they were the only ones who bothered to write about day-to-day life. I'm telling you, if you want to find what people didn't think to preserve, listen to outsiders, and listen to women."

He sets his jaw, and I do my best not to notice the cut of it, or the breadth of his shoulders as he crosses his arms. That feeling in my center—my wolf, I try to remind myself—does something weird when I look at him. It makes me uneasy.

"If you want to be wrong about this, fine," I add, pushing the feeling aside. "But it's just going to make the list of ways I beat you longer."

At this, I see the corner of his mouth tug just slightly.

"What?" I snap.

"Nothing. You're funny. That's all."

"Yeah, I'm funny, *and* I'm smart, *and* I'm good at what I do. And you don't need to take me seriously, but you should. Because believe it or not, for a mainlander I also have some good things to say."

For just a half-second, his eyes flicker over me. I almost miss it; almost convince myself I made it up. But there's a barely-perceptible second where I notice him, *noticing* me. The world quiets again, the way it did that day at the market. For a moment I find myself searching for something in his face, trying to figure out why he feels familiar to me.

"Got it," he says finally. "Thanks."

It takes a second to realize he's quoting me from a minute ago.

"God, you're so annoying," I say, rolling my eyes.

"What? What did I do wrong now? I'll fund your little ad campaign, won't I?"

"My 'little ad campaign'—that's exactly the problem. You're *so* condescending!"

"I—"

"Just because you have a connection to your history, you think you're better than anyone who doesn't, or can't—"

The feeling in my chest is getting stronger, and I can feel my wolf scratching, getting close to the surface. The sensation sends a jolt of anxiety through me, and then suddenly everything's cracking and falling and I'm on the ground. The sweater Saga found for me is on the floor, and I feel humiliation and anger surging through my body as I realize what's happened.

"*Uikbaane,*" Seb murmurs.

I snarl at him, snapping my teeth. He crouches close to the floor to meet me at eye-level.

"Maren, look at me."

I snarl. The wild part of me is in charge now, and she's not in the mood to listen.

"You need to calm down," he says.

It's a good thing I'm not in my human form, because my internal monologue is already shouting that that is the *last* thing any man should say to a woman, at any time, ever. Some kind of bark comes out of my mouth in protest.

"No, really." His voice is softer now—resigned. "You're angry, I know. But you need to take a deep breath and try to let it go. If you feed the anger, you'll be stuck in it."

I shake my head, and then he reaches out a hand and places it on my head, stroking down to the back of my neck. He leaves it there, the heat from his skin seeping into my body, and he looks me in the eyes.

"You're okay," he says, his voice low. "It's gonna be okay."

The words catch me by surprise, but his momentary kindness creates just enough ease in my body to have the desired effect. I feel the part of my conscious mind and give into it, and then my body's unfolding, unfurling, until I'm sitting on my knees in my human form, naked.

I see him swallow as his hand lingers on the back of my head for a split-second longer than it needs to. The tension crackles in the air between us, burning, and I realize that the part of me that needs to be told not to notice him lives in him, too.

He stands and turns from me.

"Get out," he says, his voice raw.

"What? I—"

"I said *get out*."

My eyes are stinging, and I reach for the sweater and sweatpants I've now torn through and walk towards the door. As I reach the exit, I can feel a lump in my throat, and I know the words will come out uneven, but I decide to say them anyway.

"This isn't easy for me, either. You act like you're better than I am because of your connection to history. But that's something that was never offered to me, and I'm trying. Can't you see that?"

He turns over his shoulder to look at me, and the second he sees I'm still naked, the ball of clothing bundled up in front of my chest, he winces and looks back at the desk.

"You're an asshole, Seb," I say, and I can hear my own voice break. "I'm not embarrassed to be naked because I have nothing to be ashamed of. But if I'd acted the way you have to me, I couldn't meet my eyes, either."

And with that, I leave and head downstairs to wipe my eyes where he can't see.

15

MAREN

Gabe doesn't come home for hours, and at some point I hear Seb leave the house and finally dare to leave my room. I want to spend some time reading the *Eijna,* but I'd rather die than go back to the library. So instead, I wander the second floor until I find what looks to be Em's room. I find the door open, where I see her sitting on her bed, reading a book.

"Hey," I say, leaning against the doorframe. She looks up.

"Oh, *heij* Maren." The way she says 'hey' comes out different, like the e is shorter and the y is more pronounced. The second her eyes land on me, I can see her expression take on a look of pity. "Tough day?"

"Seb told you?"

"No. I just meant what happened over breakfast."

"Ah. Well. It happened again."

Her hand comes to her mouth. "Oh no, I'm sorry."

"Yeah. With Seb." I flatten my mouth into a line. "And then he was a total dick to me, so I wanna steer clear of him for a while. Can I take you up on your study date suggestion?"

I lift the hand holding the *Eijna* and wave it.

"That sounds great. I have an exam next week, and I could use some accountability."

She swings her legs over the edge of the bed, and I step into her room to take a closer look. It's similar to mine—plain white linen sheets, simple wood furniture. She's tacked some water-color paintings to the wall, all the same size, like they come from the same notebook. Other than that, it's basically empty.

"How long have you had this room?" I ask.

"Since I moved in when I was nine. Why?"

"Nothing. It's nice."

To be honest, I have a hard time imagining myself living somewhere for even a few *months* and not making it feel more my own. But I know most people have simpler taste than I do, and maybe she likes it this way.

"What are you going to work on when I study?" she asks.

I hold up the *Eijna* again. "I'm trying to do my own translation so I can learn a little Fakari. I wanted to make some changes to the Saroan Salts website, but Gabe won't be home for a while and I don't want to be around Seb right now. How about you?"

"Botany and herbalism. It's a required unit for healers." She walks over to the desk, where she grabs a notebook and a handful of highlighters. "Learning Fakari will probably be easier by ear, you know."

I shrug. "Maybe. But I want something to do."

"Okay. Want to study upstairs? Have you seen the library yet?"

"I want to study literally anywhere *but* the library."

She gives me a look. "*Ayagaayuni.* What did he *do?*"

I shake my head. "I don't want to talk about it."

"Okay. How about the living room?"

"Sounds perfect."

EM LEARNS QUICKLY that I'm more of a distraction than a study partner. We head to the living room and settle in, with my Fakari *Eijna*, dictionary, and English translation spread out around me like a mushroom colony. Em makes flashcards, sorting them in neat little color-coded piles in front of her. But within twenty minutes, we're doing more talking than reading.

"I'm surprised you feel like reading the *Eijna* with everything that's going on," she says, her eyes on an index card where she's trying to draw a little plant diagram.

"Like with this shifter stuff?"

She nods, and I shrug.

"I don't know. What else can I do? My options are to stay here and learn or go home and never think about it again."

"There's not much practical information about shifting in the *Eijna*, you know," she says. "Mostly folklore. The edicts are more about how to live a good life."

"Did it take you a long time to learn to control it?"

She hesitates. "I don't really shift."

My brow furrows. "You don't have a wolf?"

"I do. I just don't like to shift."

"Oh," I say, eyeing her. "Does that happen a lot? Are there many people who have this... quality, and don't use it?"

If there are, that could be a game-changer for me. Maybe there's better ways to tame it—things that don't involve drugging me without my consent. But she shakes her head.

"No. I don't know anyone else like me."

I nod. "Why don't you... Sorry. It's none of my business."

"It's okay," she says, looking up at me with large gray-blue eyes. I realize for the first time that she has a gold ring on the outside, like Seb and Gabe, but that hers is much thinner and more faded. Just a hint of gold.

"I don't like it. I associate it with a bad part of my life, I think. And honestly, it just... freaks me out a little." She smiles. "You know. Your body changing. You not being in control."

I snort. "You're telling me."

"Do you think you want to learn how to control it, eventually? Or would you rather be like me?"

I think about it for a second. "I don't know. I don't think I'm that far yet. For now I'm just surviving."

She nods. "It's doable, living here without shifting. It's inconvenient sometimes—since it's the main way to get around, our infrastructure is kind of built around it."

I nod, remembering the walk I did with Gabe from the harbor to the *fikarig*. We didn't pass a single car. I thought that was the European-style charm, but now I realize...

"But I have a bike," Em adds, "and if we're going out with the group, Kieran lets me tag along."

"What do you mean?"

Her complexion gets a little rosy. "I mean, you've met him. He's a pretty big guy, and his wolf is huge, too. So he lets me ride on his back when it saves us time."

I feel my eyebrows raise before I can help it, and the rose tint in her cheeks grows darker and spreads across her face. I'm dying to ask what their deal is, but I like Em, and I figure one day she'll tell me herself. So instead, I look back at the *Eijna*.

"You guys seem close," I say noncommittally.

"Yeah, we are. He's my best friend. Has been for decades, basically."

"So can I ask a question, then? Just, like, logistically."

I meet her eyes again as she nods.

"Officially the *fika* is made up of you, Seb, Gabe, and your parents. Or, aunt and uncle I guess, for you. But Kieran basically lives in the *fikarig*, too. And he's not part of the *fika*, right?"

"I mean, he doesn't... He doesn't technically live here," she says awkwardly. "He just sleeps over some nights."

Most nights, I remember her telling me. But I nod.

"There's no hard and fast rules, but anyone who lives in the *fikarig* is usually a member of your *fika*. A *fika* is basically just a pack. It's who you share your life with."

"Why doesn't he just join?"

"He probably will, one day." At this, she blushes again, and she brings her hands to her lap. "But usually, you don't have adults joining a *fika* where they're not one of the founding elders. It's more likely that once our generation starts pairing up, we'll start our own. Then we'll be the elders of that *fika*."

"When you start pairing up?"

She nods. "Yeah, like when the first of us start finding our mates."

"Oh my God." I put my hands up. "You guys have mates. I can't, that's so weird."

She laughs. "I mean, you have mates on the mainland too, right? Like spouses? Life partners?"

"I guess, but the word sounds so much less primal." I shudder. "How does it work? Is it someone you choose, like marriage?"

She shakes her head. "No. I mean, some people think so. But the traditional belief is that it's someone who's meant for you, and that your souls are tied together."

"Is everyone supposed to have one?"

"In theory. Of course, life is messy, so sometimes it's more complicated than that. Some people end up alone, or have multiple life partners at different stages. And some people don't really feel a need for romantic partnership—for them, a mate can be more like a best friend you share your life with. But yeah. Theoretically, everyone has someone."

"Do you know who your mate is?"

Her mouth twists, and she shakes her head.

I nod, thinking it over. I wonder if I'm supposed to have one, in their belief system. Not that I really believe in that sort of thing.

"So if you guys made your own *fika* eventually, would you still live in this house?" I ask.

She shakes her head. "We'd buy our own *fikarig*, if we can. Nothing as nice as this, of course. I don't know what we'll be able to afford when that time comes."

"Would it still be on this island?"

"Probably." She shrugs. "Seb, Gabe, and I all grew up on Saroe. Plus, now that I work with Saga, it just makes sense. Kieran's from Halluk, but he moved here for high school, and his wood shop is here now, too."

"Which one's Halluk again?" I ask, trying to draw up a mental map.

"The north island. We have a vacation house there, so you'll probably see it for yourself during Fire Week."

"What's Fire Week?"

Her eyes light up, and she leans forward in excitement. "Oh, Gabe hasn't told you? It's the best. It's a week-long festival in the summer. Officially it's to mark the summer solstice, but in practice it's become a big party to celebrate the end of the school year. Usually the young people from all the other islands go to Halluk for a week-long party. And this year, I'll have just finished my exams, so we'll actually have something to celebrate."

I nod, wondering if I'll still be here in three weeks to celebrate with her.

"It sounds fun, I bet I'd like it." I conjure up that mental map again, trying to imagine what Halluk will be like. Something tugs at my memory.

"Hang on. Can I ask something else?"

"*Iija*, but after that I really do need to study. My first exam is at the end of the week."

"Yeah, okay." I pull my knee towards me. "I wanted to bring up the thing I had you translate in the bookstore, about the 'island of death.' Why is it called that?"

"Oh, that's easy. Fajje." Her voice is soft and lyrical, and she pronounces Fajje like a whisper: *fah-yay*. "There have always been native Fakari people on the islands, but Fajje was the first island to be reached by European settlers. We've found artifacts that tell us that there were probably a few earlier waves of people who stayed, from longer ago—I think the first Viking settlers reached here around the year 1000? But the big waves of settlers were in the 1500s and after, and they always reached Fajje first."

I nod, thinking of the church ruins.

"I think the last attempt was a few hundred years later, but it's been a while since I interned at the museum, so I'm not sure. But one of the issues we clashed with the Europeans on was what to do with the dead. It's Fakari tradition to bury the dead at sea."

For a second, her vision clouds over, like she's remembering something unpleasant.

"Yeah?" I ask, nudging her back to the present. After a moment, she nods.

"Yeah. The settlers disposed of the dead the European way, by burying them underground. But the *Eijna* says it's bad luck to keep the bodies locked on land. Eventually, as far as I understand, the few Fakari people who were still living on that island left. There's some people who live there now, of course—it's mostly superstition, and it was so long ago. But it's still the least populated of the islands to this day. And if you're not from there, I think the idea creeps most people out."

"Island of death," I say, nodding to myself. "Sounds pretty metal."

She laughs. "Yeah, I guess. If you like this sort of stuff, you should go to the history museum sometime. We can go together, if you want."

"Sure, that sounds fun."

At exactly that moment, Seb and Gabe walk through the front door. I gather my books and get up.

"I should probably get going. Good luck with the rest of your studying," I say to Em, and without a glance at Seb, I walk upstairs to my room.

16

SEB

A week passes, and every fucking night I have the dream.

Me, walking into the ring. The haze of blood and teeth and fear. A strong black wolf appearing out of the mist, as though sent directly by the gods.

Maren. It was Maren, and with that realization, the memory haunts me as much when I'm awake now as when I'm sleeping. Every time I look at her, I feel that churning in my gut: the cruel turn of fate. The gods twisting the knife.

It wasn't her, not really. It was the ghost of her—some version that the ancestors constructed to torture me. It can't possibly be the same Maren who shifts at the breakfast table every time Gabe or Kieran looks at her sideways. Not the same Maren making snide little comments each time she passes me in the hall. And not the same Maren who, six days after I agree to fund her Instagram ad campaign, walks into my bedroom and slams her notebook on my desk.

"I win," she says, crossing her arms in front of her.

"*Agaayit,* can you give a guy some warning?"

I turn from my book to face her. She looks great today. She

must have showered this morning, because her curls are tight and shiny, and she smells like coconut. Immediately, I resent myself for noticing. Even more so when my wolf sits up and wags his tail as he stares at her. *Stupid dumb animal.*

"No." She smiles sweetly. "I win. You sold fifty jars of salt today."

"What?" Immediately, I start doing the math. I was able to fix our broken radiator earlier this week, and with that we've been making enough salt to keep production a little higher than our current sales average. But fifty orders in a day is way more than we can handle.

"Stop making that face, I already took care of it. Gabe held back any product from going to Halssel this morning, and we packed orders together. He's taking them to the ferry tomorrow, to ship on the mainland."

I cross my arms. "Hang on. If you sold fifty orders online instead of fifty in-person on Halssel, then you basically made zero extra profit on the website."

"That would be true, if I were an idiot," she says sweetly, in a tone that makes it very clear she does think *one* of us is an idiot, and it's not her. "But I sold them at a mark-up. $26.50 U.S. dollars per jar."

"*What?* I've been selling these for $5! You can't raise the price that much. My customers will riot!"

"Please. Your customers are old people who visit Halssel for one weekend and will never come back. We're catering to a new demographic, and you can afford to charge them more. Didn't they teach you this in Fakari Business School?"

"We don't—" *Have a business school,* I want to say, but I realize that I'd be making her point for her, so I stop. "Okay. So you made fifty sales and you packed the orders, and they're already out the door? And so you made..."

"$1300, or ₭1,700 *króna,* before lunch."

I blink. We usually make that much in a week, and that's if

it's tourist season.

"I... How did you..."

"I started making Instagram reels, and one of them blew up. And I sent PR packages to a few people I know back in Boston the day after we made our agreement. Once they started posting, that made a big difference. Plus, Gabe helped me update the website to show the new texts I wrote, and I made the page with product recommendations per ailment. That's really what sealed the deal, I think. We're focusing on brand storytelling."

"I... Maren..."

"The correct answer is *thank you*."

"Thank you," I say, and I mean it. "That's huge. You have no idea what a big deal this is."

I meet her eyes, which I realize I've been avoiding for this whole conversation. The second I see them, I feel my wolf startle in my chest. Where they were dark brown before, they now have a golden outline rimming the iris, same as anyone else who's *pakka*. The eyes from the rite, even in human form.

My brow furrows as I stare at her. She's been shifting a lot lately—three, four times a day if Saga's to be believed, whenever her anger gets the better of her. I'd always assumed the shifter ring is genetic, but it must reflect how well or how often you access your inner wolf.

"Yeah, well. Whatever," she says, looking down at her notebook. "Anyway, we're low on stock now, so I need you to make more salt so I can keep doing my job."

I swallow. "That's gonna be tough. The one radiator we have right now is enough to heat one evap pan. That's about a hundred jars of salt a week."

"That sounds like a you problem. I could have sold a hundred *today* if you'd had the stock. We have a waiting list now."

I curse under my breath.

"What?" she asks.

"'That sounds like a you problem.' You mainlanders are only concerned with yourselves."

"Excuse me, it *is* a you problem," she says, crossing her arms as she leans against the desk. I do my best not to notice the way the outline of her ass is made visible leaning against the table.

"This is *your* business, Seb. I agreed to help you make sales. Helping you figure out how to keep up with me is not my responsibility. And before you accuse me of being selfish, please remember that I made you a *week's* worth of income this morning."

I bite the inside of my lip, staring at her.

"Sorry." I nod. "You're right. I'm an asshole sometimes."

"Only sometimes?"

"Yeah. You just haven't gotten to see the other parts of me."

"And whose fault is that?" she asks, straightening herself.

I roll my eyes. *"Agaayu, vaare,* will you let me off the hook even once?"

"Not even once." She smiles. "What's *vaare?*"

"It means woman."

"Oh, I knew that." She nods, thinking. "And *mand* is man, right?"

I nod.

"So if I say, *ije heit tuyyur mand,* I'd be saying..."

I feel a small smile tug at the corner of my mouth. "That you hate thighs man."

She laughs, and the sound is rich and warm and free. My inner wolf rolls onto his back, happy and playful. *Cut it out.*

"Okay, nevermind. What's 'this' again?"

"Deije," I say.

"Okay. So, *ije heit deije mand."*

"You hate *this* man."

She smiles. "That I do."

I want to laugh, but something pulls at my chest.

"Sorry for being a dick to you this week," I say. "You're right

—figuring out the production is my responsibility. I should be grateful to you. And I am."

"Thanks," she says, and stands to leave the room.

"I... I heard from Saga you've been having issues with shifting," I call after her. "I've been there. If you want, I can help."

She hesitates in the doorway, her hand on the doorknob.

"I don't need your pity-friendship, Seb."

"It's not..."

"And I don't need your help. Actually, Kieran is gonna help me with shifting."

Instinctively my head rears back. "What? Why Kieran?"

"Because he offered. And mostly, because he isn't you."

She smiles and shuts the door behind her.

As soon as she's out of sight, my wolf sits up and starts pacing in my chest. I let out a low breath and turn my attention back to my work. Who she spends time with is none of my business—I shouldn't care. I don't. But the thought of her naked and vulnerable after shifting with Kieran, the way she was with me in the library, makes it impossible for me to keep my eyes on my book.

"*Kuunalle*," I command my wolf under my breath. *Cool it.*

He snarls, but after a minute I can feel the burning in my chest die down, and I huff out a breath. As I bring my eyes back to my book, I see something she's circled in the notebook she's left on my desk, under the math on how many sales she made this morning.

61 people on waiting list

I let out a sigh. This woman will be the death of me.

17

MAREN

Mom: Call me

Mom: Maren, CALL ME

Mom: You're very lucky I had my lawyer kill the parking lot video. But we need to talk. TODAY.

Mom: WHERE ARE YOU?? Answer your phone. If you don't get back to me by Wednesday I'm calling the police for a wellness check

I chew my lip. In the week since I left for the Fakaris, I haven't spoken to my mom once. There's no way I can tell her where I am—I wouldn't be surprised if she called the National Guard if I told her I'm out of the country, let alone on the islands. But if I keep ignoring her and she *does* call the police, I don't know how long it'll be before Boston PD breaks down my door.

I think of my landlady—sweet, frail, and nearing 70—and decide I can't do that to her.

My thumbs hesitate over the little keyboard on my screen. Finally, after a minute, I write,

> Maren: I'm safe. I'm out of state for a break. I don't want to talk for a while.

I STARE AT THE MESSAGE, debating.

"Hey. Ready?" Gabe says, peeking his head into my room.

"Uh—yeah. One sec." I hit 'send' and turn the phone off, then place it on the bedside table.

"Everything good?"

"Yeah. Just my mom." I make a face. "She doesn't know I'm here. She was worried."

"Did you tell her?"

I shake my head, and he lets out what looks like a small sigh of relief.

"Well. From what my mom has told me about her, that's probably for the best." He offers a smile. "Are you ready to go?"

"Yeah, coming. Just a sec."

He nods and turns to walk down the stairs. I stand and take a quick moment to calm myself down in the mirror.

I let out a low sigh as I meet my own gaze. These are new eyes to me: marked with a thin golden ring, same as Saga and Gabe and everyone else. I look into them, uneasy. *This* is what everyone was looking for when they stared so intently at me after I first arrived: proof that I was *pakka*. Proof that I belonged.

"You can do this," I say quietly. "It's not a big deal. You're gonna be fine."

I look down at my hands. My skin is clearer now than it was when I came here, and I try to tell myself it's just another sign. Saga was right—maybe my eczema was a reaction to all the stuff

I've been slathering on myself. Maybe my body knows I have a place here, even if I'm not so sure.

Something in me quiets. Finally, I gather myself and turn for the door, walking down to meet the others.

At the bottom of the stairs are Gabe, Kieran, and Em. I'm not sure why I said it was just Kieran helping me shift when it's really more of a group effort—but, after seeing the look on Seb's face, I don't regret it. Anything that gets under his skin works for me.

Kier's wearing workout clothing: a black tank top and loose-fitting joggers. Up and down the seams are magnetic clasps to accommodate shifting—not something I knew how to recognize when I came here, but now that Saga's found me clothing that has the same feature, I notice it on almost everyone. No wonder Em didn't want me shopping for clothes the other day. Now they're a total godsend, because I ruined literally three pairs of pants this week by tearing through them.

Em is the only one in the group wearing normal clothes today —a loose-fitting blue floral sundress. Under one arm, she's carrying a giant canvas beach bag.

"I brought a blanket," she says, holding the bag up as proof. "To cover you at the gym in case you get embarrassed."

"So there's gonna be other people there?" I ask.

Kieran shakes his head. "It shouldn't be too busy."

"But there will be *some* people?"

"On a Tuesday afternoon? Some." Gabe shrugs. "You'll be okay."

I swallow. "I just would love for the entire island not to see me naked, if I can help it."

"It's different here," Gabe says, as Kieran gestures towards the door. We head outside, walking in the direction of the common house as he keeps talking. "Shifting is a normal part of everyday life. When you shift into your human form, people are trained to look away until you're clothed."

"Hm." I think of the times I've been in the gym changing room with other women. It's true that we don't look at each other, but still. It felt different.

"Really, it's pretty normal," Em says. "There's even clothing boxes outside a lot of the communal buildings, for if people shift and don't bring their clothes with them."

I nod. I've come a long way since being embarrassed of my body in middle school gym, but being completely naked as an adult in a literal gymnasium is a bit much, even for me.

"It's gonna be fine," she says, reaching out to nudge my arm. "It makes sense you'd be nervous. I can even talk to the other people in the gym to give you some space, if you want."

"It's okay," I say as we near the woods. "If you guys say it'll be alright, we'll just see."

We walk for about ten minutes, until Em gestures to a building ahead of us. Through the trees up ahead is a large wood structure, multiple stories tall. The arched roof makes me think of a Viking movie, but the rest of it looks more like a hunting lodge. There's a large porch in front, where I can see two old men on one side playing some kind of card game.

"That's the common house," says Gabe to me. "It's where we have community gatherings and council meetings."

"Ah. So this is where you all voted on if I could come."

Em laughs. "No, only pack elders can vote. None of us are elders, just Seb."

My brow furrows. "Wait. You're all adults, right? What makes someone a pack elder?"

"You have to do the elder rite," Gabe says as he leads us around the side of the building.

I nod, trying to remember what Saga told me about this at dinner on my first night. Something about the northern lights; a personal test of strength...

Oh. And the salt ritual. The one Seb's obsessed with restoring.

I turn it over in my mind, trying to find the words for a question. The reason his hunt seems so personal... The way everyone froze when he came to dinner on the first night, just as we were talking about medical care...

"Did... did Seb's elder rite not... go very well?" I ask.

Even from a few feet away, I see Kieran's posture stiffen. Gabe glances over his shoulder at me.

"He was okay, in the end," Em says quietly. "He made it."

"Do people ever... *not* make it?"

She nods, and there's a weird expression on her face. "Sometimes. But it's been a long time since that happened. No one expected—"

"Em," Gabe says, and she looks up. He shakes his head slightly, a nudge.

"What, I can't know?" I ask.

"You should ask him yourself," says Gabe.

I roll my eyes. "Like that man would ever tell me anything."

Gabe shrugs. "If he doesn't want you to know, that's his call. Not ours."

I swallow, feeling slightly stung.

"Guys? We're here," Kieran says as we reach a set of side doors.

We step inside, and I look around to see what looks like a large school gym. There's padded mats along the floor, with punching bags hanging from one wall and some weight-lifting equipment stacked along the other.

"So *this* is where you work out every morning," I say to Kieran.

"Nah, there's a nicer gym with better equipment down the road. But this one's for everybody—you don't need to pay for access. They use it for school games, too."

"Werewolf basketball?" I ask, and he smiles.

"Wolf lots of things. Wolf volleyball, wolf high school dance..."

I snort. "Please tell me you guys have seen *Teen Wolf*."

Gabe, who's already getting the memo that I'll never run out of stuff to say, ignores the comment. "This is also where the kids have shifting practice. That's why we brought you."

"We are *not* letting a bunch of middle schoolers see me naked." I look around, but the gym is, mercifully, relatively empty. There's a few elders on the far end walking laps, but other than that we're alone.

He shakes his head. "They're all in class right now. Are you ready?"

I nod uneasily. Em walks over to a bench along the far wall and sets her bag down. Kieran and Gabe lead me to an area of the mats about ten feet in front.

"Okay, so I did some reading—" Gabe starts.

Kieran shakes his head, waving a hand. "Dude, you can't learn this stuff from a book. Don't you remember what they did with us when we were in school?"

Gabe gives him a look, then turns back to me. "Like I said, I was reading about it, and I think the best place to start is getting you to work on relaxing through the triggers that make you shift. Eventually you want to be able to shift back and forth on command. But in the short-term, just getting you not to shift at random is already a win. Right?"

I nod. "Right. How?"

"Well, it looks like anger is your main trigger right now. You're mostly shifting when someone says something that upsets you."

I think of Kieran making an off-color joke at the breakfast table and Seb getting under my skin in the library. I nod.

"Okay," says Gabe. "So I think step one is recognizing what's going on in your body when that happens, and then being able to talk to your inner wolf."

"My inner wolf?"

Kieran puts his hand in the middle of his chest. "The feeling inside you whenever you have a big reaction. That's your wolf."

I put my own hand on my chest, mirroring him, trying to tune in. I know what he's talking about—the clawing, frantic sensation when I get anxious, or the snapping feeling whenever Seb's looking at me. Or that weird third thing I feel when I look at him.

Nope. Not gonna think about *that*.

"Do you feel her?" Gabe asks.

"It's a her?"

"Unless you have something to tell us," says Kier.

I shake my head, feeling. "No, it's a her."

"Okay. You feel her now?"

I nod, tuning in. She's lower than Kieran said—in my gut somewhere, noting the situation. Just watching us.

"Okay, great," says Gabe. "Can you try talking to her?"

"....Hi?" I say awkwardly.

Kieran snorts.

"Well, what am I supposed to say?!" I snap at him. In my stomach, I feel the sensation of something rising, and a kind of snarl forming. I turn to Gabe, my eyes wide. "Oh..."

"Yeah," he says, nodding enthusiastically. "Your wolf feels a lot of the same things you do."

"But bigger," I say.

He shakes his head. "Sort of. It's kind of like an inner child, if you've ever been to therapy."

I bark out a laugh. "Oh dude, you've heard about my mom. I've abso-*lutely* been to therapy."

He smiles. "Right. Well, it's like that—it's what you feel deepest. Sometimes, if your wolf and your mind aren't in alignment, it's because you're not really in tune with yourself. That makes being able to listen to your wolf, and connect to what she's feeling, its own skill."

I think of the feeling I had when I looked at Seb in the library again. Out of alignment is right—whatever my inner wolf feels for Seb beyond anger is *all* physical. Good thing my brain is in charge, because she's the one who knows how to call a red flag when she sees one.

"Okay, so what now? How do we practice?"

Gabe and Kieran glance at each other.

"In grade school, they taught us some mindfulness skills to speak to our inner wolves when they got scared. But if your wolf mostly responds to anger right now..."

I laugh. "Oh my God. Tell me you're gonna try to piss me off for practice."

Kieran grins. "Too easy. Nah, for now we're just gonna teach you some calming tricks to use when you feel your wolf getting riled up. You can use the same stuff to calm down when you've shifted, to help you get your skin back."

I nod, and Gabe leads me through a few mindfulness exercises.

"Gabe, this is so boring," I say, after learning a third way to breathe. "I thought we were gonna do wolf practice."

"This *is* shifting practice. You need to learn to feel your wolf and work with her. If you can connect to her, and get yourself to calm down when you get overheated, you're halfway there."

Connect with her. I put my hand over my core, trying to feel for her presence. Sure enough, she's in there—antsy and a little playful, just like I feel right now. As I tune in, I can visualize her lowering her front legs, wagging her tail like a dog, wanting to play.

I hear something from behind us—the doors to the gym opening. I turn my head to look, and it's Seb, probably here to check on whatever Kieran and I are doing.

"Hey!" Em calls from the bench, waving at him.

I try to suppress a smile. I have an idea, and it's way more fun than breathing exercises.

I focus on my inner wolf again, and in my mind I give her a

little nudge: *go ahead. You can play.* It takes a few seconds—I'm pretty sure my muscle memory needs some time before this becomes second-nature. But after a minute, I feel a kind of surge under my skin, and then I'm falling forward, my body cracking and breaking, and I'm on the ground on all fours in wolf form.

"Look at that," I hear Kieran mutter to Gabe. "All it takes to get angry enough is *seeing* him."

But it's not rage that's fueling this—it's the desire for some fun, if at Seb's expense. Before he has time to react, I'm bolting for him at all-out speed, snarling. He startles at the sight of me, but it only takes him a second to react. Moments later, just as I reach him, he's in his wolf form, too.

I haven't seen it before. His wolf is big and dark gray, just a few inches taller than mine. My plan had been to tackle him to the ground, but now that he's on all fours, I end up leaping half onto his back. He rolls to the side so that he's partially crushing me, and where I expect it to hurt, it feels gentle, like he's aware of his own weight. I paw at his side, trying to push him off. He gives way easily, then lowers his head, his tail swishing like he wants to play.

From the side of the gym, I hear Gabe and Kieran's footsteps coming towards us. I let my wolf pounce on Seb's, but where it's meant to be intimidating—or at least a challenge—I feel my own tail wagging, too. He gets me off of him with ease, then pins me to the ground.

"What the fuck is she doing?" Kieran asks.

Gabe comes to a halt close to us. "I think they're... play-fighting?"

Seb's wolf nips lightly at my neck, and I manage to get him off me. I bolt across the gym, running from him, but he keeps up. A minute later, we're on the far end of the hall, and he pounces.

I fall to the ground under his weight, and Seb cages me in with his arms and legs. My tail swishes side to side with satisfaction. I realize somewhere in my conscious mind that my wolf liked being caught. She wants the game, yes—but she also wants to let him win her.

I feel something small crackle in the air. It's playfulness, and a tiny hint of something else—that same feeling I had when I looked up at him in the library. It's coming from him, I realize.

Desire.

Oh my God. I'm fine tackling Seb in front of the others, but there's no way I'm gonna let anything sexual happen in what's basically a high school gymnasium—that chapter of my life ended when I let my ex-girlfriend feel me up under the bleachers the day before graduation.

I tune inwards again, trying to feel for my inner wolf with my conscious mind. I find her, impish and playful, and wordlessly ask her for the reins. She resists for a minute, but I push, and then I'm shifting, human arms and legs unfolding onto the wood laminate. I move quickly, trying to gain the upper hand mostly through surprise. Seb gives in—the wolf is more generous to me than the man. A second later, I get the advantage, and then he shifts. We end up with me on top of him, straddling his core and pinning his wrists over his head.

He's breathing heavy from the exertion, and I am, too.

"Good game," I say, like I've just won a wrestling match. And maybe I did.

I hear footsteps coming up to us, and it's Em with the blanket.

"Here," she says, and I look up as she wraps it over my shoulders.

"Oh. Thanks." I lift my hands from Seb's wrists, holding the blanket in place.

It's true, what Gabe said—I glance around the gym and realize that no one is looking at us. But everyone seems *aware* of us—stiff shoulders, intentional glances to other parts of the gym. And how could they not be, I think, since I basically attacked a man in broad daylight and then wrestled him to the ground?

Under me, Seb is still breathing heavy, gazing up at me with a dazed look on his face. Kieran comes up to us and tosses a ball of clothes at him. I climb off his body and he scrambles to his feet, turning from me as he snaps on loose-fitting black pants.

I have to remind myself to look away. But not before I catch sight of my effect on him, once his pants are on—just the outline of something against the fabric. I feel my cheeks warm, some combination of embarrassment and satisfaction, and I bite my lower lip to suppress a smile.

I wanted to fight him and win. But psychological warfare works, too.

"Nice work, Maren," Gabe says as he reaches us. "You shifted on purpose?"

I rise to my feet, keeping the blanket wrapped around my shoulders. "Yeah. And back."

"So that was planned?" He nods towards Seb, who's turning back towards us, running a hand through his hair. He's pulled his shirt back on too, now, a tight blue tee.

"I mean. I wouldn't say planned. But it was intentional." I glance over at Seb. "All good?"

He nods, a little breathless. "I, uh. I came here about the business. But we can—we can talk after you're dressed."

I smile and let the blanket slip an inch or so off of my shoulder and smile innocently, still aware of the effect of my body on his.

"I can talk. What's up?"

Seb looks back and forth between the guys and me, clearly a little winded.

"Uh. I worked it out. I think with slightly different settings, the radiator can handle more volume than what we've been using until now, so I'm gonna try increasing production a little bit. But I also talked to someone at the bank, and I showed them your sales numbers from yesterday. Based on that and the rate I paid off my last loan, they're letting me borrow enough for a second radiator and evap pool. It should get here during Fire Week, so we can set it up after. Until then, we should have enough to sell maybe 130 to 150 jars of salt a week. After that, double."

"Nice," I say, nodding. "That was fast."

"Yeah, well." He nods awkwardly. "You were right, I guess. I was being stubborn. And if we're able to sell that much, I think I'd be able to upgrade to a better space, with access to a better geothermal heat source, within a year. So. Thanks."

He waits, as though expecting me to say something or thank him for his great magnanimity. But instead, I turn to Em.

"Cool. I think I've had enough wolf practice for today. Do you wanna get some ice cream or something? I'm taking the rest of the day off."

18

SEB

When I come back from swimming at the hot springs the following night, I find the rest of the gang sitting on the back porch.

I can smell the rich acidity of red wine from halfway across the yard. Maren is in the middle of a story, and I can tell because her words are coming a mile-a-minute and Em and Gabe are doubled-over in laughter. Kieran's smirking behind his beer, and Maren seems to be fighting to get to the punchline before the others' laughter drowns her out.

I walk up to the back steps. Halfway through her sentence, she hears the tread of my feet and stops.

"Oh. Hey, Seb."

The others look up, smiling from behind their drinks.

"Hey." I lean against the wood railing of the porch. "Drinks night?"

"Oh, we were just... hanging out," she says. For a moment I can see awkwardness on her face, like she's fighting herself. She feels obligated to invite me to join, I realize, and she doesn't want to.

I clear my throat. "Well. Don't stop on my account."

I give the rest of the guys an awkward smile and head inside. Saga and my mom are at the dining room table playing *kateijtko*, the cards in neat little rows between them.

"*Heij piu,*" Saga says to me. Mom, for her part, just gives a little nod. Saga's always been much warmer and more affectionate with me than my own mother.

"*Heij Aja. Ama.*" *Hey, Aunt. Mom.* I lean over the table, looking at the cards. "Who's winning?"

"Your mother, as always," Saga says, winking at me. "Ever the strategist."

"Want to join us?" Mom asks. "We're almost done with this round."

"*Nekkaaa,*" Saga scolds, drawing the second syllable out. "He should be out with the kids. Why don't you join them, *piu?* I can get you a drink."

"I... I have stuff to do. Thanks, though."

"What stuff?"

"Just work."

She shakes her head. "You work too much. Take a break every once in a while."

Just then, a peal of laughter erupts from the balcony, and I find myself glancing over my shoulder. I swallow and bring my attention back to the table.

"I'm good. Thanks, though. Good luck with the game."

I head for the living room, where I give a quick wave to Viggo and Dagmar on the couch. As I take the stairs up to the second floor and walk to my room, I run my balled fist over the front of my right thigh, trying to ease the muscle. My leg is especially achy today—it's been a few days since I did my physical therapy stretches. To be honest, I'd hoped that upping my swim routine and honing in on the salts would mean I could do less PT. Instead, my leg's been nagging me for a week, and I can feel the pain building with each passing day.

I enter my bedroom and see Maren's notebook left out on my desk. She's added up some new numbers for me, and as I drape my towel over the back of the chair, I take a look. Including the first day, she's now sold 170 jars, or $4500 of product. She subtracted the amount from her goal—$20,000—and circled the amount left.

I sigh and turn from the desk towards my dresser. I didn't *just* come to the gym yesterday to tell her about the generator; I came to apologize—and honestly, to keep an eye on Kieran. It's none of my business, but Kier has gone out with basically every girl we've ever met, and the thought of him with Maren does something to my wolf I don't like. Her wolf barrelling towards me was totally unexpected, but what took me more by surprise was what happened after...

I swallow, remembering how it felt to play with her, taking turns wrestling each other to the ground. I can't blame my wolf for how he feels around her—Maren is beautiful, and the thick, rounded curves of her body are enough to make anyone do a double-take. Add that to the fact that the ancestors have tied us together in some fucked-up way ever since my rite, and I can't blame my inner animal for taking note of her—for better and for worse.

But it's not just that. When we were play-wrestling in the gym, I *felt* something.

I walk down to the hall to wash my face and brush my teeth. As I do, I pore it over, remembering how it felt to be with her. My inner wolf has an easier time living in the moment than I do, but even in my wolf form, it's been a long time since I felt any kind of happiness or joy. But with her? I felt lighter. Almost like the kid I was before I first went to the ring.

And the thought of her straddling me, leaned over to pin me down, her chest almost directly in line with my face? I can't think about *that* for too long.

I meet my own eyes in the mirror and try to pull myself back to reality. Over the sound of my electric toothbrush, I can hear someone climbing the stairs. I wait, and then in the bathroom mirror I see the back of Maren's head as she walks down the hall into her room. I let out a breath and rinse, then wash my face and head back to my room. I hear the click as her bedroom door shuts.

As I pull off my clothes and climb into bed, I can hear her breathe through the wall again. I know the layout of her room, and our beds are each pressed up against the wall that separates us. The first few nights she was here, I found the sound of her light snoring grating, but now I'm kind of used to it. I hear it again now, and for a second I'm surprised that she's already asleep.

And then I realize I hear something else. There's a faint buzzing in the background.

My jaw clenches, and I feel my pulse quicken as I realize what I'm hearing. As she lets out a breathy sigh, it's all but confirmed.

She's touching herself.

My body responds almost instantly, a surge of desire rushing through me at the thought. I let out a low breath. It's been a long time since I've shared a bed with anyone—since before I did my consecration, during which I needed to fast and abstain from earthly pleasures for three months. I've been taking care of myself in the years between, but still, I'm more reactive now than I used to be. The sound of Maren's breath growing heavy, the little gasps—the unmistakable gasped *"oh"* that falls from her lips—does something to me.

I close my eyes, trying not to picture it: her parting her legs, her head falling back with pleasure. The sound is muffled enough that I can almost convince myself I'm mistaken, and I start muttering some random verse from the *Eijna* to try to get myself to think of something else. But then, a minute later, I hear a low moan, and I feel my inner wolf respond at the same time as my body.

I put a hand on myself, easing the pressure. My wolf is nagging me, wanting me to go to her, and I shove him away.

Down, boy. It's not like that.

I can hear her sounds grow more rhythmic, the pitch of her moans getting higher. I can't bear this—I can't be around to hear her climax, can't bear to live with the knowledge of how that sounds.

I swallow, pulling myself from the bed, and put on some loose-fitting pants and a sweatshirt. I tuck my cock into the waistband of my pants and leave the room, the breathy sound of her moans following me as I make my way down the first few steps. I rush all the way down, into the living room.

"Aeijs kut, jenge?" Viggo calls after me, checking that everything's okay.

I nod wordlessly and head for the door, into the dark, warm cover of summer night.

I ARRIVE at the temple breathless, my leg aching even more than before. My body shifts back into my human form, and the clothes I was carrying in my mouth fall to the floor. Snapping them on over myself, I stagger up to the temple, my footsteps uneven. *Uikbaane*—I've been doing too much, and if I don't slow down soon, I'm going to regret it. Still, I needed to come here, if only to be as far away from the sound of Maren's breathy little sighs as possible.

I reach the top of the steps and I grab three *loter*, writing my name in the logbook. Once inside the temple doors, I wash my feet in the selenite pool, and then step into the main hall.

The tension in my shoulders eases as the soft light of a dozen candles falls over me, welcoming me into the space. I look down at the strips of paper in my hands, then up at the wood carvings of the gods in their niches.

With a low exhale, I walk up to the statue of Tinnúr. I dip the first *lot* into the small dish of oil before him, then bring it to the flame.

"Gracious Tinnúr, champion of peace," I mutter under my breath in Fakari. The scent of the smoke is rich and faintly sweet, and I take a deep breath before saying the prayer I've repeated in this temple a dozen times.

"Thank you for the life of my father, Filip, and for the ways he taught me to become a man... Bring his spirit into full unity with the ancestors, bringing him to peace."

The words bring a tightness to my chest. Saga always tells us the spirits of the ancestors stay on the islands, giving us guidance. And I *do* believe it—I even know people who claim to have seen them: shadows of beloved grandparents or lost friends visiting them in dark moments. But the last time I saw my father was the day he died.

I'd hoped to see his spirit that night in the ring. Instead, I left on the brink of death, so close to the veil that I almost prayed for it to take me.

The flame eats the last stretch of the *lot*, and I let go before it reaches my fingers. I don't like to admit it, because I'm almost afraid that letting the thought to the front of my mind will somehow make it true. But I've wondered before whether maybe it's why I feel the need to come here so often, praying for my father's soul to be at rest. Some part of me worries that the fact that I've never seen his spirit means he's not with the ancestors yet, somehow. That his soul is trapped in the past, the way it was when he was still alive.

The thought makes something roil in my gut, and I clear my throat, looking at the two *loter* still in my hands. Feeling every muscle in my body rebel as I do, I pick up the next *lot* and dip it in the flame.

"Bring the soul of David Winterwood to peace, and into unity with the ancestors."

I let out a low breath, watching the flames lick up the paper, willing myself to say more. But I can't bring myself to plead for his soul the way I do for my father's, so finally, I just let go, the last of the prayer going up in smoke.

I know what's next—I knew it the second I chose three *loter* as I came to the temple. I turn right and walk to the niche for Fjarayya, goddess of love and healing. Feeling my pulse beating in my throat, I dip the paper into the oil before her, where flower petals on the surface part to make way. I bring it back up to the flame and watch as the flame engulfs the oiled tip. Smoke, sweet and rich, wafts up towards the carving of the goddess.

"For Maren," I say quietly, and I watch as the flame consumes the rest of the *lot*. Finally, as it reaches my fingertips, I let go.

I turn to leave the temple, walking towards the heavy wooden doors at the back. As I reach the front steps, I'm about to step out of my clothes and shift when I see something up ahead.

Far in the distance, a blue light. It's a single orb, floating gently on the horizon.

Agaayu. Could it be?

I strip off my clothes immediately and shift, bolting towards it. I've never seen a spirit for myself before, and as I run towards the light, I try to make out something in it—a shape or movement that would confirm it for me. The dark wave of his hair; the way his whole body shook when he laughed. The sound of his voice. I'll take anything.

I run and run, feeling my leg ache in pain as I go. But the farther I get, the farther the light seems to stay, dancing like a little flame. I tear through the woods, heading south past the *fikarig*.

Please, Dad. Wait for me. Just hang on.

The light doesn't leave, but it doesn't come closer, either. I run for what feels like hours, till I reach the edge of the island, coming to a halt at the raw edge of a low cliff. A dozen feet below me, I can hear the dull roar of the ocean, and I take a moment to try to catch my breath. The light stays on the horizon, dancing gently off in the distance. To my eye, it almost looks like it's hovering *on* the line of the horizon, where the sky meets the sea. And then, to the right, I see another—a second light, also blue, farther somehow. And another, to the left of me.

My wolf lets out a bark of surprise, and I scramble back from the cliff's edge.

What are they?

I sit and wait for a few minutes, watching as the lights dance, willing them to come close. But they stay far, and finally, almost an hour later, I turn back in the direction of the *fikarig*, my leg aching with every step.

19

MAREN

The next week passes in a blur. I spend most of my time with Em, who's studying for her final exams, or preparing orders with Gabe. Every once in a while, Seb comes to hover like a ghost in the doorway as Gabe and I sit on the floor, packing boxes.

I do my best to be polite. "We don't need any help, thanks!" And then he leaves to haunt someone else, presumably.

Gabe and I do shifting practice another one or two times, but it's *so* boring, and with my new snap-on clothes, once I get down to only shifting by accident once or twice a day it feels manageable enough to go without. Em's exams are at the end of my third week here, spilling over into the Monday after the weekend. She won't know if she's passed until later, but Saga and I still make a cake to celebrate the tests being done. And finally, on Monday, we pack to leave for Fire Week.

"You're gonna love it," Em says, putting her duffle in the back of Saga's beat-up Jeep. It took her basically thirty seconds to pack —unlike me, who spent a whole hour figuring out which, and how many, pairs of underwear to bring for a five-day vacation.

"Yeah? What's Halluk like?" I hoist my purple suitcase into the back. It slips halfway out, and Kieran stops behind me to lift it for me.

"I mean, Halluk during Fire Week is different than Halluk the rest of the year," Em says, giving Kier a grateful look. "Fire Week is like a festival. The rest of the time, it's pretty quiet. But it's beautiful, and the house is really nice."

"Why do you guys call it Fire Week, anyway?"

Kieran leans against the car, folding his arms in front of him. "On the night of the big party, we burn a giant statue of Beiyyur, god of the harvest, on the beach."

"Oh my God." I look at Em. "You're taking me to wolf Burning Man."

She shrugs, confusion written on her face. "I... guess? What's Burning Man?"

"American Fire Week," I mutter, and eye the car.

It's a tight fit—the Jeep can fit exactly five, and with Kieran's height, it's decided that he'll ride shotgun while Gabe drives us to the north shore. That leaves Em, Seb, and me in the back seat.

"Em, don't you want to sit next to me?" I ask from outside the car as Seb shoves past me to climb into the middle. He's been even more sullen than usual lately, and as I let out a huff, I do my best to make sure he hears it.

"Em needs to sit next to a window or she throws up," says Gabe.

"That was *one time*, and I was twelve years old."

"One time was enough," Seb grumbles, buckling the seatbelt around him. He looks up at me, standing next to the car side door. "So? Are you coming?"

I sigh and step into the Jeep, reluctantly cramming myself between Seb and the car door as I shut it behind me. Gritting my teeth, I buckle the seatbelt and press my elbows as far inwards as they can, the way I have had to on every plane ride since I was 13 and hips, thighs, and waist sprouted outwards practically overnight.

"Ready?" Gabe asks. "Everyone buckled? Everyone's stuff packed?"

"Yes," Em and I say at the same time, as Seb grumbles "Just go."

Gabe peels out of the driveway, and as we turn onto the wooded main road towards the north shore, I feel the gentle pressure of Seb's leg against mine. Instinctively I jerk my knee away, but there's no room for it to go, so within seconds it's brushing against his again.

He shifts uncomfortably, and I cross my arms in front of myself, trying to make myself smaller.

"It's fine," he mutters under his breath.

"What's fine?" Gabe asks, glancing in the rearview mirror.

"Nothing," we both say.

We drive in relative quiet until Kieran puts on some music. After a few minutes, I start to let go, and finally my hands come to rest in my lap again. Seb, trying to make more room around us, puts his arms behind Em's and my headrests.

I swallow, taking in the scent of him and the nearness of his body. I've never had an especially strong sense of smell, but since I started shifting, it's gotten deeper somehow. Em smells like rose water and some kind of spice; Kieran smells faintly like wood and salt. But Seb smells *good*—the kind of good you could bottle and sell for $300 at Tom Ford. It's rich and deep, like amber and warm spices and a hint of tobacco, although I can guarantee based on uptightness alone that this man has never smoked a thing in his life.

And there's something else, too. He smells like sex.

Not the *scent* of sex. His scent *reads* as sexual to me, and the closer he is to my body the harder I find to ignore. Gabe drives us through a large valley with mountains on either side, and I'm not paying attention to the view because I'm paying attention to Seb's body and the gentle vibration of his leg next to mine as we hit bumps in the road. He's aggravating and annoying and, sometimes, a total dickhead—but much as I hate to admit it, Seb is also *fine*. Dark eyes, sharp jaw and cheekbones, that brush of stubble... Broad shoulders, the way his strong arms fill out the sleeves of his shirt.

I didn't know I had a type until I came here, and now I wonder if he might be it.

I tune out as the guys start talking about something, and am brought back to earth by the feeling of Seb's full-body laughter, the warmth of it vibrating through both him and me. At the sensation, I can feel my inner wolf loll onto her back, happy and lazy. I bring my arms back tightly around myself, crossing them over my body.

"Put your arm down. I'm going to try to sleep," I say to Seb, and he glances at me and does as told. And then I rest my head on the window and pretend not to think about him.

WE GET to the house on Halluk about two hours later, after waiting for a ferry and then wading through the crowds gathered at the receiving harbor.

"Woah, this is gorgeous," I say, looking up at it as we near the top of the hill. It's large, painted blue with gambrel roofs like something out of Martha's Vineyard.

"I love it here," Em says happily, glancing over at me.

I step closer to her as Gabe finds the spare key and opens the front door.

"When did they get this house? It looks totally different from the *fikarig*."

"A few years before I joined." She runs a hand over her arm, warming herself against the breeze that's coming in from the sea on the other side of the hill. "All the houses here look different than on Saroe. The island was populated last, out of all of them, so the style is different. You should ask Kier sometime. He grew up here."

I nod.

"How many bedrooms is it? Are we doubling up?"

"Nah, there's enough. Kier and I will, um, probably share a room anyway. But we'll have more than enough space."

"Alright, get in," Gabe says, finally getting through all three locks on the front door.

Seb storms through the door first and immediately heads right, up a large staircase to the second floor. *Typical.* He's probably taking the best room for himself.

"I'll take the blue room at the end of the hall," Em says, glancing over at Gabe. "So Maren can have...?"

"Maren, you can take the master, since it's your first Fire Week," Gabe says. "I'll take the green room."

"Are you sure? I don't need a lot of space."

His and Em's eyes immediately fall to the suitcase I packed— by far the biggest out of all our bags.

"Really, it's fine," Em says warmly. "I just want you to have a good time."

GABE AND SEB make dinner in the evening, and we eat outside on a large veranda overlooking the shore. There's a fire pit in the middle, which Kieran lights after dinner. We linger after with drinks—Gabe and me with a glass of wine, the others with beer. While the guys joke with each other, Em scooches close to me, telling me a little about the traditions she looks forward to every year.

"Tonight's the opening celebration, all along the south shore beach," she says, curling her feet under her. "It goes for hours, but you don't have to come for the whole thing. I think it's probably already started, if you want to go soon."

"Yeah, I don't know," I say. "It's been a long week, and I'm kind of tired. Do you mind if I stay back?"

Her face falls just slightly.

"I'm gonna have a great time here, I promise," I say. "It's just that I packed nine million salt orders this week, and with that and learning how not to shift through the last clothes I own, I'd love to be able to slow down for like, one day."

It's not *just* that. As humiliating as it is, Seb's been on my mind since I tackled him in the gym. After the car ride to the harbor together, I can feel my body's awareness of him swirling through me. I'd rather take care of that alone, at home, than go to an event where I'm more likely to drunkenly work through my frustrations with a stranger.

As if to drive the point home, at that exact moment Seb barks out a laugh, the sound rich and heady. I can practically feel it reverberating through me, and my wolf sits up, attuned to his presence. Em and I both glance over at the guys, and then she turns her attention back to me.

"Yeah, of course," she says, nodding. "I mean, there will be parties all week. We'll make sure you get to see the best of the celebrations."

"Thanks."

"Em," Kieran says from across the fire pit. "It's getting late. Do you want to head out soon?"

She nods, and I watch as her face lights up from the way he says her name. She's got it bad. I wonder if she ever admits it, even to herself.

The others start to get up and head inside.

"You don't want to come?" Gabe asks, and I shake my head.

"Long week. You have fun, I'll stay back here and rest."

"You sure?" Kieran asks. "It'll be a good time."

"I'm sure, thanks. Enjoy," and I wave as the others go inside.

I stay out there for what must be a half hour, staring at the fire, thinking. After a while, I hear the front door slam shut, and the sound of the others' voices face away as they walk down the hill towards the party on the south shore.

I let out a sigh and tilt my head back to look up at the inky-black sky above. It's hard to believe it's only been a few weeks since I arrived here on the Fakaris. It feels like it's been months, between me getting to know my new family, finding out new parts of myself, and getting involved in Seb's business.

Seb. At the thought of him, I instantly remember that day in the gym, tackling him to the ground. I've thought about it—the two of us wrestling, me ending up naked on top of him—more often than I'd like to admit.

God, I could hate myself for it. For the way I find him hot even as he drives me insane. His stupid, irrational temper. How he gets angry over nothing—and even worse, how quick he is to apologize. It always catches me off-guard.

The way he throws his head back when he laughs, and how the sound feels like it hums through my whole body. That golden glint in his eyes...

I feel the stirrings of desire between my legs, and that heady, fluid feeling in my gut. I know I shouldn't—that as soon as I finally give in to these thoughts, I'll make them a hundred times worse. But in a moment, I decide I don't care. I've been through enough this year, and I deserve a break. Everyone's left already, and I'm home alone. No one has to know.

I finally give into the thoughts that I've been suppressing for weeks. I imagine Seb's body over me; the weight of his chest on mine, the pressure of him between my legs, hard and needy and insistent. I slip my hand into the drawstring of my shorts and find the indent in my underwear for the crest between my lips. I strum my fingers over it, sending a shiver of my skin, and imagine Seb's head in my neck. I picture him muttering unspeakably dirty things to me: telling me he hates me and needs me and can't get me out of his head. I think of his fingers entering me, and slip my own under the cotton of my underwear, finding the sensitive curve of my clit. At the rush of pleasure, my eyes flutter shut and I hear a breath escape me.

I circle it as I imagine Seb burying himself into me, losing himself in my body. I want him to lose control; I want to see the look of desire on his face and know that I've won. I want to be so fucking good that he surrenders himself to me.

"Maren."

My head snaps up and I almost scream as I see Seb standing at the entrance to the veranda, directly across the fire pit. He's in his gray sweatpants, shirtless, his hair damp. And he's staring at me with my hand in my pants.

"Oh my God!" I cry, pulling my hand out and curling my legs under me, trying to rearrange the blanket to cover as much of my body as possible. "Oh my God. I'm sorry, I thought you all left together. You didn't see anything."

But I can see from his body language that that's not true. His breathing is deep and rough, and the look in his eyes is slick, like he's hungry. His whole body is stiff, as though he's afraid that moving even one muscle will break his composure.

At the hunger in his gaze I feel myself warm, and the heady flow of my desire comes back, swirling through my core. I see him flex his jaw, almost like he can tell. His hand twitches, like he wants to reach out to me, but he swallows and drags his eyes back to mine, so slowly I almost think it hurts him.

"Tell me you were thinking of me," he says, his voice dark.

"I wasn't."

He steps forward. "Liar."

His voice is low, goading. It's doing something to me and I don't know what, but it's something I like.

I huff out a sigh. "Not everything is about you, Seb."

"But *this* was, wasn't it?"

I meet his eyes again and say nothing. He looks hungry, like a predator, and I realize I want to be prey. I want *him*. Not in my fantasies—in *me*.

The drink and desire flow through me, making me bold. I know I'll regret this tomorrow, but tonight...

I keep my eyes locked on his and bring my hand slowly back to the spot between my legs. He doesn't move, but I see his breath draw deeper, and I slip my hand back under my shorts and let out a low murmur as my fingers find my clit.

"Fuck. Mare," he breathes, and I find that I like the sound of my nickname on his lips.

"Mm," I say, running my fingers slowly back and forth. "Is this what you had in mind? That I was lying here, touching myself like this, thinking of you?"

I lower my fingers and slip them into myself, letting my head fall back.

"Oh, Seb..." I murmur, my voice exaggerated, mocking him.

He walks over to me, his stride confident and masterful. In a second he's over me, grabbing my wrist and pulling my hand from my pants.

"Stop," he commands. The ownership of his words sends yet another ripple of desire through me, and instinctively my hips writhe forward, craving the pressure he's just taken away.

"You like messing with me?" he asks, sinking to his knees on the ground between my legs. His eyes are still on mine, his hand still wrapped around my wrist, as I nod.

"You can joke as much as you want, but I know you were out here thinking about me as you touched yourself."

"How are you so sure?" I try to twist my wrist out of his hand, but he clamps down harder, and I feel the animal in me respond.

"Because I can feel your wolf under the surface, wanting to play," he says, his voice low. "Because your hips are bucking at my face being so close to you."

It's true, I realize. His face is just inches from the crest between my thighs, and instinctively they're grinding towards him. *Traitorous, horny body.*

"And because I can't stop fucking thinking about you, either," he says, and lets go of my wrist.

He brings his hands up to my shorts and pulls them down. Instinctively, I lift my hips so they slip down over my ass, and my pussy is exposed.

"Here's what I'm going to do," he says, his voice low as he brings his fingers between my legs to stroke over my lips. "I'm going to taste and touch you until you're crying out for me."

I nod, moving my hips towards him.

"I'm going to eat until I've had my fill." He brings his dark eyes up to me. "And then, when you say my name, I'm going to leave, so you remember who's really in charge."

The hell he is, I think. As soon as this starts, neither of us are going to be able to turn it off. But I nod breathlessly, inching my hips towards his mouth, wanting it. At the indication of consent, he brings his mouth to my clit and I gasp.

At first, his tongue is feather-light. My body moves for me, trying to get closer and make him taste me fully. He looks up at me from under an arched brow, then brings his hands to my hips, his fingertips pressing firmly into the softness of my body. His hands are firm, holding me in place.

"Down, girl," he murmurs, and I try to hide the shiver of pleasure that ripples through my body.

My hips grind towards him again, but he grips me firmer, and I realize I like it—letting him be in charge, just a little. I watch as he brings his mouth back to to the crux between my legs, and then, a moment later, I can't see what he's doing because my eyes are closing and I'm arching for him, gasping as he makes me feel something so good that all the words fall out of my head.

OhmyGodohmyGodohmyGod. If I thought my emotions were on a dimmer switch before my wolf came out, then this is like a whole new level. Is *this* what I've been missing all these years? Sex that makes me feel like the whole world could end and I wouldn't notice?

His tongue runs up and down, tasting me, working me. I don't know what he's doing, but it feels so incredible that I'm crying out already, gasping for air. The sound of him groaning against my body sends a secondary ripple of pleasure through me as I realize he likes it, too.

"Fuck, Maren," he murmurs as he pulls away. I look down in time to see him slip two fingers in his mouth, then bring them to my lips.

"Your pussy is so pretty," he says, reverent, almost under his breath. One hand comes to rest on my inner thigh, possessive, and I watch him part my lips with his thumb and let out a low groan at the sight.

I like it—watching him watch me. Instinctively I spread my legs a little wider, showing myself off for him. I see his breath grow deep and ragged as he brings the two fingers to my slit and runs them up and down, parting my lips.

"I've thought of this," he says, his voice a low murmur. "I thought of you, spread out like this for me."

I moan as his fingers find my entrance and he dips his fingertips into me.

He swallows. "I wondered what you'd look like. How you'd taste."

"And?"

"So fucking good." He sinks his fingers into me, and I let out a gasp as his mouth returns to my clit, sucking gently. Pleasure coils through my body, curling through my muscles and around my bones, sparking to the surface of my skin. I can hear myself moaning and bring a hand to my mouth, suddenly worried about being too loud.

"Don't bother," he says, the heat of his breath warming the skin between my thighs. "Everyone else left. And besides. I like hearing what I do to you."

He brings his mouth back to me and I'm moaning, gasping, my back arching off the seat as his fingers work in and out of me.

"*Agaayu*, Maren," he groans. "God, you taste so good. You're so wet for me. Tell me who made you so wet."

I can hear the ache in his voice, the tone low and rough and warm. I want to respond—want to tell him that, despite myself, *he*'s the one who does this to me. But I can't say anything, because the only sound coming out of me is moaning, wild and primal. I've never heard myself like this. I've never *felt* like this. But the sensation of his mouth on me—and more than that, the realization that he *likes* it, that he's delighting in the sight and taste and sound of me, that he's longed to know what I'd look and taste like—gives me pleasure so intense it's almost unbearable.

Instinctively, my hands find his hair and grasp onto it as I grind myself against his mouth. After a moment, I let go—I don't want to hold him in place if he wants to stop. But he keeps working me with his mouth, and his free hand reaches back up for mine and brings it to the back of his head again.

"*Nekka*, I like it," he says, his voice raspy. "Grind into my face."

He doesn't need to ask twice. I grab onto his hair, my hips rocking back and forth against his mouth.

"Oh my God," I'm crying out, gasping. "Fuck, I'm close. Oh my God, oh my God. Seb—"

And then he stops, pulling away. I'm gasping, and I hear a whine escape my lips as his fingers leave me. I sit up, confused.

He's looking up at me with dark eyes, the gold in them glinting in the light of the fire. His breathing is deep and ragged, and I watch as he brings the back of his hand up to wipe his mouth. As he stands, I see that he's rock-hard, the pressure of his erection stretching the fabric of his sweatpants. There's a small wet mark near the head, his precum telling me that his body is hungry for me even if his mind wants to win the game.

It takes a second for my brain to come back online. *This is what he said he'd do.*

He turns away from me and starts to leave the room.

"Wait," I call after him. I stand, leaving my shorts and underwear on the ground. *Two can play at this.*

He turns for me and I press my body against his, feeling the pressure of his hard-on against my hip. I snake one arm around the back of his neck and bring the other hand to my clit.

"You were thinking of this?" I whisper into his ear. "Wondering what my pussy would look like? How I taste when I'm wet for you?"

He lets out a shaky breath, and his hands find my hips as if to steady himself. "Maren—"

"Wanting to know what it'd sound like when I moan for you? From your mouth?"

I love the feeling of his hands digging into the softness of my hips. I can feel my nipples harden, and I rock on the tips of my toes just slightly, rubbing my chest against him so he can feel it. He lets out a breathy sigh, and the sound comes out broken with the weight of his need.

"Mm?" I say, goading. "Tell me."

"*Agaayu*, Maren," he groans. "God. You feel so good."

"Or were you wondering what it'd sound like when I cried out your name?" I ask. "Tell me, did you stroke yourself, imagining it? How it'd sound when I came with your name on my lips?"

I start circling my fingers around my clit, and I feel the orgasm that was building when he was on his knees for me begin to near again.

"Seb," I moan in his ear, pulling him closer. "*Oh, God.* Seb."

His posture tightens, his hips rocking back and forth almost imperceptibly against my hip, seeking the pressure from my body.

"*Mare,*" he breathes.

"Seb," I say, the pleasure building in me. I was doing it to tease him at first, but I'm not teasing now. "Oh, God. Oh my God. *Seb.*"

My fingers circle my clit, tighter and faster.

"Oh my God," I gasp, my mouth next to his ear. "Fuck. Let me come for you. I want to come for you."

He keeps his hands on my hips but pulls his face away so he can look in my eyes. And then I'm coming, my body writhing against him from the work of my fingers, crying out his name again and again, my eyes locked on his until my eyelids flutter shut. As I come, I can sense his posture tighten—feel the tension in his back and shoulders as I say his name, and then he shudders as my eyes open. I watch him swallow as his body relaxes, shaky under my touch.

I take a step back, dropping my arm from around his neck, and eye the mess he's made for me. The gray fabric of his sweatpants is streaked dark and wet in the place where he came against my body. Dragging my eyes back up to his, I bring my fingers to my mouth and suck them clean.

"Are you sure it's you who's in charge?" I ask.

And then I walk back to the chair, pick up my shorts, and leave for my room.

20

SEB

uck. I shouldn't have done that.

I feel the hot water of the shower run over my body and try to let it wash off my shame. I didn't plan to—when I first scented her desire and heard her touching herself by the fire, I didn't want to let it get as far as it did. But then she was touching herself for *me*, moaning *my* name, and I couldn't resist.

The scent of her arousal in the air... The sound of her breath hitching...

I *needed* to taste her.

I swallow, scrubbing my body with soap until the skin stings. *Nagaayu,* I chastise myself. She doesn't know what I know—that our souls are tied to each other somehow, even if we can't stand each other. Is it even fair for me to touch her if I know that and she doesn't?

The memory of her pressing her body against mine comes back to me. *Let me come for you,* she gasped, and I swear I'd never heard anything better in my life, until she cried my name over and over as she came.

I swallow. No—Maren takes what she wants. And besides, who knows if we even *are* connected to each other? It wasn't *her* there in person with me in the ring, but something the ancestors brought. Maybe just a symbol. A sign.

My wolf rebels at the thought, snarling in my chest. He's right—I know even before I can finish the thought that it's not true. Our wolves *are* tied to each other in some stupid, primal way, even if we clearly don't belong together. And then, especially, I owe it to her to keep my distance. I can't give my wolf more of this, or it'll only make things harder when she leaves.

This *can't* happen again.

I turn off the water and dry myself off. Without the rushing water, I can hear the sounds of the beach party outside—pops and bangs signaling that people have brought their own fireworks to light as part of the celebration. And, now that I'm no longer washing myself, I realize I can still scent Maren on my skin: warmth and honey and some kind of sweet, clean undertone that makes my inner wolf loll happily on his back.

I run my tongue over my teeth and let out a sigh, thinking. I've hidden enough teenage hookups from the *fika* elders to know that a shower isn't going to be enough to get the scent of her off of me—I need things to mask it, and the only things that work are mud or sweat. Maybe I'll go for a run tonight. I hate running, but it's the fastest thing that'll do the trick.

I look down at my leg as I towel myself off. I try to be extra gentle as I run my towel over the scarring, but even with great care, it aches and burns in protest at the touch. It had already been killing me in the days before my last temple visit, but running after the lights I saw that night has only made it worse. A run will probably do me in for all of tomorrow, but I can't deal with Gabe's comments, or Kieran's knowing look, when they get home and smell her on my skin.

Although... it's not like Mare will know how to mask the scent, herself. They'll probably know anyway.

The memory comes rushing back to me again. *Fuck. Mare,* I'd said, the syllables falling from my lips like calling her a nickname is the most natural thing in the world. I shake the sound of her climax from my mind. I can't dwell on this. I need to forget it ever happened.

I walk out of the bathroom towards the bed, but just as I reach the door, pain shoots through my leg and I feel my right knee almost give out. I clutch onto the door frame, hissing a curse under my breath.

"*Ayya,*" I mutter, looking down. There's no way I can run off the scent off tonight. I'll just have to deal with the looks I get in the morning.

I limp towards the bed and climb in, pulling the covers over me and trying to blot it out of my mind. I don't mean to, but for a second I find myself listening for Maren's breathing, before I remember she's down the hall tonight. I'm probably the better for it.

But still, as I listen for the sound of her, I realize I feel something in the ether. I sense her, in the same way that I can close my eyes and tune in to feel for the presence of Em, Gabe, or my mom—any of the members of our *fika*. The *fikaband* is nothing near the bond between mates, but any of us can broadly sense the presence of the people in our pack: how far away they are, and how they feel. Like a candle in the window of a house down the road, letting you know someone's home.

The absence of that feeling was the moment I knew my dad had died. Fumbling for the feeling of my mom, Saga, or Gabe in the months after was one of the only ways I kept myself sane when I was in that mainland hospital. And if I can feel it for Maren now, it means she's becoming one of us.

I set my jaw. It means nothing. It'll only make it hurt worse for the others when she leaves.

I turn over in bed, closing my eyes and trying to regulate my breathing. I choose a verse of the *Eijna* to mutter to myself, hoping the words can lull me to sleep before my mind can take me back to that night. But there's no way to stop it once it starts, and before I know it, my mind is tumbling into darkness, taking me back, back, back. Back to the night I lost most of my leg; the night I almost died.

The night Maren saved my life.

I'm standing in the ring, waiting. My posture is even; my leg is normal, pain-free in a way I didn't know to be grateful for yet. And I'm stupid: way too young and reckless to have taken on the rite having trained as little as I did. Maybe somewhere, in the back of my brain, I already know that.

The kiyyulit *slowly fill the ring, mystical light dancing off of the rocks that form the outer perimeter. Blue and green and violet, they reflect off of the white snow under my feet. I can hear the roar of the sea hundreds of feet below, and my hand reaches nervously for the knife strapped to my leg as I watch the lights swirl together, taking the form of whatever thing I'm supposed to fight to the death.*

I know what to expect—or at least, I think I do. The ancestors take the form of your greatest weakness, and if you can't overcome it, you aren't strong enough to represent the pack as a council elder. I've spent weeks preparing for this. Months less long than I should have.

Stupid, stupid. Get out of the ring. Get out—

The lights come together, and I can feel my adversary's presence take shape. I hear the snarl from his throat, and scent his fury in the air before I see him. I can feel the wolf inside me snapping, getting ready for the fight. My hand grips the knife's handle and I pull my blade and set my jaw, ready to kill. And then my enemy walks through the mist towards me, and I freeze.

It's me. My own wolf form stalks towards me, large and feral, full of rage. I can see the bloodthirst in his eyes; smell his incandescent fury.

What the fucking is happening?

I blink, taking a second to collect myself. But before I can wrap my mind around it, he lunges for me, coming for my neck. Instinctively I shift, ripping through my body armor—the only protection I have. A fatal mistake.

The fight is brutal. The other wolf is stronger than I am; a bigger version of myself, almost comically exaggerated in its size and strength. It takes hours—not because he can't kill me immediately, but because he's having fun with it, toying with me, torturing me. He rips into my stomach and chest, then backs off just enough for me to stumble up. And then as I rise, shaky and gasping, he comes for me from a different direction, tearing into my body, pulling me apart.

I'm going to die here, I know it. There's too much blood; somewhere late in the night, hours into the battle, I shifted into my human form and now I'm too weak to shift back. The muscle on my left leg is almost gone, hanging off in tatters so I can see parts of the bone beneath. The snow stings my exposed skin. Everything burns.

I'm near the edge of the ring now, by the raw edge of the cliff. I can hear the soft crash of the waves hundreds of feet below. The sky is starting to turn lavender at the edges, and I know that when the sun rises over the horizon, the beast will be done with his games and finally end this. The thought strangely fills me with relief; I'm so broken, so close to the veil, that death feels like mercy.

At least this will be over. At least I'll see my dad again.

But just as he comes to stand over me, his blood-stained mouth snarling and wicked, I hear something else. From the far edge to the ring, another voice.

I can sense she's female, and she feels familiar somehow. For a second I think maybe it's Saga or my mom, but I turn my head to the right, and it's a wolf I've never seen before. Her fur is black, her body strong and sturdy, and her golden eyes are fixed on the wolf above me.

The adversary bares his teeth at my neck, ready to end this, and I hear the other wolf bark out a warning. His head snaps up and he snarls at her. I try to tell her to get out of here, to spare herself and just let me die, but there's blood and bile in my mouth, choking me, keeping the words from getting out.

She barks again, and he gets off of me, prowling towards her. He's bigger than her by a large margin, but she doesn't seem afraid. I sense something change in the air as he recognizes her as a challenger—the feral part of him gives way for just a moment. He hesitates for a fraction of a second, and that's when she attacks.

The fight is wild, nonsensical. She shouldn't be strong enough to take him on, but somehow, through her sheer determination, it sounds like an even fight. I can't sit up to see what happens, but I hear snarling, barking; scent his blood in the air. They tussle, and I hear a sharp yelp pierce the winter sky. A moment later, he manages to get out from under her and rise to his feet.

I can see him from the corner of my eye, blood streaming down from his neck. She bit him badly, and he's losing blood fast. She must have cut an artery.

He's about twenty feet from me now, and she stands between the two of us, guarding my broken body. The sun is starting to rise higher. I'm so close to the cliff's edge that I can feel the low breeze roll over my skin. If I had the energy, I'd pray for the ancestors to let me fall over the edge and end this. Even if she kills him, it's too late for me. But he doesn't seem to think so.

I see the adversary eyeing me, the blood falling from his neck into the snow. He'll bleed out before too long, I think, and he's deciding whether or not to take me with him. But the she-wolf raises her head and howls—a warning, maybe. And then I hear a faint echo: howls from the rest of the island, somehow from the sky and the sea, far above and below. And with confusion, I watch as the adversary falls to the ground, his body admitting defeat.

The she-wolf eyes him, and we both watch as his frame slowly turns into mist and the kiyyulit take back his form. Then she turns and walks over to me, lowering her head to mine. Her golden eyes meet my gaze, warm and sparkling as sunlight.

It's too late, I want to tell her, but I can't muster the strength to move my lips.

No, I hear in my mind. I blink, my lips parting in surprise.

You hear me?

There's only one way for us to communicate without words; only one person we can do that with. She's speaking to me through the mate-bond.

A shiver runs over my skin. This wolf is my mate.

The sun is rising, *she says through the bond. Her voice is rich and warm in my mind, like heat and light and honey.* You need to get up.

"I'm too weak," I sputter, these words falling from my lips. My throat is hoarse, and I taste blood as I choke them out.

She moves her head low, beckoning me to put my arm over her. I take a deep breath and muster everything in me, lifting my torso just enough to lean my upper body over her shoulders. She's smaller than me, but she's strong, and I find myself surprised that she can handle the weight. It doesn't seem to faze her at all as she slowly, carefully, carries me towards the exit of the ring and down the mountain, my tattered leg dragging limply behind me on the ground.

As she weaves her way down the cliffs, the sun rises higher in the sky. It must be seven or eight in the morning, and I'm barely here, barely conscious. Finally, we reach the bottom of the cliffs, and I can see Saroe's common house far in the distance. I think I see people standing outside: surely the elders and my fika, waiting for my return. But rather than carrying me to them, the wolf drops to the ground, bringing me down.

You go now, *she says through the bond.* They'll take care of you.

She begins to fade, her body turning into mist.

No. Don't go, *I say, fumbling for the bond.* I need you. *But before the words reach her, I feel the space between us close, and she's gone.*

I WAKE UP IN A SWEAT, breathing heavy.

It's not real, it's not real, it's not real, I try to tell myself. It wasn't Maren, not really. Just a vision—an apparition from the ancestors. It means nothing.

But as I think it, I can feel something burning in my throat like acid. I can't pretend anymore. Since the moment I first saw Maren shift in the woods, I knew what this meant for us.

Maren is my mate.

I swallow the taste of bile in my throat, returning again to the question I've been obsessing over since the night I first saw her shift.

How could the *agaayit* do this? For years, I wondered about my mate—since I was a kid, even before my rite. And in the months after that horrible night, when I was stuck in a mainland hospital—grieving my leg, my youth, learning how to walk again —the only consolation was *her*. That somehow the ancestors had given me a glimpse into my future; allowed me to have a preview of what awaited me at the end of all this.

For years, I waited. Every time we visited one of the smaller islands, I found myself noticing the people around me, looking for her.

Would I know her when I saw her? Would I hear it from her voice? Or would I just feel it, the way Mom talks about how it felt to be around Dad? Like it was someone I'd known forever? Like I was home?

I feel a stinging in my eyes and set my jaw, blinking it away. Not home—far from it. Instead, the gods bound me to a mate whose life, whose heart, whose entire *world* is an ocean away and committed to everything I'm against. Financial success, greed, social capital—

I turn over in bed, remembering last night. I can't pretend anymore that there's been some kind of misunderstanding, and maybe my mate is still someone else. What happened with Maren at the fire pit felt almost unpreventable, like two magnets colliding no matter how hard you've tried to pull them apart. And until she knows what I know, it can never, ever happen again.

"Morlaa'."

Gabe's alone at the breakfast table when I come down,

drinking coffee. The scent of cinnamon in the air would be enough to tell me that it's Em who made it, even if I couldn't make out the lingering scent of her in here, too. She and Kier must have just left.

"You're up late," he says, looking up at me from over his mug.

"I wanted to get a workout in."

He glances down at my leg as I walk to the kitchen island, and I do my best to make my limp as minor as possible, even as it makes the ache worse. I shouldn't have gone running this morning, but I wanted to mask her scent and needed to get out of my head. And, as my mom always says, there's no cure for pride.

"You good?" he asks.

"I'm fine."

"Your leg's been acting up?"

"I said I'm *fine*."

"Okay." He returns his gaze to the table, and as I start loading my plate with breakfast—scrambled eggs, sausages, and sauteed spinach, undoubtedly made by him since he's the only person who thinks to cook for the rest of us—I feel a twinge of regret.

"Sorry. I've had a lot on my mind," I say, grabbing a fork and walking towards the table.

"Want to talk about it?"

I hesitate but shake my head, setting my plate down at the table and taking a seat beside him. "I'm good. Thanks."

It's at that exact moment that Maren comes in. The second she enters the room, I pick up on it—her scent and mine together, heat and desire and honey and amber emanating from her skin, even under the mask of soap from her morning shower.

"Hey guys," she says.

Gabe's eyes flash to me, wide and accusing.

"Dude," he mutters under his breath.

"*Ijweiyyet,*" I say quietly in Fakari, so she doesn't understand. *I know.*

"Fiya eijlonni!" She's my cousin!

"Ijweiyyet."

"What's going on?" Maren asks from the kitchen.

"Nothing," we say in unison.

She glances over. "Real convincing. Seriously, what is it?"

"I was just telling Seb about our night out," Gabe says, looking up at her. "What about you? Did you manage to get some rest?"

"Yeah, kind of," she says lightly, piling eggs onto her plate. "I had a late night."

"I bet," he says, glancing at me.

She looks up again, realization dawning in her face.

"Oh, is that what you guys were whispering about? Seb told you we hooked up?" She gives me a sweet smile. "Didn't take you for one to kiss and tell, *Sebasteijen.*"

She drags out the syllables of my name, and even with the American rounding of the vowels I feel my inner wolf respond to the sound. *Nagaayu.*

"I didn't say anything," I grumble, taking a bite of my eggs. "He can smell me on you."

Maren's eyes shoot to Gabe, horrified. "What?!"

"It's a wolf thing," he says. "It's not a big deal."

"It's a big deal to me!" She walks towards the table and sets her plate down next to mine. "Maybe I don't want people to know who I happen to be hooking up with on a Monday night."

My inner wolf doesn't like *that.* He snarls, sitting up angrily in my chest. I cough to hide the sound.

"Why didn't you warn me?" She swats my arm in annoyance.

"My mouth was otherwise occupied," I mutter, reaching for the coffee pot.

"*Agaayu,*" Gabe says in disgust, pushing his chair back and getting up. "I don't need to hear this."

Maren ignores him, crossing her arms and looking accusingly down at me. "You should have told me. You owe me that much."

"Is that right?" I stand to face her, ignoring the hissing pain in my leg. Behind me I can hear Gabe head for the stairs. "And why's that? If I remember right, you were pretty eager to show me you were the one in charge."

I take a step closer to her, for a split-second her eyes fall to my hands, then come back up to my face. I sense her breathing grow just a touch heavier, and then the color rises in her cheeks. It's a good thing Gabe left, because under the scent of me on her skin, I can sense something else—the tiniest hint of her arousal, flickering in the air between us.

I shouldn't be doing this, I know. But somehow my wolf's in charge already, reacting to the hint of gold in her eyes and the scent of her, desire blossoming between our bodies. The mark of my scent under her skin. My wolf *likes* that, I register somewhere in the part of my brain that's still functioning. He wants to mark her with it again. And somehow, when she's this close to me, even the man in me wants to let him.

"What else don't I know?" she asks, crossing her arms over her chest and leaning back against the table. "Is Em going to come back from her walk and see a list of my dumbest horny ideas tattooed on my forehead?"

"No," I murmur, "but I'd like to see that list."

"Seb," she says admonishingly, but the scent of her warmth grows a tic heavier.

"You should know, though, that any of us can scent your arousal when you get turned on."

Her eyes grow wide, and my hand finds her waist.

"It's how I found you, last night, when you were touching yourself," I say into her ear. "It's how I know that this—" I press my good thigh between hers, and she lets out a little gasp. "Will feel so good."

"Seb," she says, the sound part protest, part relief.

I shouldn't be doing this. Pull back.

"Good, *eijtna*," I say, *sweetheart*, nuzzling my mouth against her hair, to her neck. "Again."

"Seb," she gasps, grabbing onto the table for support.

"*Iija*, I like that." I start kissing and nipping at her neck, and as the hand holding onto her waist pulls her towards my body, I feel myself grow hard against her.

"You smell so good with me on your skin," I mutter, running my lips over her neck, then her collar. "You look so fucking good when you come with my name on your lips."

"Oh my God," she groans. "Seb—"

"You're so beautiful," I whisper, and it's the primal part of me that says it—the part of me I can't control. I'm lost to the world; lost in her, *for* her. I press my good leg deeper into the crux of her thighs. "You're so gorgeous, Maren. Your body. Your hips, your thighs. *Agaayu*."

I sink my mouth over her collarbone, sucking at the skin. She brings a hand to my back, pulling me closer to her.

"Don't you want to come for me again?" I mutter against her neck. "Don't you want me to finish what I started?"

She lets out a low, guttural sound, and I feel her hips rock gently against my leg. Somewhere inside me, the better part of me is telling me to stop, to pull back, but I don't care to listen. Even if I'm in my human form, it's my wolf who's in charge right now.

"I want to," I say, running my teeth against the skin of her collarbone. "I want to worship your body." I bring my lips to her ear and whisper, "I want you to come on my face."

She moans for me, desire building. I nip and suck at her neck, listening to her breath grow deeper, little groans falling from her lips.

"Oh God," she says again, and somewhere in my mind I file away the knowledge that her neck is sensitive, that she cries out when I run my teeth over the skin just so. That she likes—

Oh, fuck. Of course she does. It's where our mate bite would go.

I shove myself back from the table, forcing as many feet of distance between us as the space between the table and kitchen island allows. She's still leaning back against the table, breathing heavy for me, her pupils blown wide with desire. I can see the shape of her nipples pressing against the fabric of her shirt.

What else don't I know?, she'd asked me. Fuck me. I'm an asshole.

"Seb," she says, confusion on her face.

"A shower won't get rid of my scent on you," I manage, my voice coming out raw. "Mud or sweat will do the trick. A twenty-minute workout should be enough."

"Hey—" she says, reaching a hand out for me, but I shove it away, and her brow furrows in what looks like disgust. Well-earned.

"We can't do this, Maren," I say. And I shake my head and turn for the stairs.

21

MAREN

We can't do this, Maren.

Asshole.

I listen to the *thud-thud-thud* of my feet on the cobblestone street and the rush of blood in my ears, so loud it almost drowns out the grunge song coming through my headphones. I'm not typically a grunge girl, but I guess Seb has me doing a few things that are out of character lately. Like almost climaxing against the breakfast table. What the hell?

I run faster, hoping somewhere that the pace will blot out the memory of his mouth on my neck; the waves of desire that rolled through me as he whispered what he wanted to do with me, for me, to me.

Twenty minutes of sweat to cover the scent of his body on mine. How long until I don't feel the indent of his fingertips on my waist, or the warmth of his breath in my ear? How long until I forget what it felt like to have him, for just a moment?

We can't do this, Maren. After laying me bare.

I run harder, until I can feel the rasp of fresh air in my throat, the slight taste of metal when I swallow. I have no idea where I am—some random street lined with little houses. I passed a school a way's back, I think. I'm getting closer to what looks like a busy street, but I don't want to deal with people, so as I get closer I turn into a side alley.

I let my anger fuel me for another thirty, forty minutes, until I'm gasping for air and standing at the bottom of the hill where the *fika*'s beach house is located. I swallow and start climbing, listening to the soft rush of the ocean on the other side, creating a backdrop for the music coming through my crappy earbuds. If I'm lucky, they'll all be out when I get home, and I can shower and take a nap in peace.

I get to the heavy wood door and push it open, and immediately I'm hit by a wave of scent. Wood and amber—Kieran.

Flowers and herbs—Em.

And tobacco and sex.

Seb.

Fuck.

I try to shut the door quietly and slink to the stairs so I can get upstairs to my room before they hear me. But if my sense of smell has gotten better in the last few weeks, theirs must be supercharged, because the second I reach the bottom step I hear Em say,

"Hey! I was looking for you!"

I turn to look over my shoulder. She's curled up on the living room floor, her watercolors spread out on the coffee table. Kieran is behind her, sprawled on the couch, and across from them on the other sofa is Seb, who looks up at me from under a heavy brow.

"Oh, hey Em," I say. "I was just on a run. I'll shower and then we can hang out."

"Where were you running?" Kieran asks, sitting up.

"Oh, I don't know, really. Downtown, I think? Just little side streets and stuff."

"There's way better routes around here," he says. "The woods are just behind the house. It's nice in summer."

"Oh. Well, maybe next time." I offer a smile, and I'm about to reiterate my intent to go shower when I see Seb glancing uncomfortably between Kieran and me.

"Sure," Kieran says, not taking any notice as he leans back against the pillows of the couch. "I can show you around. Just let me know when you go for your next run."

At this, Seb's shoulders tense visibly. I feel a smile tug at the corner of my mouth, and bite down on my lower lip. He's jealous. I almost let out a snort. As though that man has any claim on me.

"Absolutely," I say, leaning my weight on one hip. But almost before the words are out of my mouth, my gaze falls to Em, sitting on the floor. I can't do that to her, even if it's just to mess with Seb.

"And you should join us," I say to her. "You can show me the parts of the island you like best."

"Oh, I don't run. But you two should go. It sounds fun."

I hesitate. "Are you sure? Wouldn't it be better with the three of us?"

"No, you should do it," she says, smiling brightly, and turns to Kieran over her shoulder. "Kier, you should take her to Hannigan's after. Make a date of it."

At this, Seb clears his throat, and I swear I can almost hear a little growl underneath.

"What's Hannigan's?" I ask.

"Oh, it's a bar we used to go to. They're only open in the summers, and lately it's kind of too crowded for me. But I bet you'd like it!"

I look between the two of them.

"Are you *sure* you don't want to join?" I ask again.

"No, really. Have fun," she says, smiling. "Make a date of it."

"Alright. It's a date," Kieran says uneasily, glancing down at her.

"Okay," I say, and I turn for the stairs before Seb can meet my eyes.

SEB COMES to find me not a half hour later, when I'm sitting on the bed wrapped in a towel.

"You're seriously going out with *Kieran*?" he says, storming into the room.

I look up from the copy of the *Eijna* on the bed in front of me.

"It's just a run. What's it to you, anyway?"

He sputters and comes to a stop, his eyes falling to the white terrycloth I have wrapped around my body. I feel my eyes roll upwards into my head before I can stop myself.

"Can we not do this right now? I'm reading. I don't have time for your horny bullshit."

"I'm not—"

"Also, can you knock? This is my room. What's your deal today?"

He blinks, seemingly trying to collect himself, then brings his eyes up to meet mine.

"I just... Kieran goes out with everyone. You should keep an eye out."

I snort. "That's rich, coming from the guy who tried to make me come at breakfast just to prove a point. And if you think *that's* the reason I don't wanna go on a date with him, then you don't know me at all."

He stops. "So you *don't* want to go."

I cross my arms and look up at him. "I'm not doing this with you. What I want or don't want is none of your business. *Especially* after being such a dick to me this morning."

"I'm just trying to stop you from making a decision you'll regret."

"Ha. A decision *I'll* regret, or you? Because *you're* the one who seems all caught up in whatever *this* is." I wave a hand between us, and I feel my towel drop just slightly. His eyes fall to it instantly, and again, the tension in the air grows thicker.

"Eyes up here, dickwad," I snap. "I don't know what your deal is, but I'm not in the mood to be scolded for saying yes to someone being nice to me. If you have an issue with me spending time with someone else, maybe look inside and try to figure out why I don't especially feel like spending time with *you*."

"Maren—"

"Get out."

We spend a long second staring at each other, and I feel the anger in me rise closer to the surface. My gaze flickers pointedly to the door, but he doesn't move an inch.

"What's your problem?" I ask.

"I don't—I don't know," he says, and to my surprise, his voice comes out husky, a little broken. His brow is drawn, the look on his face almost pleading.

For a second, I feel a flicker of something like empathy. But there's that raging feeling in my chest again, surging, wanting him to stop looking at me like that, wanting him *out* of my room and my life.

"Leave," I say, bringing my eyes back to the *Eijna* and trying to get them to focus.

"Mare—"

"Don't call me that," I snap, looking up again. "Don't talk to me like you know me. We may like each other physically, but there is *zero* intimacy between us. You will never, *ever* know me."

His gaze hardens, and the pleading look in his eyes grows cold.

"Well, excuse me for trying."

I slam the book shut. "*Are* you trying? Because all it's been since I got here is telling me I don't belong, I'm leaving soon anyway, my marketing ideas suck—"

"*Agaayu*, calm down."

"—and then suddenly you're eating me out as a power play, but then when I'm down it's, 'we can't do this.' What game are you playing?"

"I'm not playing games with you, I'm just—"

"Just what?" I cross my arms.

"I don't know, okay?" he says, sounding exasperated. "I don't know what's going on. I'm just confused. Weapons down, alright?"

"Doing that when you're around would be very reckless."

"So, in-character for you, then."

It's happening before I can register it. I'm leaping forward, jumping towards him, and suddenly we're both cracking and shifting and on the floor, our wolves wrestling each other for dominance. I press him into the ground, wanting to attack, but his wolf lolls back, twisting his neck out of the way for me playfully. It's only when I start gnashing my teeth dangerously close to his carotid artery that he bats me out of the way, pushing me off of him and caging me in between his legs.

I snarl up at him, my paws on his chest, trying to shove him off of me. But where I expect him to fight back, instead his wolf cocks his head at me and then—to my total surprise—nuzzles his nose in my neck, rubbing his head against my dark fur.

My wolf freezes, even the most primal part of me so unsure of what the fuck is going on that she can't move. Seb's wolf burrows his snout against my neck, and I feel his body go still, relaxed.

Is he... *sniffing* me?

I shove him off and he staggers back, stumbling on his weaker leg as he bumps into the wooden dresser on the wall nearest to us. My eyes fall to it, noting for the first time the shape of his thigh. I've never seen it when he's in his human form, but even here I now notice that the leg is mangled, the left thigh muscle small, concave, and scarred.

I bring my gaze back to his, and as my wolf climbs back onto all fours, snarling at him, he shifts. In a second he's human again, squatting on the floor next to me, somewhat breathless.

"Still don't have your wolf check, huh?" he asks.

My wolf snaps at him, but as I do, I can feel that he's won—even this is proof. He grabs his clothes and rises to his feet, then staggers out the room. As he does, I register the unevenness in his gait, worse now than it was a few days ago.

My wolf slinks towards the bed, and somewhere deep inside myself, I try to reach for the reins. I can't find them. My wolf is fuming, somehow angrier than before. I shut my eyes tight, bowing my head, trying to force her to give over to me.

Nothing.

"Gabe and Kieran can't help you with that," I hear from the door.

I turn my head around and snarl. He's snapped his clothes on again and is leaning against the doorway, arms crossed over his chest.

"They've never had this issue. They can't help you."

And you can? I want to ask, but instead all that comes out is some kind of bark.

"Yeah, I can," he says.

I blink in surprise.

"Relax, I can't read your mind," he adds, rolling his eyes. "You're predictable, that's all."

Almost as if in evidence, he shields himself just as I start racing towards him, ready to attack.

"Cut it out," he says, and I snarl, rearing up on my hind legs to hit his chest with my paws. I'm expecting it to hit lightly, but his balance is off, and he falls backwards. In an instant, he's shifting again, clothes falling to the floor a second time as his wolf darts to get away from me.

It's stupid. I know I should back off, but the frustration is still surging through me and I can't control it. My wolf lowers her head and runs after him.

We rush through the upstairs of the house, down the hall and then towards the stairs. Seb leads me down and through the kitchen, where Gabe jumps in surprise as we race around the kitchen island and then through the dining room, towards the open doors to the veranda.

The conscious part of my mind—a tiny whisper in the back of my head—notices that his running is uneven and tells me to slow down. But my wolf's in charge, and she's too frustrated to listen. She only runs faster as Seb darts down the steps of the veranda onto the hill below. I feel the heated sand under my paws as I follow, the sunlight warming my skin through the fur as the scent of the ocean hits my nostrils. Seb slows to a stagger as he reaches the water, and I watch as he all but collapses into the sand.

I try desperately to get my wolf to slow down, begging her to give me the reins. She lowers her head, ready to pounce on him, and somewhere inside me, I find it in myself to grab hold of them by force. I stop her just in time, and then I'm shifting, my body breaking and unfolding as I spill onto the sand, tumbling over him.

He shifts, too, and we're a mess of arms and legs as we try to get away from each other. There's no one else on this part of the shore—it must be the private beach area that came with the house. He gasps for air as he scrambles backwards and away from me.

"Fuck, Maren," he shouts, and at the anger and stress in his face, I feel my inner wolf cower.

"You can't just do that. You can't attack people every time you get angry. You need to get your wolf in check."

"I... Seb, I'm..." *Sorry*, the voice in my head prompts, but I can't get myself to say it out loud. How did this happen? How could I have just *attacked* him?

"I offered to help you!" he snaps.

"I don't want..."

"I don't care what you want. You owe it to your *fika* to get yourself under control."

He staggers to his feet, and it's the first time I realize we're both naked. As he rises to his full height, my eyes fall to his leg.

In this form, too, the left thigh is mangled, scarring contorting the surface of the skin. Starting a few inches down from his hip bone, I see the line of the muscle curve inwards, as though a large chunk is missing.

"Don't fucking look at me," he says, his voice broken. He turns his body away from me so that it's his right leg facing towards me and he's facing the house.

"Seb, I'm sorry. I don't care—"

"*I* care," he says, and I feel something in his voice change. "I don't want... I can't... I can't have you look at me like that."

"Like what?" I ask, bringing my legs up around myself, trying to hide some of my own nakedness.

"Like you pity me."

"I don't—"

"Don't lie."

I swallow, and I take a second to listen to the rush of the waves as I try to find the words.

"Has it... has it been getting worse lately?"

He bristles, then shakes his head. "I've just been doing too much."

I nod, thinking of the way I chased him around the gym. Did he run off what happened between us last night, too?

"I'm sorry," I say quietly. "I'll... I'll gladly take your help with this shifting stuff."

He barks out a hollow laugh. "You sure sound excited about it."

"Well, are you?"

He turns his head to look at me, still keeping his body turned towards the house to shield me from the sight of his thigh muscle.

"Do you really think I hate you that much?"

I bristle, shaking my head. "Don't you? *'We can't do this, Maren.'* You couldn't even look at me this morning."

He eyes me for a long moment, and I find myself growing uncomfortable under his gaze. I turn my head to look out at the sea.

"No. I don't hate you," he says finally.

"So what's your issue, then?" I ask, keeping my eyes on the ocean.

"Nothing you did," he says quietly, but I don't quite register it. My eyes make something out in the far distance, flickering on the horizon.

"Huh."

"What?"

"Do you... do you see that?" I ask.

Seb turns over his shoulder to face the sea, and I feel something in the air still as his eyes fixate on it.

"*Ayagaayuni,*" he whispers under his breath. "They're back."

I see what looks like two glowing orbs of light far in the distance, almost at the line where the sea meets the sky. They dance a little on the horizon, flickering like the innermost ring of a flame.

"What are they?" I ask.

"I don't know. I saw them a few nights ago, on the way home from the temple. I followed them to the edge of the island, but I couldn't get any closer. I thought..."

His voice trails off, and I look up to see his face.

"Hm?"

"Nothing."

I shake my head in annoyance and look back at the lights, but then I feel something in his energy change. He comes to sit next to me in the sand, using his forearm to cover his leg.

"That night, I thought it might have been my dad's spirit," he says finally. "But I don't think so."

I turn to look at him, surprised by a rare moment of openness. We stare at each other in silence for a moment, and the air softens.

"You miss him," I say quietly.

"Yeah. I wasn't supposed to grow up without him."

His words hit me like a gut punch, and I nod. "I know how that feels. He died when you were a teenager, right?"

"Yeah, but I was basically still a kid. I hadn't even finished school yet. I had no idea..."

His voice trails off.

"How did it happen?"

Instantly, I see it was the wrong question. Seb stiffens, his posture becoming hard as his shoulders curl up just slightly.

"I'm sorry. You don't have to answer that," I say.

"I should go." He turns from me, and I hear him start to walk up the hill towards the house.

I bite my lip, inwardly chastising myself for closing whatever hint of openness was starting to form between us. But then I hear,

"Shifting practice tomorrow?"

I turn over my shoulder, taking great care to meet his eyes and not glance at any other part of his body.

"Yeah, okay."

22

SEB

The following morning, I take Maren to a clearing in the woods behind the Halluk house. The space is ringed with stones to sit on, with a large open area in the middle.

"This is beautiful," she says, looking around at the trees around us. I glance over my shoulder and see the way the sunlight falls on her face, illuminating her round cheeks and the smile pulling at her lips. Things I shouldn't notice. Things the man in me, at least, should be able to ignore.

"In Boston you'd have to go out of your way for a park like this. Here, nature is just... everywhere."

I clear my throat, swallowing an acerbic remark, and step to the center of the clearing.

"Come here."

She does as told, still looking up and around us, and comes to stand before me. I let out a deep breath, and she looks down to meet my eyes.

"So," she says. "You're gonna teach me."

I nod. "Shifting into your wolf form is pretty easy for you, right?"

She thinks for a second, then nods her head. "I guess. I can do it. It takes some effort."

"Okay. And, when you shift on purpose, is shifting back an issue?"

"I don't really know. I don't shift on purpose much—just that once in the gym."

I nod, refusing to let the memory come to me. "Can you try it now?"

She hesitates.

"If you get stuck, I'll help you come back," I offer.

She nods, and I watch her throat bob slightly as she swallows, seemingly gathering her nerve. It takes a second, and then her body falls forward, her body shifting. The tank top and shorts she was wearing fall on the ground around her.

"Okay, good," I say. "Now shift back."

But she doesn't. Instead, her tail swishes, and she looks up at me playfully, cocking her head.

I let out a sharp breath through my nose, smiling. "Okay. So it looks like your wolf likes to be in charge. That's not a surprise, I guess."

She lets out a little snarl, but her tail is still swishing, and I can tell she's more playful than angry. I squat down, meeting her at eye level, and put my hand on the back of her head.

"The wolf can come out and play again later," I say, trying to make my voice soft for her. "Can you shift for me?"

Maren's wolf turns her head, and a second later she's shifting again, her human limbs unfurling onto the ground before she rises to her feet.

I stand, too, and clear my throat, averting my eyes. But she just stays there, waiting.

"I'll give you a second," I say, gesturing to the clothes on the ground.

"To get dressed? Why? I'll shift again in a minute anyway."

"Maren." I bring my eyes to hers, resolute not to look at anything else. "Come on."

She raises an eyebrow, and I see a smile tug at the corner of her lips. "I don't need to be clothed to focus."

I feel the heat rise in my neck. "Maybe *I* need you to be clothed to focus."

"Fine," she says lightly, grabbing just the tank top and shorts from the ground and snapping them on around her. On the ground, she leaves her bra and a little pile of magenta lace I'm trying desperately not to imagine on her body.

"Mare," I say again, and the sound comes out pleading. She raises a hand, cutting me off.

"I don't want to make this hard for you, but if I'm going to be shifting back and forth, I'm *not* messing with *that*," she says, pointing to the bra. "You don't even want to know how they configured shifting snaps to work with an underwire. It's a nightmare."

I do want to know, I feel from somewhere inside myself. I want to feel how it would be to tear it off of her. She seems to register something in my face, because I see that flicker of humor form behind her eyes again, and she bends over to pick both items up, along with her socks and shoes.

"I'm just gonna hide these behind a rock so you can do your job, okay?"

I clear my throat again and nod.

"Alright, I'm back," she says, coming to stand before me. "So now what?"

"I have a theory for what might work for you," I say, keeping my eyes hyper-focused on her gaze. "The way we were taught to rein our wolves in when things got out of hand was to work through our anger. Or sadness or fear, or whatever was causing the shift."

"You can shift from things other than anger?" she asks, her

brow furrowing.

"Your wolf can take over from any big feeling."

"Okay... but so you want to try something different."

"Yeah." I swallow. I never talk about this—not with Gabe, not with anyone. When I finally make the words come out, they come faster, and I can hear my own nerves in my voice.

"So... When I was in the hospital, for..." I gesture awkwardly to my leg. "I was so angry I could barely think about or do anything else. I was on a lot of pain medication, and some things to suppress shifting. But when I was well enough to come back to the islands, I'd shift at the drop of a hat. Kieran would say something over breakfast, and..."

She smiles. "Yeah. I know how that goes."

"Right. And working *through* my anger just wasn't possible. No matter how much I prayed or meditated or went to the temple—" At this, I see her brow furrow, something flickering behind her eyes, but I keep talking. "Nothing was going to give me back my leg, or the things I'd lost. I couldn't get over it, but at some point, my random shifting started being a problem for the others, and I realized I had to find something else."

The tension in my chest starts to ease as she nods gently, listening without any trace of judgment.

"So... what did you do?"

"I needed to give my wolf an outlet. He kept bursting out of me because... I... because I felt things that were too big for the man to work though."

I eye her again, waiting for some kind of snicker or mocking remark, but it doesn't come.

"But the wolf serves a purpose," I continue. "It was supposed to be a gift. So instead of trying to keep myself shifting, I took it as a sign that I had... *stuff* I had to work out. And that if I couldn't work through that mentally, they needed to be worked out physically."

"So you'd shift on purpose," she says, nodding. "To make an

outlet."

"Yeah. I'd spend some time as the animal every day. I'd let myself run and be angry, and work through that physical need. And by the time I got to the hot springs to cool off, I usually felt better."

"Did it work?" she asks gently. "Like, long-term. Did you start shifting less?"

I nod. "Yeah. It really helped. And my brain... I don't know. It finally got quiet, after months of feeling like I couldn't escape the noise."

"I feel like that, too," she says quietly. "Back home. It was like I could never outrun my thoughts. I took boxing classes for years, and after a while, even that didn't help."

"And now?"

"Some of the time it's quiet, since getting here. But most of the time I still feel that constant... *noise* in my head."

"You have a physical need to work out."

She looks at me for a moment, considering.

"Physical need, huh?" she asks, raising an eyebrow. "Did you ever find other ways to work through it? *Physically?*"

I purse my lips, feeling my jaw flex as I fold my arms across my chest.

"Mare," I say. "Come on, take this seriously."

"I am taking it seriously. I'm here, aren't I? With you. I'm just saying, there's more than one way to work through your frustration." She steps closer to me, placing a hand lightly on my chest.

"I... You can't just fuck your problems away."

"You won't know until you try," she says teasingly, looking up at me. "My wolf comes out most around you. We both bring out a lot of that frustration in each other. Seems only fair to work it off together."

I swallow.

"Maybe it's good for me," she says, coming closer. "Tames the wolf, and all."

I let out a breath as her other hand reaches around me, coming to rest on my back, the scent of her washing over me as her body pulls close to mine. I should say no, but the truth is that I don't want to. I want her around me, under me, taking me. Pulling her name from my lips. Climaxing under me from my mouth between her legs.

"Come on," she murmurs, pulling close to me. "It doesn't have to mean anything."

Her words hit me like a cold shower, and I put my hands on her shoulders and gently push her off of me.

"I don't want to do this with you. Now come on—get serious. You're going to *run* this energy off today, and nothing else. Now shift."

A FEW HOURS LATER, Gabe comes home to find me surrounded by books at the dining table, talking on the phone.

"Yeah, thanks," I say into the phone, waving at Gabe as he enters the kitchen. "No, if you could set it up, that would be great."

Finn? Gabe mouths, referring to Saroan Salts' part-time employee. I nod.

"Okay, sounds good," I say over the phone. "Call me if there's any issues. Alright, bye."

I hang up, and Gabe sets a bag of groceries down on the kitchen island.

"The new radiator came in, so he's setting up the second evap bin today. By the time we get back, we should already be producing double."

"Is that what the books are for?" Gabe asks, nodding at the table.

I glance down at the table, where I've spread out six books on Fakari myths and legends that I was able to find at the local bookshop. So far, nothing about blue lights.

"Uh, no. Not exactly. This is for... personal research."

"...Alright." He eyes the table warily. "Where are the others?"

"Uh, Maren and Kier are on their run, I think." I clear my throat, trying to suppress the frustrated growl of my inner animal. "Em left to take a walk along the shore a little while ago. Where were you?"

"Just getting stuff for dinner. I wanted to try a fried rice dish tonight, so I'm gonna start on the rice now so it can cool off before evening. Wanna help me prep?"

"Sure, I guess." I put my hands on the table in front of me to help me get up. I let out a low hiss as soon as I manage to get my feet under me. I can sense it in the air the second Gabe registers.

"You know, actually, I've got it," he says lightly. "Why don't you just stay there and tell me about your morning."

"I'm fine," I grind out from between clenched teeth.

"Seb."

"Stop it. I don't need your pity." I take a few steps from around the table to get towards the island.

"It's not pity, it's care. I'm not going to let you hurt yourself for fried rice—it's not that deep. Now sit down."

I hold his gaze and finally relent, sitting at the head of the table.

"You and Maren were gone this morning," he says carefully, pouring some dry rice into a small saucepan.

"She attacked me yesterday. Her anger keeps getting the better of her, so I told her she needs to practice reining it in. Actually—" I let out a small laugh. "You know what I said?"

"What?"

"She said she didn't want to, and I said, 'I don't care what you want. You owe it to your *fika* to get yourself under control.'" I shake my head, smiling. "I'm not kidding. Word for word."

"*Ha.* That sounds familiar."

"If you'd told me when you said that to me three years ago, that one day I'd be saying it to someone else, I would never have believed you. Guess who turned into the responsible one."

"So it worked." He smiles over at me, then adds water to the saucepan and places it on the stove, covering it with a lid. "Do you think it can work for her?"

I shake my head. "Fuck if I know, man. I feel like there's just as good of a chance she'll go home and spend the rest of her life suppressing her wolf with those creams and pills."

He looks up at me. "Do you really think that?"

"Yeah, you've seen her—that energy is unstoppable. In a few weeks she'll be bored and on to the next thing."

He shakes his head, reaching into the paper grocery bag for some shallots. "Have you actually *asked* her what she plans to do?"

"No. I mean, I don't think *she* thinks she's leaving. But you watch—in just a few weeks, she'll get sick of this and start talking about her article or some new career idea, and—"

"How long has she been here now?" he asks, reaching for a knife. He peels the shallot's outer shell and starts cutting it into neat little cubes.

"I don't know. A couple weeks?"

"And what has she done since she got here?"

I think it over. *Start a wager with me. Follow me to the hot springs. Attack me upstairs—*

"I'll tell you what," he says. "She learned she's *pakka*, is trying to learn Fakari, started translating the *Eijna* for fuck's sake, and started doing this marketing stuff for Saroan Salts. The business has seen more sales with her in charge in the last few weeks than we've seen in the months before that. I've been telling you for a year to get a new generator, and you didn't listen. It took *her* sales numbers for you to take that shot. She's saving your ass."

"Because I made her a bet, in exchange for an interview."

"Because she *cares* about this place," he says, shaking his head. "Because she cares about *us*, and she wants to belong here.

Why else would she make Em that cake for finishing her exams? And I heard her and Kier planning something for Em's birthday. She's trying, dude. She wants to be a part of this *fika*, whether she knows how to say that or not."

"I... Nah," I say, shaking my head. "Cakes and birthdays and stuff is just what women do for each other."

He puts his knife down and gives me a look. "Are you serious?"

I throw my hands in the air. "What do you want from me?"

"I want you to admit that the way you've been treating her is unfair."

"Whatever," I say.

He bristles. "This isn't even about David. It's about your dad, and your own unresolved shit."

That makes me pause.

"It *is* about David," I say. "She's her father's daughter. You've heard how Saga talks about what he was like—he had big, crazy ideas and that same directionless ambition. He let that lead him wherever he wanted, and look where that left us."

"Look where that left *your dad*," he corrects.

"No, *all* of them," I snap. "*Pakka* is supposed to share life. Our parents made an agreement. They'd made the plans they needed to secure a *fikarig*. Once you have that, you can't just leave—it tears a *fika* apart."

Gabe shakes his head, focusing on the cutting board before him.

"Haven't you heard them talk about how it used to be?" I ask. "They were different, before. They used to be happy once. The grief that hangs in our *fikarig* wasn't always there."

"That's just what loss does, dude," he says quietly, shaking his head. "They loved him, and he died too young—of course that stays with you. Grief is just what love leaves behind. But that doesn't make him responsible for what happened to your dad."

"Doesn't it? He abandoned them, and it scarred them all for life. It shaped both of us to grow up around that kind of loss."

He sets the knife down. "Take some responsibility for yourself. You're not the only one in this *fika* with a dead parent. My dad died defending the work that *your dad* and David started. You don't catch me walking around blaming *you* for that."

His words hit me like a gut punch. I swallow, eyeing him.

"I never thought about it like that," I say.

"Yeah, well, I don't go around blaming other people for my problems." He shakes his head, crossing his arms over his chest. "You miss your dad. I get it, I do too. Filip mattered to all of us. But at least you had seventeen years with him. At least he got to see you grow up."

I watch him swallow, like he's collecting himself. When he speaks again, his voice is measured, even.

"His life was too short. David's, too. Sometimes that's just how the *agaayit* let things unfold—and it's okay to be angry about that. But if you take your anger out on the rest of us, you don't bring him back. You don't resurrect the past. You just cut yourself off from a future where you could actually be happy."

We stare at each other in silence as I let his words wash over me. A moment later, the stove starts hissing, and he turns around to see bubbles coming out from under the lid. As he walks over to deal with it, I hear the front door open, and Maren's bubbly laughter fill the hallway.

"Oh, hey guys," she says, stopping as she spots Gabe and me through the archway to the kitchen.

"Hey Mare," Gabe says. His voice is even, but I can tell from his shoulders that he's still angry. "Good run?"

"Yeah, really good," she says, letting out a breath. Kieran comes to stand behind her, visibly sweaty. "I took a page out of Seb's book, actually—we ran in wolf form, to see if it helps me get some of my energy out. I think it worked. I don't know, my head feels clearer."

I look at the ground. I don't like the thought of them shifting, but I *especially* don't like what comes after. Her, naked—vulnerable with him in a way I only want her to be with me. Not that I have any right to feel that way.

"I'm just gonna take a shower, and then we can head out," Kieran says, running a hand through his hair.

"Okay, sounds good," she says. "I need, like, fifteen minutes and then I'm ready to go."

They walk towards the stairs, and I wait until I hear their bedroom doors close before I speak again. Gabe says nothing, focusing on his work on the stove. I pore over the words that change all of this, wondering if I can share them.

"She's my mate," I mutter finally, in Gabe's direction.

He whips his head around *"What?"*

"Yeah."

"How do you know?!"

"I can't tell you, it's from my rite. But I know."

He shakes his head. *"Agaayu.* How long have you known it was her?"

I hesitate, unsure how much I can say. The *Eijna* is clear—you can't tell others what happened during your rite, or you risk the wrath of the ancestors. Some people make exceptions for mates, but even then it's better to err on the side of caution. I haven't spoken a single word about what happened that night with anyone since the day it happened.

"Since she started shifting," I say finally. That shouldn't be too much.

"Uikbaane, man. And you still treat her like this?"

"Don't you see that it makes it worse?" I say, my voice lowering to a hiss. "The *agaayit* chose her to be a part of my *fika,* even knowing she belongs somewhere else. They've given me my father's fate."

"Or they've given you the chance to undo it." Gabe shakes his head, eyes fixed on mine in anger. "I'm sorry dude, but I have no sympathy for you. The *agaayit* gave you a mate, and the ancestors have brought her to your literal fucking door step. The only thing standing between you and your happiness is yourself. Because I'm pretty sure the only thing keeping Maren from feeling like she belongs here, is *you*."

He turns off the rice and leaves the pot covered, then leaves the room, shaking his head. A few minutes later, I hear the front door open and close. I'm tempted to follow—if we were back home on Saroe, I might have, knowing where in the woods he usually goes to retreat. But here, all our routines are different— and my leg is hurting too much to walk more today, anyway.

I stay seated, stewing. A little while later, Kieran emerges from upstairs, and Maren comes down a moment later, smelling like honey and that coconut stuff she puts in her hair. I smell her first, but as she comes into view through the archway separating the kitchen from the hall, my wolf rises, watching her.

She's wearing a red dress that hugs the contours of her body, cut to look like bandages and leaving a few inches of skin here and there exposed. Her hair is down, thick and wild, and she's wearing little black heels.

I watch as Kieran opens the door for her and they head outside. As the door shuts, I can hear her laugh through the door, flowing like a brook.

My wolf snarls. I don't have the words to explain to him what's going on—and maybe I don't totally understand it myself yet.

I stay at the table, poring over Gabe's words. If he's right—if this wasn't doomed from the start, if there was ever any chance for Maren and me—then I've done this all wrong. The way my wolf feels when I'm around her, the way it felt to hear my name on her lips...

I put my head in my hands.

What the fuck have I been doing?

23

MAREN

"So how long have you been in love with her?"

"Who?" Kieran asks. He brings the beer to his lips, and across the bar, a group of guys erupts into cheers at something happening on the TV.

I roll my eyes. "Who do you think? Em. The person whose bed you're sleeping in every night."

He scoffs, but I see the color rising a little in his neck. He takes another swig of the beer to buy time.

"It's not like that," he says finally.

"No? So what's it like?"

"She's... I don't know." He sets his beer down and rakes a hand through his hair. "She's my best friend. But we're just..."

"Just best friends who sleep next to each other."

"I... Yeah. I mean. That's a thing."

I press my lips together, trying to suppress a smile. "I mean, I used to have a best friend who slept over at my house every weekend. And I *thought* that was a thing. But then we realized we both had a crush on each other, and she became my girlfriend."

His eyebrows shoot up. "You're gay?"

"I'm bi."

"Ah, okay. That makes more sense."

"What's that supposed to mean?"

"Nothing. Just that I see the way you look at Seb."

"Oh my God, shut up, I do not!" I say. "Stop changing the subject. You're deflecting. This is about you and Em."

"There's nothing between me and Em," he says, clearing his throat. "And besides, I don't sleep next to her because..." He shakes his head. "It's different. She just doesn't sleep well, and she feels safer if I'm there. I just want her to feel safe."

I cock an eyebrow.

"What?" he asks.

"That's love, dude."

He clears his throat. "No. Friend-love, maybe."

I roll my eyes again. "Why does everyone on these islands think I'm stupid? I may not know much about Fakari history, but I know 'down bad' when I see it. And you, Kieran, are down bad. Stop lying to yourself."

He coughs again. "I'm not... I just..."

He swallows, seemingly thinking, and I wait.

"Can I ask you something?" he says finally.

"Yeah. If I get a question, too."

He nods, putting forward a large hand to shake.

"Deal," he says, as I take it. "You and that girl. Your best friend and then girlfriend. How... how did it end?"

"Between us?" I shake my head. "We dated for a few months. But we were kids—like, fifteen—so it was on the down-low. She wasn't out yet, and it was just too hard. Eventually we broke up."

"Did you stay friends after?"

I shake my head again. "I don't think I've spoken to her since graduation."

He nods, looking down at the beer in his hands. "How long were you friends before you dated?"

"Years." I lean forward, tilting my head, trying to get him to meet my eyes. "Is that what you're afraid of? That if it doesn't work out..."

He swallows and sits back, and I watch as the shield goes up behind his eyes again.

"I'm not afraid of anything," he says, shaking his head. "But *if* someone starts dating a friend, then... Yeah. That's always the risk, right?"

I nod. "My turn for the question?"

"Sure."

"Why this?" I gesture between us. "Why are you going out with all these girls if it's her that you're coming home to, anyway?"

He eyes me, thinking. Finally, after another swig of his beer, he shakes his head.

"I don't know how to do this," he says finally. "I don't ever talk about this kind of stuff."

"Well, try, because we're staying in this bar at least until I finish my drink."

It takes him a while to find the words, and I watch behind his shoulder as a crowd of men jumps every few minutes, cheering on whatever match is on the big screen. Finally, Kieran leans forward again.

"*If* you had feelings for someone—and I'm not saying I do. Just, like, hypothetically—" he adds hastily. "And you knew it would never be like that between you two. Wouldn't you look? Wouldn't you want to try literally everything else out there, in case any of it made the way you feel when you're with her?"

"Oh, Kieran," I murmur. "Is that what you're doing?"

"I don't know. But *if* I had feelings for Em. Then it might be."

"I think she loves you," I say quietly.

"Like a friend."

I shake my head. "No. Like *love*-love."

He says nothing, and I watch as he starts absentmindedly

peeling the label off his beer. I wait for him to speak, but after he doesn't for a minute, I sit back.

"Come on," I say gently. "Let's get you another drink, and then we can get back to your girl."

AN HOUR LATER, I find Em on the floor of her bedroom, working on some watercolors.

"Hey," I say, leaning against the door frame.

She looks up and smiles. "Hey! How was your date?"

"Not a date. Just a drink between friends." I smile, registering the slight softening of her posture and what looks like relief in her eyes.

"He's not really my type," I add.

"No? Why not?"

"Well, for one thing, I'm pretty sure he's taken."

Her brow furrows in confusion, and I nod my head to the bed behind her, where his sweater is balled up on the edge of the bed.

"Oh," she says, a blush rising in her cheeks. "I mean. We're not like that."

"Okay." I shrug. "But in America we have this thing called girl code. And I just want you to know that, if you ever *were* like that —or even a little bit into him like that—I would never get in the way. I'm Team Em, okay?"

She chews her lip, and I can see a smile tug at her lips.

"Yeah, okay," she says. "Thanks."

"What are you painting?"

She hesitates, then turns the sketchbook on the floor to face me. It's us—me, Em, and Gabe at the lake, on my second day here.

"Oh my God, I *love* it," I whisper, walking into the room and getting on the floor close to her so I can see better. I feel my eyes start to sting, to my own surprise.

"Sorry, that's so embarrassing," I laugh, bringing a hand up to my face. "I don't know why it's making me tear up. I'm just really touched."

I point my finger to the little drawing of me, hair piled on top of my head while I'm wearing my black bathing suit.

"Little me looks so happy," I say, smiling. "She looks like she belongs."

"You do belong," Em says, smiling. "If you want."

I nod, thinking. "Yeah. I don't know. I don't know if I really belong anywhere."

She brings her knees up to her chest.

"So do you usually wear this kind of thing for drinks with friends?" she asks, gesturing to my dress. Her eyebrow is raised, and I can see she's teasing. I let out a laugh.

"You wanna know a secret?" I ask, leaning in. She nods, and I glance over my shoulder to check that we're along before I tell her.

"I may have worn this for Seb."

Her eyes go wide. "What?! No way. Are you guys...?"

I shake my head. "We're not anything. But there's something there, and he embarrassed me the other day, so I wanted to make him a little jealous."

She giggles, throwing her head back. "*Ayagaayuni*, we're so different. I would never be brave enough to do something like that."

"To dress up for a guy?"

She shrugs. "I don't know. To, like... Put yourself out there."

"Well, that's the great thing about a bangin' dress. It does all the work for you."

"We don't have clothes like that here on the Fakaris," she says, gesturing to me.

"Next time I go back to the mainland, I'll bring something back for you."

She smiles.

"What?" I ask.

"Nothing. You called it the mainland. You're starting to sound like us."

I look down at the illustration again. *You do belong, if you want to.*

"I love how you did my hair," I say, leaning in to look at it closer. "It really looks like me."

"I love your hair. I wish my hair had more texture."

"There's ways to do that," I say.

She shakes her head. "I don't have a curling iron."

"You can do it without heat, too. I can braid your hair, if you want. If you sleep in it overnight, it'll be wavy tomorrow."

She pulls her knees closer and rests her chin on them, looking up at me.

"My mom used to braid my hair for me at night," she says after a minute. "No one's done that for me since she died."

"Do you want me to?"

She thinks for a minute, then nods.

I stand up to go to my room, and a few minutes later I come back in my pajamas, holding small hair elastics and a rat-tail comb.

"Here, I'll sit on the bed and you can stay on the floor."

She nods and sits up straight, folding her legs in front of her butterfly-style, the way my friends and I all did in countless childhood sleepovers.

"This is perfect," she says as I run the tail end of the comb over her head to create an even part. "Tomorrow's going to be a big day, and now I'll look extra nice."

"What's tomorrow?"

"Fire Night. It's the big party at the heart of Fire Week. They're hoisting up the statue of Beiyyur today, and tomorrow we light it on fire. Will you come?"

She turns her head to look at me, and I use my hands to gently turn it back in place, laughing.

"Girl, I'm braiding your hair, hold still. But yeah, for sure I'll come. We'll make it a night."

"Awesome, everyone's coming. Well, except maybe Seb—he said he's not feeling well."

I nod, thinking as I weave new pieces of her hair back into the braid.

"Was he different before?" I ask quietly. "I mean, before what happened with his leg..."

Em shuffles, growing quiet. "Yeah. I mean, he's always been Seb—it never took much to set him off, even before everything happened. But he changed after his dad died. And after the rite... I guess it felt like the parts of him that had calloused over got rougher."

I nod, starting on the other side of her head.

"Do you miss how he was before?"

She shakes her head a little, and I use my hands to gently hold it back in place.

"Not really," she says. "He's like a brother to me, but we were never that close. It was always him and Gabe, and me and the elders. Until Kier came around."

"Mhmm."

"So, you guys...?" she asks tentatively.

"I don't know what it is," I say. "I mean, it's nothing, I know that. But there's a little spark there, for sure. Just physical, nothing more."

"You'd be good for him," she says after a minute. "I feel like he could use someone who knows how to laugh."

"Well. My days of dating men because it would be good for *them* are behind me. I'm not getting tangled up in anything unless it's good for *me*."

At the words, I remember the feeling of his face buried between my thighs, and how it felt when he basically seduced me against the breakfast table the morning after. *Some* things about

Seb are very, very good for me. But annoyingly, they seem to be the very things he won't let me have.

"I saw you on your laptop this afternoon," Em says. "I tried to talk to you, but you were totally engrossed. Were you doing something for the salt company?"

I shake my head. "Nah. I saw something weird recently—these blue lights on the horizon, over the shoreline. I was trying to figure out if they could have been something."

"What kind of something?"

"I don't know. A... magic something." The words feel stupid as I say them.

"Like a sprite?"

"Yeah, maybe. My dad named me for this Fakari nymph thing. I was trying to figure out if that's maybe what that was."

"The *mareijnit*," she says. "Guide-lights."

"Yeah, exactly." My fingers work my way down her hair, finishing off the braid. "But I remember those are gold. These were blue; it must have been something else."

I reach for an elastic and finish off the braid.

"There, done," I say.

She turns around, putting her hand on my knee.

"You know what? We should go to the Fakari history and culture museum when we get back. If I pass my exams, I'll schedule something before my rounds start. And if I don't, it'll be a consolation prize."

"You'll pass," I say, smiling. "But yeah, sure. Sounds great."

24

SEB

I let out a low hiss as I ease myself slowly into the couch in the den. From outside, I can hear the pops and bangs of fireworks from people partying along the shore. It's Fire Night tonight, and this year the biggest party will be along Halluk's western shore—but even on this side of the island, people are pregaming and kicking off celebrations.

I glance down at my left leg, currently concealed by gray sweatpants. The truth is that, even if I hate the reason why, I'm grateful I get to stay home tonight. I used to love the big party at the heart of Fire Week, but it's been different these last few years. Now it just feels like watching other people have fun in a way I don't remember how to.

I reach for the open book on the coffee table, bringing it onto my lap. It's an old, illustrated book of Fakari folklore—the last of the books I managed to find yesterday. It won't be comprehensive, but I've read enough of the *Eijna* to know that there's nothing about blue lights in there. If I'm lucky, this will include later legends...

I start flipping through, looking for something familiar. The book is chronological: at the beginning are the stories about the old gods, then the legends about the earliest Fakari people. As I keep going, I reach the section on mythical beasts. First is the *amreija*—the mythical winged wolf-dragon that protects lost children and returns them home. I flip past that to selkies and sirens, and something gives me pause.

A golden orb of light, and within it, the barest outlines of a woman's features.

Of course. *Mareijnit.*

I skim the page, searching for details in the text as I try to recall what we learned about this from grade school.

In Fakari lore, sirens are deep sea dwellers—dark beings who call to sailors of their deepest wishes and desires, distracting them from the realities of their homes, lives, and families to pull them into the depths. Mareijnit are the opposite: beings of light who serve as guideposts to return sailors to safe land. For hundreds of years, sailors have reported hearing the call of the siren's voice and being tempted to dive into the dark, cold waters, only to—at the last minute—see a golden being floating on the horizon, bringing them home. To this day, the Fakari word for lighthouse is taken from the name of these benevolent guides.

COULD IT BE? Are the lights we've been seeing supposed to serve as some kind of guideposts?

I reread the description, wondering. But *mareijnit* are gold, not blue, and I remember searching for my father's face in the light I saw outside the temple. I would have noticed anything resembling human features, if it had been there...

I close my eyes and let out a low breath, trying to bring to mind any other kind of light beings from primary school Fakari culture classes. Nothing—even the *mareijnit* were barely discussed. I'd almost think I made them up completely, if it weren't for Maren seeing them, too.

Maren. I sigh as my conversation with Gabe yesterday comes back to me.

"They've given me my father's fate."

"Or they've given you the chance to undo it."

Is it true? I've been praying to the *agaayit*, burning *loter* to change my fate. But is it possible that Maren was the key to doing that all along?

A shiver of unease runs over my skin. She's her own person, I chastise myself—not some kind of tool to make my life better. But I know that, don't I? Because it's that very loud, outspoken, totally irrepressible Maren-ness—the essence of her, totally unpredictable, wholly separate from me—that makes it somehow impossible for me to stay away. It drives me insane; and also, maybe, it's the thing about her I like best.

I swallow and bring a hand over my face, trying to sort out the jumble of thoughts. The *Eijna* tells us that the *agaayit* don't do anything in a vacuum—that all our paths are interconnected, any one person's fate rippling outwards to affect the fates of those around them. So Maren's here for her own story—but maybe, in some small way, she's here to play a role in mine, too.

"The only thing standing between you and your happiness is yourself. Because I'm pretty sure the only thing keeping Maren from feeling like she belongs here on the Fakaris, and in this fika, is you."

I let out a low breath, letting Gabe's words hit me a second time. What would Maren's relationship with the Fakaris look like if I'd treated her differently? What would *our* relationship look like if I hadn't tried to shut her out before she could do it first?

Leaning back on the couch, I close my eyes, the memory of our night by the bonfire coming back to me. I'd be lying if I said I haven't thought about it a hundred times since then—in moments by myself, in bed or in the shower. When I'm near her, the scent of her skin is so close that it takes next to nothing to bring back the taste of her desire on my tongue; the memory of that liquid, molten look in her eyes when she came for me; the sound of her climax rolling through her like an ocean wave. I've thought of her body, wet and needy and waiting for me, every night since.

But there's something else, too. Something soft and vulnerable, way more uncomfortable to think about than the way my body craves her. It's the little flicker of eagerness that sparks inside my wolf when she's around, even when we're fighting. It's what led me to nuzzle my face in her neck when we tussled on the floor of her room in wolf form. It's the part of me that can't stop thinking about the fact that, while I've run my tongue up and down her slit and heard her come... I've never *kissed* her.

I feel my neck heat in shame. The truth is that, when I'm falling asleep, I'm not thinking about Maren under or over me. I'm thinking about her lips, and the way her face lights up when she laughs.

And maybe, the only thing that's standing between me and being the reason for that look on her face, is myself.

I hear my own breathing grow deeper, and somewhere in the back of my mind, I register that I'm drifting closer to sleep. The world grows soft and dark, and I find myself falling into a dream again—me, walking my way up to the cliffs—when I feel something tug somewhere deep in my mind.

I blink my eyes open, searching for the feeling.

Something's wrong—I can feel it in the ether, in the space connecting me to the rest of the *fika*. Em's scared and upset; but that happens relatively often, and I can feel Kieran's presence somewhere, not too far from her. But it's not Em's fear that's pulling me from sleep.

It's Maren's.

I sit upright, fumbling for that feeling in the *fikaband*. My ability to sense her presence at all is stronger than it was a few days ago—I feel it more strongly now than I did yesterday, and I wonder if my verbal beating from Gabe has anything to do with that. But where this morning I just felt the soft glow of her presence somewhere far away, I now feel her tense and angry. There's rage there, and something deeper than fear—panic.

I try to feel for Gabe's presence, but it's farther away. And as I check again for Kieran, I realize they're getting farther from Em and Maren. *Why aren't they together?*

Another pang of fear tugs at my mind, coming from Maren again. I rise to my feet, letting out a low grunt as my weight comes to rest on my left leg.

I shouldn't go after her—Gabe will reprimand me the second he sees me staggering up to them on that beach, knowing what the run there will have cost me. But as Maren's fear surges through my mind again, my feet make the decision for me, and I run for the door.

25

MAREN

"Seriously, back up," I snap, putting my hands out in front of me.

"What's wrong? We just wanna dance," the tall one says, stepping closer to Em. He sways slightly under the effect of the drink in his hand. Next to him, his two friends snigger, and one of them mutters something to the other over his drink.

"She doesn't want to dance with you. Leave," I say, stepping between him and Emerson.

"*Heij*, we should just go," she mutters behind me.

"No, we're not going anywhere," I say to her, keeping my eyes on the guy. "We came here to have fun. We should be allowed to do that without being bothered."

"Come on, *eijtna*," he says, lowering his voice. "You don't come to Fire Night dressed like that if you don't want to get at least a *little* hot and bothered."

He winks, and his friends laugh, egging him on.

"Seriously, I said *back the fuck up*," I say, stepping back and putting my hands between us. From where she stands next to me now, I see Em glance over her shoulder. Kier and Gabe left to get us drinks ages ago. *Where the hell are they?*

"Lighten up," the tall one says, slipping his hand around my waist. I step back again, but I can feel a ripple of anxiety slither through my gut. One of the guy's friends mutters something to the tall one in Fakari, and as he laughs darkly, I see Em stiffen next to me.

We should go, she mouths.

I look around again. The beach is crowded, and most people seem too drunk to take notice of what's happening. If we leave this part of the beach, Kieran and Gabe won't be able to find us— and I'd rather not end up being cornered by these guys again when we're alone, and no one knows where we are.

I bring my gaze back to the tall one. He's staring at me with slick, dark eyes, and I can smell the sting of heavy liquor on his breath. If I knee him in the groin, there's at least a fifty percent chance he or his friends attack me. Too risky.

"Listen, guys, we just came here to have fun," I say, smiling and cocking my head. "Our boyfriends will be back in a minute, anyway. But why don't we buy you a round of drinks before you head out, so everyone has a good time?"

"You hear that? Their *boyfriends* are coming," says one of the friends.

"So where are they, huh?" the tall one says, leaning in, grinning. "I don't scent anyone on you."

Just then I hear a loud bang from the left. I look up to see a firework that's gone off at the wrong angle, just a few feet above the head of some women dancing. Next to me, Em starts at the sound. Her breathing gets heavier, and she glances back and forth between the guys and me. I know that look in her eyes—I saw it in my college roommate just before she had her first panic attack. Em brings her arms up around herself, like she's boxing herself in.

"Em, *go*," I say. "Get out of here."

She hesitates, but one of the other guys steps closer to her, and I see her anxiety rise in the way her shoulders come up around her ears.

"*Go,*" I repeat, and she nods, turning to run down the shore.

The friend starts to follow after her, but I turn to put myself in front of him.

"*Nekka,*" I say, hoping somehow the word will do more in Fakari than it does in English. He glances at me and then up at the shore again, but Em's already woven herself into the crowd. Hopefully to find Gabe and Kier. *Please.*

The tall one slips his hand around my waist again, coming to rest it on my lower back. I take a step back, but I feel my heel gets stuck in the sand and I lose my balance, falling backward. He stumbles forward, catching himself before he falls on top of me, and laughs as I fall onto my ass in the sand. By now that coil of anxiety has sunk into cold, hardened fear.

Another bang goes off behind us, this one uncomfortably close. I jump and the guys laugh again. Inside my chest, I can feel my wolf start pacing, anxious.

"Come on, *streikna,*" the shorter one says, reaching for my hand as if to help me up. "You came dressed like that to dance, didn't you? So dance for us."

I scramble up from the sand myself, brushing it off of the short, skin-tight pink dress. Glancing over my shoulder, I search for Gabe and Kieran's heads in the crowd, but can't make them out.

Please, someone.

As I turn back to the men, I realize that the tall one's closer now. His clammy hand reaches for my wrist, and instinctively I pull it away, hard. He grabs at me again, and over his shoulder I see his friends give each other a look and turn their backs to us.

Oh, fuck. That's not good. I have ten, maybe fifteen seconds before this goes from bad to much, much worse. I can run, I can fight, or I can call for help. But over the sounds of the music and the crowds laughing and dancing, I don't think anyone will hear me.

Help, help, help.

I turn away and bolt, but his other arm comes to wrap around my waist, the drink in his cup splashing over my front. I grunt and try to pull his arm off of me, but instead we just fall into the sand. I raise my right elbow, trying to slam it backwards into his body. I don't feel it hit, but suddenly I hear him grunt and feel him let go, then hear some kind of roar as his body hits the sand.

I scramble up and away, trying to put as much space between us as possible. But as I look over my shoulder to see what happened, I freeze. Seb is wrestling the man to the ground.

Oh my God.

"Leave her alone," he yells, rising to his feet. And those are the only words I can make out before all hell breaks loose.

The other guy shifts and lunges up to attack him, and Seb's wolf emerges from him just in time. Their clothes fly off as their bodies collide, slashing and gnawing and violent. The crowd on the beach makes way to watch, clearing a space to fight. Sand flies as their wolves fall over each other, wrestling each other to the ground. I see a flash of red and scent iron in the air as someone bites; I hear a cry from, I think, the other wolf. Over my shoulder, I hear a woman scream in surprise as blood hits the sand, and then I realize my mouth is open and I'm the one screaming. The guy's friends run up, and I hear footsteps and turn to see Gabe, with Em and Kieran behind, making their way up the shore.

"Where the fuck were you?" I shout, over the sound of the two of them snarling.

"The line for drinks was really long. I'm sorry, we didn't—What's going on?" Gabe asks, breathless.

"This guy, I don't know. He was trying to corner me. And then Seb—"

I turn just in time to see the other wolf's leg scratch at Seb's thigh as he tries to get him off of himself. Seb lets out a yelp of pain, and before I can stop myself I'm running forward, Gabe behind me, reaching to pull Seb's body off the other guy as his two friends come in to do the same.

"Stop, stop," I'm yelling. Across the clearing made by the crowd, the other guy shifts back into human form, his friends lifting him up by the shoulders.

"Cunt!" he shouts at me, followed by a string of words in Fakari.

Seb lunges forward again, but Gabe manages to grab him before he reaches the other side of the clearing. The crowd beside us parts for two men in dark blue uniforms—they must be police. As one of them charges towards the man and his friend, the other walks up to us.

"What's going on here?" the man asks Gabe, who shakes his head and turns to me.

"That guy tried to attack me," I say, gesturing across the clearing. "My friend tried to step in to help. He didn't do anything wrong."

"Are you hurt?" the officer asks Seb. Seb shifts back, panting, leaning forward on his knees.

"I'm okay," he says, but I can hear instantly that it's not true. His voice comes out strangled, constricted. Instinctively, I put my hand on his back.

"And you?" the officer asks me.

"I'm... yeah, I'm fine," I say, nodding. "I don't... I don't know, I wouldn't have been if he didn't come in. If it had been five minutes later, it would all have gone south. Please don't punish my friend."

The officer shakes his head. "We won't. This kind of stuff happens every year."

"Well, it shouldn't," I say, crossing my arms in front of my chest. "You need to get that guy and his friends out of here. If you don't, I won't be the only woman they try to hurt tonight."

The officer eyes me and nods. "We'll take care of it. I'm sorry about this."

He turns away, and I feel the anxiety and adrenaline coursing through my gut as I turn my attention back to Seb. Behind him, I see Gabe reach for his clothes in the sand, bringing them over for him to put back on.

"What happened?" I ask, wrapping my arms around myself as he steps into his pants. "How did you know to come?"

"I don't... I don't know," he says, shaking his head. He seems bewildered, the look in his eyes glassy. Gabe hands him his shirt to snap around his torso.

"Are you hurt?" I ask. "Did you get hit on the head? Where did he bite you?"

"He didn't—" He blinks, shaking his head, and turns to Gabe. "Where the hell were you, man? How did you almost let this happen?"

"We were here," Gabe says, shaking his head. "We just went to get drinks. We were gone for maybe fifteen, twenty minutes, max."

"You shouldn't have left the two of them alone. One of you should have stayed. You know how people get."

"*Heij*," Gabe says, putting his hands up. "Calm down. Everything's okay."

"How did you know?" Kier asks, and it's only then that I even register his presence in the group. I glance over and see Em standing in front of him, wide-eyed and shaken, with his arms wrapped protectively around her, one hand moving gently up and down her shoulder.

"I felt it," Seb says, waving a hand. "In the *fikaband*. She was scared."

"You felt Maren?" Em asks, looking between us, her brow furrowed.

"Yeah. Don't you?"

"What's going on? What's a *fikaband*?" I ask.

Gabe looks between us, something passing behind his eyes. Just then, I hear a loud chorus of cheers erupt from down the beach. I look up and see the large wooden structure at the end of the shore, shaped vaguely like a man, erupt into flames. To the left, the two police-like figures are leading the man and his friends down the other way of the shore.

"We should talk about this later," Kieran says, shaking his head. "Let's just have some fun for now. Don't let those guys ruin Fire Night."

"It's fine, we can just go home," Em says quietly, wrapping her arms around her waist.

"No, *heij*, you love this," Kieran says, tilting his head down, looking at her. "Let's go."

I look at Seb, whose face is twisted in pain.

"You guys go," I say. "We'll join in a little bit. I just want to stay here for a second and make sure Seb's okay."

"Gabe?" Kier asks, looking over at him.

Gabe looks at Seb and me for a long moment, then turns to walk with Em and Kieran down the shore.

"Hey," I say quietly, looking into Seb's dark eyes. "Are you okay?"

"Are *you* okay? When I came, all I could see was that *freijyyuk* with his hands all over you."

"I'm fine. I was fine," I say, wrapping my arms tighter around myself. "I would have been okay. You didn't have to..."

But I feel my voice waver for a second, and I stop myself.

"Thank you. For coming," I say quietly. "Are you hurt? I saw him kick your hip."

"I'm fine," he says, but his voice comes out broken, exhausted.

"Do you want to get a drink or something?" I ask, gesturing down the shore towards the bar Gabe and Kieran had disappeared to. "Apparently the wait is forever, but..."

"I don't know if I can walk there." He takes an uneasy step

forward, but his knee buckles in the sand, and I reach out my hands to help catch him.

"You shouldn't have come," I mutter admonishingly, helping him straighten to his feet. "You shouldn't have hurt yourself like this for me. You'll be in pain for days."

"I'm fine," he says, and I give him a look.

"Really," he continues. "You should join the others. I'll wait here. I just need to rest for a bit before I can head back."

"I'm not leaving you here in pain by yourself."

"Maren—"

"Seb," I say quietly. "Will you please let me help you? Just put aside your pride for once."

He stares at me for a long moment.

"Okay," he says finally.

"Can we get you home? I can find a cab. I'll call an Uber or something."

He smiles softly. "We don't have any of that stuff here."

"How long is the walk?" I ask, looking around. "Twenty minutes, maybe? Can I— Here."

I come up beside him and slip my shoulder under his on the left side, wrapping my arm around his middle.

"I'll help you walk."

"You don't have to do this," he says quietly, and I can hear the edge of shame in his voice.

"I want to. Really." I look over at him, holding his gaze in mine. "It's fine. I can handle the weight."

26

SEB

Maren all but carries me through the front door of the Halluk house.

"Careful," she says quietly, her voice straining, trying to help me over the threshold by lifting her shoulder higher.

"Sorry," I mutter, doing my best to put more of my weight on my good leg.

"Stop. I'm here because I want to be here. Now, where do I need to take you? The couch? Your room?"

"The den is fine," I say, my voice worn with the sound of the pain in my thigh. She nods and helps me in that direction, past the kitchen and dining area, into the room at the far end of the house.

We near the couch, and she helps lower me onto the pillows.

"Do you need to elevate it? I can grab a pillow."

"I'm fine."

She gives me a look.

"Yeah, okay. Thank you," I say quietly.

She nods and walks around the couch to grab one, then sets it down on the coffee table, moving the open book out of the way to do so.

"Can I get you some water? Or tea? What usually helps?"

"I don't know. Rest. The hot springs."

She stands. "Are there hot springs around here?"

"Not with the same kind of salinity, and that's what helps."

"Can we do anything to recreate what they do? There's a bathtub upstairs, right?"

"I don't know if we have enough salt. It's fine. I'll just sit here for a while until it gets better, and then try to sleep it off upstairs."

"Hang on," she says, and walks out of the room.

A minute later, I can hear her on the phone in the kitchen.

"Hey, *aja*. Yeah, everything's fine. No, everyone's okay. Yeah. I just wanted to know if you have salt here? Like, Epsom salt, or those Fakari healing salts? We need, like, a lot. Yeah, really, everyone's fine, I just wanted to take a bath. ...Oh, really? Okay, perfect. Where? ...Okay, hang on a sec."

She disappears from the kitchen, and I listen as her footsteps trail up the stairs and down the hall, in the direction of the master bedroom. Five minutes later, she emerges downstairs again, and I can hear the faint roar of rushing water coming from the other end of the house.

"Okay. Here's what we're gonna do," she says, crossing her arms. "I'm running a bath upstairs for you. I found a metric ton of Epsom salt and Fakari sea salt, and I've made the bath about as salty as the Dead Sea. You're barely going to be able to *enter* the water with how salty I made it."

"Mare—"

"Shush," she says, raising a hand. "I'm gonna help you up there and then I'll shower down the hall. That guy spilled his drink on me and I smell like the MBTA bathrooms. I know you don't know what that is, but trust me, it's gross." Her voice softens slightly, and she tilts her head to look at me. "And I know that you don't like people taking care of you, so here's the deal. I promise I know you can take care of yourself. But you did something really nice for me tonight, so I want to do something nice for you. And tomorrow, we can go right back to hating each other and pretend this never happened. Okay?"

I swallow. *Is that what I want?*

"Okay."

She comes over to the couch and gently helps me lift my leg from the pillow, placing it down on the ground.

"Like this?" she asks, coming beside me to wrap an arm around my waist.

"Yeah, I— hang on," I say, rising to my feet with some difficulty. I put my hand on the coffee table for balance, but it lands on the open mythology book and almost slips.

"Hey, hey," she says, steadying me. "You're good. What's that?"

"Oh, nothing, I was just reading earlier. I was looking for..."

"Something about the lights?" she asks, looking up as she leads me out from behind the coffee table. "Yeah, me too."

I lean on her shoulder, trying to put as little weight on her I can handle. "Did you find anything?"

She shakes her head, her hair brushing against my arm. "Nothing that seemed relevant. You?"

"Nah." We reach the kitchen, and I take a break for a second, leaning against the kitchen island. "There's this being called a *mareijna*—the plural is *mareijnit*—but those are supposed to be gold, not blue."

"Oh, yeah, I know. Like spirit lighthouses, right?" she says, smiling. "That's what I was named for. It's one of the only Fakari mythology things I knew before I came here."

"Wait. What?"

She shrugs. "My dad wanted my name to be Mareijna. Mom wanted a spelling that would be easier for Americans, so it was between Marina and Maren. Dad liked this better." She shrugs.

"It's basically the only Fakari cultural thing my mom ever told me. Mostly because she wanted to tell me how grateful I should be that my name was easy to spell." She rolls her eyes.

"Do you know why he wanted to name you that? Had he ever seen...?"

She shrugs. "No clue. Maybe he just liked how it sounded. Are you ready to head upstairs? I don't want the bath to overflow."

I nod, and she comes up by my side again to help me towards the hall.

"There we go," she says quietly, bringing me to the first stair. "You can use the railing, if it's easier."

"Yeah, thanks," I say, and slowly heave myself up the next few steps.

Once we're at the top of the stairs, she helps me to the master bathroom, where the large tub is already more than halfway full. I lean against the sink as she walks over to the tub to turn off the water.

"I guess you don't need help getting changed, right? That's the nice thing about clothing with snaps." She laughs a little. "I, uh, put a bath mat down, and some towels over there. I'm just gonna go down the hall to shower and you can take as much time as you want."

"I..." I hesitate. "I don't need help with my clothes, but..."

She looks up at me, waiting, and I feel the heat rise in my neck.

"It's fine, forget it," I say. "Thanks, I'm good."

"No, what is it?"

I bring my hand to my forehead. "I don't... *Agaayu*, this is embarrassing. I, um..."

She crosses her arms. "Seb?"

I swallow. "I might need some help getting into the tub. I just, I'm sorry. My leg—"

"Oh, yeah. No worries." She smiles, but I can see her cheeks color just slightly.

"It's not like I haven't seen you naked enough in the last week, right? Part of the culture here." She laughs again, but this time the sound is a little airier, more nervous than before. "Okay, I'll turn around and you can take your clothes off, and I'll help you get in. I promise not to look."

My face burns as she turns her back to me, but I pull off my shirt and, with some extra care, manage to remove my sweats along the snaps at the seams.

"Okay," I say quietly.

She turns to me, bringing her wide, dark eyes resolutely to mine. It's the same gaze she gave me the other day by the shore —showing me that she won't cross my boundaries. The wolf in my chest sits up straight, his gaze as focused on her as hers is on me. I find myself unnerved by it.

"I'm gonna put my arm around you again, okay?" she says softly.

"Yeah. Okay."

She brings her shoulder to mine and wraps her arms around my middle, clasping her hands together at my waist while looking towards the ceiling. I bring my arm around her shoulder, and she helps lift me enough to get both feet into the bath. I bring my good hand to the edge of the tub, and together we lower me into it, where I let out a low sigh of relief as the hot water laps around me. Immediately, the salt content of the water practically makes me feel weightless.

As my body enters the tub, a small wave of water splashes over the edge, onto the pink fabric of Maren's dress.

"Fuck, sorry," I mutter, but she laughs.

"It's fine. Like I said, not the first thing that was spilled on this dress today. Maybe the water will even help get the stain out."

I nod, and I feel something weird happening behind my eyes.

"I..." I swallow. "I'm sorry. You're being so good to me. You don't have to do that. Thanks."

She shrugs. "You saved me out there earlier. You didn't have to do that, either."

"Yeah, I did."

The words come out before I can really think about them. I watch as they reach her—as her brow furrows just slightly, as something in her posture softens for just a second before growing firm again.

"I'll be back in a few," she says, and leaves the room.

A HALF HOUR LATER, she comes back wearing a gray cotton tee shirt and the same shorts she had on that night on the veranda. As she enters she's looking pointedly down at her feet, and comes to sit on the floor, leaning against the tub. From where I'm sitting, I can see the profile of her face against the thickness of her hair, clipped up and back.

"How's it feeling?" she asks, resting her arms on her knees. Her gaze is pointed resolutely at the far wall.

I shrug—not that she can see. "It doesn't work right away. This helps in the moment, but the long-term effects will take a while to kick in. Hopefully doing this a few times will start to take the edge off."

She nods, and I feel her energy grow soft and curious. There's a question forming in her mind, and I make myself wait, giving her the space to ask.

"Seb?" she asks finally.

"Yeah?"

"What's a *fikaband*?"

Of course. I feel the heat creep up my neck.

"It's... like a mental connection between a *fika*. You can feel everyone's presence—kind of roughly where they are, and how they're feeling."

"You can feel the others? Like, right now?" she asks.

I nod and close my eyes. "Yeah. Gabe, Kier, and Em are together. They're not far from here. Em's feeling good. Gabe's... not. Probably from what happened earlier."

"And the elders?"

"I can feel them, too, but more distantly. I just feel that they're there. Alive, but farther from us. I can't tell what's going on with them."

"And me?"

I swallow. "Yeah. I feel you."

"How am I feeling?"

A smile pulls at my mouth. "That's different. I can tell that from you being in the room."

"So tell me, then," she says, and I watch her profile as she raises an eyebrow. "Pop quiz."

"Curious," I say finally. "Tentative. Safe."

She lets out a low breath.

"I don't like that," she says finally. "That you can just tell how I feel. That you can... *smell* how I feel, sometimes."

"Sorry. Trust me, we wish we could turn it off."

"Do you have it with everyone?" she asks, turning over her shoulder to meet my gaze. She's washed off her makeup, I realize. Her skin looks softer, a little grayer under the eyes. I like it—knowing what she looks like when she takes off her mask for the rest of the world.

"The scent thing, yeah. And if *you* feel bad about it, imagine how it was in high school for the rest of us." I laugh uneasily. "The other stuff, I don't know. It depends. I'm better at reading Gabe than Kieran, 'cause we're closer, and we grew up together."

"How long have you been able to... *feel* me?"

"Just a couple days," I say quietly. "Since... that night."

"On the veranda?" she asks.

"Yeah."

"Oh." She nods. "Is that why?"

"I don't know."

She looks away again, thinking. Finally, she asks, "Does it mean anything?"

I feel a little ripple of nerves run over me, and clear my throat. It means more than I'd like it to.

"I think it means my wolf is starting to recognize you. As part of my pack."

Among other things.

"When will *I* feel it?"

"I don't know. I've never met someone like you."

She snorts. "Someone raised in the US?"

"Someone who got to know her wolf in adulthood. We don't have anyone like that here. I don't know how it works."

"Hm."

Have you asked her what she plans to do?, Gabe asked.

"Do you..." I try. "Do you miss the mainland?"

She shrugs. "I miss some things."

"Like what?"

"Like... Like things being available all the time. If you need a chainsaw or a bag of frozen chicken nuggets at 3 a.m., you can get it in America." She smiles. "There's always *something* open. Here, it took days to get me a new converter for my laptop charger."

"What else?"

She hesitates. "Strangers are friendly. You make small talk at the grocery store and people don't act weird about it. Oh, and the nature is so beautiful. I mean, you have that here, too, of course. But it's so varied there. You can have a totally different experience of nature in Arizona versus Connecticut versus Virginia. In three different spots in California, even. It's breath-taking. It makes you feel small, in a good way."

I nod.

"Do you miss your friends?" I ask. "Or work?"

She shakes her head. "I've had a lot of friends, but people

kind of come and go. That's life. And my jobs do that, too, as you like to remind me." She sighs. "I've never really found the place where I feel like I fit."

I swallow. "Do you... Do you imagine yourself fitting here?"

She looks over at me again. "I'm still trying to figure that out."

"I think you could."

"Yeah?" her eyes widen a little, soft and hopeful.

"Yeah. You seem like you could fit in anywhere."

It's meant to be a compliment, but I watch her deflate at the words.

"I mean, but—specifically here," I add. "Like, you're building relationships with people. Em, Kieran. Me."

She smiles softly. "Just for tonight, though, right? Temporary truce."

"Yeah. Right," I say, and that same spot in my chest aches. "But really. You're connecting with people. You're doing a great job with the salt company. That's huge."

She grows quiet again, and I watch a question form on her lips.

"Seb?" she asks again.

"Yeah?"

"Since I'm helping with this... Can you tell me why you're so passionate about the salts? Like, beyond the obvious." She gestures broadly to the bath.

The only thing standing between you and your happiness is yourself, I hear in my mind.

"I... It's a long story."

"Oh. Okay."

"No, I mean—I can tell you. But I just want to give you a head's up."

She looks over her shoulder at me again. "I have time."

"So... Saga told you about the rite, right? It's the coming-of-age ritual. You do it to become a member of pack council."

"Yeah, I remember."

"You need three pack council members to secure a *fikarig*. It's an old Fakari law—it mattered more when there was a scarcity of housing, but the laws haven't changed. But so... when my dad died, a, a pack council seat opened up for me."

She nods, watching me.

"I didn't have to do it. Between the remaining elders, we still had four council seats. We weren't in any danger of losing the *fikarig*. But I think I just... I just wanted to feel closer to him, I guess. By doing the rite, and taking his seat. By becoming a man of the house. And... if I'm honest..."

I feel my voice waver a little.

"I don't know. During the rite, the ancestors come to you. They take the form of your greatest weakness, but the ancestors also guide you through the rite."

"You wanted to see your dad," she says softly.

"Yeah. It's stupid."

She shakes her head. "It's not stupid."

I let out a slow breath. "I didn't take enough time to prepare. I was reckless, and I figured that whatever the ancestors threw at me, I could hack it. And I couldn't."

"What happened?"

I shake my head. "I can't tell anyone the details. It's part of the ritual—I can't tell other people what I fought up there. It was horrible, so much worse than I'd ever imagined. I almost died. At some point, I *wanted* to die. But I didn't."

I look at her, remembering the black wolf who saved me. Her, somehow. When I speak again, my voice comes out raw.

"Saga and the other healers thought I was too far-gone for Fakari healing. They had me airlifted to Toronto, where I had part of my leg muscle removed, and spent months recovering. And when I came back, I just became obsessed with the rite. I started reading everything the *Eijna* says about it, over and over. I found history books. And I learned that the preparation for it used to look totally different. They had a whole series of rituals in the lead-up, but we don't know what those are anymore. And they had a salt regimen that used way, way more of the salt made the old way. But we don't have that, either. Now we just get a fraction, and fill in the rest with modern stuff."

She nods. "You said the *Eijna* describes that in a different way than salt now, right?"

"Sort of. The effects are different—it sounds like it was protective in some way. It had a different effect on the body."

She looks pensive for a second. "And so you think, if you'd had access to the old salt and the old rituals, maybe it would have gone differently for you."

I bristle. "I don't know. But I feel like, at the very least, the Fakari people deserve to know what we're missing. We should at least know the way it was before."

"What do *you* deserve?"

The question throws me off guard. *A second chance*, comes a voice from somewhere deep inside me, and I find myself unnerved by it. It's not that I want to do the rite again—I'd rather die, and I think it would literally kill me. It's just that, maybe if I had the right salts, the right rituals, the way the ancestors intended...

"I don't know," I say finally. "But until I do, this is a start."

Maren tilts her head back, eyeing the ceiling. I watch as two of the corkscrew curls from her clip hang perilously close to the water.

"Finn's been setting up the new radiator," I say. "Production is already up. Thanks for that."

She shrugs. "I didn't do anything."

"You created a demand for it. You made me think this was possible. So, thanks."

We sit in silence for a few minutes, and I watch her face as she eyes the far wall.

"Em used to work at the Fakari museum," Maren says finally.

"We were talking about taking a trip, since I want to learn more about the history and culture of the islands."

I nod, waiting.

"You should come," she says carefully. "Maybe they'll have something about the salt rituals."

I want to say, *They won't.* I want to say, *I've been to that museum a thousand times since I was a kid,* or, *thanks, but I've got it.* I would have, a week ago. But instead, what comes out of my mouth is,

"Thanks for inviting me."

She glances over her shoulder at me.

"You know, it's a shame this truce is just for tonight. I almost like you."

"Yeah. I almost like you, too."

27

MAREN

The car ride home from the harbor two days later is relatively quiet. Em, Seb, and I climb into the back seat, and this time there's no grumbling or annoyance when Seb has to put his arm around the headrest to make room for me. This time, I don't fight myself when I notice how good he smells. And when we run over a bumpy stretch of the road and our legs brush against each other, it takes a second before I pull mine away.

We arrive at the *fikarig* a little while later, and I watch as Gabe and Kieran grab Seb's bags from the trunk so he doesn't have to. When we get inside, Viggo and Dagmar are there to greet everyone, but Seb turns for the stairs and starts pulling himself up, using his hands on the railings to put as little weight on his leg as possible. I follow, reaching out to grab his arm once we get to the second floor landing.

"Hey. Are you okay?"

He shrugs. "I'm fine."

"Your leg?"

He shrugs noncommittally.

"Okay, well. Is there anything I can do?"

"There's nothing anyone can do. It just hurts sometimes—once I overdo it, it takes a while to get back to normal. And it's hard to see..."

He gestures downstairs, and I glance over my shoulder.

"What? Gabe and Kier?"

He shrugs again and turns from me, heading towards his room.

"Hey," I say, and he stops. "What's going on?"

He turns, letting out a low sigh, and brings his eyes up to mine. "It's stupid."

"So what? Tell me anyway."

"Everyone does this thing where they kind of... dance around me. No one asks if I need help. People just see that I'm in pain and fill in the gaps. I hate that they have to do that."

"That sucks."

He shrugs. "I wish it wasn't like this. But it is, and there's nothing I can do about it. So I'd rather just be alone until my leg is feeling better."

"Are you going to the hot springs today?" I ask. "That usually helps, right?"

I see him set his jaw, and he looks away.

"What?"

"I don't— It's been a long day. I don't know if I can make it there."

I nod, eyeing his face. His eyes are tired, and in them I see a vulnerability that's new for him. Or, new for us, maybe.

"I can take you. With the car."

"You don't have to go out of your way for me."

I smile. "Dude, if you think it's a hardship for me to spend my evening at a natural hot tub, you don't know me at all. Come on. It's not a big deal. We'll have a good time."

"Are you sure?"

"Yeah, of course. Let's do it."

A few hours later, the two of us head downstairs and for the car. The Jeep doesn't have a stereo system I can hook my phone up to, so I play some pop music directly from my phone speaker and wait for Seb to tear it to shreds. To my surprise, he doesn't, and I even see him nodding his head to the beat when he thinks I'm not looking.

By the time we arrive, the sun is setting. It's humid out, and I can feel the thick halo of frizz around my hair, brushing against my neck and shoulders. As we get out of the car, I grab a bag with towels and a clean change of clothes for me, and we walk to the water's edge.

I turn my back to Seb as we start to change, stipping my shirt off and stepping out of my running shorts to expose my bathing suit underneath. I wait until I hear the splash of water as he gets in, then slide in, too, turning around to see his face.

He lets out a low sigh, leaning his head back and closing his eyes.

"Good?" I ask.

"Yeah. Thanks."

"Better than a DIY hot spring in a bathtub, I guess."

He opens his eyes to look at me, and I expect him to tease me, but his gaze is soft.

"No, that was good, too. And kind."

I shrug. "I aim to please."

"You always do."

"A week ago you were claiming the opposite," I say, laughing, but I feel a stirring of something in my gut. His words are innocent enough, but I'm suddenly reminded of the things he muttered to me against the dining table last week. *You're so beautiful. You're so gorgeous, Maren.*

Something prickles in the air between us, and I have the feeling he's remembering the same thing I am.

"Sorry," he says, clearing his throat. "That came out weird."

"It's fine. This *is* weird."

"What is?"

I gesture at the space between us, as if to say, *us.* I see his eyes fall to my hand and then back up to my face, and I feel something warm in them, just slightly.

"Can you stop doing that?" I ask.

"Doing what?"

"Looking at me like you're remembering what I look like naked."

"I've never seen you naked."

My brow furrows. "I've shifted in front of you like twenty times."

He shrugs. "I've never let myself look."

I laugh. "Damn. You might be the first person who's ever gone down on me but hasn't seen me without clothes on."

"I've never kissed you, either," he says without missing a beat.

I snort. "I'm sure you spend a lot of time thinking about *that.*"

"Maybe."

A little ripple of surprise runs through me, and my inner wolf perks up, turning her head. I feel a flicker of curiosity.

"You won't deny it?"

He closes his eyes and leans his head back, bringing his arms up around the water's edge to hold himself in place.

"I'm tired, Mare," he says finally. "There's a lot of things I don't really have the energy to fight myself on anymore. And *this* —" He waves between us, the way I did a moment ago. "—is one of them."

I feel my breath catch as I stare at him, willing him to continue. I watch as the water gently laps around his skin, the golden glow of the setting sun coming in through the trees to paint his face in light. Something simmers under my skin— something hot and sensual and uncomfortably close to affection.

It's too new. This is all too fast.

I clear my throat. "Now that we're back on Saroe, we should start talking about the business."

He lifts his head to look at me. "You want to do this *here*? Now? We're in a hot spring."

"We made our first business deal in this hot spring, if I remember correctly."

My voice is clippy, but he doesn't meet me there. Instead, he says softly,

"I'm tired, Mare. Another time, okay?"

The sound of my nickname on his lips—for the *second* time this evening—brings back a glimmer of that feeling, and it blooms for a second before I can shove it down.

"Em reached out to her old boss at the museum to make an appointment," I say, my voice weirdly tight. "She's starting her rounds soon, but she's trying to set up something for us next week. I've been thinking about what I said to you in the library, about the outsiders. I know it's a crazy idea, but I just think... I don't know. It's worth a shot, right? To figure out something about the old salt rituals. For marketing, of course."

He looks over at me again. "What has you so interested?"

I'm not sure.

"It's my history, too, right?" I try. "I don't know. I'm doing it as much for me as for you."

As I say it, I wonder if it's true.

Silence falls between us, and I blink as the light dances off the surface of the water, so bright it almost burns my eyes. I think back to the conversation we had in the library—me holding my clothes to my chest, cursing at him for thinking he's better than me. That, at least, felt simple—uncomplicated. Sparring with this man was easy; whatever *this* is feels dangerous.

He lifts an arm to scratch at the back of his neck, and I can't help but notice the cut of it—the corded muscle, the dark brush of hair under his arm. My breath does something weird, and I see the second his eyes flicker up to me, registering. I watch as he swallows; as he tries to suppress the little hint of interest in his eyes.

A smile tugs at my lips. *This*, I know how to do.

"So you think about kissing me," I say lightly.

"I've *thought* about it."

"And? How was I?"

He smiles, just barely.

"Did I taste as good as I look?" I ask coyly. "Did I taste as good as you remember?"

"Maren," he says carefully. But I see his breathing fall a little heavier, and I hold his gaze, daring him to suppress the memory.

"You said you're tired of fighting yourself," I say quietly. "Maybe I am, too."

I watch as the words register in his posture. Something changes just barely in his shoulders, in the tension in his neck. But he keeps his eyes on me, even, like he's trying to stop himself from giving away too much.

"So what if we stopped fighting it?"

"Maren." Firmer now—a warning. But I can see the wolf in his eyes, glinting gold.

"Don't you want to?" I ask quietly. He stares wordlessly at me, his breath growing deeper. My hands reach up to the bathing suit ties at the back of my neck, and I feel his eyes lingering on mine as my fingers gently pull on the tie holding it up.

He lets out a broken sigh as I loosen the knot and let the top half of my bathing suit fall down into the water, exposing the bare skin of my chest. His gaze is still resolutely on mine, not daring to move.

"Come on," I say, my voice low. "Look at me. I *want* you to look at me."

His eyes fall down my body, lingering on my breasts. I hear the soft intake of breath as he admires them, eyeing the full, round shape; the large, dark nipples. His shoulders tense, and I see something shift in him, hungry and primal.

"What is it?" I ask, willing him closer.

"I don't know how to stay away from you," he lets out, his voice strained.

"So don't," I whisper. "Come on. Let's just let ourselves have this."

He moves towards me, the look in his eyes hungry, and I wrap my legs around his waist as he presses me back into the rock edge of the hot spring.

"Mare," he breathes into my ear, and I shiver as I feel the warmth of his breath on my neck. There's still strain in his voice, and at the sound of it I feel my back arch, dying for him to break through that resolve for me.

"Tell me I can have you," he groans, bringing his lips to my neck. I feel them brush against my skin as the muscles in his back tense, hungry, waiting for me to say yes.

"You can have me," I whisper. And he finally lets go of all that self-control.

His hands find my waist as his mouth crashes against my neck, his tongue and teeth immediately uncovering the spot that makes my knees go weak. I gasp and bring my hand to the back of his neck, and he groans, low and needy, as my head falls back.

"You're so gorgeous," he murmurs, his hand finding its way up my ribcage to cup just under my breast. "How am I supposed to stay away from you when you look like this?"

"Tell me," I murmur, hooking my feet, pulling him in closer to me. "Tell me what you like so much."

"All of you," he says, his hands working their way up to my breasts. He lets out a low groan as he cups the fullness of them, and I gasp as his thumbs find my nipples, running over the tender skin.

"You feel so fucking good, Mare. Your body is so gorgeous. I can't stop thinking about your pretty pussy on my face."

A shiver of pleasure runs through me, and he pulls away to look in my eyes.

"Tell me," I say again. "Tell me what you think about."

I see a flicker of hesitation register in his features.

"It's hot for me," I say, and swallow. "I like it. Tell me."

He nods, and under the water, I feel his fingers run over the seam of my bathing suit.

"I love your pussy," he murmurs, gazing intently into my eyes, his pupils dark. "I love how she looks when she gets all swollen and wet for me."

I let out a small gasp as he slips his fingers under the fabric, running over my lips.

"I love how soft she is," he says, bringing his mouth to my ear. "I love how pretty she looks when you're gasping and spreading your legs wide."

"Seb," I moan as he slips one fingertip between my legs.

"*Agaayu*, Mare. You're already so wet for me."

My back arches for him, my hips wanting to find the angle that makes him go deeper. He grins, the look in his eyes dark and playful.

"And I love *that*. The way you're so hungry for me."

"Hypocrite," I tease, and then he sinks his fingers into me, making me moan as if to prove a point.

"Yeah, I am," he says, sliding his fingers slowly out of me, then back in again. "I'm a hypocrite, because my body is so fucking hungry for you I can't sleep. Because at night, I get so hard that I need to get myself off to the memory of the taste of you. How good it felt to make you say my name."

His breathing is ragged, and the look in his eyes is wild as he sinks his fingers into me again, the pace growing faster.

"Do you like that?" he asks darkly. "That your pussy is so good that it's the only thing I think about when I get off? That it gets me so hard I can't sleep?"

"Yes," I gasp.

"God, Maren," he moans, pulling his body closer to mine. The look in his eyes is glazed, like he's losing himself in me, not even fully here anymore. "I love the way you sound when you come. I never want anyone else to hear that sound, unless I'm the one doing it to you."

I smile, and my breath catches as his fingers slip deeper into me.

"You're a long way off from that," I say.

"Let me earn it."

His thumb finds my clit, and I gasp as I feel his fingers curl inside me, hitting my G-spot.

"Oh, God," I groan.

"I love making you feel good," he murmurs into my hair, pulling me close. He kisses my ear, my neck, my collarbone. I gasp as his teeth run over that spot again, making the pleasure from his hands ripple through me, richer and deeper.

"Yes," I gasp, bringing my hand to the back of his neck again, pressing him into me. "More. Harder."

"Mare—"

He pulls away, his eyes searching mine. His fingers stop moving inside me, and I groan in frustration.

"There are things you don't know," he says finally. "Things about your wolf nature. Things about this. I don't feel right—"

"I don't care," I say, pulling his body closer to mine. "Please. Just make me feel good."

"That spot on your neck—"

I shake my head. "I don't care right now. Don't tell me, show me."

He brings his mouth back to my neck again and begins kissing me there, in the exact spot that always makes me go wild. His fingers start up again and I gasp, my hips instinctively rocking towards him to take more.

"You want me to bite you here," he says against the skin, and I can feel the tension and heat and desire in his voice. "Your wolf wants me to bite you. I'm not going to. But I'm going to use it to make you feel good, okay?"

"Yeah, okay," I say breathlessly, pulling him closer to my body. "Whatever, I don't care."

He lowers his mouth to the place and kisses me furiously, the scruff of his stubble brushing against the skin in a way that sends shivers through my body. I feel his teeth brush over the spot and almost cry out. It feels so *good*—slick and sensitive and wild, the combination of rough and soft sending ripples of sensation through my body. At the response in me, he tenses, and I feel the hardness of his cock pressing against my thigh. Slowly, deliberately, he brushes his teeth against me again, nipping at it. He's not biting hard—just tugging at the skin between his teeth, lightly enough not to break the skin. But at the feeling of it, and the low, animalistic growl of pleasure he lets out as he does it to me, I feel myself tighten.

He's right, I realize. I *want* him to bite. I want, somehow, just for a moment, to let him have me.

"Oh, God, Seb," I say, my hips rocking against him, the words coming from me almost unintelligible. "Please, God, yes. That feels so good. More. Oh my God, more."

His fingers move faster, pumping harder, and I feel him groaning against my neck, pressing his body into me. The pleasure inside me coils and tightens, and as his thumb works my clit it crashes around me, my climax rocking through my body so hard that it's all I can do to hold on to him to keep myself above water.

He slips his fingers out of me and puts his hands on my hips, as if to steady himself.

"Oh my God," I say, tugging at the waistband of his shorts. "If *that* was the warm-up—"

"Mare," he groans, catching my wrists. "I'm not gonna... We can't have sex tonight."

"What?"

"No, not because I don't want to, but—" He hesitates, and I

can see something tortured in his gaze. "It wouldn't be fair. The things you don't know..."

"Didn't you hear me?" I ask, placing a hand on the back of his neck. "I don't care about that. Come on, let's have this..."

But he shakes his head, looking intently into my eyes. He pulls himself close to me, and I can feel his hardness pressing against my thigh.

"I'm not going to fuck you tonight," he murmurs into my ear, "because when I do, I'll have earned it. But tonight, I want to give you what you deserve. I want to finish what I started. Okay?"

The mind is hazy, and I nod wordlessly.

"Sit up on the edge," he orders, and I nod, putting my hands on the edge of the rock to lift myself out of the water. The humid summer air suddenly feels cool to my skin, and I glance over my shoulder.

"What if someone sees?" I ask, but he shakes his head.

"They won't. No one comes here in the evenings. And if they do—" He grins, the gaze in his eyes wicked. "Let them. I don't care if people know what I get to do to you."

Pleasure, slick and molten, runs down my spine, and I nod. His hands come up to my bathing suit, hanging halfway down my waist, and he pulls it down.

"Lift your hips for me," he says as he pulls the fabric down to my ass. I do as told, and he groans appreciatively.

"Good girl," he murmurs, and I watch as his gaze falls to the space between my legs, his breath growing deeper. "*Agaayu*, you look so good for me. Your pussy is so pretty," he says, bringing his hands up to run his thumbs over the lips. "Even better than I remembered."

My hands reach for his head, running through his hair.

"Yes, good," he murmurs. "Now lie back for me and let me take care of you."

I do, lying down onto the soft grass along the edge of the

spring. I feel his arms loop around my thighs, and he gently pulls me closer to him so my ass is resting on the edge of the rock. He brings his mouth to my lips, gently kissing along the seam between them, and then he slips the edge of his tongue up to my clit.

I gasp, my head falling back and my legs spreading open wider for him. His tongue works circles around my clit, and I feel him bring his fingers up to my entrance, slipping them inside me again. The sensation is immediate and overwhelming, and my hands grasp at his hair for something to hold onto.

"Good," he murmurs, slipping his fingers in and out. "You do such a good job for me."

I moan and pant as he brings his mouth back to my clit, and then his fingers start to work faster, finding a cadence that makes my mind go hazy. The sensation changes as he closes his mouth around my clit, sucking gently. My climax is closer to the surface now that I've already come once, and I can hear my moans start to grow louder and higher in pitch. My hips grind up towards him, and I feel his arm clamp harder around my thighs to hold me in place, the pressure only making the sensation better, headier, more overpowering.

"Oh, God," I cry out, my hands letting go of his head and reaching up instinctively for my breasts, my body, my hair, anything. "Oh my God, Seb."

He murmurs appreciatively, and I feel the sound of it and the sense of his pleasure ripple through my body.

"Seb," I say again, and his fingers work faster, making careful work of me. "Oh my God, Seb. I'm close."

"Good," he says, pulling his mouth away to look up at me. "Good job, *eijtna*. You're doing such a good job for me. Will you come for me?"

As he brings his mouth back down to me, I feel more than just my own pleasure—I feel his, his appreciation and praise washing over me, his desire swirling through me and around me.

I feel it all crashing again, sparking at the surface of my skin. And then I'm coming, crying out for him again and again, his name on my lips.

"Seb, Seb. Oh my God, Seb."

As I come down, I look up to see him lifting himself from the water's edge, coming to lie beside me. His hardness strains against the green fabric of his swim trunks, and I reach for it instinctively. He pushes my hands out of the way.

"Please," I whine, and he smiles, shaking his head.

"When we do that, I'll deserve it," he says again.

"What does that even mean? Don't you want to come?" I ask, my voice still soft and hazy through the cloud of my own pleasure.

He shakes his head. "I want to kiss you."

I blink and then nod, gently tilting my head up towards his. He brings his mouth down to mine, and our lips come together, soft and tender.

I can still taste myself on him, and I feel the brush of his stubble against my chin, the contrast between hard and soft sending a shiver of delight over me. I pull myself closer. I feel *him*, somehow, the essence of him in this: steady, purposeful, intense. He kisses me like he's proving something; like he's staking a claim, making a promise.

As he pulls away, the look in his eyes is serious, and I find myself made strangely breathless by it. Again, that uncomfortable feeling blossoms under my skin; something close to tenderness.

"What does *eijtna* mean?" I ask.

"Hm?"

"*Eijtna*. You called me it the other day, and then again now. The guy at the beach did, too, before you came to help me."

He clears his throat and looks away. "It's like sweetheart. He doesn't get to call you that."

"Do you?"

His eyes come up to mine again, and I feel all of it—all his intensity in me.

"I don't know. That's up to you, I guess."

I'm the one who clears my throat now, trying to ease this.

"See?" I ask, looking away from him and up at the branches above us.

"Hm?"

"I told you we'd have fun if we came here."

28

MAREN

"You did *what*?" Em whispers, her eyes growing wide. She looks over the top of the car to make sure Seb hasn't come out yet. "*Ayagayuuni*. Was it good? Wait, no, ew. Don't answer that."

"It was *so* good. Better than anything I've had in a long time," I whisper, and glance over my shoulder, too. "It's not the first time, either. Something happened during Fire Week."

She hits my arm playfully. "*Agaayu!* Why didn't you tell me?"

"I don't know. I was still feeling it out."

"So are you two a thing now? Are you together?"

I shake my head. "No, it's casual. We're just spending time together. It doesn't mean anything."

"Does Seb know that?"

My memory flashes back to the hot springs, three days ago now. *You're a long way off from that*, I'd said. And he said, *Let me earn it.*

"Yeah, I'm sure," I say. "I mean, he has to, right?"

We hear the front door to the *fikarig* slam closed, and I look up to see Seb walking down the front steps, his gait slightly more even than a few days back.

"You ready?" he asks. "Em, are you coming after all?"

"No, I just wanted to see you guys off. I wish I could come, but since I've officially passed my exams—" At this, a little *eek* from me, even though I've known for days. "—I have my first rounds later today. I'm sorry, they started earlier than I thought. Please say hey to Andreas for me!"

"I will. And good luck!" I pull Em to my chest in a quick hug, then open the passenger seat to get in the car. As Seb gets in, too, I glance over at his leg.

"Do you want me to drive?"

He shakes his head. "Nah, I'm good. You're on DJ duty."

I smirk, pulling my phone out of my back pocket. "You're gonna wish you hadn't said that."

"Somehow I'm regretting it already," he mutters as some 00's hip hop blasts from my phone speaker.

I look up at the driveway and wave goodbye to Em as Seb peels out of the driveway. He takes a left, and we pull into the main road to disappear into the woods.

THE DRIVE TAKES ABOUT AN HOUR, and I spend the first half introducing Seb to 00's rap, which he pretends to tolerate. By the time we pass the low mountains, we've transitioned from Ludacris to Omarion, to Bow Wow to the *Like Mike* soundtrack, and he finally asks for a break. In the silence, the space between us grows languid and easy. I watch as the forest turns to bright green fields, and low mountains appear in the distance.

The sun is out in full force today, beaming onto the car and seemingly warming me from the inside. After a while, Seb rolls down the windows to let the breeze in, but it does nothing to detract from the warm, rich scent of him, which fills the car and seems to have taken up permanent residence somewhere on my neck since that night at the hot springs.

"I'm glad your leg is starting to feel better," I say after a while, keeping my eyes on the road before us. "I guess the rest has been helping."

He nods silently.

"You're working out less than you were," I try, after a minute of silence.

"Are you telling me I'm getting soft?"

"No, I—" I look over. "You didn't work out, after the last trip to the springs?"

I see the corner of his mouth turn up, and he glances over. "You're asking if I worked off the scent of you."

"Yeah. I went running that night. I thought—"

He shakes his head, and the look on his face is casual, easy. "I have nothing to hide."

Something flickers in my chest. I take a second to tune in: my wolf, sitting up.

Down, girl.

"You don't mind if the others know?" I ask.

"I have nothing to hide," he says again.

I swallow and pull out my phone again. A few seconds later, the sound of 12-year-old Bow Wow's rap fills the car.

A HALF HOUR LATER, we reach the cobblestone streets of another town. Seb asks me to help with navigation, and within a few minutes we're nearing a set of three large buildings, arranged into a C-shape. The buildings on either side are long, painted red shiplap. The center building looks oldest, made of stone with a thatch roof. Seb parks the Jeep on the gravel before one of the side buildings, next to two other cars. The rest of the area seems basically deserted.

I climb out of the front seat of the car to see someone

crossing the lot.

"*Morlaa'!*"

A middle-aged man with thinning red hair walks towards us. He's dressed in what I'm starting to think of as the Fakari Old Guy Uniform: worn light wash jeans, hiking boots, and a dark Fakari sweater over a button shirt. He comes up to us and grabs Seb's hand, shaking firmly.

"*Heij*, it's nice to meet you," Seb says. "You must be Andreas. I'm Em's *fikalid*, Seb. Thanks so much for taking the time to meet with us."

"Oh, of course. Any friend of Emerson's is a friend of ours. And you are?" He turns to me and extends his hand to shake.

"I'm Maren. I'm also in their *fika*, sort of. I just moved here. I'm Saga Taguit's niece, if you know her?"

"You moved here! From...?"

"Uh, it's complicated. How much time do you have?"

I laugh, but he doesn't seem to register that it's a joke, so after an awkward second I keep talking.

"My dad was Fakari, but I grew up on the mainland," I add. "I moved here in May. But that's why Em suggested we come here—I'm trying to get a better sense of the history of the islands. And Seb here has been talking about the old salt rituals, so we wanted to come by and ask you some questions."

"Right. Well, we don't have much about the oldest salt rituals, I'm afraid, beyond a handful of artifacts. But I'll do my best to answer any questions you have. Why don't you tell me a little more about what you're interested in?"

"Yeah, okay." I nod, feeling the patter of my heartbeat in my chest. "Um, I'm really curious about the history of outside influence on the Fakaris. When did people from other countries first immigrate here? Or try to?"

He laughs. "I thought you were interested in learning about Fakari history."

"That *is* Fakari history, right?" I glance over at Seb, as though to confirm.

"Yes, yes, of course," Andreas says, waving a hand. "I just mean, Fakari *culture*. Well, alright. There were several waves of European immigration. There was already some Viking presence here by the year 1000, and for the most part, they seem to have integrated into Fakari life. Starting in the early 1500s, there were several failed European attempts to colonize the islands by Dutch, Danish, and English settlers. The last of those groups left in the mid-1700s, and we've remained successfully independent ever since."

"Do you have any artifacts from that time?" I ask.

"Which time?"

I shrug. "I... I don't know. I guess I'm hoping for writings from the settlers."

His eyes crinkle at the corners, and I can't help but feel that somehow I'm not in on the joke.

"Not here, no," he says. "Again, this is the *Fakari* history and culture museum. We had a small exhibition a few years ago, but there wasn't much interest. If you're interested in settler history, I believe there's a small archive on Fajje."

I swallow. The patter of my heart has gotten faster, and I can feel some kind of adrenaline in my throat.

"Sorry, I don't want to waste your time—" I say, but Seb cut's in.

"You're not wasting anyone's time," he says, his voice kind but firm. "Andreas, maybe you could show us what you *do* have in the collection when it comes to the salt rituals."

"Yes, of course." Andreas smiles, and his eyes flicker back to me before he turns around. "Come, follow me."

He gestures towards the museum, and the two of us follow him towards the front doors. I reach to cross my arms over my chest, but Seb's hand finds mine and clasps it gently. I swallow as

I feel his thumb run over the back of my palm. As we near the front doors, I look up at him.

"It's fine," he says quietly. "We'll make it worth the trip. Promise."

I nod. Once inside, the curator leads us through a maze of glass displays, towards a staircase at the back. As we pass by the display cases, I admire artifacts of old Fakari life—traditional embroidered dresses, an old wooden boat, and little dolls before old ceramics. We follow Andreas down the stairs, and he takes us into another large room, this one darker, the glass display cases lit with soft, low light. He leads us to a cabinet towards the end of the hall, and gestures to a collection of old wooden bowls with carvings etched along the outer rim. The wood is dark and warped; I can see a small split in one of them, cracking it down the center.

"These are the oldest artifacts we have attesting to Fakari salt traditions. These bowls were used for the salt rituals preparing people for major life milestones. We know from the *Eijna* there was a coming-of-age ritual around the age of fifteen, as well as a ritual before claiming someone as your mate. Both of those traditions are lost to time, but the carvings on these bowls show us that they were happening as late as the 1500s."

"Right, okay," I say, thinking. "And, um... Can you remind me when the *Eijna* is from?"

"The writings themselves are from the 13th century, but they likely reflect an oral tradition that goes back further than that."

"So... that's after the Vikings, but before the other countries came here," I say.

"Yes, correct."

I look at the little wooden bowls for a minute, trying to gather my thoughts. So the lost salt rituals in the *Eijna* disappeared somewhere between the 13th century and now.

"What about the elder rite ritual?" I ask. "Do you have anything about that?"

"Oh, yes, of course. The elder rite is the most elaborate ritual we had on the Fakaris. We have a number of artifacts attesting to its history."

He leads us further down the corridor and shows us a large display on the left, featuring a beaded and embroidered outfit, a dozen bowls of different sizes, and something that looks like an old tin tea kettle.

"We don't know exactly how it used to be practiced, but there was once at least a seven-stage ritual to prepare. You can see the different bowls here. One of them shows the remains of charcoal, but we don't know exactly what it was used for."

"What's the latest you have about it in writing?" I ask.

"Describing the rituals? Nothing after the *Eijna*," Seb interjects next to me. "The ancestors thought it was bad luck to put any of it in writing. Right?"

The curator makes a face, as though it's a little more complicated than that, but he nods.

"So they could have lasted for a long time," I say. "They could have overlapped with the periods of colonization that you mentioned, Andreas. Maybe the settlers wrote about it."

"Overlapped in *time*, yes," Andreas says. "But culturally, there was barely any contact between groups. The Fakari people had to stay isolated for our own safety. It's unlikely any settlers would have come close enough to Fakari culture to truly experience it."

"Do you know for sure?"

Andreas furrows his brow. "Almost certainly. Very few foreigners even made it past Fajje. And we've found very few Fakari artifacts on that island. They were isolated until they were forcibly removed."

My mouth twists, and I chew on the inside of my lip.

"Do you have other questions about the salt, or the elder rite?" he asks.

"There is one other thing, actually," I say. "Um, my aunt Saga was telling me when I came here that you have a stockpile of ancient salt, made the old way, that you still use for rituals."

He nods, waiting. Suddenly, I feel stupid that I haven't asked about this before.

"When was that stockpile made?"

"Over about a fifty year period. They stopped adding to it in the 1750s."

I blink. "Around the time the last settler group left?"

He nods.

"Is that connected?"

He sighs, his voice betraying his impatience. "Did the settlers have any impact on the stockpiling of salt? No, of course not."

"Why were they saving it?" I ask.

"There was a storm coming," Seb says from beside me. "We don't know how they knew in advance, but they knew it would interfere with their ability to make salt for a while."

"But so... " The gears in my brain are churning now, and I feel a spark of excitement somewhere in my gut. "That last wave of settlers might conceivably have had some interaction with the people who were stockpiling the salt."

I see his mouth tense. "Again, that's highly unlikely. They were culturally completely separate."

"Unlikely, but possible."

"Theoretically, yes."

I nod. "Okay. Were there any Fakari people living on Fajje at the time of the last settler group? You said there were some artifacts found there."

He shrugs. "Some. A very small number. There was a difficulty with growing crops in that period, so more people had moved here even before the settlers left."

"So they *could* have interacted."

He lets out a sharp exhale, and I see the annoyance register in his features.

"If you'd like to learn more about the settler periods, I'm

afraid I can't do much to help you. That isn't my specialty. Nor that of anyone at this museum, unfortunately. There's an archive on Fajje with some records from the monastery, from before the 1500s. And I know—"

He hesitates.

"Hm?" I ask.

He sighs. "It's probably not worth your time. But there's a little house museum there—I wouldn't even really consider it a museum, really, it's more of a hobby project—that focuses on a small gathering of settler history artifacts. It's more of a curiosity, really. I believe it's an old woman with a curio cabinet of family artifacts that she's set up in the living room. It's not much. But if that's *really* what you're interested in, it's worth a try."

"Okay, thank you." I turn to Seb and swallow. "I mean, it's a long shot. But those records could show you a side of Fakari history that the people here didn't think to write down."

Andreas glances at his watch, then looks up. "I'm afraid my lunch period is over soon, and I have a meeting at one. You're welcome to stay, but I can't show you around much longer. Is there anything else I can help you with?"

"No, I think that's everything. Thanks again so much for your help," Seb says, his tone firm and polite.

Andreas nods and walks past us, towards the stairs at the back of the room. We wait until he's out of earshot.

"Are you okay?" Seb asks, his voice low.

"Yeah, I'm fine. He was a little condescending, but it's whatever."

"He was more than a little condescending. He totally dismissed your questions."

"Really, it's okay."

"It's *not* okay," he says, putting his hand on my arm. I feel the heat of it warming me through my shirt.

"No one should talk to you that way," he says.

"I mean, you did. What is this, an apology tour?" I try to keep the humor in my voice, but a thread of vulnerability seems to find its way in. I clear my throat, looking away.

"Maren..." His other hand comes up to my arm. "I'm sorry. Your ideas matter. And this one—it's good. Seriously."

I want to trust him, and something in his voice feels safe. But this is still too new—too fast.

"We should go to Fajje," I say, straightening to look him in the eye. "We can talk to that lady. You never know."

"Yeah, okay. But let's just... slow down for a second."

I swallow. *No.*

"Why?"

"Because you're sad."

"I'm not."

"Don't lie to me," he says gently. "I can feel you."

I sigh again and shrug his hands off of me. "I'm just... I'm frustrated, okay? I *know* you all think I don't I belong here, and my ideas suck, and the very *idea* of any mainland Fakari crossover is *so laughable*—"

"You *do* belong here."

"Okay, but what changed?" I ask, crossing my arms and shrugging his hands away. "Is it because we're hooking up now? Because a few weeks ago you were telling me I was already halfway out the door."

He stares at me for a long time, and the look in his eyes is careful, pensive.

"Can I show you something?" he asks.

29

SEB

We pull up a few hours later, and the sun is hanging low in the sky, the hour close to dusk. Maren steps out of the car, looking up and around at the trees above us. Her shoulders are easier now; we spent a little more time at the museum, and then had lunch nearby before we headed this way. I step out of the front seat, too, and close the front door of the Jeep behind me.

"Where are we?" she asks. Her eyes fall on the front of the building before us. "Is this another common house?"

"No. This is the temple."

She looks over, her brown eyes gleaming in the light. Curiosity flickers over her face.

"Come," I say, walking over to her. "Let me show you."

We walk together towards the wooden front steps, and I lead her to the side, where the logbook lies open in the little niche in the wall.

"These are *loter*," I say, reaching for a handful. I lift a few out of the cup, then open my hand for her to see them up close. "We burn them before the gods so they hear our prayers. When you come here, you write your name in the logbook, alongside how many *loter* you take. They reach out to you once a month for the charge."

I reach for the pen and write my name in the book.

"There's not a lot of names in here," Maren says, looking over my shoulder at the book. "None I recognize, anyway."

"Not a lot of people practice the old religion anymore. Most peoples' practice revolves around the ancestors." I put the pen down.

"So why not you?"

"You'll see," I say. "Come on. Let me show you."

I lead her through the heavy front doors, and we enter the hall.

"Take off your shoes," I say quietly. "We have to cleanse our feet."

She does as told, slipping off her shoes and following my lead as I dip my feet in the selenite basin. I reach for a towel on the rack beside, and watch as she dries herself off. Then I reach for her hand and lead her through the entrance to the main part of the temple.

I feel her energy still as we step into the main room. The golden glow of candlelight washes over us.

"My dad used to take me here," I say. "This is where he taught me to pray. This is where he taught me about the ancestors. About the islands."

I swallow and look over at her.

"About you."

Her brow furrows as she looks at me. "Me?"

I nod, and gently tug her hand as I lead her to the statues up front.

"Here. This is Tinnúr, god of peace and stability," I say. "He would take me here every week, and we'd light *loter* for your dad to find peace and prosperity in his new home. Like this."

I reach out and dip one of my *loter* into the oil before the statue, then lift it up to the flame.

"Gracious Tinnúr, champion of peace," I say—in English, for Maren's sake. "We ask for your protection and care over the spirit of Maren's father, David. May he be at rest in full unity with the ancestors."

We watch as the smoke curls up towards the wooden statue.

Maren reaches for my hand and grabs another *lot*, dipping it in the oil and raising it to the flame.

"And for Seb's father, Filip, too," she adds.

The wolf in my chest reacts to her words in a way I don't know how to explain. We stand there for a minute, watching the smoke for our fathers' memories curl around each other. Something hurts and feels hopeful at the same time.

"We prayed here for you," I say quietly. "I didn't know you by name then. But we prayed for David and his wife and daughter."

"Always here? At this statue?"

I shake my head. "Sometimes in front of Keijgur. We used to ask for David to come home, in the beginning. And then, after he died, I think my dad asked for justice for you. For the rest of your family to come around you and help, so you would grow up with community."

She shakes her head. "They didn't. It was just me and my mom, for years. She wanted it that way. Which one is Keijgur?"

I nod in the direction of his niche, and we walk towards it together.

"This one. He's the god of justice. I spent a lot of time here after my dad died. Even more after my failed rite. I did a consecration to him."

"What does that mean?"

I shrug. "It's like a special devotion. You abstain from earthly pleasures for three months and do special fasts and prayers. In theory, you make yourself available for that god to use in the world to achieve their aims."

"And in practice?" she asks.

I shrug. "If I'm really honest with myself, I don't think it was about that for me."

"What was it about?"

I look up at the wooden statue, eyeing the sharp cuts of his face.

"I just wanted justice for myself," I say. It's the first time I've admitted that out loud, and I feel the heat of shame in my chest at the same time as relief. And then she surprises me, her hand reaching for mine.

"Do you want to say any prayers to him today?" she asks.

I hesitate, then shake my head. "No. I think I'm good."

She turns to look up at me. The candlelight in the temple washes over her face, painting her soft, round features gold.

"You prayed here for me," she says quietly.

I nod. "For years."

She swallows and looks around the room.

"Tell me about the other gods."

I nod and lead her through the hall, stopping one by one before each statue.

"This is Móra, the moon goddess, and her brother Toreijet, god of the sun. As kids, we prayed to him for good summer weather."

She smiles, and I point across the hall. "There's Eisja, goddess of snow, ice, and war; she's Tinnúr's wife. You know Beiyyur, the harvest god, from Fire Week. And the empty niche is for his wife Núra, the goddess of fire, death, and rebirth. Fakari temples always keep that one empty. In the legends—"

"Oh, I know this one," she says, dropping my hand and bringing hers together in front of her chest. "She betrayed him, right? So the other gods kicked her out and she had to leave the islands."

"Right."

"That's weird, that they still keep a niche for her."

I shrug. "They say it's so we don't forget what she did, but some people still pray to her. Saga, actually. She's one of the only people I know who does."

Maren's energy stills, and she looks to the last statue in the room.

"And who's that?" she asks quietly.

I swallow. "That's Fjarayya."

"Goddess of plants and love," she says, and I nod.

She looks up to meet my eyes.

"Why did you take me here?" she asks.

I clear my throat. "I owe you answers. I... I treated you badly. And I need you to know it's not your fault."

She stares at me, waiting.

"Our dads were kids in the same *fika* together," I say. "Did you know that?"

She shakes her head.

"They grew up as best friends. As close as brothers, like me and Gabe," I say finally. "My mom and dad were mates, but I think, in some ways, my dad was closer to David than my mom. From what I've heard, once David left, my dad was never the same. I remember stories about how they were together, but I never got to know the version of my dad. I only knew the version of him who got left behind when David left."

Her mouth twists in what looks like sympathy.

"He got sick when I was in high school. Cancer. Not anything any of us could do something about." I swallow, then look up to her. "But my mom always said she thought it was the loneliness eating away at him. When he got sicker, he eventually kind of lost touch with reality. He'd talk to Viggo or Saga, thinking it was David. Cooking up all these wild ideas about how they'd open up the islands, bring a whole new stage of life to the Fakaris. It was the only time I ever got a taste of the person he was before."

I feel her hand find mine, our fingers clasping together.

"I was alone with him, the morning he died," I say quietly.

"He looked me right in the eyes and told me, 'David's here. He's taking me home.' A half hour later, he was gone."

"Oh, Seb," she says quietly.

I clear my throat, trying to wring out the sound of grief.

"I wasn't supposed to grow up without him," I say finally. "And after he died, I... I blamed your dad for killing him, as stupid as it sounded. Not in that moment, but all those years before, when he left. All I could think about was the way the loss had eaten away at him, how everyone said he'd had so much more life before David left. We're *pakka*—we're supposed to be pack animals. David and my dad had planned to share a *fikarig* together, along with Saga and the others. And once David left, he never got over the loss. I imagined that, if your dad hadn't left and they'd been able to share pack life, it might have ended differently. So when you showed up..."

She swallows, and I meet her eyes.

"You're not temporary," I say finally. "But I think I was guarding myself."

"I'm so sorry about your dad," she says. "I know how it is to grow up without someone who should be there."

She looks at her feet for a long time, and I can tell she's trying to find the words for something.

"Saga told me a little bit about my dad, on the night I found out I was... *pakka*," she says finally. "She told me how hard it is to be away from your *fika*, and she said the loss was killing him. She thought that was part of the reason, maybe, that my mom hid my shifter nature from me. So I wouldn't have to experience that."

I nod. "It's why they closed the islands again."

Her brow furrows, and she looks up at me. "What?"

"Our dads worked together to try to usher in a new chapter of Fakari history," I say. "They fought together to open up the islands. For the first time in hundreds of years, people were able to travel here. That's how David met your mom, and that's when they started the new *fika* with my parents and Saga and the others. But—I mean, I wasn't there, but from what I've heard from the elders—once your mom knew she was pregnant, she didn't want to raise you here. They left for the mainland so you could have a more normal life. Mainland-normal."

"So what happened?"

I shake my head. "I don't know everything. None of them talk about it so explicitly—I think it hurts too much. But the *fikaband* is really strong, once it's formed. From what I can tell, being separated from each other was hurting all of them. Saga said once that your dad was spending a lot more time in wolf form, to try to feel more connected to them. But then, when he was shot..."

I can see the pain in her features, and I bring my hand up to her face.

"It brought an end to everything," I say. "My dad considered the whole thing a failed experiment. He said opening the islands caused way more pain than anything else. They shut down everything but Halssel to visitors."

She blinks. "So our dads fought to open the islands. And in the end, it killed them both."

I shake my head. "Maybe. I saw it that way, once."

"I'm so sorry. I wish it had been different."

I swallow and lean my forehead against hers.

"I think maybe it gets to be different," I say quietly. "I spent years wishing we could go back in time and undo the mistakes of the past. That's not possible. But the *agaayit* brought you here. We can't rewrite the past, but maybe they're giving us a chance to write a different future than our parents did. Together."

She looks up at me, her eyes wide and soft and vulnerable.

"Yeah. Maybe," she whispers.

I lean down to kiss her, our lips pressing together. She smells like honey and warmth and—my wolf growls happily at the realization—a little bit like me. I kiss her intently, trying to say the things I can't bring to words yet.

You're my mate. Please, stay.

I pull back, shoving the words down.

"Let me take you to Fajje," I say, looking at her. "We'll make a trip of it. I want to go to that house museum and test your theory. Maybe the settler records can give us new insight into the salt traditions. And if not, it'll just be a vacation."

"Okay," she says, and I see a smile tug at her lips.

"I wasn't fair to you," I say. "Let me make it up to you."

She cocks an eyebrow. "That stuff at the hot spring was a pretty good start."

I grin. "So you want to go swimming tonight?"

She steps closer to me, putting an arm around my waist. "Maybe. But we have one more *lot* to burn."

I look down into my hand and realize she's right.

"Any requests?"

She takes it from my hand wordlessly, then crosses the temple. I watch as she dips it into the oil in front of Fjarayya and lifts it to the flame. She closes her eyes, and as she lifts up a silent prayer, I look to the statue and do the same.

Help me win her trust, I ask. And when we're on Fajje… help me find the words.

30

SEB

I hear a soft rap of knuckles against my door frame.

"*Heij.* What are you up to?"

I look up to see Gabe leaning against the door, and instantly shut my laptop.

"Nothing. What's up?"

He raises his eyebrow and stares at me silently for a minute. Reluctantly, I open the screen again.

"Looking at hotels in Fajje. There's next to nothing."

"Big surprise," he says, walking in and sitting on my bed. "With a tagline like 'the island of death,' it's not exactly a tourist hot spot. How long are you guys staying?"

"I don't know. Two nights, maybe? I'm not sure how long it'll take to find what Maren's looking for, if they even have it."

He says nothing, and after a second I turn my chair around to face him.

"So. Things are better between the two of you, huh?" he asks.

I shrug. "I'm doing my best."

"It seems like it's working, if your state after you came back from swimming last night was any indication."

I set my teeth as I try to figure out what I can say. The two of us went swimming together again last night. *And then some.*

"We're not..." I hesitate. "I'm not sleeping with her yet, if that's what you're asking. It doesn't feel right if she doesn't know."

"That you're mates?"

I look over my shoulder and reach over to shut the bedroom door, then lower my voice.

"Yeah. I don't even think she'd know what that meant if I told her."

"Have you tried?"

I shake my head again. "We *just* started actually talking. I don't think that would go over well."

"I don't know about that."

"What do you mean?"

"I think she's looking for a reason to stay. A way to prove she belongs."

"She does belong."

His eyebrows raise, and I see a sardonic look in his eye. "That was quick."

I roll my eyes. "Whatever, dude. Why are you here again?"

"I just wanted to see how things were after that night on the beach."

I wince, remembering. "Yeah. I don't know what happened."

"You don't?"

I shrug. "I felt her through the *fikaband*, I guess. I came to help."

"You know we don't feel her like that, right?"

My brow furrows. "You don't?"

"No. I mean, I feel her presence, kind of. But not the way I feel you or Em, or Kieran, even. You say she belongs, but I don't think she knows that yet. And I don't think she'll really be part of the *fika* until she does."

At that, I feel a small tug in my chest.

"So why do *I* feel her, then? If it's not the *fikaband*?"

"The mate bond?" he asks.

I shake my head. "No. We haven't claimed each other."

He shrugs. "Your situation is different. You knew she was your mate before you made the choice to claim her. I don't know anyone who's had that story. Maybe..."

"You think you can form a mate bond with someone without marking them?"

He shrugs. "What do I know? I'm the last person to ask."

His voice is glum, and for a second, it gives me pause. Gabe's never shown interest in anyone, and I make it a point to stay out of other people's business. And yet...

"What's... been going on with you lately?" I ask.

He shrugs again. "Same old, same old. Nothing ever really changes. Selling your salt on Halssel. Cooking. Working on my dad's old place."

I nod. Ben Taguit died more than a decade before my dad did, and left his old cabin to Gabe in the will.

"Yeah, you've been gone more lately. Is that what you've been up to? The cabin?"

He nods. "Yeah, I guess. I finished installing the wood-burning stove just before we went to Halssel. I try to spend some time there most weekends. It's nice to have something that's just mine."

"Does Saga know?"

"That that's where I am when I disappear?" He shakes his head. "Nah. We never talk about Dad. I mean, she knows he left it to me. But I don't even think she knows I've been to visit since he died."

"What, she thinks it's just rotting away in the woods?"

He shrugs. "I don't think she lets herself think about it at all."

I nod, thinking of Saga—of the grief that permeates so much

of this house. There's a reason Gabe and I never talk about Ben unless we're alone. Even Em doesn't know about his old cabin, and she's lived here for over a decade.

"Well. You should take us sometime to see what you've done with the place. Maybe we can spend a weekend there or something."

"Yeah, I don't know." He shrugs. "It's tighter quarters than the Halluk house, for sure."

"That's not a big deal. What else are you saving it for?"

He gets a weird look in his eyes and stands up. "I should get going. Good luck finding a hotel. Maybe there's a bed and breakfast somewhere."

I want to ask if he's okay, but I can't find the words. Instead, what comes out is,

"Yeah, okay. See you later."

ABOUT AN HOUR LATER, I hear Maren's footsteps on the stairs, and her bedroom door open and shut. I get up slowly from my desk, using my arms to help push; my leg's been better these past few days, but it's still nagging at me. I make my way from my room to hers, and knock on the door.

"Yeah?"

"It's me. Uh, Seb. Can I...?"

"Yeah, okay."

I swing the door open to find her lying on her bed, turned onto her side. She looks up at me with a glum expression on her face.

"What's up?" she asks, her voice flat.

"I figured out some details for our trip. I just wanted to fill you in. What's... What's wrong?"

I watch as she swallows, her mouth twisting like she's fighting herself.

"It's nothing."

"It looks like something."

She sighs.

"I've been avoiding my email for the past couple weeks," she says finally. "I made the mistake of opening it today, and read a couple emails from my mom. It's…"

Her voice trails off, and I hear a choked noise at the back of her throat. Instantly, the wolf in my chest sits up.

"I'm fine," she says finally, but she blinks quickly, and I watch as her chin quivers.

"What did she say?" My voice comes out harder than I mean it to.

"Nothing she hasn't said before. It doesn't matter."

"It matters to me." I step inside, walking over to her bed and squatting on the ground next to it. "What happened?"

"She reached out to her contact at Puur and heard I haven't gotten back to them with a story or a deal. I haven't missed a deadline or anything, but she just…"

Maren shakes her head, her dark curls bouncing around her face.

"She says I'm irresponsible. She says I'm just proving that I haven't grown, and I never will. That I need her help to get my life together. And you know what? Maybe I do. I mean, look at me. I'm twenty eight years old. I have no career and no prospects. I'm basically on an extended vacation in this house, freeloading off of my aunt—"

"*Heij*—"

"—I have next to no money, I just found out I'm a fucking *werewolf* and now I have to learn to deal with that for the rest of my life. I don't—"

Her voice quivers again, and she sits up, bringing her sleeves up to wipe her eyes before her tears spill over her cheeks.

"I don't *belong* anywhere, Seb. I'm in-between everything. I don't fit."

"What do you mean?"

She shakes her head, looking away. "I grew up in America plus-sized, bisexual, multicultural, with one parent, being gaslit about who I am and where I'm from. I never, *ever* felt like I belonged. I've tried a hundred different careers and none of them made that feeling go away. And I came here hoping that I could find some piece of something—something to help me understand where I came from, how I fit into the world. Like maybe if I could learn about these salts, I'd know a little more about my dad, and I'd find something I've been missing."

"Haven't you?" I ask, and she shakes her head.

"All I've found is more questions and more things I'm not. Now I need to rebuild my whole life around a different reality. So I'm here, *trying* to learn a new language, *trying* to find a way that I can fit—"

The tears are coming harder now, and she brings her sleeves up around her face, covering her eyes. Without thinking, I climb up on the bed, sitting next to her, wrapping my arms around her. She leans over, resting her head on my shoulder, and breaks out into loud, heaving sobs.

My wolf curls up in my chest, wanting to be nearer to her. Awkwardly, I run my hand over her shoulder.

"*Heij*, it's okay," I say quietly. "You're okay."

She sniffles after a minute and sits up to look at me.

"I'm sorry, I'm a mess. You don't have to be here for this."

"No. I want to."

She looks up at me, her dark brown eyes wide and vulnerable. The golden glint in them now is getting stronger every day. I reach over and tentatively pull her hair back from her face.

"Seriously, Maren," I say quietly, looking in her eyes. "I know you think you don't belong anywhere. And I know I haven't helped with that, with the things I've said to you. But I'm an idiot. And I... I really think you do belong here. You can, if you want to."

Her lower lip disappears between her teeth as her eyes search mine.

"Yeah, maybe," she says finally. "But it'll never be easy. There's so much stuff I have to learn. My family, my history, my culture. My *body*, now that there's two versions of it. I just... Sometimes I wish I didn't have to try so hard."

I want to tell her she doesn't need to try with me, but I know better than that. Instead, I run my hand over her hair and bring it down to her waist.

"What can I make easy for you?" I ask.

She smiles at that, tilting her head away. "I don't think you can help with this."

"Let me try."

She hesitates for a moment, and then I feel her posture soften. She pulls herself closer to me, resting her head against my shoulder.

"Tell me what you found for our trip," she says quietly.

I wrap my arm around her shoulders, carefully leaning my head against hers. I've never done this before. Sex, yes. But cuddling? That's new for me, and I don't quite know where to put my arms.

"I looked at the archive in the old monastery," I say, running a hand over her arm. "But their materials are only up to the 1500s, and I think you're onto something with the later stuff, so I looked into the little house museum the guy mentioned. It's open by appointment only. I reached out and arranged a time with the owner. And I found a bed and breakfast we can stay at for a few nights, in case we need more time to find what we're looking for."

"How much is it per night?"

"Doesn't matter. It's a business expense."

I feel her head tilt upwards to look at me. "Seb Greenleaf. I never thought I'd see you spending company money on something that feels even vaguely extra."

"Yeah, well." I shrug. "Maybe I can change."

"Yeah. Maybe you can," she says quietly, and burrows her head against my chest again.

31

MAREN

We make the trip to Fajje a few days later. There are no direct ferries from Saroe, so Em drops us off at a small harbor on the eastern shore and we take a boat to Marit, then a private boat to Fajje's southern coast. We reach the harbor around four o'clock, and by then I'm thoroughly nauseous, so seasick from the ride over that it takes everything in me not to hurl onto Seb's feet as we disembark.

"Are you okay? You look pale."

"Nggh," I mumble as we step onto the dock.

"Do you need some food? I think I see a fried fish stall over there."

"Oh my God, please don't talk to me about food. *Especially* things that are fried and *especially* fish."

He nods. "I kind of thought you'd be used to boats by now."

"I'm not here for your judgment," I say, smiling faintly even as my stomach churns. "How far are we from our hotel?"

"It's about a half-hour drive. I rented us a car to use while we're here."

I nod and take a deep breath. The air smells like salt and brine, and somehow it makes me feel even worse.

"Here, let's get you off the dock. I'll figure out the car, and you can just sit on a bench for a bit while I work it out."

"Yeah, okay."

I nod and he leads me to a little bench not too far from the dock. I take a seat, and as he leaves to pick up the car, I try to get my center of gravity under me. I take a few low, deep breaths, keeping my eyes affixed on the view.

It's beautiful here—much quieter than the harbor on Saroe or even Marit. The air feels a touch cooler, but maybe that's just my imagination. Behind the harbor are low rolling hills in rich green, and I see small houses that seem almost nestled into them, their roofs covered with moss. In front of me, a quiet cobblestone street leads from the harbor through the hills, in the direction of a small town I can see part of in the far distance.

A few minutes later, my stomach has started to settle when Seb drives up to the bench in a dark gray truck.

I laugh. "Oh my God. You're driving a pick-up now?"

He raises a sardonic brow, but there's a smile pulling on the corner of his mouth.

"It was all they had. Get in."

WE DRIVE through the rolling green hills until we reach the small, historic town center. The buildings here feel a little closer here to the ones I know on Saroe—stone builds with shingled roofs, but nestled more closely together. We park behind a three-story building with a little sign hanging in front. Seb leads me inside to a charming, if dark, reception area, and I can smell soup for dinner coming from the kitchen behind.

"*Anftu'kut,*" the woman behind the counter says to Seb. "Are you checking in?"

"Yes, we have two rooms."

"Name?"

"Greenleaf," he says, setting my bag down.

The woman scans the paper logbook before her. "We only have one room for Greenleaf."

I shoot Seb a look, and he clears his throat, the color rising in his cheeks.

"Uh, it should be two. Can you check again?"

She looks down at the book. "I only see one for Greenleaf."

"Could you try Winterwood?" he asks, clearly flustered. She scans the list with her pen, and I see her eyes light up as she finds my name.

"Ah, yes! Here it is. Nevermind, two rooms total. And Winterwood has the suite?"

He clears his throat again, and if I'm not mistaken I can see visible relief wash over his face, his shoulders easing just slightly. "Uh, yeah, I think so."

"The *suite?*" I murmur, my voice teasing, but he ignores me.

"Here are your keys," the woman says, reaching for a wall of hooks behind her and grabbing two sets. "You'll be in rooms 110 and 112. This one is for the front door to the inn, and the other is for your rooms. Your fare includes breakfast; details are printed on the guide on your bedside table. Dinners aren't included, but we can add the fee to your bill. Check out on the last day is at 11."

"*Takka,*" Seb says, taking the keys from her and handing one to me. We walk towards the elevator together, and I wait for the doors to shut behind us before I say,

"You seemed pretty uneasy at the thought of us sharing a room."

He glances at me but says nothing.

"What is it?" I ask teasingly, stepping closer to him. "Do I smell bad?"

He smiles, but keeps his frame firm, his shoulders tight as I bring myself closer.

"Tell me the truth," I say, wrapping an arm around the back of his neck. "Is it the snoring?"

He rolls his eyes, but places an arm around my lower back, his frame easing slightly for me.

"*Nekka.*"

"So what is it?" I ask, pulling his face towards mine. "Don't you want to share a bed?"

"Maren." He pulls me towards him, resting his forehead against mine. The air between us changes as he brings his voice low. He swallows, and there's something vulnerable as he says,

"I just— This matters to me. I want to do this right. If we share a room, I'm going to want to do things that I shouldn't."

I feel something constrict in my chest. Behind us, the elevator doors *bing* open. I clear my throat and reach for my carry-on suitcase.

"Okay. Well, thanks for giving me the suite I guess. I'll just —"

He follows me as I walk out of the elevator.

"Hang on, I think our rooms are next to each other."

"Ha, well," I say. "That should be familiar."

"Maren—"

"I'm fine."

"*Heij.*" I feel his hand reach gently for my wrist, and my words falter. I stop and turn to face him. "Did I say something wrong?"

I stare at him for a moment. "I don't know."

"So what's up?" he steps closer. "You know it's not that I don't want you, right?" His voice lowers, and he wraps a low arm around my waist. "Because it's definitely, *definitely* not that."

"It's fine. I'm fine. Come on, we should go to our rooms."

"Are you sure?" he asks, but I nod and pull away, walking down the hall until I find the door for 112. Right next to his.

"I'm gonna get settled in and I'll see you in a bit, okay?"

"I—okay," he says. "I made us a dinner reservation at a place nearby. But if you're still feeling sick from the boat..."

I hesitate. "What is this?"

"I'm..." He swallows, running a hand through his hair. "I'm trying to do this right."

We stand there for a moment, silently staring at each other.

"We can do dinner," I say. "And I'm never gonna say no to a nice hotel room. But I don't need, like, a big sweep of romantic gestures. I liked you best when you were honest with me."

"It's not about romantic gestures."

"So what is it about? You want me, and then you don't. Or you say you do, but you can't have me, for reasons you can't explain. I thought... I thought things were changing."

My voice sounds more vulnerable than I want it to, and I hate it. Seb lets out a low breath, and I watch as his posture eases. He raises his eyes to look at me, soft and uncertain.

"I just... I'm trying to do the right thing. I don't want to sleep with you until..."

"Until what?"

"Until you know everything."

I sigh, crossing my arms. "So tell me."

"I will," he says. "I promise. I'm going to tell you everything, but I... I need it to be right."

"What does that *mean?*"

For a moment, he looks tortured. Then he drops his bags at his feet and steps forward to kiss me. In a moment, his mouth is on mine—soft and warm and tender. He pulls my body towards him and kisses me like a vow. Like a promise.

"Tomorrow morning we're going to the museum," he says, pulling away. "And then I'm taking you to the ruins. And then, I promise, I'll tell you everything."

"Why tomorrow? Why not now?"

I look into his dark eyes, searching for something I can grab onto. What I see is hesitancy, soft and vulnerable.

"Because I need time to find the words."

32

MAREN

We make it to the little home museum early the following morning. The sun is hanging low in the air, and there's a thin level of mist crawling over the hills as we walk down the narrow cobblestone streets to the museum.

"You look good," Seb says. "I like your hair like that."

I bark out a laugh. "Thanks. It's four days since wash day, so this is about as big and crazy as it gets."

He shrugs. "I like it. It feels like you."

I feel the heat creep up my neck and look at my feet as we keep going. As we reach a new area of the town—tall, narrow houses clustered together under thatched roofs—I feel something tighten in my chest, and I stop walking.

"Seb?"

"Yeah?" He turns around. "What is it?"

"I..." I bite my lip, and my voice comes out quiet. "What if this doesn't work?"

"What do you mean?"

"What if it's nothing? What if we came out here to this

remote little island because I had an idea, and it all falls apart? Will it even count as a business expense if we can't find anything?"

"Don't worry about my taxes," he says, smiling gently. "*Heij*, this isn't like you. What are you scared of?"

This is all so fast, and it's getting so serious. What if I disappoint you?

I blink, thinking. "I just... I know how much it matters to you to get to the bottom of this salt ritual stuff. We came here because I had one idea. What if it's nothing?"

He steps closer to me. "Best-case scenario, we figure out something about how they used to make the salt, and we get one step closer to making it that way ourselves. Worst-case, we're right where we started, plus a vacation. We have nothing to lose. Okay?"

"Okay," I say, nodding. Hoping that he's right.

We keep walking, and a few minutes later we reach a house on the corner of the little cobblestone street. All the houses here are old, made of brick with low, arched doors and small windows, like something out of the 1600s. This one in particular has a little green door with a metal star affixed to it. In the front window, I can see a collection of old items: a wooden doll, a globe, a silver tea set.

"Is this right?" Seb asks, looking up at the building and then back at his phone. "It says this is the address."

"The curator said it was basically a personal collection, right?"

I reach for the front door and knock.

"*Ijekommet*," we hear from inside, followed by shuffling feet.

I glance at Seb.

"She says she's coming," he says quietly.

A moment later, the door swings open to reveal a little old lady with short white hair cut to a bob.

"*Hallu! Welkommitet Neijbigmuseon!*"

Seb smiles warmly and does a little nod, and I make out

'*takka*' in his answer before he gestures towards me, saying my name mixed into a long string of Fakari words.

"Oh, from the mainland!" she says, looking brightly to me. "How wonderful. I haven't met any foreigners in years."

"She's Fakari, actually," Seb adds. "Half. But she's *pakka*."

"Ah." She looks at my eyes and nods. "Well, I'm so happy to have you both here. I'm Ingemar. Please, please, come in."

She steps back, opening the door wider for us, and Seb and I duck our heads as we enter through the low door frame and step down onto the cool black tiles of the floor of the house.

The room is dark, with antique furniture and some kind of quilt hung on a far wall above the fireplace.

"This is the old house of Richard Langdon, leader of the last major pilgrim group to come to the Fakaris," the woman says proudly. Her accent soft and lilting, and I can tell she's rehearsed this speech—even in English. "I've kept the downstairs as they would have had it when he and his wife Sarah lived here."

"It's beautiful," I say, looking at the small wooden dining table she's set up in the middle of the room, sporting a richly woven cloth on top. "How long have you lived in this house?"

"Oh, my whole life—the house has stayed in our family since that time. But I was the one who got to restoring it and making it into a community resource."

"Do you get a lot of groups who visit?" Seb asks.

"Ah, some. The primary school nearby does a trip every year. But most of the other islands don't have an interest in Fajjean history or the settler periods. You're my first appointment in a few weeks."

She smiles brightly. "But I'm very passionate about this, and I'm happy to share anything I know with you."

I lean down to admire the painted jug on the dining table, featuring an intricate Fakari pattern. Next to it is a wooden stand with what looks like an old hymnal, with an intricately embroidered fabric bookmark peeking out over the top.

"There's Fakari items here, too," I say, noting the embroidery pattern on the bookmark.

"Oh, of course. They shared the land."

I look up, my brow furrowed.

"So the groups had contact with each other?" Seb asks, filling in my question for me.

"Absolutely," she says. "Towards the end there was a lot of hostility from the Fakari people towards the settlers. But in the early period there was some collaboration and trade."

"Wait, really?"

"*Iija.* We don't like to talk about that, of course. It's much nicer to imagine keeping things neat and separate, especially in light of what happened towards the end." She smiles. "But you can't live in such close quarters without some element of community."

"What happened?" I ask.

She looks at me. "What do you mean?"

"I... I'm sorry, I just haven't heard this stuff before," I say, straightening. "I was telling Seb, I'm sure there must have been some kind of collaboration between the settlers and the Fakari people. But every single person I've spoken to—even the guy at the Fakari history museum—insisted that couldn't be true. And now you're saying there *was* some contact. How do you know?"

She shrugs. "I'm proof."

I eye her, waiting.

"My great-great-grandmother—well, my sixth great grandmother, so that's many generations—was fully Fakari, and she married one of the settlers."

I look over at Seb.

"Most of us here on Fajje are proof, even if we don't like to think so," she adds. "It's just that the others are less fortunate in knowing about their family tree. I am one of the few who is able to prove it."

"So one of your ancestors was in the last wave of settlers?"

"Yes. It's how I inherited this house. And it's why I'm so interested in all these things." She gestures around the room. "Really, it's a joy for me to have people expressing any interest. So few members of the younger generation care to learn about this part of our history."

"No, I'm *really* interested," I say, walking towards her. "I know nothing about this. Can you start at the beginning? Where were the settlers from?"

She lets out a contented little sigh, and I can see a sparkle in her eyes. Behind me, I feel Seb step closer too, to listen in.

"Well, the majority of the 1700s settler group came here from England seeking religious freedom. There was some initial fighting with the locals—we had a history here on Fajje, of course, of failed attempts to colonize. People were wary. But over time, some of the settlers endeared themselves to the Fakari people. Within a few years, they were trading with each other, and some of the settlers began forming closer relationships with the islanders. Here, see—" She gestures towards the tapestry over the hearth. "This quilt was made by Sarah Langdon, Richard's wife, as a gift for the *reijna*'s daughter. You can see that she incorporates Fakari patterns and motifs alongside her own."

"What's a *reijna*?" I ask, glancing at Seb.

"The highest-ranking woman on pack council," he answers, but Ingemar shakes her head.

"Not then. Back then, the *reijna* was the pack leader. The council system was adopted later on in Fakari history."

I step closer to the tapestry, admiring the intricate patterns along the edge. I can make out birds and branches: sweeps of wisteria and sparrows, weaving through traditional Fakari geometric patterns. In the middle is a complex scene with different areas, almost like a quilt. I can make out women sitting together in one, and another with a group of people holding hands around a fire.

"This must have taken years," I say quietly.

"It likely did," says the woman, coming up behind me. "Two or three, I estimate."

"So the period of collaboration between settlers and locals was pretty long?"

She nods. "About seven years of close collaboration and even friendship, before it ended."

"Why did it end?"

"There was an assassination attempt made on the *reijna*—a group of men, at Langdon's orders. Her son killed him in retaliation."

"Oh my God," I say, my face twisting in horror. "That's horrible. Why would they do that?"

She eyes me for a moment, as though considering something. "It's a long story."

"We have time," Seb says.

She nods. "Then, could I interest either of you in some tea?"

Twenty minutes later, we're sitting on a couch towards the back of the house. On top of the dark wooden chest in front of us, Ingemar has laid out a few framed prints and a large box of papers.

"I'm sorry, it's been a long time since anyone showed any interest in this," she says. "If I'd known you were interested in the Langdon story, rather than just wanting to tour the house, I would have taken more time to take these pieces out for you."

"It's totally fine," I say. "I'm just *so* happy to finally be able to talk to someone about this. Can I help with anything?"

"*Nekka*," she says, carefully lowering herself into the chair across from us. "Please, drink."

I pick up the teacup she's prepared for me and take a sip of peppermint-anise tea.

"So who was Richard Langdon?" Seb asks, picking up his own teacup.

"He was the leader of the pilgrim group. By all accounts a very commanding, calculating man. Not especially kind or well-liked, but commanding."

She crinkles her eyes at me as I set my teacup down.

"He captained the first ship here in 1747, with about a dozen men, and then later sent for his wife and the others. It was a small group—about sixty to start. They grew to be eighty or so in the decade following."

"And how long after they arrived did the settlers start working with the Fakari people."

Ingemar turns her head side to side, as though considering. "It's difficult to say. His wife wrote letters and kept a diary, which I still have. I know that she arrived here by 1749, and within two years she was writing about Eia, the *reijna*'s daughter, who had become her friend."

"Do you know how they got to know each other?"

She shakes her head. "She doesn't mention it. Most likely it had to do with trade, in the beginning. The settlers had a difficult time growing the crops they were used to. At some point the Fakari people began trading fish and locally-grown vegetables with them in exchange for European goods. Art, clothing, jewelry. But they were very wet years—over time, it became harder for even the Fakari people to farm as they were used to. The weather patterns were changing, and that seems to have led to more collaboration between the groups. It became less about collaboration and more about mutual survival."

I look over my shoulder in the direction of the living room and the large tapestry.

"Tell me about Sarah Langdon. You said you have her diary?"

"Dia*ries*," she says, nodding. "The paper seems strong, but I have a hand tremor, and I'm worried about damaging them. I haven't dared open them in years. But I know a lot about her— not only from what she left here, but from English records of her life before they left. She and Richard married when she was 18 and he was 32. I know from her letters that she very much didn't want to come to the Fakaris. She wrote dozens of letters to her sister, most of which I still have. She was never able to mail them, unfortunately. There weren't enough ships going back."

"God, that's horrible," I murmur, and she nods.

"It was an unhappy marriage, by all accounts. Richard was a very unkind man, and it appears she felt alone amongst most of the other wives in the settler community. She and Eia grew quite close."

"Eia was the daughter...?" Seb asks.

"*Iija*. The daughter of the *reijna*, or pack leader, on this island at the time." Ingemar leans forward over the table and pulls out a frame, handing it to me. Inside is a black-and-white sketch on a piece of faded paper, featuring an elderly woman with broad, sharp features and dark hair pulled back, wearing an embroidered dress.

"That's her—my fifth-great grandmother. This was an illustration made of her towards the end of her life. I don't know exactly how old she was, but she and Sarah appear to have been of a similar age, because she did her elder rite a few years after Sarah came here. She was likely in her late twenties at that time."

"How do you know?" I ask, leaning forward. "About the elder rite, I mean?"

"Sarah mentions it in a letter to her sister."

I feel my heartbeat quicken, and glance over at Seb. He looks at me, too, his eyes wide.

"Was she involved in the elder rite?"

Ingemar nods. "Not the rite itself, of course. But she helped her prepare in the weeks in advance."

"*Agaayu*," Seb mutters. I feel a shiver go over my skin.

"Does she mention it in the diaries?"

Ingemar lifts her shoulders, her brow furrowing apologetically. "I haven't been able to read them all. The paper is very delicate, as I said. I, myself, have only looked through them twice in the last fifteen years or so, for fear of accidentally destroying them. Light exposure, finger oils..."

"No, no, of course," I say. "I totally understand. It's just..."

I glance over at Seb.

"I work with Fakari salt," he says. "We're trying to uncover the way they made the old salt, and how they did the salt rituals before an elder rite in the old days. Like we see in the *Eijna*."

"I... I know it's crazy, but I'd had this idea," I say to Ingemar. "The Fakari people didn't write down how they used to make the ancient salt, or how the rites were conducted—either because it was bad luck or because they didn't need to. But I'd thought, if any foreigners had been close enough to the Fakari people to see..."

She nods. "They might have made note of it."

"And they could have, right?" I say, leaning forward. "I mean, Sarah could have. She was close enough to Eia to witness the rituals."

She nods. "She wrote a lot in her ten years here. I know from her letters that she became quite involved in Fakari life up until her husband's death. It's possible."

I nod, looking over the chest of documents. "Thank you so much for telling us about this, Ingemar. I'm so grateful. You definitely don't need to share the documents with us, but if you would even consider showing us any relevant letters that mention the rite... that would be incredible."

"It's not that you can't see them," she says, sighing. "It's just that there's so many, and I've been terrified for years to handle them incorrectly and have them be lost to time forever."

"I understand."

"But I'm getting on in years, and I do worry about what will happen to them. To all of this." She gestures around her. "My children have no interest in keeping up the museum once I'm gone, and while the archive is willing to take the collection, I'm worried that it'll be buried in some underground stack of boxes somewhere. I've offered what I have to the bigger history museum on Saroe, but to them, this is... marginal. I don't want this to die with me, but I don't know what I can do to prevent that."

I nod, remembering Andreas' words. *I wouldn't even really consider it a museum, really, it's more of a hobby project.*

"Have you ever considered digitizing what you have?" I ask, setting my cup down. "It seems like such a waste for future generations of Fakari people not to know about this. If you could scan what you have, it would reduce the amount of time you, or anyone else, needs to look at the originals. But it would preserve the information and make it available to others."

"Oh, I've tried," she says, looking at the chest. "I bought an expensive scanner several years ago. My daughter was helping me for a while, when she could. But she and the children moved down to Marit a few years back, and somewhere in the meantime the scanner stopped working. And people just aren't interested. No one cares about this settler group—they were too small and localized to matter, in the grand scheme of things."

"They matter to me," I say. I can feel the gears churning in my mind even faster than my mind can keep up with them. "Maybe I can help. I worked as a research assistant in college—I know it's nothing professional, but I had to scan, like, nine million books that summer just using my smartphone. Technology has come a long way; you're able to make really high-quality scans even with just something like that now. I know it'll be fragile, and I'm sure that it won't be as professional as if we got a real archivist to do it. But it's better than nothing."

She looks up at me. "You would help?"

"Absolutely," I say, without hesitation. "If you'd let us see the originals, I'll scan everything."

33

SEB

Nine hours later, Maren and I leave the museum. She's glowing, practically bouncing with excitement over the folder full of dozens and dozens of scans on her phone.

"Thank you *so* much again," Maren says. "I promise that I'll send you all the files when I'm done cropping and editing them."

"No, thank you both," she says, leaning against the doorway. "It's been a long time since we had any visitors. I'm just grateful to have people show interest—and help me preserve this piece of our history."

"*Takka,*" I say to her. "*Farvayyu!*"

"*Farvayyu,*" she says, waving as she says goodbye.

We hear the door shut, and I reach for Maren's hand.

"I can't believe this," she says. "Like, I can't believe this actually worked! And now we have all these scans—hundreds of pages of them. There has to be *something* in there. This is actually going to work, I swear. We're gonna figure this out. It's incredible."

"*You're* incredible," I say, wrapping my arms around her and pulling her close to me. "I feel—I don't know. I'm more hopeful than I've been in a long time. Thank you for suggesting this."

"Thank *you* for listening," she says, her voice playful.

"I should have done it sooner."

"Correct." She raises her chin proudly, then gives me a warm look. "And thanks for finding gloves and stuff for us to use in scanning. Where did you disappear off to, after?"

"Oh, I prepared some stuff for us. I'm taking you to the ruins, remember?"

"Oh my God, I totally forgot! Isn't it too late? We have to get dinner."

I smile. "I took care of it."

"WOAH. THIS IS SO BEAUTIFUL."

Maren looks up at the hill above us, where the stone ruins of the old monastery stand against the setting sun. They're overgrown with lush greenery and twisting vines, wisteria brushing down from the uppermost arches of what used to be stained glass windows. Along the bottom are overgrown bushes of pink and red flowers, and large beds of moss stretching across overturned stones. It's totally deserted here—we didn't even pass any cars on the drive up.

I step out of the front of the pick-up.

"I brought us a picnic," I say, walking around the back of the car with her. I gesture into the back of the truck. "It's not a full meal, but I got a bunch of stuff, including—"

"Oh my *God*," she says, looking into the back of the truck. "You brought pillows and blankets and everything. Where did you get this?"

I shrug sheepishly. "There's a couple stores in town. I thought we could use them for the picnic. And if not, I've heard with trucks like this, you can make it comfortable in the back and look up at the stars."

She beams, looking up at me with glowing eyes. Her whole face is alight, and I feel a flush of warmth and joy in my chest.

"Seb, I *love* it. This is so perfect."

"Yeah?"

"Yeah. I can't believe you did this! Come on." She leans over the truck bed to grab the blanket and a few pillows. I grab the bag of groceries and follow.

Maren leads me towards the ruins, looking up and around her at the scene. I watch as her wild mess of curls blow in the wind, the sun shining through them. I can feel my pulse in my neck, the low ripple of nerves making the wolf in my chest jittery.

I have to do this right. It *needs* to go well. And if it doesn't...

After a few minutes, we reach the top and come to stand under a large arch. This part of the monastery is completely open, all arches and partial walls reaching up towards the sky. Maren looks over my shoulder, and I turn to follow her gaze. There's an expanse of partial wall behind me, through which the arch of an old window allows for a view of the island.

"God, look at this," she says, walking towards it. "I can't believe no one else is here to see it. I mean, look at that."

I walk up behind her, looking out over the rolling hills. The sun is low on the horizon, painting the fields in shades of gold. She lets out a contented sigh.

"I love it here," she says quietly. She carefully places the blanket and pillows at her feet, then comes to sit on the wide rock making up the window edge. Maren motions for me to sit beside her. Heart in my throat, I take a seat.

She leans back against the empty window arch, and I watch as a sweep of wisteria brushes against her hair, wafting gently in the breeze.

"I just can't believe this. Like, I can't believe we're *here*. I can't believe how much stuff we found today. And all it took was *one* conversation."

"All it took was you," I say.

Something softens in her eyes, and I clear my throat.

"Alright, so. Ruins picnic. We've got..." I reach into the large paper grocery bag. "Fresh grapes. Bread. Cheese. Olives. Wine..."

One by one, I take each item out of the bag, showing it to her briefly before putting it back.

"Clementines," I continue. "Gummy worms, for you..."

"Oh my God, you're a dream."

"Are you hungry?" I ask.

She shrugs. "Not yet. But we can start with some grapes, maybe?"

I nod at pull them out of the bag, setting the rest of the groceries down at our feet. I open the container of grapes on the stones between us, then grab a bottle of water and run some of it over the grapes to wash them off. As Maren leans back against the rocks behind her, I bring a few grapes to my mouth.

"This is wonderful," she says, looking out over the hills. "Thank you so much for thinking of this."

"Yeah, of course." I swallow. "Maren..."

She looks over at me. I watch as the breeze brushes over her hair.

"What?"

"I promised I'd tell you the whole truth today. I..."

I sigh. While she was scanning documents, I spent my entire trip to the grocery store practicing this in my head.

"I think it's time."

I see her take a little breath, like she's steeling herself. "Okay."

"Maren, I..." I look out at the rolling fields beside us, hoping for a sign from the *agaayit*—anything that will make this easier. I don't know how to do this. And if I do it wrong...

I bring my eyes back to hers.

"You're a much better person than I am," I say finally.

She chews her lip. "Okay..."

"You're generous. You're so good to other people—to Em, to Kieran. To me. And you're *so* smart. If you'd been on board when I started the salt company, we'd be in a totally different place today. I'm so glad you came here."

She smiles again, but nervously this time, the color rising slightly in her cheeks.

"So?"

"I was awful to you," I say quietly. "I'm sorry. It was never about you. Or, it was, but... In a different way. You deserve to know why."

She nods, waiting, and I let out a sigh.

"When you came to Saroe, I was broken. I still am. But I was so angry—so fucked after my rite—that I couldn't see *anything* clearly. After that night, everything in my world turned dark. Every relationship I had lost color; anything I did became meaningless. And so I couldn't see you for who you were. I saw a mainlander—David's daughter, someone who was going to leave —and I hated you for it. And so when I learned something about you... about *us*... that changed everything, it only made it worse."

Her brow furrows. "What?"

I swallow, the adrenaline coursing through me, and instinctively I reach for her hand.

"I... I don't know how to tell you this. I don't know how to do it because I've never done this before, but also because I don't think *anyone's* ever done this before. You're not from here—you don't have the same understanding of what this means—and I just don't know—"

She pulls her hand away. "Seb, what are you talking about?"

I look at her for a long moment.

"You're my mate."

She blinks. "*What?*"

"You're—" I swallow. "Fuck, I'm doing this all wrong. I'm sorry, let me start from the beginning."

"No, hang on, go back. I'm *what?*"

I feel a knot forming in my throat.

"You're my mate, Maren."

"What does that mean?"

"It means our souls are tied together. That we knew each other before this place. It means we belong together."

She stares at me, wide-eyed. "You can't just say that. How do you know?"

"The ancestors showed me."

"What do you *mean?*"

I sigh. "Three years ago, I went into the ring for my elder rite. I told you—I was stupid. I wanted to see my dad again, but I hadn't trained for nearly long enough. What I faced there almost killed me. I lost so much blood I could barely think. I couldn't walk. It hurt so bad that, at some point, I *wanted* to die. Every other person who went into that ring and lost what I did, didn't come out alive. But I lived. Because of you."

She blinks again, faster now, her breathing coming quicker. Her voice is like a whisper.

"What do you mean? How?"

I shake my head. "I don't know. It was early morning—it had been hours since the rite started, and I was inches from death. I was lying at the edge of the cliff, waiting to die—practically begging for the beast to just end it and kill me. He was stalking towards me, ready to end it. And then I heard *you.*"

"Me?"

"Your wolf." I swallow. "You came into the ring and fought him off. It didn't make any sense. He was bigger than you, vicious. But you weren't afraid. I couldn't even sit up to see it, but I heard you defending me. You fought him and... you won."

She shakes her head. "I don't get it. That didn't happen. I've never been to the Fakaris before this year. It was someone else."

"It wasn't you in the flesh," I say, reaching out for her hand again. "It was the *agaayit*, intervening for me. But they did it *through* you. They showed me *you*. You came to me after you killed him, and you spoke to me through the mate bond."

"The mate bond?"

"It's like the *fikaband* but stronger. It's a soul connection—a way of reaching the other person even when they're not close. You can talk to each other without words."

"But we don't have that."

I shake my head. "You don't have it until you claim each other. They didn't bring you to me in the flesh, but they showed me you, and that you were my mate."

She looks down at her hands, thinking.

"I'm sorry. I know it's a lot to take in. I know it doesn't make sense—it didn't make sense to me. But the *agaayit* showed me you that day, and you carried me down the mountain to safety. If it hadn't been for your wolf, I would have died up there on the cliffs."

She turns her face up to look at me, her eyes wide and soft.

"I spent years looking for you," I say, and my words come out like a whisper. "Every night in that mainland hospital, I thought of you. When I wanted to die. When I had to learn how to walk again. The only thing that got me through was *you*—the idea that even after all this hell, there would be something beautiful and worthwhile and worth it."

"Seb," she says quietly.

I feel that knot forming in my throat again, and try to swallow it down.

"I tell people I almost died during my rite," I say quietly. "But I *did* die that day. The person I was when I walked up to the ring never came back. It killed the part of me that was naïve, and the part that believed in easy endings. It killed my belief that life was somehow fair. I would never have told you that I believed that before the rite, but somehow I did."

She leans forward, placing a hand on my knee, and I swallow.

"I think in a way, having the rite ahead of me was how I made peace with my dad's death," I say. "I held onto the idea that I'd see him again, and that got me through the worst of my grief. But then I *didn't* see him. And not only that, but the rite almost killed me, and I'll be in pain for the rest of my life. The suffering just felt so... needless."

She nods, scooching closer to me.

"For three years, I lived like a ghost in my own life," I say. "I disappeared from all my relationships. I didn't know how to be myself anymore, because I couldn't be the person I'd always been, and I hated the person the rite had turned me into: bitter, angry, resentful. I was so, so angry. At the *agaayit*; at every person who had let me take myself up to that ring. At everyone who pitied me, who didn't know what to say, who said the wrong thing. Everyone but you."

She brings a soft hand to my face. I lean my forehead against hers.

"What got me through was the knowledge that *you* were out there somewhere. That after all this horror and pain and loneliness, one day there would be someone who felt like home. That one day, I wouldn't be alone."

I feel an ache in my chest, and I bring my hand to the back of her head, over her hair.

"I'm so sorry," I whisper. "I'm so sorry for how I treated you. When I saw you shift for the first time, and I realized... It just made me angrier. You were still David's daughter to me then. I saw what it did to my father to lose his best friend, and I felt like —if you were my mate—I'd be reliving his fate but worse. It felt like another cruel joke from the *agaayit*; a twist of the knife. I didn't know how to accept it. I wanted it to be anyone but you."

She lets out a low breath, and I pull away, looking into her eyes.

"I was wrong," I say, my voice steady. "I was scared. Because after all those years of waiting for you, the idea that you could leave and I'd spend the rest of my life, still waiting to feel at home..."

"Seb?" she asks quietly.

"Yeah?"

"Stop talking."

She brings her mouth to mine. The scent of her is rich and warm: honey and heat and rich, deep florals. She brings her arms around my neck and pulls herself close to me, and something inside me feels like it clicks into place.

I kiss her back: deeply, hungrily. She wraps her arms around the back of my neck and pulls herself closer to me, pressing her body into mine.

"Maren," I say, pulling away and kissing her cheek, her jaw, the spot just under her ear. I bring my mouth to the place on her neck that always makes her breathing run ragged and nuzzle into it, biting gently.

"*Oh,*" she gasps, bringing a hand to the back of my neck.

"That's where your mate bite would go," I say, pulling away, my voice rough. "That's why it feels so good."

"A mate bite is what seals..."

"The mate bond," I say, nodding.

"Kiss me there again," she whispers.

I do as told and suck and gently bite on the skin, her moans hitching with the uneven cadence of her breath. I can feel myself harden against her, and I hear the moment she registers it—her gasp a little louder, delighted. As I pull myself closer, almost on top of her now, I hear a small thud next to us, and look over the edge of the wall to see the basket of grapes rolling down the hill below.

"There goes dinner," she says with a little laugh.

"I can think of something better," I say, bringing my hand to the space between her thighs.

"Seb. *Here?*" She looks over her shoulder.

"Anywhere. Please." I run my fingers over the crease of her jeans, rubbing gently over the seam. "I've waited so long."

"As I remember, we did *this* a few days ago." She brings a hand to my hair, running her fingers through it and taking a gentle grip.

"Let me have you. Let me make you feel good." I press my fingers against the seam again, creating friction in the space over her clit. She lets out a little gasp, and her hand reflexively grips tighter in my hair.

"You offer things that are very hard to say no to," she says with a breathy little laugh.

"So say yes," I murmur.

She meets my eyes and nods slowly, her breathing heavy. "Yes."

I sink to my knees before her. My hands reach for the button of her jeans to loosen it, and she lifts her hips to pull them down. Underneath, she's wearing black cotton underwear, and I can see a little damp spot over the cleft between her lips. I bring my mouth to it hungrily, kissing her over the fabric.

"Oh my God, Seb," she gasps, her hand coming to the back of my head.

I let out a low groan at the taste of her through the cotton, sweet and tangy and fully, deliciously mine. My fingers come up to pull her underwear to the side, and as I slip two inside her entrance, I bring my tongue directly over her clit.

She moans as I run tight little circles around it, and I can feel her inner walls clench around my fingers. The sensation—the warmth and wetness and heat of her, the way her body reacts to me—sends a jolt of pleasure through my body.

"You taste so good, *kamaatni*," I murmur against her skin. *My mate.* "I want to taste you every night for the rest of my life."

I feel her tense for a moment, and pull back to look at her. But when I meet her eyes they're dark and full, glazed over with desire, the pupils blown wide. The sight of it surges another wave of want through me, and I feel myself straining against my pants, aching for her.

"Tell me what you want," I say, my voice a low rumble. She brings her hand to the back of my hair and pulls me towards her, her voice breathless.

"Eat."

34

MAREN

He doesn't need to be told twice. Seb sinks his mouth into me, working his tongue and his fingers with such fervor that the pleasure jolts through my body, making me arch my back. I can feel *everything*—the humidity clinging to my skin, the brushes of flowers against my arms, the heat of his breath against me as he devours me. Sex has always been good, but with him it's more: rich and wild and vibrantly *alive*. All of my senses are heightened; everything feels closer to the surface.

He hooks his fingers inside me, pressing up into my G-spot, and the sound that comes out of me is broken and wild. He's so *good* at this, and it's not just his experience—made evident in the deft work of his fingers, or the way he knows to attune himself to the uneven rhythm of my breath. It's his clear pleasure in it: the satisfaction he shows he's taking in me by the way he groans, low and guttural, as he tastes me. Feeling his pure, primal pleasure is so good that it makes everything else better.

He works his fingers faster, and I hear my moans getting

shorter, higher in pitch. I don't want this—not yet. Gently, I push him back, shaking my head.

"No?" he asks.

"I don't want to come like this," I breathe. "I want *you*. Inside me."

He blinks, his breath ragged, and looks around us. The sun is setting now, shining through the arches of the abandoned ruins. The air is warm, hanging around us, and I feel the heat of my own desire humming through me.

"Here?" he asks.

"Yeah," I say. "I've waited long enough for you."

"I've waited my whole life," he says softly.

He grabs the picnic blanket and spreads it out near us on a soft bed of moss. I come to lie down on it before him, and he grabs one of the pillows and places it gently under my head. I part my legs for him to kneel between them, but he hesitates.

"Mare..."

"What?"

He swallows. "I— I don't know how it'll be. With my leg."

My gaze falls down to his thigh, covered by black jeans, then back up to him.

"Haven't you..."

"I haven't been with anyone since my rite," he says. "I was recovering first. Then I was celibate for my consecration, and after that..." He shakes his head.

"I don't... I don't know what's gonna be easy. I don't know what will hurt."

"Okay," I say softly.

"But I promise I'll make it good for you," he adds quickly.

Something aches in my chest, and I sit up, pulling him close to me so our faces are pressed together.

"I know. It's gonna be good for both of us. Sometimes it just takes a little work to get it right, okay? But we'll figure it out."

He nods. "Yeah, okay."

"I have an IUD," I add, "and I got tested a few weeks before I came here. I don't have anything. Have you ever...?"

"I was tested during my hospital stay," he says. "And there hasn't been anyone else since then."

"Okay," I say, and swallow. "Then I don't need to use a condom. Take me."

"Mare..." he murmurs.

He looks in my eyes, and his gaze is dark, hungry.

"I want you," I whisper, and bring my mouth to his. My hand moves lower, and over the fabric of his pants I feel the hard outline of his dick pressing against my hand. At the pressure, he lets out a low groan.

"God, I need you. Please," I say.

His hands come to the button of his pants, and he swiftly undoes it, pulling them down along with his boxers so the length of him is exposed.

I take him in hand, stroking up the length of it. When my fingers reach the top, I run my thumb over his head and feel the wet slick of precum waiting for me. I swipe my thumb over it, running it over the sensitive head, and Seb shudders.

"Can I...?" I whisper, bringing my mouth close to him.

"God. Yes, please."

I wrap my lips around him, taking it as deep as I can. He lets out a broken sigh as I bring my mouth back up, then take him again, creating suction as I go.

"*Agaayu*, Mare," he murmurs. "*Ayya—*"

I work up and down the shaft, using my hand to help with the length of him I can't fit into my mouth. Eventually his hands find my head, his fingers gently winding through my hair while still letting me move freely. It's when his breathing grows uneven and I feel his hips start to jerk just slightly that I pull back.

"Maren," he says softly, pulling his face to mine. He kisses me deeply, intently.

"*Ijekayyatik*," he whispers.

"What's that?"

"I— I love you. Is that okay?"

I nod and kiss him again. "That's okay."

He leans over me, and I pull him down onto the blanket. I reach my hands to pull his pants all the way down, and he helps, being careful as they come down over his thigh. I pull off his shirt so he's naked over me, and he reaches for mine, helping me get it over my head.

"God, Maren," he says, coming down over me, kissing my neck, my chest, my breasts. "You're so fucking beautiful. Everything about you... Your hair, your face, your body..."

He pulls the lace cup of my bra down on one side and takes my nipple into his mouth, sucking gently. I gasp and let my legs fall wider, reaching between them for the length of him.

"Take me," I whisper, pulling his body closer to mine. "Please. Just have me."

He nods and leans himself over me. It takes a moment—I move my leg out to the side to try to give his thigh some space. As he leans against me, his left leg presses against me, and I feel him tense, then pull away.

"It hurts?"

"A little. It's fine."

"What if we used a pillow?" I ask, reaching for the second one we brought, close to the grocery bag. "I can angle my hips."

"Yeah, okay."

He grabs the other pillow and folds it in half, and I lift my hips for him to wedge it under me. A moment later, he comes over me again, and this time I angle my legs up higher, so I can keep most of my leg from pressing against his.

He leans over me and takes himself in hand, bringing his head to my entrance. I arch my back as he runs the head up and down my slit and watch the look on his face as he registers my wetness. As his head brushes over my clit, I let out a little moan, and then—before I can brace myself—he lowers his hand and sinks the full length of himself into me.

I gasp as he pulls back and then thrusts in again, the motion deep and masterful.

"Oh, fuck," I say, bringing my hands to his back, holding his upper body close to me. "Oh my God."

"Maren," he groans, pulling out and then thrusting in again.

"Is this better?"

"This is perfect," he says, pressing deep. "Everything about you is so fucking perfect."

He thrusts again and my head falls back, my body reacting for me to the movement of his hips. He makes me feel so full; the angle of the pillow helps him brush against my G-spot, and with each thrust I feel my body react again. My hips rock as he grinds into me, and I can hear my own moans getting louder as buries himself into my body, pressing his face into my neck.

"*Ayya,*" he mutters, kissing and nipping at the skin. "*Ijekayy-atik, kamaatni.* My mate."

The words unlock something inside me, and as he nips at the skin of my neck I feel the warmth and heat of it take my pleasure higher. The gentle pressure of his teeth, the brush of his stubble, sets me on fire.

"God," I gasp. "Tell me why everything feels so good with you,"

"Because we belong to each other."

He pulls away so I can see his eyes, and I bring my hands up to cup his face. He leans over me, and with one hand takes my fingers and guides them to his mouth. He sucks on them gently, gazing into my eyes, and then guides my hand down between us.

"Touch yourself," he whispers.

I nod and bring my fingers to my clit, and just as I start to run circles over it, he begins thrusting again, leaning back to give my hand space. The pace and feeling is electric, and as he thrusts harder I feel the pleasure building in me, rolling under the surface of my skin.

"*Good*," he murmurs. He keeps thrusting as I gasp under him, my hips grinding in a pace I don't know to control.

"You look so beautiful under me," he says. "You look so beautiful when you come with my name on your lips. You always do such a good job for me."

"Kiss my neck again," I gasp, and he leans over me, burying his head in my neck, licking and biting and sucking on the space just over my collarbone.

"Oh God," I gasp. "I'm close. Don't stop."

"Come for me, *kamaatni*," he whispers against my skin, and I let go.

The orgasm surges through me, my body rocking as the sounds from my mouth grow louder and higher. I feel his body tighten over me, the rhythm of his hips growing wild as he loses himself.

"Mare," he groans as I feel my inner walls convulse around him. "Fuck. *Agaayu*, you feel so good. Can I come inside you?"

"Yes," I gasp, and I feel his body tense, the rhythm growing desperate. A moment later, he cries out, his groan low and guttural as he slams himself into me.

I can feel all of him—his body in me and over me and around me as he spills into me. He pulls back from my neck, his breath ragged, and looks into my eyes.

"Maren. You're so perfect," he whispers, and kisses me again.

35

SEB

We drive back to the hotel after nightfall, after sharing the rest of our picnic foods together at the ruins. Once we reach the hotel and take the elevator up to our floor, Maren starts fiddling with her room key, looking over her shoulder at me. Instead of stopping at my own door, I come to stand behind her, wrapping my arms around her waist.

"Please don't make me spend one more night hearing your breath through the wall instead of in bed next to me," I murmur into her ear.

"I thought you'd never ask." She lets out a laugh and unlocks the door, swinging it open to let me into her suite.

It's a nice room—a bit bigger than mine, mostly made into a suite by the huge bathroom with a clawfoot tub. We spend some time lying on the bed, and eventually get up to take a bath together. Afterwards, I stay in the warm, soapy water while she showers in the glass stall next to the bath.

I watch in wonder as she washes her hair, using the conditioner first to scrub the roots and then to soak into the length of it. Under the shower, her curls clump together, weighed down by the shower so they form a curtain reaching almost to her tailbone. The room slowly fills with steam and the scent of coconut.

"Did you bring your conditioner here from home?" I ask once she's done.

She scrunches her hair up to her head, gently squeezing out the water before getting out of the stall.

"Oh, for sure. You don't get hair like this without traveling with your own little arsenal of products."

She wraps her hair in an old tee shirt and piles it high on her head, and I watch with curiosity as she towels off her body and applies cream to her legs from a little glass jar.

"Is that from Saga's place?"

"The moisturizer? Yeah. I threw out most of my old products after learning my mom had been basically drugging me for my entire life. Saga was right, though—my eczema cleared right up when I stopped using that stuff."

She rubs more cream into her body, over her shoulders and arms.

"That's so horrible, what your mom did to you," I say.

Maren meets my eyes in the mirror and shrugs.

"Yeah, it is. But I think, in a way, it hurts less than the other stuff. She was always pushing me, telling me I was too much or not enough. That hurts worse than this, somehow."

"Worse than lying to and drugging you?"

She wraps a towel around her body, then turns around, leaning on the sink to face me.

"Yeah. She had all this trauma from seeing what happened to my dad, so I can kind of make an excuse for why she'd want to protect me, in her own fucked-up way. But there's no reason for the other stuff. I was never enough for her. She just... never let me feel like I had a place in the world. And I still don't."

"Even now?" I ask.

"Even now. I mean, I'm still finding my place here." She

seems to catch a glimpse of something on my face, and quickly adds, "I mean, not with you. Just in general. I'm still trying to figure out what I'm here for."

I sit up, the water around me splashing with the motion.

"I want to help you with that, if I can."

She shrugs and gives me a sad smile. "I don't know if anyone can help me. Anyway, we don't need to think about that right now. I have a purpose for *today*. You take your time in the bath, and I'm gonna start cleaning up and reading through the photos I took earlier today."

WHEN I EMERGE from the bathroom twenty minutes later, she's in bed on her laptop, wearing an oversized gray tee shirt. Her hair is still piled high on top of her head, and I feel a possessive little satisfaction from my inner wolf that I get to see her like this. Beautiful. Undone.

"*Heij*. Can I come lie next to you?"

"Yeah, of course." She pulls back the duvet next to her, and I climb in, sitting up against the headboard.

"How's it going?"

"Pretty good. The scanning app I used was decent, so I'm just kind of straightening and cropping the ones that it didn't get right right away. I'm skimming the pages as I go."

"Did you find anything?" I ask.

She shakes her head. "Not about the rite. I'm starting with the diary for now and just reading a little bit about Sarah Langdon's life. Ingemar said she doesn't mention the *reijna*'s daughter Eia by name until a couple years into the letters to her sister, but the diary was harder for her to access without accidentally hurting it, so she hasn't read most of that."

"How did Eia's family end up with Sarah's house and diaries?" I ask.

Maren gives me a look. "I don't know. And I'm kind of afraid to ask."

She turns back to the screen, and I watch as she adjusts the angle of the page, tweaking the crop to be closer.

"Can I help with cleaning up the scans?" I ask. "Then you can take more time to read through what you found."

"That would be perfect, actually. I can show you how I've been editing them, and you can send me the files as you finish, for me to read."

"Yeah, show me."

She passes the laptop to me and gives me a quick tour of the tool she's using to edit, then configures a set up on her phone to read the diary pages as they come in. I get to work adjusting the photos one by one, fixing up crops and angles, and she burrows her body under the blankets, just her head and arm peeking out as she starts reading.

"Oh my God," she mutters fifteen minutes later, bringing a hand to her mouth.

"What?"

"No, nothing. Just—her husband is terrible. What an asshole."

I want to ask, but Maren stays focused on the screen, and I get the sense she doesn't want to stop reading for long enough to tell me. Ten minutes later, she lets out a little gasp, followed by "Oh no, poor Sarah..."

I look over. "Want to fill me in?"

She shakes her head, eyes glued to her phone. I keep editing, sending her new photos as I go. After another little gasp, Maren sits up straight in bed.

"Oh my God, here! Okay. So, like, background: one of her only friends on Fajje, one of the other English wives, got really sick. The settlers don't have a doctor, but her friend kept getting worse, so Sarah decided to go to the Fakari village and see if one of their healers could help. And she talks about meeting a young

Fakari woman close to her own age, who comes to take a look at her friend and help. That has to be Eia, right?"

"I don't know. Does she call her by name?"

"Not yet. She says the woman took a look at her friend and checked her—looked in her eyes and at the color of her tongue? —then seemed to say something over her body and told Sarah she'd be back the following day. They can't actually talk to each other, because Sarah doesn't speak Fakari. But she did a thing with her hands to show that she'd be back."

Maren scrolls to the following photo of a diary page.

"Okay. She says the woman came back with a packet of herbs... She brews some really foul-smelling tea... Oh my God! Okay, she brought salt. Okay, okay, okay..."

Maren skims down over the next few pages.

"Okay, friend is feeling better... Sarah goes back to the Fakari town to give the woman bread to say thank you... Yes! Okay, the woman is called Eia. She also introduces her to her mom and her brother Theio. And—okay! They give her salt as thanks. And this is in 1704, so she's only been there for less than a year."

Maren looks up at me and grins. "We're really gonna get somewhere with this, Seb. Like, look at this. We have nine more years of the story to figure this out. And we *know* she eventually witnessed part of Eia's rite prep. We're actually going to get to the bottom of this."

I wrap an arm around her and rest my chin on top of her head, the scent of her hair products wafting up to me. And for the first time in a long, long time, I feel hope.

"Oh, shit."

"Mm?"

I turn over in bed and open a groggy eye to see Maren, scrolling on her phone with a hand to her mouth.

"Sorry, sorry, I didn't mean to wake you. Go back to bed."

"What is it?"

"It's nothing, you should rest."

I close my eyes and adjust the blanket, but a minute later, I hear another little gasp and sit straight up.

"Okay, come on. I know you want to tell me."

Maren looks at me, the blue light from her phone illuminating her face.

"I think Sarah's gonna get it on with Eia's brother."

"*What?*"

"She's been going over to their *fikarig*—she spells it Feekarig with a capital F, it's so cute—all the time. Richard doesn't know because he's totally focused on this whack-ass idea for how to help the settlers' town flourish. They're all basically dying because no one can get anything to grow. *Anyway.* Sarah just came over after dinner and Eia wasn't home. And she and Theio shared a *look*."

"A look?"

"A lingering glance." Maren looks at me intently, her eyes wide. "You know."

"I know what?"

She rolls her eyes. "Oh, come on. You and I have totally shared a look! And I've read enough romance novels to know what's up. These two are gonna get it on, I swear."

"It's two in the morning," I grumble.

"So go back to bed, then. I'm reading."

I lie back down, but this time I turn to face her, curling my legs up in the space below her knees. I nuzzle my face close to her body and take a deep breath, inhaling the scent of her.

"What are you doing?" she asks.

"I'm cuddling you. Keep reading."

I close my eyes and listen to the sound of her breathing, the occasional little gasp or whispered "Oh," telling me she's still invested. After a while, she lays a gentle arm over my shoulders, and I find myself drifting closer to sleep, lulled by the warmth of her body and the scent of her essence.

It must be an hour or two after that that she shakes me awake.

"Seb. Seb," she whispers.

"Mm? What?" I ask, sitting up. "Are you okay?"

Her eyes are wide, the expression serious.

"I found something," she says. "Something in the diaries. Something really bad."

"What is it?" I ask, rubbing my eyes.

"Sarah's learned that all the islands are pooling their salt production, like Saga told me. Because a storm is coming, like you said."

"Okay," I say, sitting up.

"Not just any storm," she says. "They call it the 'Wrath of the Gods,' and it returns every so many generations. You said we don't know how they knew it was coming, but it says so here. She says the first sign is that, after a dark winter, the sky lights up like fire."

A shiver of goosebumps goes over my skin.

"*Agaayu,*" I whisper.

"In the weeks before the storm comes, they know it's nearing because of blue lights in the distance."

"What?" I ask.

She grabs my hands. "They're not spirits, Seb. They're earthquake lights."

36

MAREN

"P*iu*, slow down. What do you mean?"

"Listen, I know it sounds crazy," I say. Pink light is streaming through the sheer curtains, painting our bedsheets in shades of pastel. The sun will be rising soon, but I've barely slept.

"We went looking for outsider accounts of Fakari life, in case they'd written about the old salt rituals," Seb says into the phone lying on the bed between us. "We found that, but we also found more information about why they were stockpiling the salt in the first place."

"The storm?" she asks.

"Right—they knew a storm was coming, but we didn't know *how* they knew that," he says. "They told us in primary school that they probably had some kind of primitive storm tracking apparatus, but these diaries tell us there were signs. A dark winter, followed by a bright red sky—just like this year. And then blue lights on the horizon, which Maren and I have seen in the last few weeks."

"I think they're earthquake lights," I say. "They can show up in the moments before an earthquake, but sometimes farther in advance—days, weeks. Something bad is coming.”

“*Agaayu*,” she mutters under her breath. “I... Okay, I don’t know what I can do with this. But send me photos of the pages. You’ve both seen these lights?”

“Yes. On Saroe a few weeks ago, and last week, on Halluk,” Seb says.

“Okay. I’ll call an emergency council meeting. The two of you come home immediately.”

“We’re already packed,” I say. “Seb’s figuring out a boat to Marit as soon as businesses open, and we’ll take the next ferry. Can someone come get us at the harbor?”

“Yes, of course. I’ll send Gabe. Or, no—Kieran.”

“Okay. We’ll let you know when we expect to arrive.”

“Oh, and *piu*—how long between the last of the earthquake lights and the storm, in the diaries?”

“Just a few days,” I say. “And the ones we saw on Halluk were more than a week ago.”

She pauses. “Is there any chance it’s not what’s happening? Or that the earthquake was so minor that we didn’t realize it had already happened?”

“Is that a risk we want to take?” Seb asks.

“*Nekka.* Come home. I’ll get the council together.”

We make it to Saroe’s harbor in mid-afternoon, and Kieran is standing in wait in front of the Jeep, Em beside him.

“*Ayagaayuni*,” she says, running up to us and wrapping her arms around me. “Saga told us. I can’t believe this. Are you okay?”

“Yeah, we’re fine. I mean, for now. I don’t know what’s coming.”

Kieran walks up and claps Seb on the back, then leans down

to hug me. As he pulls away, he takes a breath, and I see his eyebrows shoot up. He gives Seb a look.

"The answer is yes," I say, before he can ask. "We're together."

Em's eyes widen, and she grins at me, taking my arm in hers and turning her back to the guys so we can walk to the car.

"Okay, as soon as we make sure there's not a hurricane coming, you have to tell me *everything*."

"Deal," I say, and she opens the car door to fold the front seat down.

Seb climbs in back with me, and Em and Kieran get in the front. We buckle up, and Kieran drives us back to the *fikarig*.

"What do the diaries say about the storm?" Kieran asks. "How worried do we need to be?"

I scroll back in my photo folder, trying to find the right page. "Here. She talks about what sounds like a bunch of small earthquakes in quick succession. And then a huge storm that wiped out several buildings. It seems like Marit and Fajje were hit the worst, but she doesn't know that until later. Word traveled a lot slower back then."

"But why would they need to save up salt for the storm?" Kieran asks. "Sorry, I didn't really pay attention in history."

"We don't really know," Seb says. "The records we have from that time just tell us they knew a storm was coming—how they knew that, we didn't know until now—and we know that they were saving salt for a long time in advance."

"Wait, that doesn't make sense," I say, looking up. "Theio was involved in salt production on Fajje, and Sarah says he'd been saving up for three years before the storm happened. The signs only started the winter before, with the dark winter."

"But..." Em looks away, thinking. "I mean, it's a storm that happens once in so many generations, right? So maybe they just knew it was time."

"Yeah," I say, uneasy. "Yeah, that must be it."

WE GET BACK to the *fikarig* an hour later, and when we arrive, Saga's on the phone with leadership from the other islands.

"Iija, iija, neijtuurlik. Nekka."

As we walk through the front door, she spots us and rushes over, pulling Seb and then me into a hug.

"Welkommit rig, denanni," she mutters, pressing her lips against my forehead. "Welcome home."

Kieran motions for Seb to head outside with him, and through the glass doors to the deck I see Gabe, talking with Em's aunt and uncle.

"What are we supposed to do?" I ask, turning to Em.

She shakes her head. "You can't really prepare for an earthquake. I guess the thing they're afraid of is flooding afterwards. Mostly, I think the islands are preparing an evacuation plan if something does happen."

I swallow, looking down at my phone.

"What is it?" she asks. Next to us, Saga turns away and heads into the living room, still talking on the phone.

"I'm gonna call Ingemar from the museum to let her know," I say quietly. "But it's not just that. I'm... I'm worried about Seb."

Em glances over my shoulder, and I do, too, to make sure he isn't close by.

"Why?" she asks.

"I don't think they were stockpiling salt just because of the storm," I whisper. "There's all this stuff about how the settlers can't get their crops to grow, and later on, even the Fakari people are having trouble. The diaries keep talking about the changing weather patterns. I'm worried—"

"Heij," Seb says, coming up behind us. "The guys and I are gonna bring in the deck furniture and then head to the common house for a council meeting. Do you want to come?"

I look over at Em.

"I'm okay, I think," I say, smiling for Seb's sake. "I'll just stay here and keep reading. Maybe we'll get to the part with Eia's rite."

"Okay, sounds good." Seb pulls me close and kisses my forehead. "*Ijekayyatik.*"

"See you soon," I say, as Em's eyes widen to meet mine.

Agaayu, she mouths.

Seb turns back towards the deck to help the guys, and Em grabs my hand.

"Okay, we'll figure out this salt thing, but also, he *loves* you? You need to tell me what happened."

"Deal," I say. "Upstairs?"

"*Okeij.*"

We climb the stairs to the second floor, but she leads me one story higher, up to the library. Once we get inside, she shuts the door behind us and demands details—about when we first kissed, what happened between then and the Fajje trip ("ew, nevermind, no details"), and Seb's confession at the ruins.

"He said we're mates," I tell her.

"*Agaayu!* Do you believe him?"

"I think so?" I say. "I think I do."

"How do you feel?"

"I... I don't know. I mean, all this stuff is so new to me. Like, it clearly means something to him. I just need to figure out what it means to me."

"Wow," Em says. "Seb being the first of us to find his mate. I don't think I ever expected that."

"No? Who did you think would be first?"

She thinks about it for a moment, and I see the color rising in her cheeks.

"It could have been any of us, I guess," she says finally. "But this is so exciting. I guess we'll start thinking about our own *fikarig* now."

I feel something tighten in my chest as a slow drum of anxiety builds in my stomach.

"Yeah?"

"Of course! When the first of the new generation starts finding their partners, you usually pick a few people to do the rite so we can get our own place. It'll be a while, I guess—especially if the lights aren't back this winter. But if he's already told you you're it..."

I swallow.

"Have you already claimed each other?" she asks, her eyes falling to my neck. I'm wearing a light purple tee shirt today that covers my collarbone.

"No, absolutely not," I say, laughing uncomfortably. "All this stuff is so new to me. I just... I need some time."

"Yeah, yeah, of course," she says, nodding. "But okay, so, the salts. You were saying..."

I swallow, pushing my nerves down.

"Yeah. Something just doesn't feel right." I say, shaking my head. "You guys said they were stockpiling the salt for this storm. But reading this, it doesn't sound that way. It sounds like the weather conditions on the islands were changing, and they were worried they wouldn't be able to make the salt they needed anymore."

"But what about the storm, then?"

"I don't know." I shake my head. "I think I'm just worried that, *if* it wasn't the storm that made them stop producing salt... If it was just that the conditions changed, and maybe we can't recreate the old salt methods because *they* couldn't, either..."

I swallow.

"I don't know what it would do to Seb," I say finally.

"What do you think would happen?"

I chew my lip, finding the words.

"This is what he's been living for for years. I feel like it would break him. He told me that before his rite, having that ahead of him was the thing getting him through losing his dad. But since then, he's had so much pain..." I blink, remembering what he told me at the ruins. The anger and resentment that's been curdling within him in the years since.

"I'm afraid this became the next thing that was helping him survive," I say. "That he's pinning all his hopes for the business, and his leg, on *this*. Restoring the old way. And if we can't..."

I let my voice trail off.

"We'll figure it out," she says resolutely. "We have no idea what else is in that diary. I'm going to make some tea for us both. You, get to reading."

I nod and walk over to the couch by the far window, collapsing into it and letting myself focus on the diary pages. I read that Eia is preparing for her rite—she's doing some kind of physical training that Sarah's not a part of—and so Sarah is spending less time with her and more with her mother, the *reijna*, and with Theio. Sarah seems to be learning some Fakari from the *reijna*, but at some point it becomes clear that Theio is also making an effort to learn English.

By the time they offer to tutor each other, Em is back with two mugs of tea. She sinks into a book on the other end of the couch, and I read with bated breath as the Fajjean people try to fix the damage done to the island by the storm. The efforts require collaboration between both settler and Fakari men, and so for the first time, Sarah's worlds start to collide. My breath catches—I'm almost as nervous as she is at the thought of Richard and Theio interacting.

It's just as Sarah overhears Richard and a few of the other settler men plotting something that I hear Em gasp beside me. I look up to see her staring out the window behind me and whip my head around.

There, far in the distance above the trees, I see a huge blue light floating far in the horizon.

"Oh my God," I say, scrambling up from the couch.

"We can see better from the turret," she says, and rushes to the spiral staircase at the far end of the room. I follow her, and together we scramble up, then reach the top where we have a better view of the island and the cliffs in the distance.

Over the horizon are what feel like a dozen streaks of cool blue light, floating steadily in the distance. They're everywhere, in every corner over the shoreline: even stronger and brighter than the ones I saw with Seb.

"*Agaayu,*" Em whispers under her breath.

I look at her. "That can't be good."

37

SEB

Thunder cracks overhead, and as we dash through the brush, I crane my neck to look up at the sky. Heavy gray clouds are knitting together overhead, painting the world dark.

To the left of me, Kieran's wolf tics his snout upwards, a suggestion. On my other side, Gabe's wolf nods, and the three of us pick up the pace, lowering our heads to run faster in the direction of the *fikarig* just as the first drops of rain begin to hit our fur.

The pace gnaws at my leg almost instantly, but I grit my teeth and charge on. It's been a full day since Maren and I came back to Saroe, and today the guys and I spent the afternoon at the common house with my mom, boarding over the windows to make a shelter for those whose homes can't otherwise be made storm-safe. Hopefully, it'll be a few more days before the storm hits—but if it's coming now, no amount of pain will keep me from wherever Maren is.

And with any luck, maybe her discoveries will mean I won't be in pain much longer.

The thought fuels my drive, and we make our way through the woods until we reach a wide expanse of green hills. The rain is falling harder now, but I can see the *fikarig* up ahead, windows glowing warm yellow against the dark sky. We race towards it, reaching the front steps just as lightning cracks up ahead.

I shift into human form, staggering towards the clothing box we keep near the front door.

"I'm gonna check on Em," Kier mumbles as he tugs on a pair of sweatpants. He heads for the door, and as it swings shut I can hear Saga's voice, asking if Gabe came back with him.

I step into joggers and pull on a dark sweater, then glance up at Gabe. He's at the edge of the porch, looking out into the woods.

"You good?" I ask. "Wanna go inside?"

"Yeah," he says, looking away as though breaking a trance. "I wanna go check on my dad's place, in case the storm hits."

"Now?" I look out at the sheets of rain coming down off the side of the porch. "Go later, when we know more about what's coming. Come on. Your mom's asking for you."

"Yeah, yeah. Okay."

I open the front door for him, then follow as he steps into the foyer and is immediately swept into a hug by Saga. I glance over her shoulder. The other elders are here, but Em and Kieran are off already, and Maren's somewhere else. I feel the air for her, then head for the stairs, in the direction of her scent.

I find her in her room, lying on her bed with the blanket bunched around her body.

"*Heij*," I say, walking in.

"Hey," she says, glancing up. "Is everything okay? You were gone for a while."

"Yeah, I was just busy helping prepare for the storm. The common hall is gonna serve as a shelter for those closer to the coast. Saroe and Keist are the highest islands above sea level, so if there's flooding, the other islands have put evacuation plans in place. If the worst happens, our *fikarig* is elevated enough that it should be okay. For now, all we can do is wait."

I take a seat on the bed, and it's only now that I register her face. Her eyes are pink and swollen, as though she's been crying.

"Hey, what's wrong?" I ask. "Did something happen?"

"It's nothing," she says, but I can hear immediately that's not true.

"Is it your mom?" I reach out a hand to her leg, and she sits up, her phone coming into view.

"I've just... I've been reading the diaries," she says, bringing a hand to her face.

"Is this about Sarah?"

"Sort of."

"Did you find out what happened to her?"

She sighs. "I don't know. Her husband caught her listening in on his plans to kill the *reijna*. He had this idea that, if they killed the pack leader, they could access more fertile soil on the southern part of the island. But even the Fakari people were struggling to grow crops, and when her husband found out how much time Sarah spent with the pack, he beat her. She managed to get to Eia for help, and when Theio saw the state she was in, he left the house. That's where the diary ends. I don't know what happened next."

"Is that what you're upset about?" I reach a hand out to her face. "We can find out more. Maybe Ingemar knows—she inherited the house in the end, right? I'm sure she knows something."

"That's not it," she says, her dark eyes looking up to meet mine.

"Okay. What's up?"

She opens her mouth to speak when suddenly I feel something—a low rumble murmuring through the house. For a moment, the animal of my body thinks there's something happening outside: a noise loud enough to make it feel like the house is vibrating. But a half-second later, as the dresser next to us begins to shake, I realize.

"*Agaayu*, it's happening," I say. "Get down."

The bed begins to rattle, and I push Maren down onto the mattress, pinning myself over her as the earth shakes. The books lying on top of the desk across her room fall onto the floor, and from on top of the dresser, we watch as two clay vases teeter closer and closer to the edge, one falling over and smashing onto the hardwood.

From down the hall, I hear Em's startled cry, and somewhere in the *fikaband* I fumble for the others, checking that everyone's close. Maren pulls herself to me, and I hold her to my chest, closing my eyes. Above us, I hear the lamp on her ceiling swinging wildly, and feel little chunks of plaster and dust brush down on top of us.

After what must be a half-minute, the sound of rumbling finally stops.

"*Aeijsammen okeij?*" comes Saga's voice from downstairs. *Is everyone okay?*

"We're alright!" I yell back, and I hear another call of the same come from Kieran, down the hall.

I turn to Maren.

"Are *you* okay?" I ask.

She nods. "I'm fine. But... we need to talk."

"Yeah, sure. I just need to check with Saga about what this means for the emergency plan. Can we go downstairs first?"

Her mouth twists, but she nods. "Yeah, okay."

She takes my hand as I lead her out of the bedroom, careful to step around the shards of broken pottery. We make it downstairs, where I see one of the living room bookshelves is knocked over, the books spilling out onto the floor.

Saga looks over her shoulder at me, and I see she's holding a phone to her ear. The person on the other line must pick up, because she presses a finger to her other ear and begins speaking rapidly, the Fakari words coming out like a waterfall.

Next to her, Gabe and Viggo squat down to lift up the bookshelf. I walk over and help, and together we begin picking the books off the ground. Behind us I can hear Em and Kieran come down the stairs to join the group.

"*Iija, iija. 'Ts kut,*" Saga says, and as I look up at her, I see the tension in her shoulders ease just slightly. "*Iija, okeij. Ije ringe stra tikbakke. 'Vayyu.*"

She turns to face us, and Gabe and I straighten from the books. Kieran comes beside us, and Em walks over to Maren and gives her a hug.

"That was your mom, Seb," Saga says, turning to me. "She's at the common house. She's fine, she was just reporting on behalf of the council."

"What now?" Kieran asks, turning to Saga.

"We won't know the magnitude for another twenty minutes, but it's unlikely this was strong enough to cause any major ocean waves or seiches. Maybe some local flooding near the watersheds."

"We're not worried about anything like a tsunami, right?" Kieran asks.

Saga shakes her head. "*Nekka.* They're incredibly rare in the Atlantic, and this wouldn't have been big enough to cause one."

Thunder claps overhead, and out of the corner of my eye, I see Em jump. Kieran moves in her direction, coming to stand beside her.

"Okay," I say, nodding at Saga. "And so what *are* we worried about?"

"The Wrath of the Gods, right?" Em says, running a hand over her arm. "Is that what this is? The storm…"

Saga shakes her head. "No, an earthquake and a thunderstorm aren't nearly big enough to be the storm from legends. A hurricane, maybe."

"One can't cause the other?" asks Kieran.

"It's not a storm," Maren says, and thunder rumbles outside again.

"I mean, can an earthquake cause—" Kieran says.

"No, hang on." I turn to Maren. "What's not a storm?"

"The Wrath of the Gods. It's not a storm."

Saga turns to look at her. "What do you mean? The ancestors saved up salt because a storm was coming."

Maren shakes her head, bringing her golden-brown eyes to me before looking back at Saga.

"No," she says, her voice careful. "They saved up salt because they knew conditions were changing, and making salt the traditional way wouldn't be possible for another hundred years."

I feel something cold slither through my gut. "What?"

"Tell us, *piu*," Saga says. "What did you learn?"

"I've been reading the diaries we found on Fajje, and the author, Sarah, knew some of the people who were saving the salt. The Wrath of the Gods wasn't a storm—it was a period of change in conditions on the islands. Like a fallow period. The island's natural heat sources become harder to use for a few generations."

She looks at me again. "It wasn't the storm that caused them to slow down salt production, Seb. I think the geothermal energy couldn't get hot enough to produce salt anymore."

"That doesn't make sense," I say, my pulse rising. "Geothermal energy doesn't run out."

She shakes her head. "No, but reservoir pressure can change, right? Sarah didn't call it that, but I used what she wrote in the diaries to learn more online. I think that's what happened."

I feel my pulse beating in my chest. *This isn't possible. It can't—*

"So what about the storm?" Em asks. "There was a storm that wiped out parts of Fajje, Marit, and Keist. You said she even speaks to some of it, in the diaries."

Maren brings her arms around herself, and I can feel her eyeing me.

"I... I don't know," she says, but I can see she's holding something back.

"Yes, you do," I say, my voice low. "Say it."

"It looks like..." she tries. "Like the red sky and the earthquake lights were signs that the shift in conditions was imminent. But what they told you in school is right, Seb—Sarah says the Fakari people already knew to expect it using some kind of calendar. *That's* why they were saving up salt for years already, before the dark winter and the blue lights. The storm marked the turning point, but it wasn't what stopped them from making salt —that was changing conditions, making it harder to do it the old way. And I think that year, the storm just ended up being way worse that year than anyone expected."

"Why?" Kieren asks. "Why was it worse?"

Maren looks at Saga. "You know the year of the storm, right?"

"1755," she answers, without thinking.

"I... I looked it up," Maren says. "It's the same year a really bad earthquake hit Lisbon. The earthquake was so big that it resulted in aftershocks as far as Finland, and a tsunami wave in Cornwall. I think maybe that's what caused the damage here, too."

"But that wasn't the Wrath of the Gods?" Gabe asks.

"No," Maren says, looking at me. "The Wrath of the Gods is the part that repeats—it's the fallow period that the old Fakari people attributed to the gods' anger. That year, the changes they were expecting—dark winter, red sky, earthquake—just happened to overlap with a much bigger earthquake somewhere else, and that sent flooding this way."

I can hear the rushing of blood in my ears as I start putting the pieces together. Somehow it's made louder by the rain pelting down on the windows outside.

"But… but that's not happening now," I say. "It's not the same. We haven't been having crop issues. Everything's fine."

Saga shakes her head, thinking. "I don't know about that… Things are different now. We import a good portion of our produce, and we can create farming conditions through technology that the ancestors didn't have access to. It's possible we've missed the signs they knew to look for."

I feel something harden inside my chest. Maren seems to register a change in me, and starts talking faster.

"The trouble you had with your salt plant, Seb—it wasn't your fault. Sarah's diaries show that, in the years leading up to the storm, it was already getting harder and harder to use the island's geothermal energy to produce salt. I don't think you need access to a better geothermal heat source. I think, maybe, it was already too late."

"No," I say, and it comes out hoarse.

"Seb," Maren says, stepping towards me. Her voice is thick and full of pity. I can't stand it. "It sounds like we might have had the conditions to make the salt the old way a few years ago, but, I mean… These people were struggling with the same issues you are. The geothermal energy just can't get hot enough. That's not your fault. It just means—"

I shake my head. "But a hundred *years*? We won't be able to make the salt the old way for *a hundred years*? That's after my lifetime."

"Hey, it's okay," she says, putting a hand on my face. "They found new ways. They adapted—we can, too."

"I don't—I don't *want* new ways," I spit. "I don't want to adapt. I want—"

I can feel my frustration rising, anger and anxiety building in my chest.

"Seb—" Saga says, and I turn from Maren, running my hands through my hair.

"*Nekka*," I snap.

"Hang on," Gabe says, but I walk out of the room, into the kitchen.

I can hear the blood rushing in my ears, and I feel my wolf raising his hackles. Behind me, I hear Maren move, and her scent comes nearer. A moment later, the warmth of her hand comes to rest on my shoulder.

"Hey," she whispers.

"I can't take this," I say, and my voice comes out broken.

"It was always a long shot," she offers, and I feel something like a vice grip inside my chest. "It was never a guarantee that you'd be able to recreate the salt the old way."

"I just want— In the *Eijna* they talk about salt that can heal the most unfathomable of wounds. If we could get—"

"Seb—"

"*Stop*," I say, turning, and my voice comes out louder than I want it to. I see the shock of it register on her face. "We can't give up here. It's not enough for me. We have to find a way—"

"You need to let this go," she says, her voice firm. She holds my gaze with intensity. "If this whole time, all this salt stuff was about getting your leg muscle back—"

"*Of course* it was. You can see that, can't you? You have no idea what it's like to live with this kind of pain. I can't give up. I have to find a way to undo this."

She places a gentle hand on my neck.

"I just don't want you to spend the rest of your life chasing something that might never happen," she says. "You have a good, rich life. You have a promising business and people who love you. If you're always looking back, you'll never be *here* to experience it."

I take a deep breath. The part of me that wants to fight this rages within me, barrelling inside my chest. But it's the scent of her—honey and sunshine and joy and peace—that helps me slow it down. Like a lighthouse, calling me back to safe harbor.

I wrap my arms around her waist and lean my head against her shoulder.

"I don't want this," I whisper. "I don't want to spend the rest of my life regretting what happened."

"I know," she says, bringing her hands to the back of my neck to stroke my hair. "I'm sorry."

My eyes sting and I take a deep breath.

"What is my life going to look like, if it can't be about this anymore?"

She pulls her head back to look in my eyes. Instinctively I look away, not wanting her to see the pink edges and the edge of tears forming. But she takes my face in her hands and looks intently at me.

"I think that's something you get to choose," she whispers. "*You* get to decide."

I feel that rush inside my chest again, rising. Grief and anger but a little bit of something else, too. Hope.

I lean down to kiss her. She presses her body against mine, and I take her in: honey and sunshine and belonging and *home*. After a moment, I pull away.

"Thank you," I say quietly. "I don't know what we're gonna do, but somehow it's gonna be okay. We'll build a future together."

I see her swallow, and register the slight rise of tension in her shoulders.

"What?" I ask.

"No, it's nothing. I'm just... this is all new for me, you know?" She smiles awkwardly, lifting her shoulders.

"Yeah, of course," I say, nodding. "But we can take our time. I know you're still finding your place here, but I can help. I talked to the guys this morning and told them about us. Kieran and Gabe are both eligible for a council seat, and they agreed to do the rite next winter, when the lights are back. We'll be able to get our own place together, all of us."

She blinks, and her brow furrows. "Seb..."

"Em, too. Maybe my cousin Quinn—I think you'd like her."

"Hey, back up," she says, putting her hands up. "That's not really taking our time. I'm not really ready to think about a house right now—I don't even know if I'll be here in a year."

"*What?*"

My voice comes out loud again, and I see a wall go up behind her eyes. *Fuck.*

"I— no, hang on, sorry," I say, trying to backtrack.

"We've known each other for a few months," she says. Her expression is bewildered, like this shouldn't surprise me.

"We're *mates*," I say.

"I mean... yeah, maybe," she says. "But like... that means so much more to you than it does to me."

"I... okay, I get that," I say, and I can hear the strain in my voice. "But... We belong together. I told you about my rite."

I'm suddenly all too aware of the presence of the others in the living room, and I wish we were anywhere else so they couldn't hear us.

"Yeah, but you had months to adjust to that idea. I've had two days. You can't just start talking about buying me a house. I could be back in Boston next year, I don't know."

"I thought you needed a reason to stay," I say, trying to keep my voice steady. "So I'm giving you a reason. We'll get a house. You can work at Saroan Salts. Now that you know that we're mates—"

"But that means nothing to me," she says. At whatever expression passes over my face, I see her backtrack.

"No, not nothing, just—intuitively, I don't get it. I'm still learning all of this. I'm still getting to know my new body, now that I have a wolf side. I just need time to figure out where I belong."

"We belong *together*," I say. "That's what that means."

Her brow furrows. "Okay, but belonging, big-picture, has to

be about more than just *you*. If I want my future to be here on the islands, I need to figure out what it looks like for *me*."

I take her hand and put it on my chest.

"It can look like this. It can look like *us*. Think of how well we worked together on Fajje—we can build a life together. We can find a way forward with the salt company. We can figure out what's next."

She pulls her hand away.

"But it's *your* salt company," she says carefully. "You're talking about all the ways I can fit into *your* life. If I move my life here, it has to also be about what I want, and what's right for me."

I swallow. *If* she moves here. That rushing sound is back in my ears, and I can feel my wolf rising in my chest, wanting to break free.

"I'm not saying I'm leaving," she says. "I'm just saying I don't know yet that this is forever, and all of this is going a little fast for me."

"I—I can't do this right now," I say, and turn away from her.

"Seb—"

"I just... I can't lose all of this," I say, turning over my shoulder to look at her. "Not all at once. Not today."

I head for the front door of the house and get outside, tearing off my clothes before my wolf can burst out of me. The rain is pouring down in sheets, and it hits my skin as I step out under the dark cover of night.

I let myself shift, and I run and run and run.

38

MAREN

"Can I come in, *piu?*" Saga asks, rapping her fingers on the doorframe.

I look up from my bed.

"Is Seb back?" I mumble.

"Not yet," she says softly. "Gabriel went out to find him. I don't like the thought of them being out in this weather together, but he promised they'd be home soon."

Her eyes fall to the shattered shards of pottery lying on my floor. "Ah, the earthquake did me a favor. I always hated that jug."

I let out a little snort, but it comes out choked from the sound of my tears. "Really?"

"*Iija.* Your mother bought it, just after she and David got together. It's factory-made. There's no accounting for bad taste." She rolls her eyes, and I can see a smile tug at her mouth.

I let out a broken sigh.

"I don't— I don't know what to do," I say.

She comes into my room and sits on the bed. "I think you did everything right," she says softly, reaching over to stroke my hair.

"How much did you hear?"

She turns her head side to side. "Most of it."

I sigh. "I knew this would hurt him. And the commitment stuff—it's just a little too much for me. It's too fast."

She nods. "Seb has spent most of his life waiting for his *kamaat*—his mate. They all have. He's always known there was a puzzle piece missing, and now you're here and you seem to fit perfectly. But all of this is new to you."

I nod, sitting up to look at her.

"I just... It's not about that for me. Things with Seb are good. They feel right. He *could* be it. But... I need more than that, to move my entire life here."

She nods solemnly. "Your mother said the same thing."

"Yeah?" I ask, bringing a sleeve up to my face to wipe my eyes.

"*Iija*. She was a modern woman—a career lady. It wasn't enough for her to move to these islands to be with a man. And she was worried about your future. She wanted you to have choices. That's why they moved back."

I sigh, looking at the bed. "I mean, I'm not a career woman. I don't know what my job is supposed to be, or what I'm here for."

"Those aren't the same thing," she says, smiling softly.

"In America they are. I've spent what feels like my whole life trying a hundred things to see what my calling was."

"And where did that lead you?"

I shrug. "I don't know. I haven't found it yet. I mean, what about you? When did you know that being a healer was what you were on this earth to do?"

She smiles again and laughs softly. "Oh, *piu*. I'm not here to be a healer."

"What do you mean?"

"I'm a healer, but I'm more than that. I'm Gabe's mother. I'm your aunt. I'm on pack council, I own the apothecary. But I'm also just here to *be*. To play cards with Isolde and go on walks with Dagmar. To carry my husband's memory forward without him."

I see a cloud pass over her face.

"When I was a few years younger than you, I *desperately* wanted to leave this place," she says after a minute. "I wanted to go to the mainland to become a doctor of Western medicine. Can you believe that? *Me*. In America."

"Really?" I furrow my brow, struggling to imagine it. "So what changed?"

She shrugs. "David was always the true child of the islands, between the two of us. He loved Fakari history and culture. He had a daily salt practice; he read the *Eijna*. *He* was supposed to stay here, not me. And then—" She raises her hands. "He fell in love. He started talking about leaving."

"So? Didn't that make it easier?" I ask. "You could have gone together."

She shakes her head. "We had already started forming this *fika*. Someone needed to be here to take care of our parents. And when he started talking about leaving, it made me think of all the things we have to offer here. What I had to gain by staying."

"Do you ever regret it?" I ask.

She shakes her head. "Not once. But that's because this was the right thing for *me*. That doesn't mean it's the right thing for you. If you want to leave, you can. You'll always be welcome back."

"I don't know what I want. I just... I want to be happy. I want to feel like my life matters. Like I belong."

"What makes you feel that way?"

I shake my head. "I don't know."

She nods, looking down at the blanket. "Do you remember what I said to you, the first time you shifted in the kitchen?"

I shake my head.

"I said that your wolf might feel like a liability, but she's also part of what makes you strong. Our wolves are closer to our hearts than we can sometimes get with our human minds. Maybe she can be a tool to you in understanding what matters most."

I sigh, thinking back over the last few weeks—to the moments where the wolf in my core felt happiest.

"Back on the north island, there was this moment where Em showed me a painting she made of me and the gang," I say. "I felt like she saw me. And on Fajje, when I talked to that old woman and I listened to her story. I got to help her feel like she mattered. Like her work would continue on after her. Or with Seb..."

I think back on the moment we made the deal to help his salt business. Fixing up his website. The way I felt when I saw the first rush of orders come in. The moment he kissed me at the top of the ruins.

"I don't know. I think I feel best when I feel like people see me. But you can't build a life around that."

She shrugs. "Maybe you can."

I look down at the bed and let out a sigh.

"It's alright if it takes time," she says gently. "You don't need to choose anything for forever. You can just choose for today."

"It feels like Seb wants me to choose for forever."

She turns her head. "That's his problem to sort out, not yours."

"Yeah, okay," I say, sighing. "Thanks, Saga."

"Of course, *denanni*." She stands up. "I'll go get a dustpan for the vase."

"I— actually, can I ask you a question?"

She turns. "*Iija*, of course. What is it?"

"Do you know why my dad named me for the *mareijnit*?"

She smiles sadly. "Why do you ask?"

I shrug. "Seb and I thought that's what the earthquake lights were, at first. I told him that's what I was named for, and he asked why. I realized I didn't know."

She leans against the door, crossing her arms over herself.

"David never told me why, explicitly. But since you were born on the mainland, I always wondered if maybe it was about his hope for you."

"What do you mean?"

"*Mareijnit* bring sailors home to safe harbor. I wondered if he hoped that you would bring him home, in your own way."

I blink, feeling a stinging behind my eyes.

"It must have been so hard for you when he left."

She nods. "It was. It hurt all of us. But you find ways to move on. You build forward."

Saga jumps, reaching for her pocket. "That's a phone call— I'm sorry, I have to pick up. It's probably a leader from one of the other island councils. One minute—"

She turns her back and starts talking into the phone in Fakari. I lie back on my bed and close my eyes to think.

39

SEB

My wolf darts through the forest, running through wet branches as thunder cracks overhead. I can scent someone behind me, far away but picking up speed. I lift my nose, searching the air.

Gabe.

I lower my head and run harder, through routes I know he doesn't like. I don't want to talk—not to anyone, about any of this. I hear his feet pick up the pace behind me and push. *Faster, further,* until the air rasps at my throat and my leg sears in pain as rain clouds my vision. After a few minutes, the scent of Gabe's wolf disappears, and I pass through a small clearing in the woods surrounded by high rocks. I stop for a moment to catch my breath, but then hear something from above: the shuffle of feet. I look up just in time to see him jump. Within a moment, he's on me, tackling me to the ground.

His wolf bears down on me, pressing me into the dirt. I snarl, trying to wrestle him off. He barks out a sound and stands back, lowering his head, his tail swishing.

I know what this is. When we were kids, we'd race and

wrestle each other in these woods to get the energy out. Years later, in the weeks I spent preparing for my rite, we would spar for hours in the gym. I think that fighting was the closest I ever got to therapy after my dad died.

I lower my head and snarl, my tail swishing back and forth behind me. Slowly, we start to circle one another—fangs bared, eyes glinting yellow in the dark. He cocks his head in gentle challenge, and my mind flashes back to the night of my rite: large wolf, cocking its head, taunting me.

Me, fighting myself, my outsized anger. Proving beyond a shadow of a doubt that I'm my own worst enemy.

I must hesitate a moment too long, because Gabe lifts his head, leaning back to eye me. I feel my breath begin to grow heavier as the memory of the rite comes back to me: blood and fear and pain. All at the hands of my own wolf; my own fault. And here I am, still paying for it all these years later, with the knowledge that it'll never get better.

Suddenly, the ground begins to shake. Gabe's eyes lock with mine as we both jump in surprise.

Aftershocks, I think, and he must register the same thing I'm feeling—we need to get out of here, before a tree or worse lands on either one of us. I start to run back in the direction of the *fikarig*, but he barks out a sound, and as I look at him he gestures with his head in a different direction.

Right—his dad's cabin. We're deep enough in the woods that it must be closer.

He begins to run, and I follow, doing my best to keep up pace as the ground stops rumbling. Within a few minutes, he finds the stream, and we dash alongside it, heading in the opposite direction of the water. Finally, his father's old cabin comes into view.

My wolf starts at the sight, and for a moment, I stop, even as the rain still bears down in sheets. Where I'm expecting dark, decaying wood swallowed up by overgrown greenery—the state it was in the last time I saw it, years ago—the cabin is now pristine: dark wood and large windows nestled into the surrounding trees, gleaming in the moonlight. It's small, but fixed up like this it looks like a home.

Gabe looks over his shoulder at me from up ahead, and I break myself from my thoughts and follow. We scamper up the front steps to the large porch, and he shifts, running to a clothing box that looks newly built. As I shake the water from my pelt, he pulls out a handful of clothes and tosses them to me. I shift as we both pull our clothes on, still panting from the exertion of the run. I hear another clap of thunder, but it sounds farther away now than a few minutes before.

"Come on," Gabe says, reaching for the handle to the front door. "Get inside."

I follow him, running a hand over my face to remove some of the rainwater. We get through the front door, and Gabe shakes off his feet on the mat, then stands to flip on the light switch.

"You've done a lot with the place," I say, eyeing the room. I remember the whole cabin feeling small and dank, smelling vaguely like old carpet and mildew. Now, the wooden floors are gleaming, and I can see he's lofted the ceiling. The room is relatively empty—just a few folding chairs and a stack of books in the corner, before a stone fireplace that looks like it's still under construction. But in spite of the sparse furniture, the structure of the house is immaculate.

"I'm grabbing socks," he says, ignoring my comment and walking through the living room towards a small bedroom on the other side. A minute later he returns and tosses me a bundle of woolens.

"Thanks."

"Yeah. So." He takes a seat in one of the folding chairs. "Are we gonna talk about this?"

"About your dad's place?" I ask, looking around. "This must have taken you years, man. Did you do this alone? How did you learn to do it?"

"Not about this. About your life. What happened in the kitchen just now."

I swallow down the feeling of gravel in my throat. "No."

"No what?"

"We're not talking about it."

"Because that's worked so well for you before."

"What's it to you?" I snap. "Why did you even follow me out here? Isn't it obvious I want to be alone?"

He gives me a look. "I'm not doing that to you."

"Well, why the hell not?" My voice is bitter, angry.

He leans forward, resting his forearms against his legs.

"For three years, I've watched you throw yourself into a dream like it's your life's work. You just found out that it's never going to happen. So no, I'm not leaving you alone. You wouldn't do that to me, either."

Hearing him state it so plainly, I feel something ache in my chest, and my shoulders fall.

"I really... I thought this was it," I say.

"I know."

"What are we gonna do now?" I ask, sitting in the folding chair beside him. "I mean, with the business. Our dream is dead."

"*Your* dream."

I look at him. "It's *our* business. We've worked together on it for years."

"And you're still the owner."

I blink, my brow furrowing as I realize—I never even stopped to consider offering him partial ownership. But he raises his hands.

"That's fine, I don't need more than that. It was always your dream, never mine. I did it for you." He smiles, like he's surprised I didn't realize.

"You never told me," I say.

He shrugs. "You never asked."

I look over his face, suddenly realizing how much there must be I've never asked about. The cabin; the things he alluded to in my room a few weeks back, about not finding a partner. It was so easy to let myself and my own pain be at the center of our friendship. I always figured that if he wanted me to know something, he'd tell me himself.

"So what's your dream?" I ask carefully.

He shrugs, but I register a tension somewhere in his silence. Typically, I'd change the subject, but now I force myself to wait.

"I don't have much that's mine," he says finally.

I turn the words over in my head, trying to glean some insight from them. But before I get anywhere, he asks,

"So what are *you* going to do with the salt business? Now that the real dream is dead?"

"Did you always know that's what this was about?" I ask, gesturing to my leg.

"I had a feeling. You didn't have the money to get close enough in any other way."

I sigh, looking down at my hands. "I don't know. I mean, I like the work..."

"Is it meaningful to you?"

"Yeah. I really do believe in this stuff, even if I'm never going to get close to what the ancients had. Even our modern stuff has helped me. I think it can help others."

"And with Maren at the helm, you're actually getting it *in front* of others."

I shake my head. "I mean, for however long she's here. You heard her. She doesn't know where she'll be a year from now."

I run a hand through my hair, leaning back in the chair and looking up at the ceiling.

"You said she needed a reason to stay," I say finally. "I thought, if I told her we were mates, it would be enough."

"It's okay if she needs more than that."

I look over at him.

"She could leave at any time," I say, and my voice betrays how much the idea hurts.

"So could you," he says, raising an eyebrow. "That's what love is: risk."

"Is that so?" I say dryly.

"Yeah. You have to dare to be vulnerable." He shrugs, smiling slightly. "I've heard it's worth it."

I sigh. "I thought I gave her a reason. Being mates, Saroan Salts, getting our own *fikarig*..."

"Your dream, your dream, *your* dream," he says, ticking them off his fingers. "What does *she* want?"

I think of the things she told me, that afternoon crying on her bed.

"Belonging," I say finally. "I thought that's what I was giving her."

"Maybe she needs to find out what it is for herself."

We hear thunder crack in the distance, and Gabe looks out the window at the dark forest.

"My mom's gonna be losing her mind that we're out in this weather," he says, standing. "I didn't bring my phone, so I'm gonna head home. You stay here as long as you want to clear your head."

He walks to the front door.

"Gabe," I call out, and he turns around.

"I'm sorry," I say. "I've been so focused on myself these last few years. I should have thought more about what was going on with you. I should have asked."

He lifts his shoulders. "It's the way of things."

"No, really." I gesture around the place. "I wish I'd known you were working on this. I should have helped. We should have the *fika* over, show them what you've done with the place."

He shakes his head. "Nah, that's alright. I'm okay letting this be the one thing that's mine."

He shuts the door behind him, and I look through the

window as his wolf disappears between the trees, in the direction of home.

It's been so easy to center myself in our friendship these past few years; I didn't even notice. And, for the first time, I let myself wonder if that's how I've been treating Maren, too.

40

SEB

I get back to the *fikarig* hours later at close to midnight, exhausted and soaked to the bone from the rain. The living room is empty—I can sense in the *fikaband* that, although some people are awake, everyone's already off to bed—but Saga's left a light on for me. I turn it off and head for the stairs, carefully pulling myself up step by step until I get to the second floor landing.

The light is on in Maren's room, and I can see it spilling out over the floor and into the hallway. I walk over and knock.

"Yeah?"

I open the door. She's sitting on her bed, her laptop and a notebook in front of her. When she sees it's me, she folds the screen shut and flips the notebook over, crossing her arms over her chest.

"So," she says, eyeing me.

"I'm sorry."

"Yeah." I see her bite the inside of her cheek, looking down at the duvet.

"Can I come in?"

"You're soaking wet."

"Can I... get changed and then come in?"

"Yeah. Okay."

I head for my room and pull off my rain-soaked clothes, toweling off my body and hair before stepping into clean sweats and a loose black shirt. A minute later, I reappear at her door. She's rearranged the bed, making the sheets and pulling up a chair for me to sit in. I walk over and take a seat opposite her.

"I'm sorry," I say again.

She holds my gaze. "For what?"

A challenge, not a question.

"For leaving when I got upset."

She shakes her head, dark curls bouncing around her face. "I don't care about that."

"I'm not done." I lean forward, looking up at her. "For getting angry at you for needing more time. You're right. I had years to wrap my mind around having a mate, and months to get used to it being you. This whole concept—this whole world—is new to you. Of course you need more time."

"Okay," she says, pulling her arms closer to herself.

"But I think, mostly..." I sigh, looking down at my hands. "That was a symptom of something bigger. I think I've been looking at our relationship through... my own lens, I guess. I've centered myself. The salt business, this quest to Fajje, getting a *fikarig*, our future... It all felt perfect because it was what *I* wanted. That wasn't fair. And I think I'm realizing that I've been centering myself in a lot of my relationships. Ever since my rite."

She pulls her legs in butterfly style, and looks up at me, eyebrow raised in challenge.

"That's not an excuse," I say, "just an explanation. I was devastated after my dad died. And after that night on the cliffs, it felt like I'd been cursed. My suffering became the biggest part of my life, and I guess it blinded me to everyone and everything else. Gabe; my mom. You."

Her gaze softens.

"You deserve to be happy," I say. "You deserve to choose, and make, your own happiness. And I want to support you with that. Even if... even if it means you going home."

The words taste like bile in my throat, but I mean them.

"I think I want *this* place to be home," she says.

The wolf in my chest sits up, swishing his tail at the thought. "Yeah?"

"Yeah," she says, nodding. "It's what I asked for, burning the *lot* with you that day in the temple. I wanted a place to belong. And I think that place can be here, if I let it—but I need to figure out what it looks like. If I stay here, my life has to be bigger than just you. I need you to get that."

I nod. "I do. What does that look like for you?"

"I'm still figuring that out," she says. "I don't really know yet what I need to feel like I belong."

"Do you remember when you asked me about the *fikaband*, that night on Halluk?" I ask, and she nods.

"The way I could feel you then wasn't the *fikaband*, yet. It was the start of the mate bond—I think because it was the first time I was starting to recognize that you were my mate. But the *fika-band* will form between you and the others eventually."

Like how the mate bond will form with me, I think.

"When?"

"I don't know," I say honestly. "Maybe the closer you get with people, or the more this place starts to feel like home. Or maybe when you accept that you *do* belong."

She blinks as the words hit her, and then reaches to pick up the notebook.

"I talked to Saga. I'm trying to figure out what sorts of things make me happy here—what I need for a full life on the islands."

"Any ideas?"

"Too many. Famously." She smiles, then looks down at the list.

"I like working at Saroan Salts, and I think I'm good at it. I want to keep working there, but I want to pursue my own interests there, too. I want to design that bath products line. And also, now that we're making a profit, I want to be paid for my work."

She glances at my face to gauge my reaction, and I nod.

"You should be. And Gabe should be getting more than an hourly wage. I realize I've made a mistake there."

"Yeah?"

I nod. "Yeah. I want to give you both partial ownership of the company. I should have done that for him years ago—he's been there with me from the very beginning. And with you, for how much you've grown the business and how much of the work you're doing—you deserve a cut of the success."

"I like the sound of that," she says, eyes twinkling.

"It's— it's also not contingent on our relationship," I add. "I don't want it to influence how you feel about us."

She smiles, and raises her eyebrows in challenge. "How big of a cut?"

"Subject to negotiation."

The smile widens to a grin. "Something tells me that if we have our next business meeting in the hot springs, I'll have the upper hand in that conversation."

"I think you already do," I say.

She gives me a look, and the wolf in my chest perks up. I make myself focus and look down at the notebook in her hands.

"Now come on. What else is on your list?"

She reads it off. "I like writing, even if it's not everything to me. I'm gonna write that article for Puur—it seems like such a waste not to, even just for the free publicity."

"Sure."

"And I just want to try a bunch of stuff. Not career things, just life things. Like learning how to make some of Saga's apothecary recipes, or taking a boxing class here. I want to spend time with Em, and work on my Fakari, and swim in the lake. Not proving anything to my mom, or anyone else."

"That sounds great."

She nods. "And lastly, I want to keep working on this history stuff. I want to help Ingemar make her documents available to the Fakari people. I want to prove that foreigners also have a place here."

"Because you care about history? Or because it's also about proving you have a place here?"

She shrugs. "I don't know. Maybe both? Like with you and the salts. It was about the business, but it was also about... you know."

She looks down at my thigh, and I nod.

"I don't think it was ever really about the business for me, if I'm honest," I say.

She waits as I take a moment to collect my thoughts.

"I was using the business as a way to fund the thing I wanted most," I say finally. "Restoring the old salt production methods wasn't even for the greater good, I think. It was just about me and my own pain. The geothermal energy and stuff—I don't know that it matters so much now."

She shakes her head. "It *totally* matters. Heating with geothermal energy, even if it's supported with a radiator, is still probably the closest thing to how the salt used to be made. I think that's worth something—it's what makes Saroan Salts special. And who knows? Maybe one day, with enough effort and research, we can get there. The salt won't be how it was hundreds of years ago. But we can get as close as possible."

I shake my head. "No. You were right: if I'm focused on resurrecting what we've lost, I miss out on what I have now."

Her hand reaches for mine.

"I'm never gonna get the muscle in my leg back," I say, and my throat burns with the truth. "I'll never be able to undo what happened. I need to stop mourning the past and focus on building the future."

I run my thumb over the back of her hand.

"You asked me, that night in the bath, what I deserve," I say quietly. "I think I finally figured it out. To let go. To move on."

She smiles softly, and I look up at her.

"Earlier in the kitchen, I was falling into the same trap as before. I'm sorry. The salts couldn't save me, and neither can you. I don't want a version of you who exists to save me from myself. I want *you*, the full you. Loud. Wild. Messy."

"Even when I snore?" she asks, cocking an eyebrow.

I shrug. "It's cute."

She smiles. "It won't be cute forever."

"I thought we weren't thinking about forever."

Her eyes sparkle with humor, and she shakes her head. "Not *yet*."

The words send a ripple of delight over my skin, and I reach my free hand to her, running it over her hair.

"I don't want you to choose me," I say. "I want you to choose *you*. And I'm going to try to be good enough to and for you, so that if you choose what's best for you, ending up with me is a natural consequence."

"Deal," she says, pulling my face towards hers. She kisses me gently, her lips pressing against mine. I feel the rush of joy and hope and warmth bloom in my chest. Finally, she pulls away and looks into my eyes.

"Yeah?" I ask.

"Yeah." She smiles. "Let's try it."

41

MAREN

Three months later

"Mare!"

"Mare!"

I look up to see Seb hopping out of the Jeep, slamming the door behind him. In one arm is a stack of magazines.

"Oh my God, is that *it*?!" I ask, lifting myself out of the water to sit on the hot spring's edge. The cool autumn air nips at my skin, and I reach for a towel to wrap around myself my upper body.

"Ten copies. Cover story. Look," he says, kneeling beside me to show me the magazine.

Puur's cover features a gorgeous, glossy photo of light-brown garlic salt spilled over moody deep green tiles. All around are jars of salt and gold spoons with thin handles, splayed out as though you interrupted a cooking day in someone's perfect kitchen. Black volcanic salt, the light green of samphire salt, soft golden smoked sea salt. On the bottom-rightmost jar, the Saroan Salts logo is fully visible.

"Letmeseeletmeseeletmesee," I say, using the towel to dry off my hands and reaching for a copy. I flip through the pages until I find the story.

"'Finding Home and Healing on the Fakaris,'" I read, before my eyes fall to the byline. *Maren Winterwood.* No Holt in sight.

My mom will flip, I think happily. Let her.

I skim the article, looking at the beautiful photos the Puur team put together. The story ended up taking more of a personal angle than I'd initially intended. Instead of just focusing on the salts and their healing properties, I was able to find a way to tie them to my own story of finding myself here—*without* spilling any of the Islands' secrets.

I look up to meet Seb's gaze.

"And?" I ask, my voice betraying my nerves.

"It's only been out on the mainland for a day or two, and we've already seen a threefold increase in sales. Definitely enough to fund the bath product line you want to make."

"Eep!" I squeal, kicking my feet so that some of the water from the springs splashes onto Seb's jeans.

"*Heij*, watch it. You'll ruin the magazines." He picks up the stack and places it behind himself, then sits down fully to start untying his shoes. I flip through the story, skimming the paragraphs I've all but memorized.

"Did you read it?" I ask.

"You mean *after* reading it a hundred times during your editing process? No." He manages to get his shoes and socks off.

"You should," I say, and hand him my copy.

I drop the towel from my shoulders and slip into the water, then turn to look at him. He stands to pull off his sweater and jeans, then lowers himself to the water's edge and enters the pool with me.

"From the beginning?" he asks, picking up the open magazine.

"Nope." I pull myself close to him, wrapping one arm around

his waist under the water and leaning my head against his shoulder. "Just this part."

With my dry hand, I point to the last few paragraphs. I look up at his face as his eyes read over the lines of text, detailing the sense of home I've been able to find on the Fakaris—and my hopes for the future.

I watch as realization dawns in his eyes, his brow furrowing just slightly.

"Really?" he asks.

I nod. "Really."

He puts the magazine on top of the stack and pulls himself against me, pressing his lips to mine.

"So you've decided to stay," he says, nuzzling his face into my hair.

"I decided a while ago. I just wanted to make you sweat." I wrap my legs around his waist, pulling him closer to me as the warm water envelops us. "I *do* insist on an annual trip back to the States. For business reasons, of course. And snacks. I can't be-*lieve* you don't have goldfish here. The Fakari people are very bad at processed carbs."

"Fine by me," he says. "So does this mean Kier and Gabe have the go-ahead for the rite?"

I pull my head back and give him a sardonic look. "Are you trying to tell me that's *not* what Kieran's been training for every day these last few months?"

He smiles, the warmth in his eyes glowing like embers for me. "Maybe."

"You must think I'm very stupid," I say, pulling him in to kiss me.

"No. In fact, I think you're very, very smart." He presses me against the mossy rocks at the edge of the spring, kissing me on my mouth, then my cheek, then my ear. "And funny, and beautiful. And sexy."

As his hands roam over my waist and hips, I can feel him

hardening against my inner thigh. For a second I reflexively pull him closer at the sensation, before lifting a hand between us.

"Wait! I almost forgot. I have news for you, too."

"Tell me," he murmurs, kissing his way down my neck and to my collarbone. A shiver of delight runs through me at the feeling, and I push him away.

"No, seriously! I need to be able to focus for a minute. Ingemar and I finally found it."

"What?"

"The end of Sarah's story," I say, reaching for my phone. "It took forever, but she found a letter to Eia, from Sarah. Richard died—I don't want to think about how, but I have some ideas," I say, remembering how Theio left in a rage when he saw that Sarah had been beaten.

"Sarah and Theio ended up getting married and moving away. They left Eia the house and all Sarah's old possessions. That's how it ended up in the family. So now we know."

"Wow. How do you feel?"

"Happy," I say, smiling. "She got the ending she deserved. And now I get to have mine."

He looks at me for a long moment, and I feel something behind my own eyes start to sting.

"*Ijekayyatik*, Seb," I say to him—for the first time. "I love you."

"Yeah?" he asks, his shoulders softening.

"Yeah," I say softly, and pull him close. "I've known for a while now. I just wanted to make you sweat."

I wrap my arms around his neck as he pulls me close.

"Tell me again," he murmurs, bringing our faces together.

"I love you," I whisper. "I loved you once, long ago, before our souls ever made it here. And I'll love you long after we're gone."

"And in between?" he asks, and I can hear a teasing edge in his voice.

"I'll hate you sometimes. Not my fault. You have a tendency to be insufferable."

His hands tickle my waist and I bark out a laugh, yanking his hands down so they're on my legs, holding me up.

"I love you, too," he says. "You know, I've been thinking about it. I did see a *mareijna* that day with you, out on the beach."

My brow furrows. "Yeah?"

"Yeah: you. I spent years after my rite wandering—searching for justice, for restoration, for a place to land. But all that searching kept me from being *here* to experience my life. Until you."

He kisses me, and I lock my ankles behind him.

"You bring me home," he whispers, pressing his forehead against mine. "Not to a new place, but to the moment—to being present and alive. *Here*, with you."

I place my hand on his chest, and he raises a hand from the water to clasp onto it, our fingers intertwining with each other.

"*This*," he says, moving our hands back and forth between us, "is where I belong."

"Where we *both* belong," I say.

And as I do, I finally feel something inside me click into place.

He eyes me, some combination of wonder and bewilderment on his face.

"What just happened?" he asks.

"I... don't know. I think I feel—" I hesitate, looking away to focus on what's happening in my mind.

"It's the *fikaband*," he says, beaming. "It happened. You've let yourself join us."

I look up at him, feeling the tears prick my eyes.

"Yeah. I think I did."

"Mare," he says gently, nuzzling his face into my hair. "Welcome home."

I hold him close, feeling the gentle drum of his heartbeat against my skin.

Home. Forever.

"I want you to claim me," I say quietly.

He pulls away. "What?"

"It's time," I say, running my fingers through the hair on the back of his head. "I've known for a while, but I wanted to wait until the time was right. Let's make it real."

"Mare," he murmurs, and I feel his hips shift a little under the water. "Are you sure? Don't make promises you can't—"

He lets out a guttural groan as I move my hips against him.

"I'm sure," I say, gazing into his eyes. "I want you. I want this."

I watch him swallow, and see that languid look take over his eyes as he allows his desire to run through him. His gaze falls to my collarbone, and I feel a smile pull at my mouth.

"What's the matter?" I ask coyly, bringing my fingers to the exact spot. "Not so sure anymore?"

"I've just... I've wanted this for so long," he says, his voice low.

"So show me, then," I whisper. "Show me what you waited for."

He brings his mouth to my neck, and instantly I feel the sparks of hunger and desire flood over my body. I gasp as I pull my ankles tighter around him, bringing his hardness as close to my body as I can.

"*Mare,*" he breaths, the *r* rolling like a snarl. "Show me where. Like this?"

He takes the skin below my collarbone between his teeth and rolls it gently, and I feel my inner wolf respond.

"You know where," I breathe, my hand fumbling under the water for the length of him. I grip it and stroke it upwards, and feel his shoulders tense at the sensation.

"Here?" he asks, his voice coy and teasing. He brings his mouth higher, below my ear, and I groan in frustration.

"Don't tell me you haven't memorized the exact spot," I say.

"Don't try to tell me you haven't fantasized about this for months."

"Oh, *there*," he purrs in my ear, and brings his mouth just above my collarbone.

My breath catches as his tongue runs over the skin, and the little brush of teeth instinctively makes my hips buck.

"Yes, there," I gasp. Under the water I feel his hand come to the crux between my thighs, his thumb instantly coming to my clit as his fingers move against the seam. I reach for the waistband of his boxers and pull them down so I can feel the exposed skin of his hardness in my hands.

He laps at my neck, toying with the skin between his teeth, and presses himself against me. I can feel him pull the fabric of my bathing suit to the side, and instinctively I spread my legs wider to make room for him. He brings the head to my entrance.

"It might hurt. The bite," he says, pulling away from my neck briefly to look in my eyes.

"I don't care," I breathe. "Claim me."

I see the hunger overtake him, and he brings his mouth back to my neck.

In an instant, it overcomes me. I feel him slide the hard length of himself into me, and I cry out, dropping my head back just as his teeth sink into the skin. His hips find a rhythm as they pump into me, and at the suction and combination of pain and pleasure in my neck, my own hips grind back.

The pleasure of the bite is overwhelming, matched only by the fervent, needy rhythm of Seb's body, showing me how much he needs this—how much he's dreamt of taking me, claiming me, making me his. I can feel something seep into my skin— something innately *him*, strong and insistent and powerful. It feels euphoric, mixing with my own energy and overtaking my body. I can feel his pleasure in mine, swirling through me, wrapping around my bones, into my soul, bringing an incredible rush of pleasure through my hips and core.

"Oh, God," I groan, and his thumb finds my clit again, rubbing against it with a needy, urgent pace that matches his hips. I feel myself growing closer, and as he continues to suck and nip at the skin of my neck, the pitch of my moans grows higher.

"Claim me," he murmurs against my skin, the words guttural and commanding.

"Out of the water," I say, and he nods.

Seb brings his hands under my hips to help as I lift myself over the edge of the rocks. The air nips at my skin, somehow only heightening the overwhelming surge of sensations running through me.

"I want to be on top for this," I say, and he nods, moving to sit up.

I straddle his hips, bending my head to kiss him as I slowly lower myself onto his length. The heat from his cock seems to warm me from the inside as I sink into place, and he groans as I rock my hips back and forth.

"Where?" I ask, and he turns his neck for me, showing me the expanse of skin.

I bring my mouth down, running my teeth gently over it until I hear his groan grow louder.

"A little lower," he gasps, and I move my mouth as he says. As my mouth finds the right spot, I can feel it in my own body: his desire and need pulsing, hungry and needy.

"*Iija*. There," he groans.

I suck on the skin, moving my hips faster to heighten both our pleasure.

"Fuck. Maren," he says, and I hear the need in it. "You're so good. You're so good for me."

I rock faster, riding him until I feel his climax building somewhere in my subconsciousness—through the mate bond, I realize. It heightens my own pleasure, and my hips take on a life of their own, the rhythmic movement taking over.

Just as I feel my own climax begin to build, I sink my teeth into his neck.

The euphoria is instantaneous. I feel the bond between us strengthen, something strong and golden snapping together, and the climax hits us both as something ineffable from my own energy seems to swirl into his body through the bite.

He groans under me, his hips instinctively thrusting up. I ride out my own climax, feeling the waves of my orgasm overtake me. I pull my mouth from him and let my head fall back, and his mouth turns to my neck, my chest, my breasts as I feel him flood me with warmth.

"God, Seb," I moan.

"Maren," he gasps.

I feel myself coming down, and wrap my arms around him as the rhythm of my hips grows softer. His eyes are dark and beautiful, gazing up at me with a kind of adoration.

"Say it," I whisper.

"You're mine," he says, his voice a low rumble.

"And you're mine."

Fakari Dictionary

Fakari and English are the two official languages of the islands, and many characters use them interchangeably. I've tried to make most Fakari in the book easy to understand through translation or context cues, but for those who want a reference, here are a few common Fakari words used throughout this book.

Aeijsammen: everyone
Aftnu'kut: good evening
Agaayu (f. *agaaya*, pl. *agaayit*): god
Aja: aunt
Ama: mom
Apa: dad
Ayagayuuni: oh my God
Dennani: my daughter
Eijlonni: cousin
Eijna: the Fakari sacred book
Eijtna: equivalent of sweetheart
Et: and
Farvayyu: goodbye, farewell
Fika: a group of four or five families living together as a pack
Fikarig: a communal home for the families making up a *fika*
Fikalid: a member of the same *fika*
Fiya: she
Heij: hey
Iija: yes
Ijekayyatik: I love you
Ijweiyyet: I know
Jenge: boy
Kamaat(ni): (my) mate

Katalltet: you know/you speak
Kateijtko: a Fakari card game
Kiyyu: soul or spirit
Kiyyulit: the Northern Lights (literally spirit light)
Kiyyuni: my soul
Kutetkuk: equivalent to 'bon appetit'
Morlaa'kut: good morning, sometimes shortened to *Molaa'*
Nagaayu (f. *nagaaya*, pl. *nagaayit*): idiot
Neijtuurlik: of course
Nekka: no
Okeij: okay
Pakka: pack. Used as an adjective to refer to people belonging to the Fakari people (as in, "she's *pakka*").
Piu:
Reijna: wise woman; typically a healer, the highest-ranking woman on pack council
Rig: home
Streikna: slut
Takka: thanks
Uikbaane: wolf's bane; used as a curse word in Fakari
Vaare: woman
'Vayyu: bye, short for *farvayyu* (goodbye)
Weijtet: wait (as an imperative or command)
Welkommit: welcome

I love going through the reader's guide questions at the end my favorite books. I'm under no impression that this book will be read in a book club (though if it is, <u>please</u> invite me —that sounds hilarious), but I wanted to draft some questions for the main way romance books are shared, at least in my life: through recommendations from friends. Here's some questions to talk and laugh over with the romance readers in your life.

1. Seb and Maren seem allergic to physical intimacy indoors. Are they exhibitionists, or just too horny to find a bed?

2. Maren spends a lot of time defending her colorful resume. What job history would you add to truly send her application over the top? Which of her jobs would you be worst at?

3. Towards the end of the book, Saga makes the point that your career isn't your purpose. In what ways has career defined or influenced your sense of purpose? What other parts of your life feel more central to your sense of self?

4. Maren has introduced her Fakari peers to some eclectic music, including in particular the soundtrack to *Like Mike*. If you had to make a playlist to introduce the *fika* to mainland music, what would your top choices be? What would you choose to shock them?

5. In some sense, Seb and Maren are both wanderers looking for home. What feels like home to you? Is it a place, or a person?

6. Fuck, marry, kill: Seb, Gabe, Kieran.

7. Seb's journey to a healthy relationship is, in part, a journey of letting go of his anger—not just at others, but at himself. Do you think Maren played a role in this? Was she a catalyst, or a motivator? Or was this ultimately something Seb had to address within himself?

8. Given unlimited resources, what new product launch would become your personal pet project at Saroan Salts?

PREVIEW THE NEXT BOOK IN THE SERIES

Read the next book in this series, *In Her Own Rite*, featuring Em and Kieran's love story. It's already available at all major retailers.

You can scan the QR code below to access the Amazon listing, and read the first chapter starting on the next page.

IN HER OWN RITE CHAPTER 1
EMERSON

We're in the water.

It's the start of summer, and even at 8 p.m. the sun is only just starting to make its way down the sky. The lake water is rich and warm, and the surface sparkles with light so bright it's almost blinding. Seb, Kieran, and Gabe are swimming around the shallow end, laughing and jumping at each other while I tread water a little farther from the shore.

I look up at the forest across the lake and notice a gray shadow through the trees. It fades in and out of view, but the shape feels familiar. I start to swim towards it to get a better view, even as my mind realizes: *it's a dream. It's a memory. Come back.*

"Mom," I hear myself say, quietly enough that the guys won't hear. The bottom of the lake drops off as I get to deeper waters. My hair is floating around me, long and golden, and it brushes against my shoulders the same way the weeds do against my feet.

Don't go, my mind says. This is a memory I've dreamed through a hundred times. I know how it plays out, and still, each time I try to wrestle myself to a different ending. A different story. It never works.

The shadow disappears behind a tree. I swim farther, faster. The guys are far enough behind me that they can't hear me now.

"Mom!" I call out to her. "Mom, come back!"

For a moment I think that she's gone for good, but as I come closer, she emerges from behind the trees slowly, like a mirage. She's wearing the dress I last saw her in, dark blonde hair spilling over her shoulder. She tilts her head, looking at me tenderly.

"Emerson," she whispers. "Oh, baby." She kneels down to crouch by the water's edge, as if to be closer to me.

I know it can't be real. I know she's dead. But Aunt Saga always talks about the spirits of the ancestors staying on the islands, and for a moment I believe—

Something in the air shifts. I look up and see thick, dark clouds gathering ahead where there was sun and clear skies just a moment ago. The shadow of the cloud falls over me, and the water around me grows cool. A low wind rustles over the edge of the water.

"Mom...?" I say. But as I turn to look back at her, it's as though my body already knows.

In the place where she knelt is a wolf, head low, bearing its fangs at me. His sinewy frame and matted fur gives the appearance of something sick, but even the hunger pangs visible in his thin body can't mask its muscle and sheer power.

I know *exactly* what he's capable of.

The air escapes my lungs. I try to swim back, but it's like I can't get enough air. I thrash as the wolf steps to the water's edge, his golden eyes taunting me.

"Help!" I try to call, but the sound comes out like a whisper. The wolf snarls and comes closer, and for a moment I think this is it, and he's going to kill me. But suddenly I feel a pair of strong arms wrap around my waist, pulling me back.

"Hey," says Kieran's voice, low and warm in my ear. "Hey, you're okay. You're okay, I got you."

I gasp and turn to him, climbing onto his body, my legs wrapping around his waist and my arms round his neck. "Kieran," I say, feeling the adrenaline pounding through me. "Kieran, help, get me away—"

"You're okay. You're okay," he says, his voice rich and reassuring. "What happened? I saw you swim out and then you just froze. Did your leg get caught?"

"No, my dad—"

I turn around and point to the clearing in the trees, but it's empty now. I look around and realize the clouds are gone. It's warm and sunny again.

"He's gone, Em. He can't hurt you anymore."

"No. It was real, I swear."

"Okay," he says gently, nodding.

I look up at Kieran's face: broad jaw, for the first time in our lives sporting a brush of stubble. He's a year or two older than me, and his golden skin is glowing with the first hints of this year's tan. His body is so warm. I can practically feel his heartbeat through his skin, soft and steady, bringing me back down to earth.

I meet his eyes, hazel and gold.

"Sorry," I say. "I shouldn't be like this anymore. It's so embarrassing."

"Nah, no worries. When I'm here, you're always safe, okay? I'll always keep you safe."

I look over my shoulder at the trees and the clearing, and for a moment I swear I see a brush of something between the firs. But it wasn't real—it can't be. The only thing that's real is Kieran and his arms around me, holding me together.

My eyes open slowly, and the first thing I do is look to the window to see the sky. It's cloudy and overcast, *takkagaayu*—

thank God. It won't be clear enough for the rite tonight. That means Kieran has at least one more day to prepare. Not that he thinks he needs it.

I turn to look at him, lying beside me in bed. He's in his human form, so I must have slept well last night. When I wake up in a panic, he'll often shift for me, taking the form of a big, fluffy white wolf so I can curl up next to his fur and feel small and safe.

Kieran has the biggest wolf form of anyone I know. His human form is pretty big too: 6'5, his frame broad and muscular from years spent training in the gym every day with Seb. I'm grateful for it, in a way. Knowing he's strong enough to take on the world helps me feel a little safer.

I rest my head close to his, taking in the unique scent of amber, leather, and wood that seems to soak into his skin from hours at the workshop. Most people on the islands have crafts or trades on the side to make ends meet next to their regular jobs. Kieran is one of the only people I know who's been able to turn his trade into a whole career, crafting furniture that sells for a small fortune on the mainland. He started apprenticing just after we finished high school, and finished his training on Keist, one of the smaller islands, around the time I began training to be a healer with Aunt Saga.

The nights he spent on Keist were some of the last we spent apart. We never talk about it. I've never *asked* him to spend the night, and he's never commented on the fact that we've been sleeping platonically side-by-side for years. We're not "sleeping together," regardless of what people like to whisper behind our backs. And he's not pining for me, waiting for me to finally look up at him and take notice. *I wish.*

I scooch closer to him, admiring the way his red-gold eyelashes flutter gently in sleep. My eyes run over his heavy brow, the broad, blunt cheekbones, and a strong jaw that's covered by a thick beard where his teenage stubble once was.

The spray of freckles over every part of him the sun touches. I've loved him for years, even before that day in the lake. And to him, I'm just Em. I know because—no matter what we've gone through together—he'd rather go out with half the islands than even *look* at me that way. He's out with a different girl every weekend, staying out as late as three or four in the morning. But no matter what he does with them, he always comes home to me, smelling of soap and a fresh shower so I don't need to scent them on his skin. Small mercies, I guess.

Kier turns in his sleep and rolls onto his side to face me. As his large body moves in our narrow bed, one arm curls under his head, and the other comes to rest between us. I look down at his hand, admiring the strong fingers, the veins running along the backs of his palms, and the thick brush of copper-gold hair running up his muscular arms. I slip my hand beside his, pale and slender in comparison. I wonder how it would feel if he held my hand in his. I wonder how it would feel if he held *me*.

In a moment I imagine his body over mine, caging me in, pressing himself against me. His knee nudging my legs open; his thick fingers finding the crest between my thighs and slipping into me. His mouth on me, tasting me...

At the thought, a ripple of pleasure runs through my body, and I feel the warm hum of desire start between my legs. I swallow and sit up, making myself think of something else. My heat will be coming up soon, and it's already making me run hotter than usual. As soon as I'm turned on, any shifters around me will be able to tell. And if Kieran knew I was getting wet next to him in bed? *Mortifying.*

I stand and turn towards the closet, stripping off my night clothes and pulling on a pair of blue scrubs for my postpartum client checkup today. Smoothing my hair back into a ponytail, I grab my phone from the bedside table, where it sits next to the training salts I set out last night. Then I slip out of the room, heading downstairs before I can wake him. If he's doing the rite in the next few days, he should be getting as much sleep as he can.

I get down to the living room and walk towards the large kitchen, where I see Saga at the counter, making coffee.

"*Morlaa'kut*," she says, smiling at me. Her dark hair, streaked with silver, is pulled back into its signature side braid, and her golden skin crinkles at the eyes as she sees me. She's still in her robe, sage green linen tied at the waist over old flannel pajamas.

"*Morlaa', Aja*," I say. *Morning, Aunt.* She's not my actual aunt, but I love her just as much as my uncle Viggo and his wife, Dagmar, who took me in when I was nine. They're the reason I live in this *fikarig*—the large home shared by the few families that make up a *fika*, or pack—in the first place, along with Saga and her son Gabe, and Seb and his mom, Isolde. Saga's niece Maren first came to the islands last year, and once she and Seb realized they were mates, she moved in permanently.

"Did you sleep well?" Saga asks, reaching for a mug to pour me some coffee.

"Yeah, fine."

"Great. You'll need your rest, with our rounds today and the rite coming up soon."

"You think so? It's been cloudy all week. It could still be a while."

She glances up from the coffee she's pouring and gives me a look. "What are you afraid of? All the elders have done this and lived to tell the tale. He'll be fine."

I chew on the inside of my cheek.

"We've just never done something this big without each other," I say finally. "If he gets hurt, I can't help."

"He's a big man, Emerson. He can take care of himself."

She hands me the hot mug of coffee and gestures for the kitchen table. I take a seat, curling one leg under me and putting the other up to rest my chin on my knee.

"You weren't nervous for Seb's rite?" I ask.

"Of course, but I had no reason to be. Seb is strong, and he took time to prepare. Kieran has, too."

"But Seb... got hurt," I say carefully. He's walked with a limp since the night of his rite, four years ago now. I can see how Saga looks at him sometimes, watching him with pain in her eyes. He may not be her son by blood, but the people that make up a *fika* become one family. He might as well be.

"Well. We cannot avoid pain. We can only walk through it with courage."

"Is that what you tell yourself?"

"To get through? Yes." She smiles softly, and I can see the sadness in her eyes.

Saga has lost a lot in the last twenty years—a husband, Ben; her brother David; Seb's dad Filip, who lived in this *fika* before he died and was like a brother to her. If it's true that pain makes you stronger, it must be why she's the strongest person I know. And maybe it's part of why I relate to her so much.

I swallow. "Tell me again how it'll go."

"You know how it is, *piu*," she says. *Loved one.* "You can ask me a hundred times, but it's not going to prepare him, or you, any better."

"I don't care. It'll help me worry less. Tell me, please."

Saga sighs and takes a sip from her mug. "The *reijna*, the wise woman, will know on the morning of the rite that it's time. That's me now, but for my rite, that was still your grandmother."

"And how do you know?"

"The ancestors tell you. I'll feel it in my bones." She raises her mug to me. "You'll see for yourself soon enough."

I shake my head. "No, I'm not anywhere near that yet."

"All healers are sensitive to it. I started to get the feeling when I was about where you are in your training. It wouldn't surprise me if you do, too."

"Maybe." I take a sip of my coffee. "So you know it's the day. And then what?"

"I tell Kieran and the elders. He gets ready with his training pack, and you and I prepare the *kattaka*. That evening, a few hours after the sun sets, we do the ceremony. Then he climbs up to the cliffs alone, so it's just him and the lights in the ring."

"And then he'll fight," I say quietly.

"And then he'll fight."

I swallow. The rite is styled after the founding myth of the Fakari people. The story goes that a hero named Tayyakuk sailed the seas for ten years, searching for a place to call home. He found the islands, but the moon goddess Móra had fallen in love with him and wanted him to stay on the seas so they could be together. She brought storms and disaster, trying to keep him away from our shores. After three nights, he finally reached them and climbed to the cliffs, where he challenged Móra to a battle for the right to call the islands home.

They say she took the form of a wolf and they fought through the night. Finally, as the sun began to rise over the horizon, Móra admitted defeat. And because Tayyakuk won, she gifted him the power of the wolf, and promised to protect the islands as long as his descendants lived here.

Our ancestors built the ring at the edge of the cliff where they fought. Now anyone who wants to assume a parent's seat on pack council needs to climb to the ring and fight for the right to do so, the same way Tayyakuk did. The ancestors take the shape of your greatest fear to make you prove your worth. You either beat whatever form they take, or you outlast them until sunrise.

If you win, you become an elder.

If you lose, the sea awaits below. But that hasn't happened in years.

I take another sip of my coffee, thinking it over. I used to believe it was all myths and legends. *Kattaka* is an herbal drink that makes you hallucinate; it's basically like a bad trip. But that doesn't explain why some people return from the ring covered in cuts and bruises. That doesn't explain why some people don't come back at all, or some—like Seb—carry an injury for the rest of their lives. It can't *all* be in your head.

"What form did the ancestors take for you?" I ask quietly. I can't meet Saga's eyes as I ask this, and look pointedly at my coffee. Her voice comes like a cold wind.

"*Emerson*. You know I can't tell you that. Come now, finish your coffee, and then we'll get going on our morning rounds. Linnea will be waiting." She stands and heads for the stairs to get dressed.

I stay at the table to finish my coffee. As I do, I think of Kieran in that ring. Fighting his demons alone in a way he makes sure I never have to.

ACKNOWLEDGMENTS

I want to take a moment to thank the many people who contributed to making this book better and bringing it into the world.

Adelaide and Arnica, thank you for reading my first drafts of this and providing your thoughts (and live reactions!) along the way. To my mom: thank you for taking the time to read this series and understand what I'm trying to do with it—even if we have to hide some of the content behind a sticky note.

I want to provide a special and heartfelt thanks to Danelle (@biblio.barbie), Amber (@monsterinthepages), and Tash (@tash_readsbooks) for reading an early edition of this book to make sure it lived up to expectations. Thank you for loving these characters and this world enough to give feedback, and for sharing the books with your audience. I'm so, so grateful.

Thank you also to the incredibly talented artists who have brought this world and its characters to life, in particular Sean Simmons (Vimesart), Grace (Zaeyos), Rachael Ward (Cartography Bird), and Nelidian (d.i.nd).

And finally, special thanks to my husband for the many, many conversations we had about this story: on walks, in hospital lunchrooms, and at home in the late hours of the night. You give me a level of love and support without which the most joyful and beautiful parts of my life wouldn't be possible. The way you love me inspires me to dream bigger in the love stories I tell.

I love you: ten years ago, today, forever.

ABOUT THE AUTHOR

Rowan writes romance novels featuring kick-ass heroines and couples who find wholeness and healing on the path to love. As you may have already guessed, her favorite things include found family, gorgeous artisanal and homemade goods, and really good sea salt.

She lives with her husband on two continents, and is mentally camping out on a fictional set of islands between them. If you want to hear more from her, listen to her wildly unprofessional romance book podcast, *Weak Knees*, at your own risk.

www.rowanwilder.com

Instagram: **@rowanwilderromance**
Spotify: **Weak Knees**

ALSO BY ROWAN WILDER

Fakari Series

Worth His Salt

In Her Own Rite

Under Her Wing (forthcoming)

Coyote Creek

The Ogre's Bride